continued . . .

HEART OF THE TIGER

Lynn Kerstan

AN ONYX BOOK

ONYX
Published by New American Library, a division of
Penguin Putnam Inc., 375 Hudson Street,
New York, New York 10014, U.S.A.
Penguin Books Ltd, 80 Strand,
London WC2R 0RL, England
Penguin Books Australia Ltd, 250 Camberwell Road,
Camberwell, Victoria 3124, Australia
Penguin Books Canada Ltd, 10 Alcorn Avenue,
Toronto, Ontario, Canada M4V 3B2
Penguin Books (N.Z.) Ltd, Cnr Rosedale and Airborne Roads,
Albany, Auckland 1310, New Zealand

Penguin Books Ltd, Registered Offices:
Harmondsworth, Middlesex, England

First published by Onyx, an imprint of New American Library,
a division of Penguin Putnam Inc.

First Printing, May 2003
10 9 8 7 6 5 4 3 2 1

 REGISTERED TRADEMARK—MARCA REGISTRADA

Printed in the United States of America

PUBLISHER'S NOTE
This is a work of fiction. Names, characters, places, and incidents either
are the product of the author's imagination or are used fictitiously,
and any resemblance to actual persons, living or dead, business
establishments, events, or locales is entirely coincidental.

For all my RomEx friends, whose wit, wisdom, and generosity make this world a warmer and finer place. Thanks for the Sword!

*   *   *

Special regards to the redoubtable Eve Sinaiko, who knows more than any one person should, and who is funnier than any one person ought to be. I have drawn shamelessly on her eclectic store of information.

And my deepest gratitude to Candice Kohl of Savannah, writer and intrepid carriage driver, who taught me the difference between tackle and tack and showed me how harnesses are attached to horses.

To Margaret Evans Porter, doyen of all things British and Regency, thanks for the shooting lore.

I had lots of help and advice from kind friends. All mistakes are my own.

Prologue

June 1823, India

Son of the Devil, they called him. Brother of the Beast. Outlaw.

Not to his face, to be sure. Few of his countrymen dared speak to him at all, which was just as he liked it. Michael Keynes preferred a solitary life. And besides, it was dangerous to be in his vicinity.

The past few months, his vicinity had been positively lethal. His mercenaries had beaten off five concerted attacks, but three of his best men had been killed in an ambush. From all the attention being paid to his activities, the price on his head must have gone up.

It was to be expected. He'd increased the pressure to the point that the East India Consortium had not completed a successful transaction for two years. Assassination was the logical response. Nothing else was going to stop him.

In this, his private crusade, he had always taken care to break no law that anyone cared to enforce. While he efficiently put their competition out of business, Government House officials lined their own pockets with the Country Trade and secretly cheered him on.

Or they had been cheering. Now his enemies had launched an investigation the officials could not ignore. Powerful forces were demanding he be driven out of India for good, which as it happened, was fine with him. He had unfinished business in England.

But he suspected they weren't going to let him depart in one piece, if at all. A week ago, he'd barely escaped Calcutta alive. And, as usual, made even more trouble for himself in the process. Behind him, he'd left an Archangel with a broken wing.

Now the avenger, for that's what he had always been, could expect an avenger on his own trail. There was a nice irony in that, but it was going to be a bloody nuisance.

Ah, well. Not even an Archangel could find him tonight. Above the crumpled ridges of the Himalayan foothills, stars blazed through the water-clear, moonless sky. Michael lit a cigar from the fire and settled with his back against the trunk of a sal tree, his silver flask balanced on one thigh, puffing lazy smoke rings into the still air.

For once, it felt good to be alive. The fat jungle fowl, perfectly roasted over the campfire, had been crisp and juicy, and he was nearly drunk enough to sleep.

A rustle of grasses drew his gaze to the enormous man emerging from a screen of trees. Hari Singh had gone a distance from the camp to bury the bones from Michael's dinner, muttering about infidels who killed and devoured God's animals. Graceful as a deer for all his great height and muscular physique, he lowered himself cross-legged to the ground on the other side of the campfire.

Like all devout Sikhs, he wore a dull metal bracelet around his wrist and threaded a curved dagger into his wide leather belt. His thick black beard, uncut for a quarter of a century, was tightly rolled against his chin. Always alert to danger, he was careful to wear shorts even when bathing. No Sikh would confront a surprise attack in the altogether.

Michael gazed at him with something close to affection. Hari was the most spiritual human being he'd ever known, even in god-obsessed India. Michael's own soulless faith, confined to aged brandy, fast horses, and passionate women, made him a difficult companion at the best of times. After fifteen years of hellish times, he was astonished that such a man continued to call him friend.

"You needn't come with me," he said, reviving an old argument. "What's the point? You won't help, and you can't stop me."

Hari fed the sputtering campfire from a stack of dry branches. "I wish to visit England. I have Punjabi friends there."

"You have a lot more of them here. If you want to be useful, contrive some way to keep that meddling idiot busy until I'm finished."

"Lord Varden will be unable to travel for a time, Michael. And he will never be able to fight you again."

"But he can get in my way. He already has. I—"

Aung oo aongh. The cry hung in the air like smoke.

Hari cocked his head, listening acutely. "Distant, maybe three miles. Sound travels far here. It pushes off the mountains."

It came again, a little different. *Aooch aounch aoo oo aongh.*

"Tiger." The other noises of the night had gone strangely hushed. "Is that the one?"

"The man-eater is male," Hari said patiently. "I showed you the pug marks. The toes are square, thick. This one you hear is female."

"Good God, how can you tell *that*?"

Two days out of Calcutta, they'd picked up news that sprang from village to village like wildfire. A rare, dreaded man-eater had taken three people in Sarai and five more a few miles north. Every day the shikars followed a confused trail, passing word by runner and drum of new victims savaged, children carried off.

For a time, Michael and Hari had joined the hunt, but when the trail veered east, Hari continued north, summoned by an inner voice to an almost forgotten place.

In the area of Naini Tal was a sacred lake shaped like a teardrop. Hari had stumbled upon it by accident many years earlier. Its legend told of three sages on a penitential pilgrimage who arrived on the crest of a hill called Cheena and found no water on the other side. Desperate with thirst, they dug a hole at the foot of the mountain and siphoned water into it from the holy lake of Mansarowar in Tibet. When the sages departed, the goddess Naini arrived to take up residence in the blessed waters of the new lake they had formed. It was reached by way of the mountain called Sher Ka Danda, "Path of the Tiger."

The call sounded again, closer now. Michael looked a question at Hari, who shook his head.

"It is a tigress in estrus. Late for her time. Male and female keep territory near each other and he seeks her out when she calls him. Only when her cubs can survive alone, usually two years, will she call again. The male recognizes her voice and returns to her."

"That's a hell of a long time to wait in the bushes."

"Patience has its reward." Hari smiled. "During their week together, tigers mate fifty or more times each day."

"The devil you say! Still, two years without a woman—"

"Only the female mates for life. The males keep a larger territory, so to speak." Hari traced obscure figures in the dust with his finger. "This brings to mind a parable told by the Lord Buddha of a man pursued by a tiger."

With a groan, Michael stabbed out his cigar. Hari's

evening homily was as inevitable as sunset, but at least the Buddha's tales were short. He could never decide if they were deeply profound or only designed to sound that way.

"There was a man pursued by a tiger," Hari intoned. "He ran and ran until he came to a sheer cliff, where he seized a vine and swung far down over the precipice. Above him, the tiger paced and snarled his hunger. And below, at the bottom of the cliff, another tiger waited for the man to drop.

"While he hung there, two mice came near, one black and one white. They gnawed the vine with sharp white teeth, slowly cutting it through. The man clung for his life to the shredding vine with one hand, and with the other he reached out and plucked a strawberry growing on the cliff. Never had anything tasted so sweet."

The only sound was the crackle of the fire.

"That's it?" Michael said after a time. "Gather ye strawberries while ye may?"

"The parable is not so simple as that. It is different for every man, and each time I hear the tale or speak it, new harmonics flow from the center. Tonight it sings of life reborn."

Michael drained the flask in one long swallow, rolled onto his side, and stuffed a blanket under his head. "That's the trouble with this country. India never lets you finish dying."

The dry riverbed crackled under the blazing June sun. Dust billowed with every footfall as Michael and Hari plodded along Sher Ka Danda, obscuring their sight in a haze of heat and whirring insects. Hari led the horses while Michael slouched a few yards ahead, one foot after the other, lost in his own darkness. He didn't want to think, but his head spun and hummed like the gnats that clouded his eyes.

It was late afternoon when they came near an

oxbow that retained a little water. Hari dropped back to refill their canteens and let the animals drink.

Michael scarcely noticed. Hot, tense, driven to keep moving, he turned a bend and nearly tripped over an exposed tree root. Recovering, he looked up. Froze.

No more than ten feet in front of him, a sleek tigress glared at him from icy, sky-blue eyes. She was white, silvery in the harsh sun, with black stripes inscribed across her back and sides like a tocsin. Her ears were flattened with challenge. Sharp fangs curved from her snarling mouth. She dared him to move.

No chance to lift the rifle and fire in time. He wanted to look away, to let her know he wasn't a threat, but her blue gaze held his with implacable purpose. Beauty and death, poised to leap. She growled low in her throat.

He had feared nothing since leaving England, least of all death, but he found himself terrified by this silver-white, blue-eyed cat. She seemed to have his name written across her open mouth and gleaming teeth.

The sharp crack of a snapping twig sounded to his right. He swung his head toward the noise. Nothing. When he looked back, the tigress had vanished.

About fifteen feet away, to the left, Hari slowly rose from behind a shield of dry grasses, rifle poised.

Michael shuddered as black and white streaks flashed before his eyes. His flesh seemed to melt in the hot air. Dropping to hands and knees, blood drumming in his ears, he gasped for air.

After a time, he dragged his head up and looked through sweat-stung eyes at Hari, who was now crouching in front of him. "My God, man. Why didn't you shoot?"

"I could not, Michael-Sahib. For my life I could not kill her." Rising, Hari offered his hand.

Michael grasped it and allowed himself to be pulled upright. His legs quivered. He'd been that close to death many times, but nothing had ever struck a chord of terror like those endless moments facing the white tigress.

Hari let go of his hand. "I spared her life. She spared your life. It is karma."

"If you say so." And if karma was another name for large, ravenous cat.

"Shall we make camp? The water is clean here and it will soon be dusk. By now, the tigress is far away, but I shall keep watch."

Michael poked Hari's broad chest with his rifle barrel. "A lot of use that will be. If she comes back for a late supper, you'll probably dish me up on a bed of rice."

"With curried peas."

As he watched the Englishman turn away, Hari Singh felt the air crackle. He lifted his head to the sky. Like all his prescient visions, the message came and went in a heartbeat. A blast of light. A flash of truth too bright to distinguish.

He would only know what he'd seen when he saw it again.

Chapter 1

November 1823, England

"There is no hope, then?"

Grim faced, Mr. Stewart Callendar, honored graduate of the Royal College of Physicians in Edinburgh, closed the door behind him and sagged against it. "Miss Holcombe . . . Mira . . . you knew it, I think, before you brought him here."

"Yes." She kept her hands tightly folded on her lap. "You needn't protect my sensibilities, Stewart. Complete frankness will help me understand what we are facing."

"Very much the same as you have dealt with these last three years, I'm afraid. In my experience, whatever improvement there is to be will occur within the first year. Naturally, there are exceptions, but beyond his progress in the early months, your father has regained little control of his body. I find no significant improvement in muscular control."

"But his wrist is stronger, and his finger. He can lift his head now."

"Yes. But those are motions he developed early, and the added strength comes from usage and the exercises you conduct with him. Have you seen voluntary motion in some other part of his body?"

Wishing it, willing it, did not make it so. "None," she said.

"It is little comfort, I know, but his breathing is excellent, and he is still able to swallow liquids and soft foods. None of what I observed on my last examination has diminished."

"Nor has his mind. He has lost weight, though, and seems more lethargic than before. But we have been required to relocate several times in the past few months, and travel is difficult for him."

The doctor, a sturdy, compact Scot with unruly copper hair and side-whiskers that needed trimming, took his place in the chair behind his desk, hazel eyes fixed on her intently. "I wish you would consider leaving him here with us."

"Did he ask you to say that?"

"He would have done, I ken, could he speak. And you know we will care for him as we would our own father. Janet is fond of him, as am I."

"All your patients receive excellent care, Stewart. And it is perfectly true that he wants to remain here. But that is on my account."

"Then why begrudge him the good deed? Tunbridge Wells is not so great a journey. You can visit him often. He will have a regimen of healthful foods, exercise, and the company of the other patients. Surely that is preferable to the isolation of your home? And it cannot be easy for you to tend to him with so little help."

Before her father's examination, she had been compelled to describe his circumstances since last the doctor had seen him. And Stewart, bless his soul, was perniciously keen at hearing what she had not said.

"We won't be returning to Seacrest." It hurt to say that. The home where she had grown up, her father's cherished library, all closed to them now. "But our circumstances have improved a bit. You will be glad to hear that I can soon pay what we owe—"

"The money doesna matter." His dark eyes flashed.
"There is naught I would withhold from you. My feelings have not altered. Not in all the time you were
gone."

A heaviness began to gather in her chest. She closed
her eyes for a moment, willing it away. "Nor have
mine," she said as gently as she could.

They had met on only four occasions, for heaven's
sake, and he had proposed marriage on their second
and third encounters. Kind men, decent men, kept falling in love with her for no good reason whatever,
leaving her to refuse them because she could do nothing else. If they knew her as she truly was, they would
run like foxes.

"I cannot wed you, Stewart, nor any other man.
There is something I must do, and it will require all
my attention. Save that reserved for my father," she
added quickly, but he was already leaning forward in
his chair.

"The more reason to leave him with us, then."

Because it would tie her to this place, and to him.
She must make her request without giving him false
hope. "In fact, it would be enormously helpful if you'd
keep him here for a week or so, while I go up to
London to look for a residence that can accommodate
his needs."

"You mean to live in *London*?" His stubby brows
prickled with reproach. "But the air is unhealthy. And
the expense! Servants are more dear there. The houses
have narrow stairs. How will you transport him?
How—"

"I shall manage as I always have done." Which
meant frantically improvising from one minute to the
next, but she couldn't very well admit that. "And you
must not think I find it difficult. Although my father
is locked inside his body, we communicate very well
indeed. Yes, of late he has come to imagine I would
do better if he set me free of him, but he is wrong. I

shall not leave him until he requires more than I can possibly give." She smiled. "Truly, it is no hardship. To care for him is my privilege. And my joy."

She hadn't meant to say that. To reveal so much. She scarcely dared look up at Stewart, and when she did, her worst fears were realized. He positively glowed with admiration.

"We shall be pleased to have your father in residence for as long as necessary," he said. "And if you provide me your direction, I shall send daily reports of his welfare."

"Thank you." After a glance at the mantelpiece clock, she rose and brushed down her skirts, eager to escape the heated emotions radiating from across the room. "There is a mail coach I must shortly catch. I shall be in touch as soon as I have settled in London. And now, if you will excuse me, I'll take leave of my father."

At the door, she made the mistake of glancing back. Stewart was still gazing at her with hungry veneration, mentally polishing up a halo for Saint Miranda, virgin and martyr.

And she, of course, was neither of those things.

Sothingdon House, imposing and grand in a quiet Mayfair street, caused Mira to catch her breath. It hadn't occurred to her that the somewhat disreputable pair for whom she'd once done a small favor might have become so . . . well, so *reputable*.

She looked again at the direction Lady Jessica had inscribed on the letter of thanks she'd posted almost a year ago. Had it been so long? By now, Miranda Holcombe's welcome had surely worn out. How could she plunk her insignificant self on the doorstep and ask to be admitted? Pride made it difficult to mount the steps and lift the knocker, but pride and difficulty were her constant companions. She never let either of them stop her.

Before her nerves had steadied, a footman was ushering her into a bright parlor where Lady Jessica Duran opened her arms in welcome. "At last!" she exclaimed. "I have been desperately worried about you."

At the sight of her, a pain gripped Mira so sharply that she wrapped her arms around her waist to contain it. But she found a smile and crossed to where the beautiful and exceedingly pregnant Lady Jessica half sat and half reclined on a Grecian sofa. "Thank you for receiving me," she said in the soft voice that required her to draw close to anyone who wished to hear her. "I am sorry to have imposed on—"

"Indeed you have not! Sit here next to the table, because I have ordered tea, which you will be required to pour. And you needn't feel uneasy. I've six weeks more before I pop, or so the doctor assures me, although whether the babe will wait that long is another question. From all the kicking and squirming, there seems to be a great hurry to get out of me."

Envy, squirming and kicking inside Mira, made any response impossible. She settled on the chair, straightened her skirts, and reined in her stampeding emotions.

"Miss Holcombe?" Lady Jessica's voice was edged with concern. "I . . . Your father?"

Mira, following her gaze, realized Lady Jessica was looking at her black bombazine gown, the black bonnet covering her hair, and the black gloves she wore. The footman had taken her black cloak. "Oh dear," she said, untying the ribbons and removing her hat. "I forgot how this all must appear to you. My father is well and being cared for by his physician while I am in London. When I must travel, I find it useful to disguise myself in mourning clothes. People are often undeservedly kind, which causes me to feel guilty for deceiving them, but at least I am permitted to go my way without interference."

"It is difficult for a female to travel alone. I cannot

like it that you do so." Lady Jessica laughed. "Good heavens. I just realized what I was saying. I am *preaching* at you. It must be impending motherhood that has transformed me from a ramshackle rebel into a tedious old fuddy-duddy. Do you know, I have stoutly resolved to forbid my daughter, should I have one, to behave as I have always done. Not that any daughter born to the likes of me and Duran would pay us the slightest attention."

Wincing, she spread her fingers across her swollen belly. "I swear there is a fandango being danced inside me. How good that you have come to provide a distraction. Duran will be sorry to have missed you, though. We have bought a small property in Sussex and he has gone to see it made ready for us. Where are you staying?"

Mira was spared from answering by a knock at the door. Soon, maids and footmen were spreading before her on the table a pot of tea and plates filled with small sandwiches, lemon tarts, poppyseed cake, scones, clotted cream, strawberry jam, and almond biscuits.

"Are you shocked?" Lady Jessica regarded the assortment with evident delight. "Duran says an army could travel for a week on what I eat in a day. He also says I have developed a remarkable likeness to an ascent balloon, except that it would require a cyclone to launch me into the air. Mind you, he says these things from a safe distance."

Mira strained tea into a pair of Wedgwood cups. "You don't appear to object."

"Oh, there is no accounting for male behavior at times like this. The moment a pregnancy is confirmed, they strut around as if no other male had ever accomplished so great a feat. Then they grow annoyingly solicitous, as if we females have suddenly become too frail to spoon sugar into a cup. The next stage, the one Duran occupies now, is excessive teasing to cover his fear of what might happen to me or the babe. I dare not think what he will come to when I begin to deliver. Two of the tarts, if you please, and as many sandwiches as will fit on one of those plates."

After placing the dishes where Lady Jessica could reach them, Mira took a sip of tea. It tasted bitter.

"You are too thin, Miss Holcombe," said Lady Jessica. "And too pale. Yes, I know it is none of my business, but I suspect you are in some sort of difficulty. I also believe I've some idea what it is, but I'd rather you tell me directly."

"If you wish, but I am sure you overestimate my troubles. Since my uncle's death I have felt a trifle harried, that is all."

"I read in the *Times* that he had died. Did the Duke of Tallant swoop in, as you predicted?"

"Oh, yes. But by that time, Father and I had left the castle. And I am afraid that we took with us nearly everything I thought to be of value. Lacking your expertise, I was for the most part guessing, but I tossed any promising items into the pot. Or in this case, into the icehouse."

"Good for you. It is no more than Tallant deserves, to lose what he is attempting to steal. I recall that when we were searching for the Golden Leopard in your dungeon, Duran uncovered a number of valuable antiquities. Did you wish me to sell them for you?"

Mira looked up in surprise. It was why she was here, of course. After a week of sleepless nights—her recalcitrant pride!—she had wrenched up the courage to beg a favor from a virtual stranger, entirely overlooking the fact that Lady Jessica routinely dealt with clients exactly like herself. Not that it signified. In her present circumstances, Lady Jessica could scarcely set about flogging a hodgepodge of artifacts and gewgaws.

"I can see it is out of the question now," Mira said. "But perhaps you could recommend another dealer."

"Indeed I can. My secretary, Helena Pryce, knows far more about my business than I ever did, and in the past few months, I have weaned my clients from the habit of speaking only with me. Now we work together, Helena and Duran and I, and you may be sure we will get you the best price for everything you put on offer. One other thing. I will not hear of taking a commission on the sales. You would insult me by creating a business transaction between us. What is more, I insist on advancing you a portion of the anticipated return. Now pass me another lemon tart."

Mira did, and smiled, and said nothing. Relief had set her heart thumping. Without money she could do nothing that she must do, and the little she had got by pawning her mother's wedding ring and few bits of jewelry would soon be exhausted.

Lady Jessica brushed a crumb from her bodice. "Where are you staying, Miss Holcombe? Not a hotel, I hope. Duran and I will soon remove ourselves to Sussex, but you are welcome here for as long as you like. Helena will be glad of the company."

It had come to the sticking point. To why she must not associate herself with these good people, except in secret. "Thank you. I wish it were possible to accept your kind offer. But Tallant is both tenacious and vindictive, and I must not draw his attention to my"— she scarcely dared say it—"to my friends. If you would help me, then you must also permit me to set the terms."

"I see. Well, it is no great thing to oblige you, since all my business transactions are confidential and my personal relationships no one else's concern. How is this? I shall offer you whatever favors I wish to supply, and you will select those you are willing to take. Even better, you must tell me what you require. It may be something I would fail to consider."

In the face of such generosity, Mira chose her words carefully. "Tallant has had everything his way because my family, what little remains of it, is obscure. But that wasn't always the case. While we have never been

wealthy, our home in Kent was invariably thronged
with my father's friends, and until his illness, they kept
up a lively correspondence with him. I want to find a
place here in London where we can live a public life,
surrounded by people. Father is determined I shall
find a husband, which I assure you is the very last
thing I am looking for, but it will please him to imagine I am in the marketplace and enjoying myself there.
More important, if we become known to influential
people, Tallant will not find it so easy to persecute
us."

"All perfectly logical," said Lady Jessica with a
frown, "although I'd rather you felt able to confide
the truth. But how could you, to someone you have
met only once before? What happened to your cats?"

"My—?" A wave of sadness swept over Mira. "Oh,
we couldn't take them on our travels, but I found a
family willing to keep them together in their home.
How astonishing that you should remember my cats.
You never even saw them."

"No. But since they helped us escape from the castle, I wondered what had become of them. And I have
in mind the perfect residence for your purposes, except that the proprietress does not accept pets. It is
truly an ideal location, if a little bizarre. I shall write
to Beata Neri, and Helena will deliver the letter in
person. We are of long acquaintance with her, so
Beata will not think of refusing us."

Mira gulped. "Is it terribly expensive?"

"I expect so, but Helena will negotiate a bargain
price. To reside there, however, you will be required
to cut a fashionable figure. I'd send you directly off
to a modiste, at my expense, but you would feel
obliged to refuse the offer. In consequence, I must ask
you to do me the service of accepting my castoffs."

"The *service*?"

"Oh, indeed. I'll not fit into a single thing I own for
a considerable time, and by then I shall be longing for

an entirely new wardrobe. Besides, there must be a dozen gowns I've never worn, dating back to the time I bought all the wrong colors and fabrics, ones that didn't suit me at all. How delightful that my mistakes can be made over to flatter you, as they will."

Lady Jessica held out her hands. "Will you lever me upright? We'll go to my chambers and get you measured and start trying things on you. My lady's maid has had little to occupy her since I swelled up like a melon. She will be pleased to take on this project, and by the time we're done fitting you, Helena Pryce will have returned from wherever she goes on Tuesdays. Then we shall discuss the disposal of your pilfered hoard."

Mira laughed, as she was meant to do, and helped Lady Jessica lurch to her feet. But this welcome, this largesse, made things too easy, she was thinking all the while. And as she had learned by painful experience, what looked to be a blessing was always a trap.

Chapter 2

The music sparkled, cool and crisp, like snowmelt from the Himalayas. Michael closed his eyes and relaxed against the comfortable chair while David Fairfax's limber fingers rippled over the keyboard. Precise, orderly Bach, mathematical as the stars, a world away from the throb of sitar and tabla. Clean and transparent, its devious simplicity appealed to him as Indian music never had.

As the last notes of the fugue spun away, David bowed his head for several moments, looking displeased. "Well, what do you think?" he asked at length. "I didn't play well. I was . . . nervous. But I've got better since you left."

"Bound to."

Sighing, David pulled out a monogrammed handkerchief and wiped his forehead. "Your own fault, y'know. Never would have thought of it m'self."

"I should have left well enough alone." Michael stretched broadly. "I'd figured the harpsichord would give you something to do besides get on my nerves. I miscalculated."

"What did you expect? Sonatas in a week?"

"It sounded like you were trying the beat those

scales to death with your bare hands. In the mountains you'd have started an avalanche."

"And I told you to stuff cotton in your ears."

Michael folded his arms behind his head, amused. The chubby, tongue-tied, bumbling David Fairfax he had shared rooms with at Christchurch was gone, replaced by this fashionable man who looked ten years younger than his four-and-thirty. The earnest brown eyes were precisely the same, casting about anxiously for approval.

The harpsichord had belonged to the Duchess of Tallant, brought to her arranged marriage along with a considerable fortune, and it was the only thing Devil Keynes had let her keep when he stashed her and her young son at a remote estate in Scotland. The one good memory Michael retained from his childhood was listening to her play and sing. After her death, when he'd finally raised enough money to bring the instrument south, it was almost unreclaimable— scarcely valuable even as firewood.

Greatly disappointed, he offered the remains to an elderly retired organist who collected antiques and was astonished when it was presented back to him, months later, fully restored. No charge at all, the man had insisted. Made him feel young again to do something useful. Would Mr. Keynes be interested in lessons? Laughing, Michael had invited him home and introduced him to David Fairfax.

Now the lovely harpsichord shimmered in the late-afternoon sunlight, seeming to vibrate with fifty years of music enshrined in its gleaming wood.

"It belongs to you," David said. His fingers caressed the keys soundlessly, like a lover.

"Don't be an ass." Michael crossed to the bow-fronted sideboard and poured two snifters of brandy. "What the devil would I do with it? By the way, this is terrible stuff." He handed David a glass and lifted his own in a salute. "I'm not the best of judges, Maestro, but you've impressed the hell out of me. *Slainte*."

"I hope that means something good," said David, taking a sip and putting his glass aside. "I haven't asked you . . . well, anything. I'm sorry. The minute I saw you at the door, all I could think was to play for you. I've become vain, I think, since you left. Have you come home to stay?"

"Just long enough to finish a job." When David's mouth opened to speak, Michael shook his head. "You don't want to know. And once this gets under way, you don't want to be seen with me. That's why I came here first, before it's known I'm back in England."

"Does this involve your brother?"

"Doesn't everything? Do you know where he is?"

David frowned. "When he's in London, he can be found at Palazzo Neri two or three times a week, but I haven't seen him there lately. You should keep away from him, Michael. He has become . . . worse. Monstrous. Utterly ruthless."

"It runs in the family." Michael drained his glass and set it down. "I have to go. If you get word of him, let me know."

"But how? Where are you staying?"

"For the time being, we're at a flea-ridden posthouse in Hammersmith. I'm looking for a place closer in that won't object to a Sikh."

"What's that?"

"In Hari Singh's case, something like a bear wearing a turban. He's conspicuous, and I can't shake him loose."

"You could both stay here," David said brightly. "There isn't much room, not enough for three, but I could move to Beata's. Or she might take you in. She likes having odd birds around, if you know what I mean. Except it would be expensive to stay there. Do you need money? I have plenty now."

In some ways, David hadn't changed at all. Still overeager, tongue tripping over his thoughts. "So do I," Michael said, moving to the window and gazing down at the busy sunlit street. A wagon piled with turnips and cabbages rolled past. A pretty girl and her hooknosed chaperon lifted their skirts to cross a puddle left by the morning's rain. Two men paused, arms waving as they argued about something.

Everyday life. He knew nothing about it. He had always preferred the shadows, with a quick escape at hand from wherever he chanced to be. Not for a moment had he considered making a public display of himself, and just imagining it put a sour taste in his mouth.

But this time, it was going to be Jermyn Keynes, Duke of Tallant, who required stealth. This time, he was the only one with something to lose. So long as Michael stayed out in the open, the duke would find killing his troublesome younger brother—without being caught at it—all the more difficult.

Michael had learned better than to pass up any advantage, however slight. And lacking the slightest concern for the consequences, he was free to strike at will, even with fifty witnesses looking on. Turning, he grinned at David. "Tell me about Beata's."

"Oh. You'd like it. Good wine and brandy. Gaming. Other things you wouldn't like so much, like dancing and musicales—I play there rather often—and . . . Well, you'll see. She built a villa on the Thames not far from Chelsea Hospital, and just lately she added cottages and flats for residents. I'll take you there to meet her, but"—he flushed—"but you'll need to clean up first. Shave. Haircut. Decent clothes."

Michael glanced down at his scuffed boots, buckskin breeches, open-necked shirt, and leather waistcoat. "I've only one change of clothes, and it's worse than this. All I could carry with me had to fit in a saddlepack. The luggage I sent on a trader won't be here for another month or two."

"Oh." David looked him up and down. "We can't wait that long, can we? But I know a tailor who can outfit you overnight, for the right price. We'll call there now, and by tomorrow morning, you'll be fashionable enough to meet Beata Neri."

"Don't count on it," said Michael under his breath.

Beata Neri had the sort of lavish beauty that caused men to strike poses and write bad poetry. Enthroned on a canopied gilt chair in her elaborately decorated parlor, she was wearing an iridescent gown of velvet and silk in the colors of a peacock's tail. A soft velvet hat crowned her mass of heavy black hair, with a sapphire clasp holding the feather that curled over her smooth cheek.

Michael, approaching the dais, guessed her age to be a few years above his own six-and-thirty. She had elected to receive him alone, in state, and she was smiling.

He stopped just beyond the expected spot, decided not to bow, and regarded her with open curiosity. As exotic and confident as a maharani, she was clearly a woman accustomed to getting her own way.

"You needn't play up to me," she said in a rich, slightly accented contralto. "I have already decided to have you."

"I wasn't going to," he said. "And I haven't decided to stay."

"But you will. Are you as uncivilized as you look?"

"It's the other way around. I look a good deal more civilized than I am." He glanced down at the black greatcoat he could hardly wait to shed. He had already untied his cravat and tossed a starched collar out the carriage window. "Fairfax dragged me to a tailor, who did his best on short notice. You must pardon them both."

"He has become quite the fashion plate, our David.

Because the younger men emulate him, he cannot bear to set a poor example . . . or to sponsor one."

"Then he is sure to find me a continuing disappointment. How long is this inane conversation to carry on?"

"Would you prefer to do something else?" She arched an elegant eyebrow. "I wouldn't mind. And I see you have already begun to undress yourself."

He gave a bark of laughter. "Is *that* why you've decided to have me?"

"Not originally. But the idea has considerable appeal. You would be a distinctive change from my previous lover, and I do relish variety."

"So do I. But you, Signora Neri, are very like my own previous lover—intelligent, beautiful, and demanding. Also treacherous. She sold me out."

"I trust she got a good price."

"I wouldn't know." The signora's cynicism was nearly a match for his own. "Is there a minimum acceptable fee for betrayal?"

"I count it a few pennies above whatever she can earn by other means. How else is a woman to make her fortune, unless she inherits one or elects to whore herself, in marriage or out of it? I chose to wed three men with large fortunes and poor health. Do you find that shocking? Perhaps you did not pay your mistress enough to retain her loyalty."

He thought of David Fairfax, that paragon of misdirected loyalty, who would not sell his devotion at any price. He had known a few others of such integrity, but not many.

He thought of Priya Lal, who had revealed his secret hideaway to the Earl of Varden. It wasn't the lack of money that led her to betray him, because he had long since made her wealthy. It had been the lack of attention.

He looked at Beata Neri and knew he could not

give her what she plainly wanted, although an unruly sector of his anatomy clamored for a recount. On its behalf, perhaps he ought to reconsider. Were he to seek a relationship, it would have to be with a woman as soulless as he. And he'd just met one.

He grinned at her. "Is there enough money in all the world, signora, to buy your loyalty?"

"There is scarcely enough to buy my interest for half an hour. But I expect you could hold it, *birbante*, if you tried. And I rather expect you won't try, which I regret. Still, I shall offer you one of my new *casinas*. The rent is high and the tenure day-to-day, because someone who interests me more might later apply for residence. In such a case, I would ask you to depart."

"Understood. I presume there are advantages to staying here?"

"Beyond the one you have rejected?"

He released a whoosh of air. "You have taken insult. Don't. I am poison. Just having me here will put you at risk, and before I am finished with what I came to London to do, there will be more trouble than you can manage."

He thought that had done it. He'd spoken the exact truth, and she was astute enough to hear it in his voice. When she rose, shaking out the sleeveless caftan edged with gemstones that she wore over her gown, he was sure she meant to dismiss him.

Instead, she descended regally from her dais and took his arm. A tall woman, she turned her black eyes, deep with mystery, to his. "*Vieni*, rogue. Let me show you my home. We are in the Sala dei Medici, and beyond that door is the gaming room. I claim five percent from the losers and ten percent from the winners, who are more likely to pay. Do you gamble?"

"Devotedly. I also drink."

"My cellar is excellent. I'll not charge for what is served you in the public rooms."

"Because you want me there? Why is that?"

"For the same reason I wish you to become my tenant. Fate did not decree me to be born a queen, so I built for myself a palace. Now I contrive to draw to it the most fascinating people in England. They come for many reasons, to be sure. I offer gaming, musicales, masquerades, theatricals, and banquets. Scholars enjoy my library. Politicians and investors gather in private rooms for private meetings. I select the guests who are admitted here, and I ensure their return by providing what they most delight in. Can you guess what that is?"

"No. And I don't like crowds."

"But I require them. And it is scandal that draws them to my Palazzo. Unpredictability. A frisson of danger. You will give them everything they wish and probably more than they had hoped for. Perhaps I shall place a notice in the *Times* that you can be found here."

He laughed. "Do that and you'll be sorry for it. Bad enough you want to put me on exhibit, like a monkey in a cage."

"Ah, no." She stepped back and regarded him for a moment. "Not a monkey. *Un lupo*, I think."

"There are no wolves in England."

"Not until now."

They were passing through a large courtyard with a fountain at its center, weaving through a maze of neatly trimmed box hedges studded with ornamental trees. "My lover went out to India a little more than a year ago," she said. "Perhaps you have met him."

"India's a big country."

"He should not have gone there," she said reflectively. "For all his considerable intelligence, there is a naiveté in him I find troubling. Or perhaps it is an overrefined sense of honor that does not permit him to see the lack of it in others. I advised him to refuse the errand on which he was sent, but he assumed I spoke from pique. Not so, although it is true I regretted losing him. But when he returns, I shall not have him back."

"To punish him?"

"To educate him. In all his life, he has been denied nothing. To always get what you want is unnatural."

"You appear to manage it."

"Not today. Are we not agreed that I want *you*? But you would remember, I am sure, if you had encountered him. He is exceedingly beautiful, in a way quite different than you are. People call him the Archangel."

Michael barely caught himself before he stumbled over a box hedge. He swore.

"Ah." Stopping, she turned, a smile on her full lips. "Then you did meet him."

"After a fashion," he said between clenched teeth. "We . . . quarreled. I hurt him."

"Then I was wrong. On that occasion, he did not get what he wanted."

"I cannot stay here, of course." Michael scanned the maze and had just decided to plow through it to the nearest door when a hand wrapped around his wrist. He looked down at slender fingers tipped with long manicured nails.

"I thought you had come here to face trouble," she said. "Not to run from it."

He shook her off. "That doesn't mean I want to draw it to me. Your Archangel has already got in my way. The next time, he won't survive the experience."

"If you say so. But before you turn me down altogether, come see the rest of my palace. You might change your mind."

She led him through a bewildering assortment of rooms, and then out a wide set of French windows. They were at the top of a long sloping hill, and beyond it, the Thames surged with the force of the incoming tide. Near to where they stood were several buildings, a pair of cottages to their right and three tall houses to their left. "My guest residences," she said, "completed only a fortnight ago. One of them could be yours. Ah. I see the tenants of the Chioscho delle Rose. Shall we go meet them? Perhaps they will provide me a reference."

Shading his eyes against the early-afternoon sun, he saw three people near the river. One sat in a wheeled chair with his legs extended on a platform. A female wearing a black cloak and bonnet stood beside him. And Hari Singh, crouched behind the chair, appeared to be examining its wheels.

Chapter 3

It had seemed a good idea at the time, Mira was thinking, to convey her father down to the bank of the Thames for a bit of sunshine and fresh air. He had enjoyed watching the river traffic while she fed a heel of stale bread to the ducks. But when she'd tried to push the chair back up the hill, something went wrong with one of the wheels. It refused to turn, and despite the strength she'd developed during three years of steering him around, she was unable to make any progress. Nor did she wish to leave him alone while she went in search of help.

She had been on her knees, wrestling with the recalcitrant wheel, when a deep, accented voice spoke from behind her.

"Might I be of assistance, *memsahib?*"

Turning her head, she looked up, and up, and up. The man, wearing a loose tunic over khaki trousers, was built like a tree and seemed nearly as tall. He had a heavy black beard that appeared to be rolled up around his jaw, full cheeks, a beaked nose, and the kindest eyes she had ever seen. They were the rich brown of molasses, under bushy eyebrows and a red turban.

"Indeed you can," she said, rising. "I am most grateful. This is my father, Edgar Holcombe, who can understand you perfectly although he is unable to respond. We need only transport him to our cottage at the top of this hill, but the left wheel refuses to turn."

He bowed to her father. "I am honored, *sahib*. My name is Hari Singh. Might I examine the wheel?"

Mira watched him drop to one knee and run his thick fingers around the axle.

"With the proper tools," he said, "I can easily repair this. In the meantime, *sahib,* will you permit me to carry you to your residence?"

"That would surely be a great imposition, Mr. Singh. Perhaps you could fetch footmen from the—" She saw her father's index finger move up and down. "I beg your pardon. It seems my father would be pleased to have you carry him. You don't mind?"

"Not if he will be comfortable to travel in my arms. How did he convey his will to you?"

He looked so interested that she felt compelled to oblige him. "We communicate by several means. Father is able to blink, and his lips move a bit. I can tell when he is amused, or when he is displeased. But mostly he tells me 'yes' or 'no' by moving his right forefinger. There are other methods, much slower, which we use in private. I can pass beneath his hand a large card with the alphabet inscribed on it, and he lowers his finger to the letter he wishes to choose. In that way, he speaks to me."

"A most impressive achievement, *memsahib*. It is kind of your father to trust me. If you will hold the chair steady, I shall lift him now."

As Mira took hold of the grips, she felt a strange tingling in her head, heard a sound that wasn't a sound. She glanced up the hill and saw Beata, her lapis and turquoise robe billowing in the cold November breeze. Beside her was a wide-shouldered man with overlong black hair and a bronzed face.

Mira froze in place. She took a deep breath, willed her heart to cease pounding.

Hari Singh's voice came to her as if from a great distance. "Here is Michael. Together we will transport your father without the need to remove him from his chair."

Not Tallant, then. Not the duke. Only the younger brother, athletic and forceful as he strode beside Madonna Beata, who always tried to give the impression of floating when she walked. Clasping her trembling hands, Mira lifted her chin and awaited his arrival.

"Ah," said Beata, addressing the man as they drew closer. "This must be the Sikh person David spoke of. He is your bodyguard?"

"My friend."

"It appears your friend has found your neighbors, then." Beata stopped a little distance away. He halted as well, his gaze fixed on Mira.

A cold shiver passed through her. His eyes, the famous Keynes eyes, were nearly colorless, transparent as water. They seemed to look through clothing and skin and flesh. Revealed nothing of his thoughts.

Beata laid a possessive hand on his forearm. "This is Mr. Edgar Holcombe and his daughter, who took residence a few days ago. They keep too much to themselves. Mira, several gentlemen acquainted with your father are to be here this evening, and they will be disappointed if you fail to join them. Eight o'clock, my dear, in the Camera Dorata. Michael, your friend is very large. I shall therefore put you in the Casina del Pavoni. It is a good deal more expensive than the other *casinas*, but you will enjoy a view of the river. And now I must go. My steward will make the arrangements."

She rose on tiptoe, brushed a kiss on Michael's jaw, and swept back up the hill.

And all that time, as Mira was blisteringly aware, he had not taken his gaze from her own heated face. Nor had Beata troubled to introduce him to her. A clear sign, Mira understood, that she had reserved him to herself.

"The chair is broken," said Hari Singh, pointing to the wheel. "If Mr. Holcombe is agreeable, we shall transport him to his residence."

At last Michael Keynes turned his attention away from her, although the intensity of it continued to burn her skin. He gave a slight bow to her father. "Sir, I am sure Hari could manage by himself, but I will gladly help, if you will entrust yourself to us."

Hari Singh was watching her father's hand. "He has no objection. The gentleman is unable to speak, Michael, but he communicates quite well. You should take the front, I believe."

To her astonishment, Michael Keynes peeled off his caped greatcoat and jacket and held them out to her. "Do you mind?"

"Of course not," she said, taking them, relieved that her hands remained steady. "We are grateful for your assistance, Lord . . . That is, I don't know what title you hold."

"None." A corner of his mouth quirked with amusement. "There's a courtesy title floating around for the second son, but I never attached myself to it."

While she watched, he hunkered beside the platform on which her father's legs were stretched, examining the underpinnings of the chair. "It looks secure enough," he said over his shoulder. "Tilt it up, Hari. Are you ready, sir?"

With the only good view of her father's moving finger, she voiced his response. "He is."

"Here we go, then."

A little fearful, she stepped back to give them room to maneuver. And although she observed them closely, she could not later have described how they lifted the chair. It seemed effortless, for all that it could not have been, and in a short time her father had been raised over their heads. Hari Singh, bent a little because he was taller than his friend, was holding the axle bar between the wheels. She couldn't tell what Michael Keynes had chosen to grasp. The two men were off before she knew it, moving with ease, bearing the heavy oak chair and its passenger as if they weighed no more than a pair of umbrellas. She had to rush to catch up.

"Where are we going?" Michael Keynes asked as she came alongside him.

"Our cottage is to your left, the one nearest the villa."

He corrected his course, and she found herself looking at his back, the buff-colored waistcoat stretched tight across it, the muscles of his shoulders and arms outlined by his cambric shirt. A powerful man, slim hipped and lean, fearsomely attractive. If she hadn't known who he was, and if she were capable of admiring a male physique, he might have stirred her.

But she felt numb, as always. Encased in ice. And deeply resentful because he was here. To deal with one Keynes monster, as she had resolved to do, was a nearly hopeless task. How could she possibly take on both the Devil's sons?

At the Chioscho—Beata's word for their small cottage—Mira waited in the sitting room while her father was settled on his bed. Her gloved fingers stroked the black superfine coat she held. A Keynes's coat, while a Keynes tended to her father.

She could not bear his kindness.

After a few minutes, Hari Singh came out of the bedroom carrying the wheeled chair. "I shall see this repaired. You will have it back in time to take Mr. Holcombe to meet with his friends this evening."

"Thank you," she said, wanting to say more, unable to find the words. It had been so long since there was kindness like his, since there was someone she felt could be trusted. But she had no trust to give, especially to a man in league with her enemies. He left without the gratitude she owed him, and she added one more weight to the scale of debts she owed, debts she would likely never be able to repay. She carried them with her with every step she took.

It was a long time, or so it seemed to her, before Michael Keynes emerged from her father's room. "A remarkable man," he said, taking his jacket and coat from her stiff fingers. "How long has he been like this?"

The frank question startled her. Most people tiptoed around her father's incapacity. "Nearly three years. He had a seizure—a brain attack, his physician calls it—and has regained only a little control of his body. His mind is unimpaired."

"A good mind. And a brave man. I admire him."

"You were able to communicate with my father?"

"Not in any significant way. He seemed to want me to talk to him, so I did. The intelligence in his eyes was unmistakable. As was his courage." He had propped a shoulder against the doorjamb and folded his arms. "Hari can be a great help to you, if you aren't too proud to accept it."

Anger sent heat to her face. "You are insulting, sir."

"Being insulting is the least of my vices. But you appear to know me. I wonder how. The minute I walked into range, you looked at me as if I'd just crawled out of a termite mound. Why is that, Miss Holcombe?"

She went cold. Fumbled for a way to deflect his question. "I could ask you the same thing, Lord . . . sir." He did not seem a commoner, as she was, nor common in any way. She had always thought little of inherited rank, given that the likes of Beast Keynes was a duke. But Michael Keynes had the sort of confidence that bumped against arrogance and bounced off it again, as if he couldn't be bothered with arrogance. "When first you came within sight of me—"

"I couldn't look away. I know. You seemed familiar, as if we'd met before. But that doesn't seem likely. I remember the name, though. Holcombe."

"My uncle's small estate bordered your family's large one. I grew up close by, at Seacrest, which is on the coast. But I don't recall meeting you."

"You wouldn't have. I grew up in Scotland. The inconvenient members of the family were stored there to keep them out of the way. It seems my father, or perhaps my brother, has caused you difficulty. May I inquire how?"

She all but summoned the will to dismiss him, but it slipped away before she could get hold of it. Why not go ahead and tell him? He could find out by other means. And really, there was little he could do to her that had not already been done.

"You brother wishes to acquire our property," she said, gazing at the wall just above his shoulder. "He has a claim on it, or so he insists, because of gambling debts owed him by my cousin. Robert went out to India several years ago, hoping to acquire the money to pay his debts, but we have not heard from him for a considerable time."

"How is it a cousin's debts have put your own home at risk?"

"It's complicated. When my uncle died last year, his entailed estate in Kent went to his brother—my father—while his unentailed property in Somerset was willed to his late sister's son, my cousin Robert. But straightaway, Tallant came in and looted both houses, seized the livestock, and filed claims for the land."

"Did he provide legal grounds for the claims? Did you demand them?"

"If you ask that, you must not know your brother well. Who was to stop him? I cannot hire a solicitor to match the ones he employs." She clasped her hands behind her back, they were shaking so. "I do not understand the law, Mr. Keynes, but I do recognize power. Tallant will get what he wants, one way or another."

A pause. "Has he threatened you?"

"Of course. Frequently." She oughtn't to tell him so much. And yet, she could not seem to stop herself. "But first he made an offer. If we signed everything over to him without a fuss, he would permit us to live at Seacrest until my father's death. After that, he would find employment for me in his household."

She had nearly accepted, God help her, so that her father could live out his days in the house where he'd been born. But she had been unable to summon the courage. "When I refused, he threatened to have my father declared incompetent, removed from my care, and placed in an asylum. We went into hiding for several months. Now we are here. From now on, he will have to deal with us publicly. And I shall fight him publicly, every step of the way."

Well. That was theatrical enough. She had neglected to stamp her foot, and she hadn't cried because she couldn't, but in every other way she had made a proper fool of herself. Her gaze slid from the wall to the polished wood floor. What had possessed her to say these things, and to *this* man of all men?

"You will do better to keep away from him, Miss Holcombe. He'll not be permitted to carry out his threats."

"Who will prevent him? *You?*"

"Your skepticism is understandable. But to this extent, you may trust me. I will see to it you come to no harm." He bowed. "Your servant, ma'am."

"But why?" she said as he turned to go. "Why would you wish to help me?"

After a moment he looked back at her, his eyes somber. "There is a Hindu saying, difficult to translate. *If you feed the tigress, she will not devour you.*"

"I don't understand."

But he left without saying anything more.

Chapter 4

"You there! Keynes!"

Voices stilled as everyone in the gaming room looked first in the speaker's direction, and from there to a table at the other side of the room.

Michael, holding his best whist hand of the day, folded the cards and glanced over with resignation at the tall, tawny-haired man standing in the doorway. Damn and blast. Trouble had a thousand ways of tracking him down.

Loose limbed as a cheetah, trouble sauntered into the room and stopped at the first table, where two piquet players were sitting. They leaned back in their chairs, jaws tight with apprehension. "Did you fail to hear me, Keynes? I'm waiting for a greeting. Then I want an apology."

"I heard. An apology for what?"

"Any number of offenses. For one, you stole my horse."

A new figure appeared at the doorway. Beata Neri, regal in purple and gold, wore an expression of delight. Behind her, half a dozen wide-eyed females jockeyed for a good view of the scene.

He owed Beata a scene, Michael had to concede. And who better to engage with than the fellow at the other side of the room, his hands splayed on a gaming table? He had to be got rid of anyway.

"*Borrowed* your horse," Michael corrected, putting down his cards and slowly rising. "I returned it."

"Six months later. And it was a different horse."

"A better one. Not that you would notice. Left to your own devices, you'd ride bareback on a pig."

People were milling into the gaming room now, lining the walls, their eyes round as oranges. Beata stood in a circle of light cast by a wall sconce. It was still morning, but several rooms at her Palazzo, including this one, had been designed to create the effect of eternal midnight.

"I could call you out for that," came the inevitable challenge.

Michael grinned. A heartbeat later, the point of his knife pierced the table between the forefinger and index finger of his antagonist's hand.

Two chairs crashed to the floor as the piquet players sped to safety.

Alone at the table, the long blade still quivering between his fingers, the man chuckled. "Is that the best you can do?"

"I don't know." Michael put steel in his voice. "Shall we try again? What part of you should I target?"

Looking a trifle confused, the man pulled the knife from the table and backed toward the doorway. "While I have this," he said, "what can you throw at me?"

"What indeed?" Michael held out his arms. He was in shirtsleeves and waistcoat, with his jacket draped over the back of his chair. His hands were notably empty. "Unless I have another knife."

The man had reached the doorway. He moved aside as two ladies darted past him into the room, curiosity brazen on their faces. "Have you, then? And can you throw it before I—"

A second blade, more slender than the first, whizzed by the man's cheek and hit the wall a hair's distance from his ear.

A gasp went up from the watching crowd.

"I take your point," said the man after a tense moment. "So to speak. If you will excuse me now, I shall take m'self off to Tattersall's and buy m'self a pig."

Ignoring the gossip swirling around him, Michael sat down, picked up his cards, and raised an eyebrow. "Gentlemen?"

After a while, people ceased hoping he'd do something else outrageous and went back to where they'd come from. The stack of wafers in front of him grew larger. He kept an eye on the mantelpiece clock. Half an hour would do it, he had decided.

His patience ran out in twenty minutes. Ten, actually, but he forced himself to wait, the way he forced himself to leave the table and the room without looking as if he had anywhere to go.

The only exit took him through the Sala dei Medici, where Beata was poised with a knife in each of her hands. "Yours, I believe."

"Thank you." Taking them, he bowed and would have moved on if she hadn't planted herself in his path.

"Put them away," she said. "I wish to see where you conceal them."

"What fun would that be?" Dodging around her, he got halfway across the Sala before a footman loomed in front of him. Beata used hand signals, he had noticed, to give orders without speaking.

"You would deny me?" she said plaintively. Flirtatiously.

With a shrug, he turned. The dagger was already back in its sheath. With the larger knife, he was whittling on a fist-sized chunk of mahogany wood.

Her eyes widened. "Clever wolf. Very well, then,

keep your secrets. Except . . . where are you off to in such a hurry?"

"Outside. Anywhere I can move." He bowed. "You must pardon me. I cannot be penned in for any length of time."

"I thought you would wish to know," she said with the air of a magician contemplating a wand, "that the Duke of Tallant has returned to London."

"Has he indeed." He kept his breathing steady, his voice level. "Do you expect him here?"

"From a Keynes, I expect only the unexpected. Will you go looking for him?"

"Perhaps later. If he fails to come looking for me. Your servant, signora."

He heard her musical laugh as he departed, and for long time thereafter. He felt, sometimes, like an actor in a bad play who knew his role but not his lines, who could see how it all would end but had no idea what would happen next. There would be real weapons, though, in this drama. Real pain. Real blood.

No stage-prop pig's blood, which reminded him—

After retrieving Hari Singh from the mews, where he had been working on some sort of mechanical device to support Mr. Holcombe's right arm, Michael set off in the direction of the river and Cheyne Walk. As always, the two men drew the attention of passersby. Audiences everywhere, he reflected while giving Hari his instructions.

When they had come in sight of their destination, a soft voice spoke to them from a narrow alleyway. "And what was that all about?"

While Hari moved on ahead, Michael slipped into the alleyway. "Bloody fool. Where can we go?"

"This way."

Shortly, in the darkest corner of a dark tavern, Michael settled at a scarred wood table across from Hugo

Duran. "You can't be seen with me," he said. "That's what it was about."

"All the time I've known you, I wasn't supposed to know you. And I suppose that made a degree of sense in India. But why here? What have you done *here*?"

"Nothing, yet."

A box-shaped man missing half his nose delivered two tankards of ale, pocketed the coin tossed him by Duran, and returned to the shadows.

"I went looking for you when you disappeared," Michael said, pulling out his knife and the piece of wood he had been carving. "Traced you to Alanabad, but you were already gone. There was some nonsense about a stolen icon and an emissary sent by the gods to seek for it in England."

"That would be me," Duran said. "But the Nizam of Alanabad has no love for Englishmen. I'm surprised they told you anything. More surprised you got in and out in one piece."

"Nothing to it." One broken arm, one bullet slicing off a quarter-inch of flesh near his waist, assorted cuts and bruises. It had not been one of his more graceful exits. At least he'd had the foresight to send Hari in at another time, from another direction. "I ran a diversion while Hari made friends with the locals. Did you find the icon?"

"It's a long story. Come to supper tonight and I'll tell it with all proper flourishes. Besides, I want you to meet Jessica." His expression softened. "My wife, who is carrying three-quarters of our first child."

Duran was the least likely man to wed that Michael had ever known . . . not counting himself. "You never listen," he said. "No contact with me. None. Congratulations, and from now on, stay the hell away."

"We're setting out for Sussex day after tomorrow." Duran frowned. "I presume you're going to warn me against your brother. Do you imagine I fear him?"

"You should. *I* do. Not for myself, but he won't go

for me directly unless I force him to. He'll go instead for my friends, for anyone he thinks I might value. Call attention to yourself, Duran, and he will look past you to your wife and child. There is no allowance for swaggering here, or for repaying old debts to me. You have obligations more compelling."

Duran's gaze dropped from his face to the knife shaving at the wood. "What do you intend to do, then?"

"Whatever is required. And there isn't much time." Which reminded him . . . "What do you know about the Earl of Varden?"

"The Archangel? Not a great deal. I met him once at Beata's. Come to think of it, he was in company with your brother. Others were there as well, stockholders of the East India Consortium, most of them reputable. As I recall, Varden was about to sail for India."

"He got there." The fire inside Michael roared to life. With effort, he tamped it down again. His temper, Hari kept saying, would be the death of him . . . that and his lack of interest in staying alive. "Anything else?"

"I can ask Jessica. She knows everyone. You have a problem with Varden?"

"Something of the kind. He doesn't like what I was doing to the Consortium's country trade, and he sure as hell doesn't like me. When Hari and I left, he was still gathering evidence against me, and I presume that when he gets here, he'll try to prosecute. Which means I have to finish with the Beast before the bloody *Archangel* flies in."

The plank table in front of him was littered with shavings. Whittling kept his hands busy, focused his energy. He'd done it since he could remember, shaving away bits of wood until there was nothing left of it. Then, a year or two ago and only to please Hari, he'd started trying to create recognizable shapes be-

fore using them for firewood. No point saving them.
By necessity, he always traveled light.

"When will that be?"

Michael had lost track of the conversation. He went
looking and found it again. "When he gets here. I'd
counted on two months' lead time, assuming Varden
caught a trader shortly after I left India. Hari and I
came the quickest way, through the Red Sea and across
Egypt, but bandits attacked the caravan we'd joined.
After we shook loose of them I went down with a bout
of malaria, and later, we ran into bad weather on the
Mediterranean. At this point I figure a month at best
before he arrives, and probably half that time."

Duran took a drink of ale, winced, and set the tan-
kard down again. "Foul stuff. Look. I'll put my wife's
secretary to compiling a dossier on Varden. It will be
thorough. Helena Pryce can track down a white
feather in a snowstorm."

Michael had always valued information, and the
slightest detail could be the one that gave him the
edge. Besides, with Duran wanting to be of help, this
was a way to get him off his back. "Very well, then,
if it's no trouble. Thank you. But have her send it
to"—he scrambled for a name—" 'John Blackstone'
in care of my banker, Charles Whitehead, at the Bank
of England."

"If you say so." Duran propped his elbows on the
table. "I'm almost afraid to ask, considering your reputation, but there's a young woman living at Beata's,
a Miss Miranda Holcombe. I was wondering if you
had met her. Tallant has his sights on the Holcombe
family, and he's already stripped her father of his
home and his inheritance."

"She told me. Some of it. The young lady gives
little away."

"I know. To that extent, she reminds me of you.
And, like you as well, she once did me a great service.
Keep an eye on her, will you?"

"Yes." Simple enough. He'd been able to do little else since first he saw her. "I'll make sure she comes to no harm. Or I'll try. But if I fail—"

"Jessica and I will protect her. That's assuming she'll let us, of course, because there is no creature on the earth more formidable than a proud, independent woman. I know that because I married one."

"You don't look the worse for it." Michael finished shaping the bit of wood, now reduced to the size of his palm, and returned the knife to its sheath. "If you're actually going to Tattersall's, I won't."

"I'm not, and you should. There's a special auction starting at noon, and if you require a mount, you won't easily find a better one. Lord Fenborough kept an exceptional stable, but he's forced to sell the better part of it to pay his gaming debts." Duran's lips curved in a sly smile. "Debts he owes the Duke of Tallant."

"Worth a look-in, then." Michael stood. "It was good seeing you, but I don't want to see you again. Understood?"

"Quite some time ago." Duran picked up the wood carving Michael had left on the table. "What's this supposed to be?"

"A bird. Or maybe a cabbage. I couldn't decide."

Duran held it up. "I can't tell either. Mind if I keep it? I'm collecting toys for the infant."

With an indifferent shrug, Michael left the table and the tavern without a backward look. When Duran first mentioned Tattersall's, he had understood he was supposed to go there by the most obvious route. And sure enough, Duran had been waiting for him along the way. But the ultimate goal had always been the auction house, so he had sent Hari ahead to evaluate the horses on offer.

Duran, who knew him uncomfortably well, had set him on this course. Now, with luck, he'd find a good mount.

And with better luck, he'd find his brother.

Chapter 5

A little distance from Tattersall's Repository, Hari intercepted Michael. "I have found what you are looking for."

"Tallant?"

"He is there. But I speak of the horse you should purchase. Spanish bloodlines, imported by Lord Fenborough to race, but of a temperament that did not abide close quarters. We should enter from the other street, near to where he can be found."

"First my brother. Then I'll buy a horse."

"It must be the other way, Michael. If the horse is put on the auction block and you show interest, the duke will not permit you to have it. I have asked Lord Fenborough to accept a preemptive sale at six hundred guineas."

"Good God. I hope you're paying."

"I shall, if you wish. As the Lord Buddha—"

"I've heard that one. Take me to the damn horse."

They came in unnoticed and wove toward the stables through a hodgepodge of vehicles on offer. All the action was the other side of the courtyard, where Michael saw a crowd of fashionably dressed men clustered under an arcade with their backs to him, looking at something he could not see. The auction must be under way.

Hari led him to an enclosed area lined with stalls where a handler was leading out a chestnut mare. Standing nearby, a thin man with sagging jowls and sad, protruding eyes watched the horse being taken away. Then he lifted his unhappy gaze to the men walking toward him, and Michael saw the familiar recoil as a Keynes was recognized. He was getting used to that recoil, the nervous pretense it hadn't occurred, the too-friendly smile that followed.

In this case, the smile never appeared. Fenborough looked as if he hadn't smiled in a decade, and the bloodshot eyes and trembling hands betrayed a dive into a bottle the night before. Michael knew the symptoms.

"You are the gentleman for Loki?" Fenborough said in a squeaking voice. "I have held him for you, on your servant's promise. But perhaps—"

"If I had a servant, he wouldn't be making promises for me. Where's the horse?"

"I'm afraid I didn't know you were a relation. I must pay everything I acquire to the duke, you see."

"What's that to do with anything? Where—"

"In the corner, that way." Fenborough shrank back, letting Michael pass. Fear rose from the man like steam.

Impatient to get on to his brother, Michael quickly examined the horse. Large, black, restless, and angry, just like himself. As Hari had realized, Loki would suit him very well.

Fenborough's attack of nerves had got worse in the short time Michael was gone. "I won't release the horse without payment," he kept saying. "Nor Mr. Singh's horse neither. You could ride off and leave me with nothing."

"You'll be left with nothing in any case," Michael

pointed out, not sure why he continued trying to strike a deal when he was unlikely to be needing a mount for very long. "I'll bring you the price of both nags, in banknotes, within two hours. But the horses are taken away now, because if they aren't, my brother will prevent me from having them. Then you'll make half the amount at auction, and less if the duke intimidates other buyers."

"But how would that benefit him? I'm selling everything I own to pay what I owe."

"Did I say he was reasonable? You're a gambling man, Fenborough. Have you ever won, dealing with Tallant? He'll hound you until you're dead. I, on the other hand, will pay you, my word on it, and you can draw up a false receipt for half the amount. He need never know how much you got."

"But then you might only pay what's on that receipt, and—"

"I'm finished here. Hari, buy your own horse if you can come to terms with this idiot." Michael was halfway across the yard when Fenborough scuttled after him.

"Banknotes. Slip them to me in private. And quickly. He'll wonder what happened when that horse don't go under the hammer."

"Very well. Hari, meet me across the street. I don't know how long this will take."

"You must not cause trouble here. It would be unwise."

"And when did that ever stop me?" He knew the signs. Knew he·was close to slipping his own leash, didn't much care. But to protect Fenborough, he took the precaution of edging back the way they'd come in and then reentered Tattersall's through the main gate. By that time he had cooled down, marginally, and his temper was in check.

Little had changed since his first arrival. Most of the gentlemen were where they had been before, clustered around the arches that separated the arcade from the courtyard. He found a position in the shadows and scanned the crowd for his brother, seeing no one with the height and hair and shoulders of a Keynes. After a time, he set off to explore the buildings that lined the perimeter of the compound, cursing himself for wasting time with Fenborough. By now, Tallant might have gone.

He was about to abandon the hunt when just ahead of him, emerging from a door that sported a pair of crossed whips above the lintel, came a tall man who suddenly paused, as if scenting danger, and turned to look directly at him.

Eyes the transparent gray of water under a cloudy sky, black brows arching above them with amusement. Michael held the sardonic gaze. Nearly two decades since last he saw his brother, born seven years before him to a different mother. Twenty years since he'd sworn to destroy Jermyn Keynes by whatever means it required. He had never thought it would take so long.

The silent confrontation was broken off by a man coming out the room behind the duke, talking to someone and not seeing that his path was blocked until he ran into a broad-shouldered obstacle. Swearing, the duke swung around and backhanded the man's face.

Michael slipped his knife into his hand, the blade concealed in the folds of his greatcoat, and waited for his brother to come to him.

He did so moments later, flanked by several onlookers. The duke's attack on the hapless bumbler had drawn attention, and soon others began wandering over from the auction to see what was going on. They formed a half circle several yards away, leaving the brothers to have at it.

Too many of them, Michael was thinking. Too close. And Tallant's heavy coat had a collar and lapels of thick fur. The knife might not penetrate deep enough for a kill. Letting go the rage to attack straightaway, he took a deep breath and studied his target.

All this time, he had imagined Jermyn looking exactly like himself, aging in all the same ways. Whenever he looked in the mirror, he saw his brother, and his conviction had been reinforced by those who had met both men. They never failed to remark on the resemblance. Miranda Holcombe had . . . Well, he mustn't think on her.

In fact, Jermyn stood a little taller than his own six feet and one, was wider in the shoulders and fuller in the chest, had thinner lips, and sported lines of dissipation at his temples and the corners of his mouth. He looked as if he could hold his own in a fight, but more like a man who preferred to let others do his fighting for him.

Even if they were meeting for the first time, Michael knew he would instinctively despise the man who stood regarding him with an equal mix of curiosity and contempt.

"My little brother, is it?" said the duke. "I'd heard you had been driven out of India. But with all the charges arrayed against you, I'm surprised to find you here, within the grasp of your accusers and the law."

"I'm here because your enterprises in India have dwindled to the point that gutting them no longer keeps me occupied. And because we have unfinished business."

"Ah, yes. The duel. You were, what? Seven-and-ten? Was I to take your challenge seriously?"

"I did. I still do. Shall we get on with it?"

Tallant chuckled. "But what will you do for seconds, Brother? You can't have any friends here. And do you imagine you can get away with killing a duke?"

"I don't expect to get away with it. I expect only to *do* it."

"Well, it will be amusing to watch you try. But if we are to make arrangements, let us converse without an audience." Using his walking stick, Tallant cleared a path and struck out for an absurd little Grecian folly plunked in the center of the courtyard. There, they would be entirely visible, but no one would risk the duke's anger by venturing close enough to eavesdrop.

After a moment, Michael returned the knife to its sheath and followed his brother. He might have made a try, but the odds weren't good. And if his first strike failed to kill, he'd be taken down by the onlookers before he could strike again. "You won't fight me," he said, stepping onto the marble foundation. "So why are we here?"

"To demonstrate my goodwill, of course. And no, there cannot be a fair fight. I haven't been hacking about with primitives and living, as you have done, like an animal. I grant your physical superiority, for what that is worth. I also reckon you a little mad, for so you must be to return here and openly defy me. You will regret it."

"Let's dispense with the theatrics. I've told you what to expect. If that's all—"

"But I like being at center stage. It took me long enough to get here. I don't imagine you enjoyed poverty and exile in Scotland, but you may be sure that I had no easy go of it either. With you out of his reach, I was the only one at the end of the Devil's whip. And when he finally turned up his toes, I had to rebuild everything three generations of Keyneses had destroyed. I succeeded because I had the will to do what was necessary. You would not have done so well. You haven't the stomach for it."

"Then you have nothing to fear from me, do you?"

"Only the chance misdirected shot. I think you are too soft to kill your brother, my lad. You could not even bring yourself to dispatch native rabble when they got in your way. Oh, I concede you did significant damage to my business interests, but had you not been so squeamish, you might have wiped me out entirely."

"You misunderstand," Michael said, propping his back against a marble column and folding his arms. "A mercenary relies on the goodwill of the locals for supplies and intelligence. And because my dealings with them were invariably honest, not to mention generous, they never sold me out for the price you put on my head. On occasion, they even plucked off some of the assassins you set on my trail. I have no difficulty killing when necessary, but I do like to be practical."

"That's as may be." Tallant regarded him thoughtfully. "You have, in fact, been a costly nuisance, and if you stay in my reach, I shall be forced to punish you for it. I rather hope you'll give me the opportunity. But the pleasure, I am sorry to say, must be delayed. A few nonessential assets require to be disposed of, and the errand will take me away from London for at least a fortnight."

"Perhaps I should come along. Keep you company."

The duke laughed. At the sound, startled faces turned in his direction. "You're welcome to join us. But I'm traveling with a contingent of armed men, and there's a good chance we'd lose you along the way. A little friendly advice, Michael. Use this reprieve to take ship for somewhere beyond my reach. Create for yourself a principality there, like the one I am building here for myself. This is your chance to escape. I promise you will not otherwise survive."

"Survival doesn't concern me." Michael's body strained to pull out the knife and slice it across Jermyn's throat. Even through the layers of coat and cravat and collar, it might do the job. *Self-indulgence,* his mind kept warning him. *You'll have only one chance. Make it good. Better than this.*

"Now who is being theatrical?" Tallant poked him in the chest with his walking stick. "Come near to me again, and I shall spring the blade at the end of this staff, or fire the bullet in its handle. Or simply whip you like the puppy you have always been. Take yourself to New South Wales, Michael, or to the Americas. A little brotherly advice."

Michael gently pushed the walking stick aside. Not a bad strategy, he thought with a degree of admiration. From the start, relying on his younger brother's volatile temper, Tallant had been inviting a public attack. Self-defense, the witnesses would claim when the sword cane or the bullet did its work.

"I'll think it over," Michael said, grinning. "You hurry back, now."

He strolled away, leaving Tallant in lone possession of the Grecian folly, and met up with Hari at Hyde Park Corner. Loki looked ready to bolt, and Hari's new mount, an enormous bay, was cheerfully nuzzling his turban. "Follow Tallant, will you?" Michael swung onto the silver-studded saddle, wondering how much extra that had cost him. "I want to know when he leaves London, and where he goes."

"I am sure to be noticed," Hari pointed out, handing him the bills of sale. "How long must I track him?"

"Just long enough to make sure he's gone. I'd do it myself, but I have to settle with Fenborough. I take it you expect me to pay for that glue bait you'll be riding?"

"A generous deed will repay you a hundredfold, Michael. As the Lord Buddha remarked when—"

"I'll settle for you repaying me onefold," Michael said, guiding Loki toward Hyde Park Turnpike. "Fob off the Buddha sermon on your horse."

Chapter 6

Attached to the library, accessible only if you knew the way, was a small room, little more than a cubbyhole, with a bay window that gave a view of the grounds and the river. Mira had come upon it while seeking a book her father especially wished her to read to him, and ever since, she had brought him there most afternoons. The room offered privacy and, when the weather permitted, a few hours of afternoon sunlight in which he could bask.

Because he insisted, she was generally required to leave him there and go in search of companionship among Beata's guests, preferably the masculine variety. Edgar Holcombe would not rest easy until she had snagged herself a husband. It did no harm to let him imagine she was trolling for one, but most times she found a quiet place in the library and enjoyed the solitude. On this afternoon, however, he refused to let her depart until she gave him her promise.

"Very well," she said, not surprised he had figured out her deception. "I'll take myself to the public rooms and soak up all the gossip."

His eyes glowed approval.

"In here," said a male voice just then, so clearly the

speaker might have been standing only a few feet away. "Lock the door."

Startled, Mira looked at her father. His finger moved over the alphabet card. "Nxt rom."

"If you doubt me, read this." The man's voice was soft, almost bland, but anger edged his words. "The losses are staggering."

The sound seemed to come from the picture-crowded wall. There had to be an opening, but until the man spoke again, she could not pinpoint the source. Several minutes passed while she examined the paintings and their frames, the carved wainscoting, the ornate silk wallpaper. Then a loud thud, as if someone had just slammed closed a heavy ledger.

"What do you intend to do?"

Footsteps, muffled by the carpet. And from a distance, a different voice, a deeper voice, one that sounded familiar. "You have summoned me here to no purpose. I intend to complete the personal business you interrupted. When I return, we shall speak again."

"That will not suffice."

"It will have to. We'll make up the losses. They would not continue in any case, as you must surely have observed. But if it eases your mind, I shall soon see to it there is no more trouble from that source."

A door opened and closed. Mira listened hard. After a time, the door opened and closed again.

Well. No wonder her father didn't mind being left alone here. When he wasn't snoozing in the sunshine, he had been eavesdropping on private conversations. She smiled. How could she blame him, now that he could do little more than listen to what others had to say? He had always been partial to a good story, but he never broke a confidence. And if he knew the identities of the two men they had overheard, he would not tell her.

She moved his chair closer to the window, gave him

a drink of water spoonful by spoonful, and watched his eyelids begin to droop. Not long after, she adjusted the blanket over his frail body and navigated the labyrinth of screens and bookshelves that separated the hideaway, for surely that's what it was meant to be, from the library.

Her promise, bitter in her mouth, had to be kept, so she endured an hour in unpleasant company before deciding she'd done her duty. Happily, none of the women at Beata's luncheon had paid her the slightest attention. It was only the men who ever noticed her, trailed after her, found excuses to approach her. But this afternoon, to her great relief, all the men were elsewhere. In the gaming room, probably, or taking part in the archery contest down by the river.

She wished it were possible to join them. Her father had put a small bow and arrow in her hands when she was six years old, and over the years she had become a good shot. A very good shot. But it was a useless talent, because she could scarcely wander around London armed like Robin Hood.

If only her father had taught her to shoot with a small pistol. Now *that* would have been worth something.

She was on her way back to the library when a tall, black-haired man came out of a room farther down the passageway.

Michael Keynes. It had to be. Except . . . The vibration that always signaled his presence had not warned her. Turning swiftly, she darted through the nearest door and closed it behind her.

She would have locked it or dropped a latch, but there wasn't a latch bar or a key. Never mind. Keynes had been turning the other direction, so there was no reason to expect he'd noticed her. She would wait here for a few minutes, here in this . . . this linen closet.

Good heavens. It was larger even than her bedchamber, lined with tall shelves on both sides, all of them piled high with table covers, napkins, towels, sheets, and pillowcases. At the opposite end from the door, a bottle-glass window admitted light while shutting off the view more effectively than curtains.

She looked around, she couldn't have said why, for somewhere to conceal herself. Apprehension swept over her like a cold wind. He had seen her. She smelled it on the air, his determination, her own fear.

Danger came closer. Reached out. Raised the latch.

She forced herself to stand in place, directly center of the room, and waited.

It was his powerful build that she saw first. The wide shoulders. The heavy black hair.

Her heart galloped in her chest.

He moved inside and closed the door behind him. "I thought it might be you," said the man she had come to London to kill.

Paralyzed by memory, she could only stare at him, wide eyed and mute.

"And what are you doing in this"—he waved a hand—"whatever it is? I had got the impression you were one of Beata's tenants, but it appears, Miss Holcombe, that she has employed you as a servant."

"Good afternoon, Your Grace," she said, her voice commendably steady. "Did you require some towels?"

His eyes narrowed. "How is it you recognize me? We have been adversaries, after a fashion, but surely we've never met."

She knew what he was fishing for. "Not that I recall, but perhaps your memory is better than mine. It was you, after all, who followed me in here and addressed me by name. As for your identity, it would be immediately apparent to anyone who has met your brother."

"Ah, yes. He is in residence here as well, I have just been informed." Displeasure knitted his forehead. "A strange coincidence, not to my liking. Perhaps knowing my . . . my *interest* in you, he has seized an opportunity to fix his own. An old habit with us, two brothers squabbling over the same toy. But do not think to find an ally in that quarter, my dear. Like all Keynes men, he is unprincipled and savage. He might befriend you to spite me, or to use against me, but when you have served his purposes, he'll spit you out again."

The duke regarded her speculatively. "On the other hand, we are both men of varied and demanding appetites. I expect there are other uses to be made of you." He sent his lewd gaze to her slippers and let it roam languidly up her body, pausing where men generally paused to look before moving on to another place of interest.

With apparent indifference, she endured the examination. All the battle was being fought deep inside her, as she compressed her fear and rage into a white-hot ball and contained it there. Fuel, she thought, stored up, made ready. One day she would strike tinder and send herself, and this monstrous creature, in a fiery plunge to hell.

His lips curled. "The shoes are nothing out of the ordinary, but where, I wonder, did you come by the funds to purchase that gown? Have I been neglectful? Have you established a concealed bank account?"

"Had we money to store in an account, I've no doubt you would have unearthed it."

"My solicitors are thorough," he agreed. "Which means you must have been stealing from me. Your uncle was a collector, I am told, and his castle stocked with a lifetime's accumulation of antiquities. It seems I let you run tame there overlong. Have you left me anything of value, Miss Holcombe? Or must I retrieve what is owed me directly from you?"

"You are mistaken, Your Grace. Everything of worth was sold off years ago by my uncle to fund the restoration of his castle, which was his obsession.

What little remains might bring you a hundred pounds from the ragpickers. As for my gowns, they are cast-offs from ladies of quality, sold in Cheapside markets and made over to fit me. I have taken nothing that belongs to you."

"But then, you dispute that anything once owned by your family belongs to me, whereas I claim everything down to the last button. Where, by the way, is the young wastrel who landed you in these circumstances?"

"Cousin Robert remains in India, so far as I know. If you are intent on collecting the debts owed you, perhaps you should go in search of him."

"He is being tracked down. But in the meantime, there is no reason I should not feast on his inheritance." Another step closer. He was enjoying this. For him, it was a game.

She held her ground. "That would be the castle, which my uncle willed to him. But you have no legal claim to the estate entailed to my father, nor to our family home."

"Except that I *do* claim them, and who is to prevent me from seizing them? An old man who can neither move nor speak? A young woman who can only whimper that she is being wronged?" He stopped directly in front of her, the yellow diamond pin in his neckcloth inches from her eyes. "Is that why you are in residence here, Miranda, where all Society congregates? Are you seeking a champion?"

She looked up, met his eyes. "Among the dandies of London? No, indeed. I seek precisely what every other female of my age is frantic to secure. A husband."

"You astonish me." He seemed genuinely amused. "Obscure family, no fortune, an old stick of a father to care for, enormous debts to a powerful man. Suitors must be queuing in the streets."

There was nothing to be said to that, and just as well. With him so close, she required all her strength to keep from trembling.

"Or perhaps," he said thoughtfully, a new look in his eyes, "there are *customers* queuing for your services. I begin to think you have acquired fashionable clothing and lodging in the time-honored manner— on your back. Is that the case, my dear? Are you whoring yourself?"

"People may begin to imagine so, Your Grace, if I remain closeted here with you. And that will make it all the more difficult to bring a gentleman up to scratch, for as you have observed, I have little to offer a husband save loyalty and my virtue."

"Is it intact, your virtue?" His expression sharpened. "Are *you* intact?"

The question was not unexpected. He was making sure, that was all, and she had prepared herself. In this one thing—the telling of lies—they were well matched. "There has been little opportunity for dalliance," she said calmly, "even were I so inclined. But a woman has only one way to prove her virtue, and that is in the very act of losing it. You must inquire of my husband, should I manage to snabble one, after our wedding night."

"Oh, I don't imagine there will be a wedding night, or a husband who wants to breed on you. For in addition to your other inadequacies, there is the small matter of deformity." He took hold of her hand. "I cannot help but notice your unusual glove. It makes me curious to see what it conceals."

Had it been her left glove he was peeling down her arm and from her hand, she would have resisted. But he'd chosen her right hand, so she held herself still and watched his eyes as he examined her middle and ring fingers, webbed together like one great, thick sausage. Or so it felt to her, especially when he recoiled slightly and let go of her hand with a snort of disgust.

"As I surmised. Your cousin was similarly afflicted, save that all his fingers were conjoined. He could not even deal cards properly. The affliction runs in the family, I take it."

"To an extent." Pride kept her voice level. "My aunt, Robert's mother, had hands very like mine. There are no other examples, but then, we are a small family."

"And one that will quickly die out, for no man will wed you at the risk of having his children inherit your disfigurement. So what will you do, Miranda, when I have stripped you of everything? When you have a father to provide for and nowhere to turn? If you have managed to preserve your virtue thus far, will you yield it on his account?"

"There are other means of earning a living."

"Not for a female with a spoiled reputation." He gripped her wrists, brought them behind her back, leaned over her. "Keep still. I want to know what you have under that gown, decide if it is worth sampling before you are put out to sell yourself on the streets."

"N-no." She couldn't help herself. Couldn't draw air. With his free hand he took her chin, lifted it as his lips came against hers, cool and dry until his tongue licked out. She thought she would be sick then, sick all over him, except that she was suffocating.

Fingers stroked down her neck. A hand passed over her breast, stopped, squeezed hard.

The pain brought her to her senses. He still had hold of her chin, and now her breast. He'd let go of her wrists! In an instant she had drawn out her knife, brought it around, slashed at the hand on her breast.

Swearing, he seized her wrist and wrenched her arm up behind her, applying so much pressure that she was forced to drop the knife. He put his foot on it and thrust her away. Her back hit the shelves. When he bent to pick up the knife, she tried to slip past him to the door, but he grabbed her shoulder and threw her in the direction of the window. She struck the wall beside it and sagged there, sucking in great gulps of air.

He would beat her now, she was sure. Her fault, her fault. She had been foolish and arrogant and unprepared. Had imagined she could confront the Beast, could emerge with him defeated and her unscathed.

She watched him, waiting for punishment, failure acrid in her mouth. He was studying the back of his hand. From the cut she'd made, blood dripped to the floor. After a moment he went to a shelf, took a napkin, and wrapped it around the wound. Moments later, blood seeped through the fabric, turning it scarlet.

He tossed the napkin aside and glanced over at her. "Come fix this, you bloody-minded little bitch." But it was said almost without rancor, and the heightened color of rage had left his face.

She gathered softer napkins and applied them one by one, exerting pressure until the bleeding slowed to an upwelling. The cut was shallow, she saw with regret, but it would leave a scar. Folding a fresh napkin, she placed it on the back of his hand and secured it with what looked to be a curtain tie. All the while he said nothing, and she focused her attention on binding up his wound.

When she was done, she took one step back, expecting him to strike her, preparing for the blow.

He gave her, instead, a smile. It was her anticipation of pain he most enjoyed, she understood then. The tightening bands of fear. The awful dread. Yes, the waiting for pain was worse than the pain itself, as he knew. But she could bear it.

What hurt more than anything, what she could not bear, was her failure. She had been alone with him, been given the chance she'd dreamed of and longed for. She ought to have been clever enough to come close to him, create a distraction, slice her blade across his throat. But when her chance came, she had surrendered like a lamb. There was nothing left for her now, save only her shame. And the beginnings of despair.

He picked up her knife and turned it over in his hands, testing the edge of its slender blade with his fingertip, studying the ebony handle set with a single cabochon ruby. "Deadly enough, if properly wielded. Somewhat exotic. From India?"

"I don't know."

"You won't mind if I keep it. A souvenir, if you will, of our first meeting, and a promise that we'll soon meet again. I had always meant to break you, when time and circumstances permitted, but I'm afraid your destruction is now imperative. Well, nearly so. First I must deal with two other troublesome females who have become an inconvenience, but that shouldn't take long."

He went to the door, where he turned and fixed his transparent eyes on her face. "When I return, my dear, the vise will close. First I will take everything from you, including your pride. I've a fancy to bring you to your knees"—he pointed to a spot directly in front of him—"begging to pleasure me. Your father will watch everything I do to you. And when I am finished, you will both vanish, and no one will notice that you have gone."

"Why do you bother?" she asked. "We have nothing you require. Our land is unprofitable, our home undistinguished and in need of repair. We are, as you say, so insignificant that our disappearance would be entirely unremarked. Is it that you dare to prey only on the weak?"

He barked a laugh. "Like every Keynes before me, I am by nature a hunter. A predator, if you like, but it is the chase that amuses me. The target is irrelevant. Weak or strong, it is eventually cornered, and tormented, and put out of my way. Michael is a hunter as well, and a good one, I am forced to admit. But he hunts only because his nature compels him to. He never got the knack of enjoying it. Unless, of course, he is hunting me."

"You persecute us, then, because it gives you pleasure?"

"That is one reason, yes. And because you have defied me." Lifting her knife to eye level, he sighted down it as if taking aim at her. "And because I can."

Chapter 7

After a while, she didn't know how long it took, Mira had regathered her composure and put everything else—her rage, her terror, her defeat—into the small corner of herself where her nightmares lived. No one else would ever know they were there.

They could all see the blood on her hands, though, and on her gown, unless she made it to her cottage without encountering anyone. Not easy to do any time of the day or night at Palazzo Neri, where the devil himself might come out of a room directly in front of you. But she scrubbed her hands with a rough towel while plotting a route through courtyards and back passageways, and when she left the closet, her arms were wrapped around a stack of linens. They concealed the worst of the stains on her bodice, but there was nothing she could do about the ones on her hem and her shoes.

Luck was with her. She made it outside without passing anyone except a footman, who glanced at the towels and gave her a puzzled look before continuing on his way. Only a short distance to her door, and then she could strip off her dress and burn it in the fireplace while she scoured every trace of the Beast from her body.

But quickly. Soon her father would be awake and needing her. He saw too much, she knew, probably more than she suspected. By the time she returned to the library, she must have herself well in hand.

Planning ahead made her careless about the present. She became aware of that infernal humming and looked up to see Michael Keynes striding toward her from the archery field, wearing leather breeches and a woolen shirt open at the throat, bronze skinned and aggressively male. A hunter, like his brother, even to the bow slung over his shoulder.

His thoughts must have been elsewhere as well. She saw the moment he realized she was there, the break in his stride as if he meant to shift his direction. His gaze went to the linens she was carrying, slid downward to her shoes.

There would be no escape for her now.

Seconds later he was planted in front of her, sawing a gesture at her skirts. "What happened? Is it your father?"

"My—? Oh, no. He's having a nap in the library. I cut myself sharpening a pen, only a little cut, but it bled rather a lot before I found a cloth to stop it."

"Rather a lot of cloths," he said. "Where did you cut yourself?"

"In the library." They were relentless, the Keynes men. And this one looked concerned, which was worse than all his brother's cruelty. "You must pardon me. I haven't so many gowns that I can afford to ruin one because of a small accident. This dress must be put to soak in cold water straightaway, and I must return to my father before he wakes up. Good day, sir."

She cut around him, but he was at her side in an instant. "Almost convincing. Now, what really happened?"

"Nothing of consequence, as I have already explained. Not that it is any of your business."

"Unless I make it so. You don't have to like it, Miss Holcombe, but I intend to assure myself you are not injured."

"Oh, bother!" They had come to the small veranda at her front door. Opening her arms, she let the pile of linens drop to the tile flooring. "See? I am perfectly intact. It was a maid hurt herself. I wrapped her injured hand and sent her off to the housekeeper, who will better tend to it. The maid abandoned the linens she was carrying, and to keep her from getting into trouble, I gathered them up. When I return to the villa, I shall see them returned to wherever they belong. Are you satisfied now?"

His eyes saw right past her words, she knew as she stood there all but melting under the intensity of his regard. But she could scarcely tell him the truth. Or bear another instant of his company, even if it meant . . . well, what? When she'd had her knife, she had not been able to fend off his brother long enough to draw a breath.

Unexpectedly, he began to gather up the linens. "Have it your way, Miss Holcombe, I cannot squeeze the truth from you. But Hari will tell you I never give up, and however you twist and turn, I intend to help you." He shoved the pile of towels into her arms. "*Fide, sed cui vide.*"

And then he was gone, loping toward the villa, and she stood looking after him until he was gone from sight. Robin Hood, a bow curved across his back, his black hair shining in the sunlight.

"Trust," he had said, "but be careful whom you trust."

Or something like that. Her Latin had never been better than adequate. And in this instance, accurate translation mattered not at all.

She trusted no one. Not her father, who kept a secret that belonged only to her, and kept it only because she wanted him to. Rather, she suspected that he knew, or had guessed. She could not be sure. Neither of them dared to broach the subject.

Never, not ever, would she trust a Keynes.

Most times, she could not even trust herself.

Michael stormed into the villa, wondering how the devil he was to find out what had happened to Miranda Holcombe without mentioning her or suggesting an interest he wasn't supposed to have. If the gossips ever linked her name with his, scandal would be the least of her problems.

He'd got used to being stared at, and since he was dressed like a peasant and carrying a yew bow, the attention he drew wasn't surprising. But it made things more difficult, and he spoke to no one as he went from room to room, hoping to spot something out of the ordinary.

He saw nothing.

What had he expected? A trail of blood?

In the end, there was little he could do that would not compromise Miss Holcombe or worse, put her in danger. And she hadn't appeared to be injured, which was the most important thing. But she'd been hiding something, lying through her pretty teeth, and he hadn't stayed alive this long without being alert to trouble.

To be sure, a female, especially a beautiful female, had troubles of a different sort than he encountered. Had some drunken lout foisted himself on her?

Probably something of the kind. He'd been often enough drunk and a lout to know where that could lead, not that he'd at any time imposed himself on a female. But if ever there existed a woman who made him fear his worse impulses and where they might direct him, Miranda Holcombe was the one.

Out of temper, he left the villa and set off for Beata's stable, located two streets away because the owners of the land in between wouldn't sell to her. She repaid them, some said, by secretly depositing manure where it would be most offensive.

Three quarters of the people in London, he would guess, were lodged in poorer dwellings than the inhabitants of her whitewashed stable. Even the bales of straw and hay, the bags of oats, and the vehicles were better housed. The three men who had widowed her must have been reincarnations of Croesus.

He was about to enter the stable when he saw David Fairfax pacing the courtyard, kitted out in a fur-caped driving coat the color of rust and carrying in his leather-gloved hand what looked to be a carriage whip. He seemed more than usually agitated.

Striding directly up to him, Michael wrenched the whip from his hand. "What's this?"

"Only an accessory," said David. "I wouldn't use it. Are you looking for your brother? It's too late, I'm afraid. When I got here, he was driving off."

Michael froze, hand clenched around the whip handle. "Jermyn was here? What for?"

"How would I know? I was arriving, he was leaving. I didn't see him, actually. Only the crest on the panels, and the liveried outriders, and the luggage atop the coach."

"Which way did he go?"

David made a vague gesture. "But I didn't see which way he turned."

"Bloody hell." Jermyn still in London, in spite of what he'd said at Tattersall's. He must have been delayed. Michael swore again, this time in Arabic. An opportunity missed, and no telling how long before his brother would return. He wondered . . . Another oath. Miranda. Was Jermyn responsible for whatever had happened to her?

The thought sent him racing into the stable for his horse. It was stupid, he knew it, but he had to try. Saddle up and take one of the roads out of London on the off chance it was the same road Jermyn was traveling. He'd meant to ride anyway, to release some of the pressure building inside him.

Inside the cavernous stable, two ostlers and several young boys were attempting to secure a pair of wild-eyed grays to a vehicle that must have been designed by a madman. The lines of the—whatever it was— were sleek and pleasing, even to his critical gaze, so long as no one was expected to ride in the contraption. For one thing, the small front wheels and the enormous rear wheels were an invitation to disaster on anything but a straight paved road with no traffic. And the driver's bench, thrust up like a mushroom cap, would be a challenge to the best of drivers.

A white-whiskered ostler, one Michael had not seen before, jumped out of the way of the grays' flailing hooves and landed close to where he was standing. "Better move yourself, laddie," he said, the Scots unmistakable in his pronunciation. "These beasties be a mite restless."

They looked positively murderous. "Can you tell me how long the Duke of Tallant's coach was here?"

"An hour, maybe less. At first look, I thought you be him come back again."

"We're related." No point denying the obvious. "I've a message for him. Do you know where he was heading?"

"Nay. He don't so much as look at stable hands, nor we at him." With the help of two men, the ostler went back to harnessing the horses.

Michael watched them for a time before proceeding to the stall where Loki nickered a welcome. Both of them could use a long run in the countryside, with nothing more to do than stretch their muscles and feel the wind. Or he could chase after Jermyn—a waste of time, to be sure, but doing nothing was eating him up. Most of all, he wanted to find out what had happened to Miranda, and what she was hiding. Not much chance of that.

He stroked Loki's neck, glanced over his shoulder, saw the carriage and restless grays being led to the stableyard. Fairfax was preparing to climb onto that idiotically high bench. Well, that settled it.

He went to the vehicle, angled his borrowed bow inside it, and swung up onto the bench. Fairfax, wide-eyed and perspiring, had a death grip on the reins. The grays, ears pricked forward, were practically vibrating with anticipation.

"Have you ever driven before?" Michael asked.

"Of course," said David, affronted. "The phaeton is new, though. And the nags. Bought 'em at auction yesterday. The coat as well, but I bought that at Weston's."

"That's good to know. Where are we going?"

"Hyde Park. I thought I'd practice while there's not too many people there."

"Better let's go where there are no people at all. Or animals, or building, or trees. Or we could stay here, with the ostler holding on to the horses."

Biting his lip, David nodded to the ostler, who gave a resigned shrug and stepped away. Immediately the carriage lurched forward and the grays set out across the brick-fenced stableyard, aiming for the gate.

"Draw them in a little," Michael said.

"I didn't even tell them to *go*." David jerked on the reins. The grays slowed. One large head swung around to see what the fuss was about. Then they picked up speed again and pounded through the open gate.

"Left," Michael ordered. "Go left."

"But I want to—"

Michael reached across him and tugged gently on what he hoped were the proper reins. Without breaking stride, the horses swung to the left. "We need to get away from this traffic. See those buildings ahead? Just before we come to them, turn right."

Fairfax managed to negotiate the tight corner, although he barely missed sideswiping a curricle in the process. The oaths of the driver followed them for a considerable distance.

They were soon past the outskirts of Chelsea and passing between fields stubbled with the remnants of barley and wheat harvests. In smaller fields, a few workers were bent double over patches of winter vegetables. The horses settled into an easy stride, choosing their own pace, ignoring their driver. They had, Michael suspected, taken his measure and figured out who was in charge.

Another turn loomed ahead, this one onto a narrow road where a sprinkle of buildings, the start of a new residential area, meant pedestrians and vehicles. He was calculating which direction to take when the carriage swerved to the left. He heard barking. A woman calling, *"Willy! Willikins!"*

He saw a dog the size of a rabbit streaking toward them from the field to their right. *"Willikins!"* It hesitated. Looked back at the woman. Still yapping, it pronked up and down in place until the woman got there and scooped the dog into her arms.

But it was too late. The horses, spooked or just in a bad mood, took off at an angle across the field to their left. When its wheels left the road, the phaeton bounced over weeds and clumps of compacted soil, rocking dangerously from side to side.

They reached the road ahead just as a pony cart piled with cabbages arrived at the same spot. Fairfax pulled on the leather to no effect. The pony had the good sense to begin a fast turn. Cabbages rolled off the cart. The grays stampeded over them, sending a flurry of pale green leaves into the air.

Then they were bolting across another wide field, thick with crows that launched themselves skyward, cawing raucously. Michael looked ahead, saw the grassy expanse of Chelsea Common, and beyond it a narrow road. More traffic, more people, and on the other side a cricket field and a tavern. He made up his mind.

The ride would be smoother when they reached the grass. About ten seconds now. "Fairfax, keep hold of the reins. But whatever happens, don't pull on them. Don't do anything."

He was on his feet, calculating. One foot up on the rail. The horses went from field to grass, adjusted their stride. He caught the rhythm of it, pushed off, was airborne for a moment. It seemed longer. He landed on withers and croup, the breath thumped out of him. Startled, the horse broke stride. Regained it.

Grasping the collar, he slithered forward, dropped his legs to grip the horse's sides with his knees, and reached his arms around the long, heaving neck. Snagged the reins on each side, just behind the bit, and began to draw them in. Nothing. He glanced up, saw the road too close, saw people looking over at the runaway horses.

He pulled again, evenly, firmly, and felt the motion under his body change. The beat of the hooves slowed. The horse to his left quickly adjusted to the changing pace. No time to stop, though, not before disaster. He brought his left hand to the horse's neck, used his legs, his entire body to indicate the direction, and pulled on the right rein.

The grays responded with a sweeping arc to the right, its apex coming within inches of the road, then on around until they were headed back the direction they'd come. They slowed as well, to a fast trot that bounced him around for a time, and finally, as if aware the fun was over, to a walk. He slid off, got hold of the bridle, and drew them to a halt.

Silence. He took a few moments to recover his breath, stroked the damp gray neck beside him, began speaking softly to the horse in Arabic. From behind him, he heard the creak of wood and leather as David jumped down and came around from the back, maintaining a cautious distance from the horses.

"What are you saying to them?"

"That you're a ham-handed idiot." Michael looked over at David's white face and unhappy eyes. "But they already knew that."

"Yes." David's gaze dropped to the ground. "Will you drive back?"

"I can't drive any better than you can. Probably not as well, which is saying something. We'll walk. And on the way, you'll agree to get rid of that accident trap and sell these animals to someone who can manage them."

They set out side by side across the grass, David silent until they came to a road. "But I need them," he said plaintively. "Or something like them. Devil take it, Michael, I'm four-and-thirty, not married, not even got a mistress, something of a fashion plate, and I'm a *musician*. A fellow like me requires a manly accomplishment."

"And running down a cabbage wagon qualifies? Or should you have been let to run down something of more consequence, like a pedestrian?"

"I didn't know I was so bad at it. Some of m'friends taught me, and they let me drive their gigs and curricles. I never had an accident before."

"You astonish me." Michael shook his head. "If you must put all London at risk, you'll first lease a well-constructed curricle and a pair of peaceable horses and take lessons from an expert."

"But that won't do. I need something daring and dashing. Something that causes people to see me in a new way. It's different for you. No one ever thinks . . . That is, they look at you and know what you are."

Michael very much doubted that. "So what do they think when they look at you?"

"I'm not sure. But I have some friends, good chaps on the whole, except that they prefer the company of, well, other chaps. Not in the petticoat line, I mean."

"And which line are you in?"

"The female one. But people might think otherwise. It's a crime, y'know, to be . . . otherwise."

"Not everywhere. But yes, in England your friends are at some risk. I am sorry for it. What I can't see is how you prove anything by swaggering around with a driving whip in your hand. People are going to think what they want to think, and nothing you do is going to prove a damn thing to them. Or is it yourself you're trying to persuade?"

They walked a little distance in silence before David replied. "It used to be m'father, I suppose. But I've tried and tried, and still there's no pleasing him. He's got five sons that suit him, and I never will, and that's an end to it. What I want, more than anything, is a wife and children of my own. The trouble is, the ladies all like me, but it's the way they'd like a brother. I thought it would be different when I lost three stone and learned to control my stammering. Mostly control it. Turned out that more ladies liked me than before, but still in the same way. Sweet David. Dear David. Nice, nice David. I might as well be a lapdog."

As a man sought out by the ladies for an altogether different reason, probably the one Fairfax longed to be sought for, Michael had never looked at things from his perspective. But it seemed to him they both ended up in the same place—alone, no prospect of marriage, and in his own case, no possibility whatever of a home and family.

It needn't be that way for Fairfax, though. Shouldn't be.

"Is there one of them you want, then? One whose attention you're trying to get?"

Another silence. "Now that you ask, I have to say no, there isn't. But if there were, she wouldn't look

twice at me. I'm a middle son in a large family that
has repudiated me. I haven't a title or a fortune or
the sort of . . . of *attraction* you have, that makes every
female turn to look at you when you pass by."

This conversation was so unlike any he'd ever had
in his life that Michael was at a loss how to proceed.
He knew bloody well why women wanted him. On
fewer occasions than Fairfax would suspect, he gave
it to them. But beyond the excitement of a romp with
a dangerous, unpredictable male, they had no use for
him. Which was, of course, exactly as he wanted it
to be.

"Why," he said cautiously, "would you wish to
marry a woman who saw you as something other than
you are? Disillusionment would follow, surely, and
misery hard on its heels. I'm older than you, unmarried, not even a mistress at hand, no talent for anything but fighting. I can't advise you, except to say
you'll do better as you are than as anything else."

"That's not good enough. It hasn't been, anyway."

Michael took his wrist and lifted it. "Would you
lose this hand? Risk your music? You had a lucky
escape today, but disaster requires only one moment
of carelessness, one mistake, one act of stupidity." He
let go of Fairfax. Remembered a dark Calcutta night,
opening the door to his house. Light from a streetlamp
catching a white neckcloth, gleaming off the barrel of
a gun—

"Like Mira," David said.

Michael came to full attention. "Mir . . . Miss
Holcombe?"

"She had an accident with a horse. I was studying
in Italy when it happened, and by the time I saw her
she was well again. But she had changed a lot."

"In what way?" Michael felt suddenly cold. "Tell
me."

"She was always horse mad. It was the first thing I
knew about her. Didn't pay her much mind back then,

she being . . . um, five or six when I first started spending holidays at Seacrest. She was always trying to talk one of the guests into riding out with her, because Mr. Holcombe wouldn't let her go alone. The rest is what I was told by a friend who was staying with them at the time of the accident. I did ask her about it once, but she closed up like a clam."

David released a sigh. "On her fifteenth birthday, Mr. Holcombe gave her a prime goer for a present because she'd goaded him into buying it. The weather was bad, and I guess no one wanted to ride with her. So she sneaked out after lunch and wasn't missed until that evening. There were lots of guests, and everybody assumed she was with somebody else. It was dark before the search was called, and morning when she was found in a ditch about twelve miles from the house. Nearly dead, she was. They said she'd been hit by a carriage. Probably the driver never saw her in the rain. The horse disappeared, and nobody ever reported finding it."

"But she's all right now?"

"I suppose so. It's been more than ten years, of course. I always thought she was different after that, but maybe it was just a matter of getting older. She was such a hoyden back then, wild as a feral cat. She'd have dared anything. Now she's so calm and poised and controlled all the time, as if she'd drawn in her own reins and snipped them off at the bit. She holed up at Seacrest for years. Friends offered to sponsor her for a Season in London, but she wouldn't even go to dances and parties in the neighborhood."

David looked over at Michael, his face full of sadness. "I wish you could have known her before the accident. She used to play the lute, and sang songs that made you want to weep because they were so beautiful. Something happened to her throat when she was hurt, and now she can't sing at all. Her hair changed, too. It was guinea gold like her mother's until the accident. Then it went dead white, like an old woman's, and stayed that way for nearly two years. Now it's spectacular, of course—the color of moon-light—but her voice never came back."

Michael felt as if something was pressing on his chest. "What about her mother?"

"Mrs. Holcombe died when Mira was eleven or twelve. It was horrible. She had a cancer, and it took a long time. But afterward, Mira insisted that every-thing go on as it had done. There were always guests, to lift her father's spirits, and she played hostess. It made her grow up quickly, I suppose. Nothing much changed until about three years ago, when Mr. Hol-combe became ill. I was away again, this time studying in France, and when I returned, Seacrest had been closed down. I was told they had gone to stay with her father's brother at his castle in Somerset."

"Castle?"

"Well, Old Holcombe was always a bit eccentric. Did you never meet him? His estate borders Long-view. He was trying to make a name for himself with the Royal Antiquarian Society, or some such thing, and bought a fallen-down castle in the Mendips. To raise the money he sold about everything he had ex-cept his house and land, which were entailed to his brother. Then he moved to the castle and set about restoring it. He died not too long ago. The castle was willed to his nephew, who went out to India some years and hasn't been heard from, Mira tells me, for a long time."

That filled in some of the gaps, Michael was think-ing as they led the horses from the field and onto Robinson's Lane. But he wanted to know more about her. Hell, he wanted to know *everything* about her.

"You like her." David grinned at him. "I knew you would."

"Don't be an ass. I don't like anyone."

"You always say that. But I think you don't want anyone to like *you*."

He'd forgot how well David Fairfax knew him. "Almost no one does like me, which saves me a lot of trouble. Then there's you. For no accountable reason, you like me, and you cause me no end of trouble. There's a lesson there for one of us."

"Must be for me," said David, more cheerfully than he'd said anything the entire afternoon. "You read me more lectures than an Oxford don."

"And you pay me as little attention as you did them. Listen to me now, though. I need a favor."

"Anything. As always."

They made the turn onto Paradise Row. The horses began straining forward, sensing a rubdown and a bag of oats just ahead. "Hari has found himself a enclave of people from the Punjab, and one of them claims to be a cousin. That could mean to the thirtieth degree, but family is everything there, and tonight, the cousin is getting married. I've promised to attend, and unless this one differs from every other wedding I attended in India, it will last well into tomorrow. You are to spend the evening at Beata's, and if you find it necessary, you'll sleep in my Casina. Watch out for Miss Holcombe. Assure yourself she is experiencing no difficulties. If she remains in her cottage, invent an excuse to stop by."

"Is something wrong?"

"She says not. But I want to be sure of it. She mustn't know I've spoken to you."

"You *do* like her!" David was practically crowing with satisfaction. Then he looked up, spotted the stableyard gate directly ahead, and drew in his feathers. "I wish we didn't have to go in there," he muttered.

But they did, and stable hands and stableboys and even the stable-yard cats emerged from wherever they

had been to watch the mortifying arrival. Michael saw
them staring at his chest and looked down to see that
his shirt was torn and streaked with blood. He'd felt
the pain from his rough landing, but hadn't realized
the damage done him by harness leather and metal
studs.

"An accident, sir?" The Scots ostler regarded him
with disapproving eyes.

"Only to me." Michael let go the reins he'd been
holding and stepped away from the horses. "I fell off.
Fairfax here is a capital whip, but I couldn't keep my
balance on that bench, and down I went. When I refused to get back up there, he insisted on walking with
me. I'd better stick to riding, don't you think?"

"If you say so, sir." Reaching over, the ostler
plucked a fragment of cabbage leaf from the horse's
flank. "And what be this?"

"What's left of lunch," Michael said as David gave
the ostler a coin and began to slink away. "We
stopped for a salad."

Chapter 8

Michael poured himself another large tot of brandy and carried it to the window.

The rain had let up a bit. A rectangle of light, broken by the shadow he cast, shone on the ground outside, and lanterns from a passing ship glowed orange in the distance. It was probably after midnight. He'd stopped winding the clock because its chime woke him up, and his pocket watch had been given over to a larcenous Egyptian camel driver.

Hari always knew what time it was, with the same mysterious instinct that told him when someone was lying and where a water hole could be found. But Hari had taken to spending most evenings with his Punjabi friends, seldom returning before dawn. Sometimes Michael accompanied him, but not tonight.

He didn't want company. Nearly two weeks in London, and save for their one encounter at Tattersall's, no sign of his target. Jermyn had disappeared. A bribed servant knew only that he'd departed later than he'd intended and in a rage, leaving no word of where he was going or for how long. Servants at Tallant House in Berkeley Square were easily bribed, but unreliable. Few had worked there for long, and most were already seeking other positions. The duke, they said, paid cheeseparing wages, demanded the impossible, and expressed his dissatisfaction with his riding whip.

Like father, like son. Michael remembered that riding whip. Bore the scars of it on his back. Not the same whip, probably, but Jermyn would wield it in the same spirit.

Four generations of Tallant dukes had been stodgy supporters of the monarch and conservative politics, but then came his great-grandfather. The fifth duke, reputedly mad, risked the family's small fortune on the South Sea Bubble and lost the greater part of it. The sixth duke drank heavily and gambled recklessly—two vices that ran in the bloodline—and the seventh, Devil Keynes, lost everything that wasn't entailed.

He'd still managed to cut a fashionable figure in London, but his family had lived in squalor. The estate in Kent, Longview, had long been in near ruin, and he'd sold the last of the paintings and furniture to keep up his wardrobe and stock the London town house with candles and coal. By the time he'd exiled his second wife and younger son to Scotland, the creditors were snapping at his ankles. Years later, blackballed at White's, mocked in the newspapers and broadsheets, he'd put a pistol to his head.

That was the official report, at any rate. By that time, Michael had been in India for two years. When word came of his father's death, he'd celebrated with a bottle of good brandy and a pretty nautch dancer. He was just turned one-and-twenty then, wild as a lynx, securing gemstones on credit from even wilder Afghan traders and selling them in the south through a network of marginally trustworthy brokers. With the money, he recruited and trained a small mercenary force, their sole mission to destroy his brother's India trade.

Or it had been. He'd not yet come to terms with

the end of his India campaign, or prepared himself to confront the only thing left for him to do. A primal sin. Fratricide.

Sometimes he knew beyond question it was necessary. Other times, like Hamlet, he questioned everything he knew to be true. At the age of ten he had seen his brother, seven years older, push a young maidservant to her death under the wheels of a carriage. He had told his mother, and not long after, they were both sent to the Highlands. He never saw his father again.

One thing hadn't changed, though. Thinking about his murderous family always made him want to forget them. And the only way to do that was to drink.

He took a swallow of brandy and stared out into the wet black night. Blinked. Looked again. A shadow emerged from the screen of trees lining the property, flitted behind a hedge, disappeared again into the mist.

Or perhaps he had only imagined it. Ghosts were his constant companions. They lingered in corners, curled at the baseboards, prowled through his dreams.

And one of them lived across a small patch of grass, the solitary white tigress, tending the cub who was her father. A woman so far from the reach of Michael Keynes that she might as well be living on the moon. He avoided her because she wanted him to, but he could not stop his thoughts from following her through her days and nights. She was at the villa now, perhaps in conversation or reading, while Mr. Holcombe enjoyed the company of his friends. Later, accompanied by a servant with a torch, she would wheel him back to the cottage, and after a time, the lights would go out. Only then would he go to his own bed.

He kept vigil, like a knight before the altar, like a courtly lover admiring his unattainable lady from a distance. It was stupid. Not at all in his character. Sheer madness. Still, he longed to give her something that would keep her safe, make her happy. But he had nothing she wanted. Or if he did, she wouldn't accept it. Not from him.

He moved to the window overlooking the Holcombes' cottage, where a lantern hung near the door. No sign of the intruder, if indeed there had been one, but he decided to keep watch, just in case. And so that Miranda wouldn't catch him lurking there, he closed the curtains all but an inch and drew up a chair.

He was just lifting the glass to his lips when there came a sharp rap at the door. His hand jerked. Brandy spattered over his shirt. Swearing, he lurched to his feet and went to see who'd come to bother him at this time of night.

It was a female, her limp wet bonnet concealing her hair and most of her face. Rainwater streamed down a dark, bedraggled cloak, puddling at her feet. "It *is* you," she said in a harsh voice. "I wasn't sure. Will you let me in?"

"That depends. Who the devil are you?"

"Can't you guess?" Her laugh grated like metal on metal. "I'm your sister-in-law."

Bloody hell. He stepped aside to let her enter. Nancy? Noreen? Something that started with an "N," he was fairly sure. They'd never met. He had been at Oxford when Jermyn married an Irish heiress, had read the news in the *Times*, hadn't given a damn.

He watched her fumble with the frogged clasps of her cloak, supposed he ought to help her and went to do so. She batted his hands away. "You're drunk," she said. "I can smell it."

"Come back when I'm sober, then." But she wasn't going to leave, not after sneaking herself here in the rain, not until she'd said what she'd come to say. He went into his room, stripped a blanket off the bed, and tossed it over a chair near where she was standing. She'd got her bonnet off. Red hair corkscrewed around an angular, thin-lipped face. Her eyes were small and angry.

As he crouched by the hearth to build up the fire, he heard her cloak drop to the carpet with a squishy sound. "Do you want a drink?" he asked. "There's brandy, whisky, and claret."

"I'd like tea." She came to the fire, holding out her bare hands. She was shivering.

"There isn't any. I wasn't expecting guests. What do I call you? Your Grace?"

"I don't care. Norah, if you like. I know you are wishing me somewhere else, and I am wishing there was someone else I could apply to. But there isn't. You probably won't help me either, but I had to try."

He tossed another log on the firedogs. "What do you want me to do? Kill Jermyn?"

"Would you?" She gave a sour laugh. "Someone ought to. Did you know he killed your father?"

Michael nearly dropped the poker he was holding. "I was told he shot himself."

"It was made to appear that way. I found out several years later, when Jermyn threatened to do to me what he'd done to him. It was perfectly safe to tell me. I couldn't testify against him, even if I'd found the courage, and back then, I could never have done so."

"And now? I doubt you'd get far with an accusation at this point."

"That's not it." With a shudder, she collapsed onto a chair. "Might I have the blanket, please?"

He draped it over her and poured out a glass of claret, which he placed on the table within her reach. *Please,* she had said. She must be getting close to making her request, a request he didn't want to hear. "Was it you I saw coming through the trees? Are you being followed?"

"I don't think so. Not yet. Jermyn believes me to be in Scotland, but one of the men he left to guard us will soon let him know otherwise. He intended us to die there, a winter accident, I suspect. Or perhaps there would have been a few months' delay. For him to take us there, followed too soon by our unfortunate demise, might have looked suspicious. Although I doubt he concerns himself with being caught out. He believes there is nothing he cannot get away with, and indeed, he keeps proving that to be true."

"Exile to Scotland—and I speak from experience here—isn't necessarily a death sentence. Are you sure of his intentions?"

"Quite. I have failed to produce an heir, it is unlikely that I will, and he does not want you next in line to the title."

"On that much, we are agreed. I don't want it, either. Let the title revert to the crown and the family name drop out of history."

"An admirable sentiment, except that there are two daughters to provide for. And Jermyn has, by foul means I am sure, restored the family fortune and recovered most of the unentailed properties. Unlike your father, he has a great deal to bequeath, and he wants a son of his body there to receive it." She raised a sly eyebrow. "Are you certain the title and fortune hold no interest for you?"

"None whatever. Where are you staying?"

"Last night, at a filthy inn near Hampstead. Jermyn will find it easy to track me there. Probably anywhere I go," she added with a shrug. "That cannot be far, since I spent my last coins on tea and soup for breakfast. But I did not come to you for money or protection. I want you to find my daughter, Corinna."

He met her gaze, felt a rush of anger. His plans did not allow for unwanted relations who'd got themselves in trouble. "This is going to get complicated, isn't it? Very well. We'll take care of you first. Something to eat, something to wear, and a safe place for you to go. You can stay with me for the present, but there are too many nosy servants around for safety. And at some point, Jermyn will look for you here."

"So long as you hear my story first, and promise to help Corinna. What happens to me is of no concern."

"Understood. But if you want my help, we go about it my way." He glanced down at his brandy-stained shirt, leather breeches, and scuffed boots. A good thing Beata liked him to make a spectacle of himself. He retrieved a jacket from the armoire in his bed-chamber, ran a brush over his disordered hair, and returned to the sitting room. Norah looked to be almost asleep in her chair, but she sat stiffly erect when he spoke her name.

"Be strong a little while longer," he said, closing all the curtains and extinguishing most of the lights. "Get out of those wet clothes. There are more blankets in the bedchamber, and towels . . . Just take whatever you need. I'll be back shortly."

Chapter 9

On a rainy December night, even Palazzo Neri could lure only two score of pleasure seekers, and most of them had come to toss dice or play cards. Beata was holding court in the Sala dei Medici, and in the reading room, a handful of historians dedicated to the restoration of Richard III's good name were gathered for a meeting.

Mira had left her father there with them. Most were old friends, and two had spent considerable time at Seacrest in the days when her parents made room in their home for impoverished scholars or those with nowhere to spend holidays. It pleased her to see how well he was loved and respected, and how eagerly they solicited his opinions.

It also made her feel unnecessary, which she found surprisingly hurtful. But since these were patient men who had no difficulty with his painstaking efforts to communicate, she had no reason to avoid mingling with Beata's guests, as he so greatly wished her to do.

A few days earlier, a trunk full of Lady Jessica's made-over gowns had been delivered to their cottage, and he'd required her to parade before him wearing each one. Then he insisted she order several pairs of matching gloves, and shoes as well, even though she

still owed several hundred pounds to Mr. Callendar.
Such a waste.

And yet, he was in better spirits than he had been
for a considerable time. Instead of being inward
turned, like an invalid, he was behaving exactly like a
doting father with a daughter to fire off. She couldn't
bear to disappoint him.

So she spent her evenings fending off flirtatious gentlemen, listening to the gossip of females who were
there in hopes of witnessing a scandal, and sometimes,
unable to bear the din, she retreated to a quiet corner
with a book. Always she kept a wary eye on doorways,
prepared to slip from any room entered by either of
the Keynes brothers, her hand hovering near to where
she'd stashed her knife.

But the Beast wasn't to be seen, nor had his disturbing brother made an appearance. Michael Keynes
watched her, though, when he thought she wouldn't
notice. She had seen his shadow behind the curtains
of his Casina as he looked out though a gap he'd made
with his fingers.

In his way, he was even more dangerous than the
Beast. He made her imagine what she had long known
could never be, and want things she could never have.
It was as if he called silently to her from a covert,
called her to enter a place she dared not go.

But it was only her imagination, because he rarely
spoke to her at all. And she was careful to avoid him,
inventing errands that took her from the cottage when
he arrived to play chess with her father, as he did
most afternoons.

"I will see to it you come to no harm," he had
once said.

She rather thought he had meant it, at the time.
But her safety was well beyond his reach now.

She was alone in a quiet parlor, wrestling with her
demons between paragraphs of the book she had been
trying to read, when she heard the sound of a piano-

forte. Rousing herself, she joined the crowd streaming along the passageway to the Sala da Musica. When David Fairfax played, it was never to an empty room.

She found a chair near the wall and settled to listen, remembering when he first began to study music. He'd often stayed at Seacrest, and when he practiced, family, guests, servants and pets all found excuses to leave the house. Only her father had encouraged him. Now, listening to him play was her greatest pleasure.

After a time, the air in the room abruptly changed. Became charged, as with the oncoming of a storm. She stiffened with apprehension.

Scarcely hearing the final sonata, she applauded with the others when it was done. His faced flushed, David rose and bowed, looking pleased and surprised at the warm response of his audience. He always looked that way, and his feelings were, she knew, entirely genuine. Finally the room grew quiet. He gently closed the pianoforte and stood for a moment, detaching himself from the muse that possessed him when he played. Then he turned his open, welcoming gaze on her.

"It was wonderful," she said, coming up to him, watching his brown eyes widen with pleasure. "Thank you." She risked a glance over her shoulder. Michael Keynes was near the door, shoulders propped against the wall, unshaven, unkempt, looking directly at her. A dangerous presence blocking the way out.

But she had no excuse to linger, and besides, he would surely outwait her. He had come for her. What did he want?

"Ah. There's Michael," David said, clearly delighted. "I know he looks awful, but really, he's not so bad as he would have you think."

How could he be? she wondered as David took her arm.

Keynes's disturbing eyes glittered as she approached. He seemed to drag himself away from the wall, lurched, produced an awkward bow. The smell of brandy made her wrinkle her nose.

"Miss Holcombe," he said, ignoring David. "You are radiant. You outshine the sun."

"Simple enough," she replied, disgusted. "It's night-time. And you are drunk."

"That's the consensus."

He was repellently cheerful. Except for his eyes, which were . . . Oh, she could not say. Intense. Urging her to pay attention.

He turned to David. "Come take supper with me." His voice was slurred. "You'll have to bring the supper. Will you? I'm hungry enough for two or three people. You can stay the night if you like. Hari's gone somewhere. It's raining. Did you know it was raining?"

And just when she had decided he was altogether cat-shot, he said with perfect clarity under his breath, "Miss Holcombe, go to the Limonaia. I'll follow you. David, say something idiotic."

David, trying to think of something idiotic to say, could only manage to look idiotic. Finally he produced, in a cracking tone, a question about what Michael Keynes wanted for supper.

"Bread. Meat. Cheese." Keynes poked David on the chest. "Hot tea." And softly, almost without moving his lips, "Arrange it, and then come to the Limonaia. Miss Holcombe, why are you still here?"

She might not comprehend the purpose of it, but she recognized a staged scene when she saw it. And felt, for no accountable reason, a wish to impress this man she feared. "Sir, you are no fit company for a lady," she declared with an excess of dramatic fervor. And then she sailed through the door and into the passageway, a little embarrassed but greatly curious.

If he was planning to seduce her, which had been her initial thought, he'd not have invited David to join them. And there was something new in him, a sense

of purpose she had not seen in him before. Until tonight he had seemed to be marking time, waiting for
something over which he had no control. And for him,
she expected, that was neither a comfortable nor a
natural state of mind.

She, on the other hand, had become an artist of
waiting, an expert at marking time. But like him, she
sensed that events were about to converge with her at
the center of them. And this time, she would not be
found wanting. This time, she would control the
outcome.

The Limonaia, another of Beata's Tuscan fancies,
had been constructed in the western wing of the villa,
with a glass wall to admit afternoon sunlight. Tiles of
glass were set in the ceiling as well, and large windows
opened onto corridors connecting the Limonaia to the
section of the building set apart for meeting rooms.
All were empty at this time of year.

She slipped through the door, cedarwood studded
with medallions of stained glass, and breathed in the
fragrance of citron trees and smoke from the braziers
that kept them warm. The Limonaia, octagonal with
walls of stone tracery and glass, had floors of enameled tile, marble benches, and two score small trees—
lemon and Spanish orange—set in ceramic pots. A
few, cultivated in a greenhouse on the edge of the
property, were heavy with fruit. The others, defying
the change of seasons, flaunted lush leaves. They were
dusted weekly, she knew, by the servants.

Rain streaked the glass wall and beat on the ceiling.
It was well after midnight, and an orange glow from
the braziers and the wall sconces in the corridors provided the only light. She felt nervous, like a maiden
in the Colosseum waiting for the great-toothed cats to
be let in. And because she must reveal nothing of her
anticipation or her fear, she went to a shadowed bench
near the center of the Limonaia, sat neatly on it with

her hands folded on her lap, and waited for the electric hum in the air that always signaled the presence of Michael Keynes.

It came to her shortly after, the sound that wasn't quite a sound. She rose, arms at her sides, and turned.

In the dim light, he was a tall, wide-shouldered shadow with ghostly eyes. *"I was followed,"* he said in a tone that could not be heard beyond the small room where they stood facing each other. "You didn't have to run from me." This time his voice, a little too loud, startled her.

She moved away from the bench. "I didn't run. I never run. But I prefer to be alone."

"And so you are. Alone with me." Then, quietly, *"There is a woman in my Casina—"*

"I've no doubt of it." Her voice, always a husky whisper, required no disguise. "And I am not adept at games, sir. What do you want of me?"

A long silence. Things unspoken. She felt them, like the vibration of his presence. Like the mysterious summons in his eyes.

"What do I want?" he echoed with a laugh. "Can't you guess?" Then—*"It's the Duchess of Tallant. My brother's wife. She requires help."*

"She came to *you*?"

"A measure of her desperation." Loudly, "Why don't you like me, butterfly?"

She lifted her hands in a gesture that held him away. "What should I do, then?"

"Let me close enough to speak without being heard. But make it seem you fear me."

Oh, I do, she thought, wondering at it. At that moment she was absolutely sure he wouldn't hurt her, and even more certain he could easily destroy her.

"Stay away!" she said when he staggered forward. He was pushing her toward the marble bench, using the motion to cover his speech. She resisted to give him time, surprised that she was enjoying this dance they did, this game they played. How long since she had enjoyed anything at all?

"She has come a long way through the rain. She needs something warm to wear and advice I am unable to give her. One kiss," he demanded. "Just one."

When she felt the bench against the backs of her legs, she sank onto it. "Why this charade?"

"Dear God but you are lovely. *To keep her safe. To keep you safe.* Let me, Miss Holcombe. Miranda. 'Oh brave new world, that . . .' that does something. I can't recall what."

" 'That has such creatures in it,' " she said, sounding like a schoolmistress, rather impressed that he'd guessed the origin of her name. *The Tempest* was her father's favorite play.

His teeth, when he grinned, were tinged with red-orange light. *"I need you to come to my rooms without being seen.* I'm fond of the theater. Fond of you."

"Who is watching us? And why?"

"I don't know for certain. But anyone associated with me is at risk. If you agree to help, you must take great care. One kiss, Miranda. One little kiss. Then I'll go away."

"You can't mean that."

"I do. All of it. Let me kiss you, or nearly. I'll make it appear you are forced. Then slap me and go." He stumbled forward until he was bent over her, caught himself by putting his hands on her shoulders. *"Unless you want out of this entirely."*

She ducked beneath his arms and escaped the bench. There was the sound of his palms hitting the marble, an oath, and the shuffle of his feet moving closer. She spun around to face him. "No." she said, hands raised to ward him off. "You are foxed."

"Come on, butterfly. *Settle your father and come to my Casina. Don't be seen.* I wager you'll like it."

He took hold of her wrists and drew her inexorably

closer. His eyes glowed red, as if a fire raged behind them. One hand, large and firm, burned at her waist.

The breath caught in her throat. Frozen, she gazed helplessly at the lines of his face, the black hair limned with firelight, his mouth a little open as he brought his lips nearer hers. Fingers slipped into her hair, cradled her nape.

Her heart thumped wildly. His breath tingled at her cheek. Heat came off him like a brazier, heat and strength and purpose.

He would choke her now.

And then . . . and then . . .

"I can't believe I'm saying this, but now would be a good time for you to slap me."

The spell broke.

She wrenched loose, brought back her arm. A loud crack as her gloved hand caught him on the face. A louder oath.

She rushed to the door and fled down the passageway.

Chapter 10

Michael sank onto the bench and rubbed his throbbing check.

Something had happened there, between the moment he drew Miranda into his arms and the slap on his cheek. She had gone stiff. Cold. Her eyes had been empty, her breathing ragged.

At first he'd thought she was continuing to play her part, as she had done from the first, effectively and swift to take a cue. But something—no, *someone*— had thrown her into a panic. *He* had done it. *His* touch, and the prospect of a more intimate touch.

He needn't have taken it so far. The charade had already done its work, and he could as well have told her to bolt the moment he reached for her. But he was a Keynes, to the depths of his black, black soul. And he had wanted to touch Miranda Holcombe. Had wanted that since he first saw her, and wanted a good deal more besides. Sometimes, between his nightmares, he dreamed of her.

But even in his dreams she remained beyond his reach, floating above him in the clear, clean air. And then he would be walking on a dry riverbed toward Sher Ka Danda, and she would spring on him, the white, blue-eyed tigress, and clamp her shining teeth on his neck.

Of course she despised him. How could it be otherwise? But he had lacked the will to resist her. And had ventured only a little, really. The briefest of touches. But she could not bear even that from him.

A good man, a decent man, would be resolving to spare her such offense in future.

He was already hoping another opportunity would present itself.

Not that he expected much. The press of her fingers on his arm as he helped her into a carriage, perhaps, or the chance to help her don a cloak.

Well, it was all rather pathetic, his longing for the unattainable. He felt like a puppy trailing after a queen, hoping to be petted.

He felt like an idiot.

And where the devil had David got off to? Better go find him, get some supper to Norah, wait for Miranda. If he hadn't frightened her away altogether.

As he entered the passageway, he saw the footman who had been trailing him fade back into the shadows. Being followed was nothing new. In India, where all sorts of people had set themselves to trace his movements, he had developed an instinct for sensing their presence. It took longer to learn how to throw them off his scent, but as in most other things, he'd taken his lessons from Hari Singh.

Since coming to England, neither of them had detected any sign of pursuit, but that would doubtless change when the Archangel returned. No, sooner than that. When the Duke of Tallant made a serious effort to eliminate his brother.

Beata had set the footman on him, he was fairly sure. Confirmation came shortly after, when he turned a corner and saw her waiting for him, flamboyant in blue velvet and gold braid, her expression stern and a glint of wickedness in her dark eyes.

"You have been naughty," she chided, shaking her head.

"I thought you wanted me to be naughty."

"But in control of yourself, *malcalzone*. You are drunk, I think."

It was true. In a real crisis, he would have handled himself without difficulty. He'd had lots of practice. But in ordinary times, there was slippage at the edges. Mistakes were made. He was supposed to be helping his brother's wife, but he'd got distracted by his obsession with Miranda. He deserved Beata's rebuke.

"Miss Holcombe has difficulties enough," she said, "without an importunate wretch accosting her in my Limonaia. If you require a woman, Mico, I can supply you one. Although I expect you could see to that yourself. Have you failed to notice the many fine ladies who come here with no other purpose than to draw your attention?"

He thought she was dangling for flattery, or perhaps more than that. "I can't help but notice them. Nor can I manage to remember them. Compared to you, madonna, they are moths beating against the window glass."

"Mah! You refuse any woman who dangles after you because she offers no challenge. But Miss Holcombe won't have you, and for that reason, you desire her. Am I right?"

"Not altogether." The brandy was clouding his thoughts. "You have said *you* want me, and you are a challenge on every count. I cannot think why I went sniffing after Miss Holcombe this evening, nor do I desire her. It would be like bedding one of those virgin saints with crossed legs and woeful eyes. She is not for me."

"See that she isn't. You are free to run wild here,

with my blessing, so long as you do not torment a young woman with an ailing father to tend to."

"Do you wish me to leave?"

"I wish you to leave her be. Well, perhaps I wish a little more than that. I shall keep you around to play with for a while longer." She moved closer, lifted a hand to his throbbing jaw. "You bear her mark."

"As you see, Miss Holcombe can take care of herself."

"You escaped lightly, my wolf. When your brother imposed himself, she slashed his hand with her knife."

"Did she, by God?" Admiration gave way to concern. For such an offense, Jermyn would make her pay.

"She has many knives, all of them slender and sharp and jeweled. From India, I believe. Smaller, but much like the knives you carry."

"Thanks for the warning. Did you have me followed tonight?"

She gave a delicate shrug. "I thought it best. Will you continue to make it necessary?"

"I'll leave Miss Holcombe alone, if that's what you mean. But I hope you won't require me to relinquish the company of her father."

"It is not my intention to restrict you in any way. Your brother, however, is forbidden to my Palazzo until he begs pardon of me. Ah, there is David with your picnic supper. Good night, rogue. Unless you prefer my company to his?"

"I'm drunk," he reminded her.

"So you are, and therefore of no use to me. A pity."

He bowed and waited until she was out of sight before turning to Fairfax. Beside him stood a servant with a heavily laden tray. Damn.

"I went to the Limonaia," said David, stepping forward, "but you were gone. Where's Mira? What did you do to her?"

"Nothing. Frightened her a little." The servant had to be got rid of. "She'll need help with her father. Why don't you see they get settled? Then you can come over and have supper. Stay the night in Hari's room if you like. No point slogging home in the rain."

"I'll do that," David said aloud. "*Couldn't shake him*," he mouthed. "Don't eat everything before I get there."

The servant, a tall young man with a blaze of freckles, stood immobile as Michael went to him and lifted the covers, one by one, from plates of ham, cheese, relishes, stewed mushrooms, a meat pie, some sort of custard, crusty rolls, and the makings for tea. "Where's the sirloin?" he demanded. "Roast chicken? And I have a sweet tooth. Cakes, biscuits, tarts."

The servant bowed, not easy to do while holding a tray that size. "I shall see to it, sir."

"Come directly to the Casina, then. And bring plenty of hot water."

A few minutes later, with Norah concealed upstairs in his bedchamber and all signs of her presence swept from view, Michael admitted the servants—two of them now. When the food was laid out, he tossed each one a sovereign.

"This is unnecessary, sir," said the freckled youngster, his face scarlet. "The *principessa* pays us well."

Principessa? Beata had given herself a promotion. "I'm sure that she does. But since I've managed to antagonize almost everyone I know in the last hour, I'd hoped to bribe you into charity with me."

"Yes, sir. Thank you, sir." They bowed and left.

Good Lord, what else? It seemed a week ago that Norah deposited herself on his doorstep. Watching through a slivered break in the curtains, he saw them shake off their umbrellas and enter the villa proper. The wind was whipping up. Next, Fairfax. Then, perhaps, Miss Holcombe.

For now, though, his sister-in-law, who had snapped

at him on his return and complained at being forced to hide upstairs. He didn't blame her. She was frightened, exhausted, and likely not in her right mind after nearly two decades married to the Beast.

"Come have supper," he said from the doorway. "David Fairfax will be here soon, and later, a young woman with some dry clothes for you to wear. Then you can tell us all how we can be of service."

"So I slapped him," Mira said as she spooned the last of the broth, thickened with bits of nearly dissolved bread, into her father's mouth. "Rather harder than I'd meant to, but I was caught up in the theatrics. And I don't expect he really felt it, you know. He was more than a little foxed."

David had left a few minutes earlier, after helping her lift her father to his bed, prop the pillows behind him, and heat the broth in a pot over the fire. The routine was a familiar one, although Hari Singh or one of Beata's servants usually helped with the lifting. Then, alone with her father, she always told him about her day and asked about his, sitting beside him and moving the chart with the letters of the alphabet under his hand, watching his finger move over each letter he chose.

Few words needed spelling out. She could read so much from the slight movements he was able to make, and from his eyes, that it seemed sometimes that she could read his very thoughts.

He had ceased to care for himself, she knew with the same dread with which she watched his frail body grow weaker. All his concern was for her, for her security and her happiness, and her heart was breaking to think how greatly she must disappoint him. Like everyone else, he thought her to be something she was not. He imagined a man would love her, and wed her, and not find himself disillusioned with his bride.

He did not know. Or if he did, he could not understand. And she would never tell him.

She chattered too brightly while she cleared the remains of his sparse meal and settled him for the night. He seemed pleased that she was going to Michael Keynes's Casina tonight, was glad that she meant to help the wife of the man who had destroyed her family.

Edgar Holcombe embraced forgiveness. His daughter thought only of vengeance.

When his eyes fluttered shut, she adjusted his blankets, extinguished the lamp at his bedside, and went to her own room to change. A few minutes later, a parcel with clothing for the Beast's wife in her arms, she climbed out the back window of her cottage and flitted across the wet expanse of winter grass to her destination.

Rain was streaming from the brim of her bonnet and her black mourning cloak as she rapped on the dark, curtained window. No one heard her. She knocked again, harder this time, and soon after a small light appeared to waft in her direction. A candle, she guessed. The air had long since begun to vibrate. Then a black shadow, a break in the curtains, and a pair of hands lifting the window.

She looked up, into eyes that were familiar and terrifying, and then to the hands reaching out to help her. When one of them touched her arm, it felt as if she'd been struck by lightning. Dropping her parcel, she jumped back from the window.

A moment of silence. "I forgot myself," he said. "Wait a moment. Fairfax will come to help you inside."

It wasn't him, she kept telling herself as she gathered up her parcel and huddled close to the wall. *It wasn't him*. But it had been his eyes and his hands. So many years gone by, another man altogether, and nothing had changed for her. It would never be over, never be different. She was as frozen in her past as her father was contained in his immobile body, both of them helpless to escape.

But if the Beast were dead, she kept thinking, if she killed him, surely her own demons would vanish with him. She didn't ask for much. A little peace of mind. A few hours cut loose from her memories. Safe harbor for her father. So little, and all beyond her grasp. The rain streamed down her face like tears.

"Mira?" David's face appeared at the window.

Recovering, she gave him the parcel and let him help her through the high window. Next there would be an enclosed room in company with the Duchess of Tallant and Michael Keynes. No peace of mind for her tonight.

The duchess, sharp featured and pale, sat at a small table laid out with food and a pot of tea. She glanced up as David led Mira through the door.

"Your Grace," said Mira, stopping near the table and curtsying. "I am Miranda Holcombe. I've brought you a nightrail, a dressing gown, some slippers, and a few other things you may find useful."

"Thank you." Her reply was stiff. "Tallant has laid claim to land near our own that once belonged to a Holcombe family."

"My family," Mira confirmed. "For the moment, the land remains ours."

"I am sorry for your difficulties. But there is no stopping him, I'm afraid."

"Perhaps. But I mean to try."

At David's gesture, Mira went to a chair not far from the duchess. Michael Keynes, she knew without looking, was near the hearth. The charge in the air told her, as did the sensation of his gaze hot against her back.

He doesn't matter, she told herself. But of course, he did. When he was present, little else seemed of consequence.

As if her thoughts had stirred him to action, she felt him move and heard the sound of a log being tossed on the fire.

"Her Grace has already told us a good deal," David said, taking a chair beside her. "We'll fill you in later. Her daughter Corinna has gone missing, and she wishes us to find her."

"I can speak for myself, young man," the duchess said, her voice strained with obvious weariness. "But I shall be brief. Tallant decided that we should take residence, Corinna and I, in Scotland. He escorted us there himself, and left two large brutes to protect us, or that was the reason he gave. I am certain they had been ordered to see we met with an accident—" Her gaze went to Mira's face. "Do I shock you?"

"No, Your Grace. I can quite believe it."

For some reason, that appeared to give relief to the duchess. "Then you will understand my fear," she said more gently than she had yet spoken. "Corinna is seventeen, and like her sister, has been schooled in Ireland. Catherine is three years younger and returned home last month. Save for St. Bridget's Academy, neither girl has much experience of the world. And Corinna's health has been fragile. She said almost nothing on the trip north, huddling in the carriage and staring out the window. I thought, sometimes, she meant to open the door and fling herself outside."

"Could she have suspected the duke's intentions?" Mira asked.

"She never confided in me. I have not been a fond mother, Miss Holcombe. To deal with my husband required more resources than I possessed, leaving nothing for my children. I am much to blame for their unhappiness, and hold myself responsible for what has occurred."

"But she left from Scotland," said David. "Isn't that what you said?"

"Yes. The duke saw us to the estate—a farmhouse,

really, in ill repair—and departed the next day, leaving the two men to help us settle in, or so he said. There was a handful of local servants as well, but only the housekeeper lived in the house. The second night, the duke's men went off to a local tavern that is reputed to be a sporting house as well. It was morning before they returned, and by then, I had discovered Corinna's absence.

"If only I had heard her leave. But it was the first night I'd slept well since we set out for the north, and even though she must have come into my bedchamber, I did not awaken. She took my small box of jewelry, the little money I had stored away, and left me this note." The duchess unfolded a scrap of paper and held it out to Mira.

Do not try to find me, it said. *There is something I must do.*

Mira read it aloud for the others and returned the paper to the duchess. "Did you go after her straight-away?"

"A little after dawn, a nightmare awakened me. Something felt terribly wrong. I went immediately to her room, where she had arranged pillows under the blankets to look as if she were there. I first searched the house, then the outbuildings, and finally returned to my own chamber, where I saw the note. Shortly after, the duke's men returned. If not for Corinna's message, I'd have thought they had spirited her away and disposed of her. As it was, I pretended she was ill with the mumps, which frightens men, and I stayed in her bedchamber all day. That night, when they went off again to the tavern, I set out walking."

After her own experiences of hasty escapes, Mira was immediately caught up in the duchess's story. No money, no idea which direction to go, only the urgency. The desperation. Someone helpless who depended on her, someone she had failed and was continuing to fail.

"I had a little luck then," said the duchess. "I'd kept off the roads, but by the next evening, I felt safe enough to slip into a posthouse. As it happened, the mail coach regularly stopped there, and a servant told me of a black-haired boy who'd bought passage to London the night before. It might have been Corinna, but I cannot be sure. I'd brought along a few things of value that were easily carried—my father's pocket watch, fur scarves, some banknotes I kept sewed in the hem of my cloak—and along with my wedding ring, they got me to London."

"You took a mail coach as well?" Mira said.

"It was the fastest way, and at each stop, I made inquiries. The boy had continued south for a considerable time, but I lost track of him two days ago. Perhaps it really was a boy. But if it was Corinna, she might have changed her route for fear of being traced. Or decided to go somewhere other than London. I don't know." The duchess paused, drew in a long breath. "There were newspapers at the posthouses, and in one of them I read that the Duke of Tallant's brother had returned to England and was in residence at the Palazzo Neri. So I came to him, because I had nowhere else to turn."

Mira glanced over at Michael Keynes, slouched against the wall near the fireplace. He exhibited all the interest a piece of furniture might have done. "Did the duke's servants follow you?" she said, returning her attention to the duchess.

"I've no idea. Tallant said something about visiting property in Somerset, so they might have gone there. Or they might have fled. If they were set to kill us, or merely to keep us under guard, they failed." Her voice faltered. "To fail Tallant is to be punished beyond measure."

"What did they look like?" It was Keynes, speaking for the first time since their encounter at the window.

"Large," said the duchess. "Rough faced. One had

brown hair, the other was bald save for a fringe at the base of his head, and they were tall. They reminded me of the pugilists that used to fight at country fairs when I was growing up in Ireland. The brown-haired one had a slight accent, probably Welsh, and the other favored his left leg when he walked. I'm sorry I did not observe them more closely."

The duchess's hands quivered. Her breathing was uneven. She had come, Mira realized, to the end of her strength.

"We can do nothing until morning," Mira said, rising. "And after a night's sleep, you may recall other details of use. Mr. Keynes, where is Her Grace to sleep?"

"Top of the stairs," he said, "large room to the right. Help her settle in, Miss Holcombe. When you return, we'll make plans."

Chapter 11

The duchess had begun to weep softly into the pillows. Mira, understanding that she wished to be private, snuffed the candle in Michael Keynes's bedchamber and left Her Grace alone there. Then she returned to the parlor, settled herself primly on a chair, and looked over at Mr. Keynes.

Slouched in the shadows, arms folded, he was looking back at her, his face without expression. Waiting. He always seemed to be *waiting*.

"Where shall we begin?" she said.

His mouth curved, only a little, at the corners. "With what must be done immediately. That means winkling the duchess away before anyone knows she was ever here, and finding a place to stow her."

"She could stay in my rooms," David said. "I have a spare bedchamber."

"You're connected to me. She wouldn't be safe there."

"Oh." David looked unhappy. "But I don't see why not. Surely Tallant won't figure she came to *you* for help?"

"No one seems to think she would. Not you, not Miss Holcombe, not I. And probably not my brother." Keynes pulled himself from the wall and went to an array of cut-glass decanters on the sideboard. "But he'll know that if she did come to me, I'd help her to spite him."

Mira shivered. "Is that why you're doing this?"

Keynes, a decanter in one hand and a glass in the other, glanced at her over his shoulder. "Does it matter? Whatever my reasons, she gets what she wants."

The sound of brandy being poured, the clink as the glass stopper was returned to the decanter. Mira watched Michael Keynes take a long drink from the glass. Only the duchess had understood. This man would protect her, and his motives were, as he said, irrelevant. When it came right down to it, the motives of Miranda Holcombe could not stand up to any degree of scrutiny either. It was exciting to be in company with Michael Keynes, embroiled with his plots and . . . No. She mustn't look too closely at all that.

"I don't know London well," she said, "but I am acquainted with someone who does. Perhaps she can suggest a place to hide the duchess."

"Is she to be trusted?"

"I should think so. She is secretary to Lady Jessica Duran, who—"

"Who is married to a friend of mine. Tallant knows about him. We keep clear of that family, servants included."

"Good heavens. For a man with few connections in England, you somehow manage to be connected to everyone who might help us."

"We are acquainted with the same people, is all. The secretary is tracking down some information I require."

"You know her, then?"

"We've never met. She sends her reports to a third party. Nonetheless—"

"Very well." Obstinate man. Did he imagine himself capable of protecting *everyone*? "You have ruled out Miss Pryce, so we must find a place ourselves.

David, is there a hotel where we might conceal the duchess, or an agency that could provide us with a rental flat?"

"I'm sure there is," David said. "But I've lived on Mount Street for more than a dozen years, and the only hotels I'm familiar with are the fashionable ones where I sometimes take a meal or visit a friend."

Muttering something under his breath, Keynes refilled his nearly empty glass to the top and slumped on a chair near the hearth. "Point taken. The three of us are ineffective, so Miss Pryce it is. Duran told me she could find a white feather in a snowstorm, so perhaps she can find a way to conceal one. Meantime, let's talk about getting the duchess out of here."

"You have a plan," Mira said.

"The start of one. I've no doubt you will refine on it, but here's what I have in mind. We'll dress the duchess in your father's coat and hat, cover her with blankets, and smuggle her out on the wheeled chair. You and David will accompany her, ostensibly taking Mr. Holcombe to some public place."

She understood immediately. "The British Museum. He wants very much to go there. But if the duchess goes in his stead, what will we do with him in the interim? And how do we unite the duchess and the wheeled chair?"

"Sleight of hand. We're not being closely watched at the moment, although I suspect little goes on here that Beata Neri fails to learn about." Keynes stretched out his long legs and crossed them at the ankles. "Rig up a dummy that will pass at a distance for your father and wheel it here to collect David tomorrow morning. Ten o'clock should do it. After the duchess changes places with the dummy, the three of you will set out for the museum."

"But—"

Keynes lifted a hand. "Long before then, Hari Singh will have returned from the home of his friends. He's

been meaning to construct a bed that will raise your
father's back to help him breathe more easily—something of the kind—and tomorrow would be a good
day to get started. He'll be at your door by eight
o'clock and will help you set up the dummy in the
chair. Then he'll spend the day sawing and hammering
and keeping away anyone who drops by. No one will
guess your father is still inside the cottage."

It would work. How clever of him, and how foolish
of her to underestimate him. All this time, when she'd
been sure he was paying little attention to the duchess's story, when she'd thought he didn't care what
became of his sister-in-law and his missing niece, he'd
been sketching out a plan of action. "What of Miss
Pryce? She has been seeing to a business matter on
my behalf, so it will be quite ordinary for me to pay
her a call. Shall I do that on our way to the museum?"

"From here on out, you stay away from Duran's
residence. In the morning, I'll post the letter you are
going to write her. David, we require a meeting place
near the museum, one with a private parlor. The name
and direction have to be included in the letter."

"But I can't—" David looked up at Keynes's face
and stopped protesting.

"Will you join us tomorrow?" Mira asked, to prove
that she, at least, was not intimidated.

"Yes, but first I'm going to make sure the chit didn't
call at Tallant House."

"Will the servants admit you?"

"That would be the easiest way in. If they turn me
off, I'll find another. She's unlikely to have gone there,
but we need to cross it off our list before Tallant
returns to London."

"The Lion and Lamb in Upper King Street," David
blurted out. "It's not far from the museum."

"One o'clock, then. Miss Holcombe, there are writing materials in that drawer." He gestured to a small
table near the fireplace. "Tell Miss Pryce as much or

as little as you see fit, but impress upon her the urgency of this meeting."

"She might not be at home," said David. "What if she fails to receive the letter in time?"

"We find a night's lodging for the duchess and make other arrangements. We do whatever we must."

David glanced down at his fitted black coat and intricate cravat. "I'm going to look ridiculous touring the museum in evening dress."

Shaking his head, Keynes got himself another drink and carried it to a wing chair. "The one thing I refuse to deal with, Fairfax, is your bloody wardrobe. Be quiet and let the lady write her letter."

Rising, Mira gave David her best smile and got back a good-humored shrug. "It requires an act of faith to be his friend," he had once told her. She was only glad that her own fate did not depend on Michael Keynes.

Through the mellowing warmth of brandy and weariness, Michael watched through lowered lashes as Miranda Holcombe crossed to the writing table, settled herself on the straight-backed chair, and opened the drawer.

Her every motion was fluid and spare, like a cat stalking through high grass. Nothing wasted, nothing that was not beautiful. He felt like a supplicant unable to ask for what he most desired, holding himself at a distance, grateful for the merest glimpse of the impossible.

Or, he was drunk. A maudlin sot with nothing to look forward to but a killing and a hanging. Except that after the killing, he'd be the duke. Did they hang dukes? What of a duke that had killed a duke?

Never mind all that. He didn't much care, once the main business was done with.

Even to write, she did not remove those infernal gloves. She was laying out her implements one by one—Beata's fine linen paper, a pen and a pen knife, a bottle of ink neatly stoppered, a stick of wax, a seal with what he suspected was Beata Neri's made-up family crest. Miranda's thoughts were elsewhere, he could tell, on the words she would inscribe when she'd finished sharpening her pen, on how much she would reveal in her letter.

Her profile, an ivory cameo carved out against the firelight, enthralled him. He wondered about her voice—husky, breathy, as though she had some inflammation of the throat. Like a soft wind through grass. She could weave magic with that voice. Nimue spoke with a voice like that when she enchanted Merlin.

A beggar at the queen's gate, that's what he was. Senseless, pathetic, no hope in the world of drawing her attention or meriting her regard.

He rested his head against the back of the chair, closed his eyes for a moment, remembered who he was and what he had to do. Protect Mira Holcombe, for one thing, or give her the power to protect herself. That meant money, and he must see to it while he could. Tomorrow morning, a visit to his banker, a trust set up in her name. He had no one else to leave it to, and he couldn't take it where he was going.

Fairfax could administer the trust. Fairfax, whose soft snore melded into the patter of rain against the window glass. A good boy, Fairfax. Only two years younger than he, but centuries younger in experience. Money for Fairfax as well.

He had lots of money. How nice that he had people to give it to. Something good would come of his life after all.

She had begun to write. He let the soft sounds in the room settle over him, the scratch of her pen on the paper, the rustle of her gown, the crackle of the fire. A domestic scene, surprisingly pleasant, all but alien to him.

There had been another time like this, in Scotland. The graystone house had been drafty, stocked with worn furnishings and threadbare carpets, but he'd thought nothing of that. There had never been money in the family for niceties, even at Longview, and he'd been wildly glad to escape that hellhole. Exile meant an end to terror.

He had loved the open spaces, the rough landscape. And when he came home after a day of testing himself on the cliffs or in the icy lochs, there would be thick soup and crusty bread and no one to give him a beating.

On winter nights like this one, he would read by the fire or work on the projects his mother had assigned him. She had by necessity become his tutor—there was no school in that remote area—and Devil Keynes hadn't noticed or cared that she'd packed up half his library and brought it north.

Some evenings she would play the harpsichord while he read. Other times she'd sit at a writing table, as Mira Holcombe was doing now, penning long letters to friends she would not live to see again.

Tomorrow, though, he would see Miranda Holcombe again. Thinking of it, simply having something to look forward to, gave him an astonishing jolt of pleasure.

She read over her letter, made a little nod of satisfaction, and signed at the bottom. All the rituals were rendered with feminine precision. She aligned the corners before folding the paper. The direction was printed. The wax stick held to a candle, the soft wax applied to the paper, allowed to set for just the right amount of time before the seal was pressed into it. He could have watched her repeat it all, again and again, for hours.

She rose then and crossed to where she'd left her cloak and bonnet. After a few moments, he got up as well.

"Don't wake him," she said as he started over to rouse Fairfax.

"The window is high. You'll need his help to climb out."

"You can help me." She tied the ribbons of her bonnet, picked up the cloak, and went into Hari's room.

He started to pick up a candle, remembered what a bad idea it would be. In the dark bedchamber, she waited for him beside the window, her cloak draped over her arm.

"I am sorry," she said, "for striking you so hard this evening, and for what happened later, when I arrived here. I have an abhorrence of being . . . touched."

"Not always." He shouldn't have said it. He kept going anyway. "Not by Fairfax."

"That's different. We knew each other as children. I am fearful, that is all. It has nothing to do with you."

He reached past her, watched her steel herself to avoid flinching when his hand went by to raise the window casement. Cold wind and raindrops blew into the room. She put the cloak on a chair, hitched herself onto the sill, and after a moment, held out her arms.

His heart was pounding when he took hold of her waist. She ducked her head until she was half in, half out the window, and he lifted her until her legs were free. His upper body followed her outside as he lowered her gently to the ground. He reached back for the cloak and draped it over her shoulders.

She looked up at him, rain streaming from the brim of her bonnet. "Thank you, Mr. Keynes."

"You are right to keep your distance from me," he said. "Tonight I took advantage of circumstances for my own pleasure, and given the opportunity, I shall do so again. I understand that you carry a knife, Miss Holcombe. If ever I come too close to you, use it."

Because she was dressed in her widow's weeds, and because it was raining, and because no one would miss her, Mira sped behind her cottage so that Michael Keynes would think she'd gone in through the back window.

For a time she stood there, vibrating with the call from a place she didn't want to go. Never mind that she stole from the cottage most nights and went there, certain she'd find whatever was summoning her, only to find nothing at all.

Tonight would likely be the same, but she dared not refuse the call. The instinct was more compelling than it had been the last several days and nights. She made her way to the street and walked a considerable distance before locating a hackney, which took her to Berkeley Square. While the hackney waited for her on a side street, she slipped into the gated garden across from Tallant House and watched for an hour, the rain streaming from her bonnet and cloak.

She wondered if there was a special time she was meant to kill him. Would she be standing in front of his house on a dark lonely night when he returned home, when there would be only the two of them, and her rage, and her knife?

Chapter 12

Well before dawn, Michael claimed his horse from the stable and rode out in the direction of Hampstead Heath by way of Grosvenor Street. David had given him the name of a shop authorized to receive mail, but after winding through streets and alleys to make sure he was not being followed, he decided to take the letter to Sothingdon House himself. There was less risk of being seen than of the message failing to reach its destination in time.

It was still dark when he approached the house and slipped the letter through the narrow slot in the door. Then he continued on to Hampstead, gave Loki a good run, stopped at a chop house for breakfast, and made his way back into the city. The exercise and fresh air had cleared his head, although it had left him looking even more barbaric than usual. He hadn't troubled to shave that morning. Beneath his hat, his wet hair was plastered to his scalp, and water poured from the shoulder capes of his greatcoat. He hoped the servants weren't too fussy about whom they admitted to Tallant House.

The family had owned the tall edifice in Berkeley Square for several generations, although it was practically a ruin the last time he'd seen it. He had been there twice, once when he was seven years old and again when he was twelve, just before leaving with his mother for Scotland. On that occasion, they had been permitted to stay overnight.

The rain had settled to a gloomy drizzle. The few pedestrians in the square, huddled beneath black umbrellas, paid no attention when he rode by. He dismounted in front of Tallant House, looped the reins around an ornamental pineapple on the wrought-iron fence, jumped the low gate, and strode up the steps to the door.

The knocker was missing, and it was a considerable time before his rapping drew anyone's attention. Finally the door opened a crack and a freckled, red-haired young man wearing silver-and-black livery peered outside. His eyes went round as gold guineas. "Y-your Grace." The door swung wide. "We d-didn't expect you home today."

Grinning, Michael swept off his hat. "Just as well. It's only the lesser male twig on the family tree, directly off the ship at Portsmouth. Devil take it. Rode all this way in the rain, and m'brother's not in residence." He was inside by this time, dripping water over the black-and-white marble floor, stripping off his greatcoat and gloves and handing the lot to the excessively pale footman. "How about the duchess? The children? Time I made their acquaintance. Went out to India before the marriage, don't y'know, and ain't been home since."

"Yes, sir. I mean, there's no one in residence now. A few servants is all, until His Grace returns."

"Well, well, where's he gone, then? Longview? I should have tried there first."

"I cannot say, sir, where he is to be found." The footman looked distressed. "The thing is, he does not permit guests unless he is here to approve them."

"Guests? I'm his *brother*. And unless he's begot a

son since last he wrote to me, I'm still heir to his title, lands, and fortune. Rightly so. *I'm* the one made all the money he's been spending." Michael opened the nearest door and stepped into a large, splendidly furnished parlor. "To good effect, I see. The duchess must have refined taste. God knows Jermyn never did."

When he returned to the entrance hall, he saw two or three other frightened faces peering at him from down the passageway. "What's your name?" he asked the unhappy footman.

"T-Tom, sir."

"Well, Tom, I can see I've created a disturbance. I'd meant to stay here, but in the circumstances, I'll find m'self a hotel until the duke comes back and *approves* me. How's that? Except, before I go back out in the rain, I think I'll have a look around. Ain't been here since I was a lad, and it was all to rack and ruin then."

"Sir, I—"

"He won't like that either? Always was a strange bird, m'brother. Never mind, Tom. I won't pilfer the silver. You come along to make sure of it, and then I'll be on my way. He don't need to know I was ever here. Oh, and direct someone to keep an eye on m'horse."

The tour took half an hour, during which time every servant found opportunity to pop up and get a good look at the heir who looked so much like his brother. For once, the resemblance had proven useful. No one questioned his identity, nor his right to be there, although he doubted anyone would report the incident to the duke.

He was allowed to wander about freely, Tom and the housekeeper with her ring of keys trailing behind. Most of the rooms were kept locked, and he asked admittance to only a few of them. For old times' sake,

he said when the door to the duke's study was un-
sealed. His escorts waited in the passageway when he
went inside to look around.

Save for the floor-to-ceiling bookshelves against one
wall, all the furniture he remembered from two decades earlier had been replaced with what appeared
to be good-quality antiques. The flagstone hearth and
carved marble fireplace were the same, though. According to the newspaper reports, his father's body,
the discharged pistol in his hand, had been found
there. All traces of blood had long since been
scrubbed away, but there was a chip on the mantelpiece where the bullet had struck after passing
through his father's head.

Two wingback chairs were angled nearby, a small
table between them, and not far away stood a large
desk of polished walnut, its surface all but bare. A
few hunting prints adorned the walls, and over a pier
table hung a large, gilt-framed portrait of Jermyn Ar-
thur Anthony MacTavish Keynes, eighth Duke of Tallant. After a brief glance at the imperious face with its
sardonic expression, the eyes so like his own, Michael
turned away. His fingers itched to draw out a knife
and send it into his brother's painted chest, but of
course, there was no more heart in the painting than
in the man himself.

Upstairs, to the servants' palpable relief, he declined
to examine the duke's private chambers and asked
instead to explore unoccupied rooms that might be
suitable for his own accommodations.

Reconnaissance. The real reason he had come here.
He marked out servants' stairs, closets, connecting
rooms, rooms with balconies at the rear, the layout of
the walled back garden, and trees that he could climb
before swinging over to a balcony. All the while he
chattered about India, boyhood days at Longview, his
wish to find a bride and settle down to reproduce. His
plans to buy a London house of his own.

He unlatched windows in several of the unoccupied rooms, marking their location. On a whim, he palmed one of his knives into the hem of a curtain.

Thirty minutes after he'd entered the house, he was on his way out again. Tom the footman, the housekeeper, and the boy who'd watched his horse received handsome vails, and he'd added a handful of coins, all he had with him, to provide a treat for the entire staff. He could afford to be generous.

Next stop, the Bank of England.

Hari Singh enjoyed working with his hands. In Mr. Holcombe's quiet, attentive company, he had shared his favorite Buddha tales between periods of sawing, hammering, and testing the results. Soon, by turning a crank, Miss Holcombe would be able to raise and lower either or both ends of the bed. That would improve the circulation of Mr. Holcombe's blood and perhaps make him more comfortable. Next he intended to redesign the wheeled chair with its platform, making it easier to transport Mr. Holcombe by coach.

After a luncheon of bread-thickened vegetable broth, applesauce, and tea, Mr. Holcombe gestured for his alphabet card to be brought over and asked if Hari would allow him to dictate a secret letter to his daughter. His endurance lasted for an hour and produced only one long paragraph, but Hari promised they could add a little every day.

It was early afternoon, when he was pounding nails into the backrest, that he became aware of someone knocking at the door. Michael would have the language for this, he thought, sliding Mr. Holcombe on his pallet under a pre-arranged shelter of boards and tools. Then, a hammer in one hand and a peaceable expression on his face, he went to the front door and opened it.

Two of the Memsahib Beata's servants, their arms wrapped around bundles of undetermined natures, bowed as best they could. "We have brought the costumes for Mr. and Miss Holcombe," one of them said.

"For tonight's masquerade ball," the other added. "They had the invitations last week. The *principessa* wishes to assure herself they will be present."

"I cannot speak for them," Hari said, navigating a path of truth through his own deception. "Miss Holcombe has gone to a museum, with Mr. Fairfax joining her to arrange transportation and push the wheeled chair. I shall take the parcels, if you wish, and remind them of the masquerade when they return."

"There is one for Mr. Keynes as well. Shall I leave it here with you?"

"If you wish."

"The *principessa* especially requests his presence this evening. There is to be a surprise for Mr. Keynes."

Perhaps Tallant had returned. Or perhaps the *memsahib* was simply making mischief. "I shall convey her message," he said. "But you should inform her that Mr. Keynes does not like surprises."

When the servants were gone, Hari took the bundles into the bedchamber, retrieved Mr. Holcombe from under the tent of lumber, and told him what had occurred.

"Wht r they?" Mr. Holcombe asked when the alphabet card was put under his hand.

Hari opened the two large parcels and showed him each fantastical disguise. The *memsahib* had spared no expense for Mr. and Miss Holcombe.

But the parcel containing the costume for Michael was a good deal smaller than the others. No larger, to be truthful, than a book. Unable to resist, he carefully unwrapped the contents and held them—*it*—up for inspection.

Mr. Holcombe's eyes sparkled, and the left side of his face curved, just a little, in a smile.

To wear at her masquerade ball, Beata Neri had sent Michael a loincloth.

Chapter 13

Michael arrived at the Lion and Lamb shortly after one o'clock to find David Fairfax waiting just inside. "I'll see to your horse," Fairfax said. "The others are in a private parlor, up those stairs and second door to the right."

"Miss Pryce?"

"She was here before us. Too much female talk, so I came down to watch for you."

"How's the duchess?"

"Tired. Scared. Sharp tongued. Can't blame her, with her daughter gone missing."

"And Miss Pryce?"

Fairfax thought a moment. "Energetic. Precise. Also sharp tongued. Oh, and she has a problem with her eyes. They can't be exposed to light. She wears odd spectacles to protect them, smoked and hinged at the temples. The glasses cover her eyes altogether, and when you look at them, you wind up looking at your own reflection. Disconcerting, that's what it is."

Michael shrugged. "If there's no wine up there already, bring some with you."

The parlor was a low-ceilinged room with a small window overlooking an alleyway, and a fireplace that gave off more smoke than warmth. The women were

clustered on benches at the far end of a trestle table,
Miss Holcombe and the duchess on one side and Miss
Pryce across from them, their heads bent over an open
sketch pad. He couldn't see what was on it. At the
other end of the table lay two bonnets, one blue and
one brown, and a hat belonging to Mr. Holcombe.

The conversation ceased when he entered, and three
faces turned to look at him.

Only the duchess scowled at his disheveled appearance. Miss Holcombe and Miss Pryce regarded him
with bland uninterest, as if he were a servant come in
to clear away the dishes.

He swept off his hat and bowed. "Ladies. Shall I
assume you have resolved every difficulty without
me?"

"Indeed not," said Miss Pryce briskly. "We are
gathering information. Her Grace has provided a list
of her daughter's schoolfellows, those who live in England, and of the places she has visited on previous
occasions. Just now she has been describing Lady Corinna while I attempted to capture her likeness with a
charcoal stick. We shall require a better artist, I'm
afraid."

Miss Pryce, it seemed, was accustomed to taking
charge. He folded himself onto the bench, deliberately
choosing a spot where he'd have a good view of Miranda Holcombe, prim in a dark blue dress with a
high collar, her hair combed back into a knot. Aware
he was breathing unevenly, he took a moment to remember why they had all come together at the inn.

"You are well, Norah?" he asked, noting the shadows under her eyes.

"As can be expected," she snapped, "with my child
nowhere to be found."

Put in his place, he folded his arms and left Miss
Pryce to get on with it.

She did so without delay. "In her letter, Miss Holcombe explained Her Grace's circumstances and the

urgent need to conceal her. There is a place I know of where she will be safe for an extended period of time, although it is certainly not the sort of accommodation a duchess would be accustomed to."

"I'm not fussy, young woman. Just put me somewhere, anywhere at all, and get on about finding Corinna."

Fairfax came in with two open bottles of claret and five glasses on a tray. The women ignored him as he took a seat across from Michael and, with a look of resignation, passed over a bottle and a glass.

"The house I have in mind is clean and self-contained. Meals are served there, and each resident has a bedchamber, a small sitting room, and a privy closet."

"It sounds ideal," said Miranda.

"In those respects, yes. And the location is such that no one is likely to seek her in that neighborhood. The house stands on Little White Lyon Street."

"But that's in Seven Dials!" Fairfax erupted. "She can't stay *there!*"

Seven Dials meant nothing to Michael. Miranda wore a little frown of puzzlement.

The duchess appeared unconcerned. "I'll not be on the streets, young man. Go on, Miss Pryce. What recommends the house to you?"

During the pause that followed, Michael studied the composed young woman sitting straight as a spear, her hands folded on the table in front of her. Her spectacles were as Fairfax had described them, darkly smoked, cupped over her eye sockets and folded back at the temples, admitting no light to eyes that could bear none. Her dark brown hair, smooth and shiny, sat atop her head like a turban. Despite her drab schoolmistress dress, he could tell she had a trim figure, and her complexion was, like Miranda's, smooth and pale.

"I was born there," she finally said. "Until my

mother died when I was eight, we lived there. At the time it was the sort of house one would expect to find in that section of the Rookeries, but now it serves the ladies, those who might once have plied their trade there, in quite another fashion. They come to stay, usually for several weeks at a time, to take the cure."

Silence.

Michael, biting back a laugh, watched the expressions pass over Miranda's face and the duchess's. Fairfax flushed redder than the wine he had just spilled.

"For the pox?" the duchess choked out.

"Yes," said Miss Pryce, entirely unperturbed. "And ailments of that sort. The establishment is managed by Mrs. Teale, formerly the proprietress of a brothel, now a woman of strict religious convictions. She has three large sons who see to it no undesirables enter the house. I stopped by this morning to make sure there was a vacancy, and if Her Grace is agreeable, she can move directly into a set of rooms on the third floor. It will be quiet that high up, and I shall bring in whatever she requires for her comfort."

"Oh, my," said Miranda, regarding Miss Pryce with undisguised wonder. "What an astonishing idea."

Everyone's attention went to the duchess, whose brows had lifted practically to her hairline. "I am to pretend that I, too, am there for the *cure?*"

"That would be best," Miss Pryce replied. "Naturally you must wear a disguise, and I have taken the liberty of providing one that will get you into the house without arousing the suspicion of the other residents or the servants." She gestured to a portmanteau on the floor beside her. "Later I shall bring more clothing, books, needlework, and the like. And news as well, because of course you will wish to be kept informed about the search for Lady Corinna. I come and go in that area on a regular basis, so no one will think it unusual to see me there."

For some reason, at just the moment Michael was

draining a glass of wine, everyone suddenly looked in his direction. He looked back at them with surprise. "Don't ask me," he said when the glass was empty. "I'm partial to back streets and whorehouses. No perspective to offer here."

"I *am* asking," the duchess said. "It was you I came to for help."

The more fool she. "I won't say you'll fit right in," he said carefully. "But I expect you can carry it off. In your place, I'd rely on Miss Pryce."

"So would I," said Miranda. "If it matters."

"Very well. Shall we move on to plans for locating my daughter?" Her voice quavered at the end, a measure of her distress.

"She hasn't showed up at Tallant House," Michael said. "We need to check Longview, but none of us can go there."

"We could hire a Runner," Fairfax said. "Of course, Tallant will probably do the same. And how can we determine which of the Runners is to be trusted? I've heard that some accept bribes, while others are shiftless. Why are you all staring at me? I've never employed a Runner, but some of my friends have done so. Not all of them have been glad of it."

"Mr. Fairfax is entirely correct," said Miss Pryce. "As when employing a physician or a solicitor, one must take care when hiring a Bow Street Runner. Fortunately my own acquaintance includes an assortment of thieves, robbers, confidence artists, and scoundrels of various persuasions. They are well aware which Runners are susceptible to bribes and which can be relied on to honorably fulfill a contract. Shall I seek out a recommendation and report back to you?"

"Never mind reporting. Find someone and hire him," Michael said. "Hire as many as you like."

"The expense—"

"I'll open an account for you with my banker. You already know how to contact him. Draw upon the funds for whatever you need. Which reminds me." He fumbled through the folds of his greatcoat, found a thick wad of folded banknotes tied with a string, and slid it down the table. It came to a stop directly in front of Miss Pryce.

The ladies studied it as if a snake had just wriggled into their company. Then they looked up at Michael.

What the devil had he done wrong now? "For immediate expenses, is all. I said there'd be more. I'll see to it after I leave here."

Another of those silences that made his skin itch. At length Miss Pryce said, "You are generous, sir."

Approval, he decided, was even worse than disdain. "I'm just buying my way out of taking further responsibility or doing any of the work." He stood and pulled on his coat. "Is there anything else you require, or can I be on my way?"

"By all means," said Miss Pryce in the dismissive tone she might have used with a battlefield deserter. "Mr. Fairfax, perhaps you can help us with a small dilemma. If the clothing on the wheeled chair is to pass for Mr. Holcombe, we shall need materials to stuff into it. While Mira and I see to the duchess's disguise, will you find towels or blankets or something of the kind?"

Michael got out of the room during that speech, desperate to escape. And inexplicably, not wanting to go. He was still hovering in the dim passageway when Fairfax caught him up.

"Where do I buy sheets?" Fairfax asked.

"How would I know? Where did you stash my horse?"

"You needn't snarl at me. I'll go find stuffing and bring the horse when I come back. You can go down to the tavern and drink."

He would have done, except that he was too conspicuous to hang about in public. And it had occurred to him that if he stayed upstairs, there might be another opportunity to see Miranda. If he gave it some thought, he could probably devise an excuse to go back into the parlor.

He did his thinking on a small bench a little distance down the passageway, where he whittled on a piece of wood that had started out to be a dog but was turning out to be a duck. After fifteen minutes he'd scratched up one plausible reason to speak again with Miss Pryce, one to speak again with Norah, and none to come within a mile of Miranda Holcombe. Then Fairfax returned, his arms full of horse blankets, and Michael followed him to the door and made himself useful by knocking.

"Come." It had to be Miss Pryce speaking.

Michael opened the door, let Fairfax enter, and came in behind him. His gaze searched for Miranda and found instead the back of a woman with long, curly chestnut hair. She was wearing a purple dress that had seen better days and too many washings. "Norah?"

She turned, and at first he thought he had been mistaken. A fringe of hair met dark, arched brows. Her cheeks were painted, as were her lips, and there was a mole on her cheek. "Not Norah, m'boy." She grinned, and he saw that one front tooth was noticeably yellowed. "I be Rosie Bell. What will ye gi' me fer a toss?"

"Don't overplay it," Miss Pryce said sternly. "Indeed, I believe you had better have a sore tooth. When we're nearer the house, I shall wad up some fabric in your cheek to cover that educated diction." At Norah's slumping shoulders, she relented a trifle. "You cannot help but be what you are, Your Grace. If you speak, you will reveal yourself as an aristocrat."

"I understand, my dear. I was merely attempting to shock my brother-in-law."

"You succeeded," he told her sincerely. "I believe you'll carry it off very well."

"For Corinna, I will do whatever is necessary." She stepped forward, and with a degree of hesitation, placed her hand on his forearm.

It was, he understood readily enough, an expression of gratitude, one he did not deserve. With difficulty, he refrained from pulling away.

"Do you know," she said, "the transformation from Duchess of Tallant to poxy doxy seems to me a decided improvement."

Laughing, he lifted her hand from his arm and held it as their gazes met. "You are not to worry yourself ill, Norah. You have done all you can, and now your task is to remain hidden while we find your daughter."

"Your niece."

That relationship, the girl to him, struck him for the first time. When his mother died, he had ceased having a family. There was only his enemy, who happened to be his brother. "Yes. I look forward to making her acquaintance."

He went then to Miss Pryce of the pursed lips and invisible eyes. "I owe you a service," he said.

"The documents have been of use to you?"

It took a moment to realize what she was talking about. "Indeed. I know rather more about the man than anyone should. You are thorough."

"To a fault. You should know, sir, that Lord Varden returned to England two days ago. It is likely he will appear at Beata Neri's masquerade tonight, and beforehand, I understand he is to make a report to the East India Consortium."

Bad news. The worst news. It was all coming together, and all at one time, or nearly so. He had to stay free until Tallant returned. Then act quickly, devil take the consequences. He looked down at Miss Pryce's protective spectacles, saw his reflection looking back. "If you need me, send a message to David Fairfax. Under no circumstances are you to make direct contact or be seen in my vicinity. Understood?"

"Of course. Reports of the investigation will be delivered to your banker. You may safely rely on me."

Nodding, he turned to Miranda Holcombe and located her by the window. Pale winter sunlight streamed over her, cast a halo around her. She gazed at him without expression. He felt, as always, that he was looking at her through a sheet of ice. At the end he could find nothing to say to her, could not bring himself to bid her farewell, so he left without a word.

Chapter 14

"There you are, then." With a flourish, Miranda placed the wreath of laurel leaves atop her father's head and secured it in his white hair with pins. *"Ave, Caesar, rex convivii."*

His eyes approved the jest. Immobile in his chair, he could scarcely play Master of the Feast. But the notion of dressing up as Marcus Aurelius—his personal hero—had caught his imagination. And that made it impossible for her to disappoint him, although she longed to drop onto her bed for a good night's sleep.

Instead, draped in a filmy drift of soft muslin that no self-respecting Vestal Virgin would have dared to wear in public, she wrapped the gilt cincture around her waist, secured the jeweled filet on her head, and donned the soft golden gloves Beata had provided. They were made to reach above her elbows, but she let the fabric drop into folds that concealed the outline of her dagger.

She would need it, her deadly little knife, perhaps this very evening. The Beast had returned to London. "He will appear at Beata Neri's masquerade tonight," Miss Pryce had told Mr. Keynes. Mira had overheard only a few words of their conversation, but who else could she have meant?

Hari Singh, wearing traditional Punjabi garb, was to escort her father, freeing her to enjoy the ball. At first she had been sorry for it, but perhaps all would work out for the best. Later, if the opportunity presented itself, she might be committing a murder.

The letter to her father, brief and apologetic, had long since been composed and left where it was sure to be found. She meant to take responsibility for her crime. She meant, this time, to tell the truth.

The night was clear and cold, the villa a blaze of lights. Colorful Japan lanterns cast rainbows over the terraces and in the courtyards. Servants bearing flambeaux escorted guests from their carriages to the entrance hall. Music floated above the sounds of voices and laughter as several hundred guests danced in the ballroom, dined in the supper room, mingled in the salons. With some regret, Mira watched Hari wheel the chair into a parlor near the library, where her father was quickly surrounded by his cronies. Leaving her to get on with having a wonderful time and, if Papa had his way, meeting the man of her dreams.

Not that she had any such dreams, she was thinking as she made her way to the ballroom, where she planned to conceal herself in the crowd and watch for her quarry.

No such luck. She was just inside the door, scanning the room for a corner where she might sit, when Beata Neri materialized alongside her.

"*Vieni*," said Beata, splendidly baroque in a wealth of gold satin and blonde lace encrusted with jewels. "The two most fascinating women at the party will pose side by side over there, by the fountain, so that the beau monde may draw near and pay homage. And when they move on, I shall relate to you the most salacious gossip about them. Oh, and there is someone

I especially wish you to meet, but I see he has not yet arrived. Gentlemen and their business meetings. Mah!"

Mira took her position on the low dais, feeling as conspicuous as if she'd just emerged from her bath, smiling and nodding when strangers made their curtsies and bows to the hostess. There were harlequins and shepherdesses, satyrs and soldiers, monarchs and demons, pharaohs and faeries and monks. "Who are you meant to be?" she asked Beata during a rare interval of quiet.

Two dark brows lifted in surprise. "Why, I am myself, of course. Who else could I possibly wish to be?"

Laughing, somewhat relieved that Beata was laughing with her, Mira saw a slender gentleman with light brown hair and an unassuming smile approach the fountain. He was of average height, in his forties, she would guess, and wore correct evening garb instead of a costume. She had seen him before, always surrounded by the political set, but they had never been introduced.

"Lord Gretton," said Beata, allowing him to kiss her ring-studded fingers. "At long last you and your commercial associates emerge from your lair."

"From the meeting room you most graciously provided us," he amended with gentle reproach. "Our business could not be postponed."

"But of course it could. Nonetheless, I shall do you the honor of presenting Miss Miranda Holcombe, who has never been known to express an interest in business or politics."

"I am interested," Mira said, "but so ignorant that I dare not express an opinion."

"If only my fellows in the government would hold silent when they had nothing of use to say, Miss Holcombe. But no doubt, they would make the same observation regarding me." After favoring her with a smile, he turned again to Beata. "Do you know where Lady Gretton has got off to?"

"She is in the gaming room, I believe."

"Just so." Sadness darkened his eyes. "Perhaps she will favor me with a dance. Ladies, your servant." With a bow, he moved away.

Mira wished she could go with him. Go anywhere but where she was, appended to Beata like a corsage, while the Duke of Tallant prowled every room but this one. He was not, she felt sure, a dancing man.

"A powerful man," Beata was saying, presumably about the one who had just departed. "But a trifle dull. Ah. There." She gestured with her fan. "By the door. He has stopped to speak with Lady Drendle and her mother. The most beautiful man in all of England."

There was no mistaking the gentleman she meant. Tall, slender, elegant in formal evening dress, he had hair the color of flax and the sort of classic profile generally sculpted from marble. Always conscious of hands, she immediately saw that he was wearing well-fitted black leather gloves. "Is he in mourning?"

"No. Why do you . . . ah. The gloves. Alas, he suffered an injury while in India and his right hand was—how do I say this delicately?—*crushed*. A great sadness. But heaven, I think, could not allow so perfect a creature to remain without flaw. Or perhaps it was the devil sought to unravel him. When lesser creatures gaze on him, they either wish to be better than they are, or they wish to destroy the image of what they can never be."

Mira released an imperceptible sigh. Beata was at her most theatrical tonight, which was saying a great deal. And she was annoyed with herself as well, because her own gaze kept returning to the light-haired gentleman by the door. She liked the attentiveness with which he favored the two ladies, who were old enough to be his mother and grandmother. Unlike so many others in the room, he did not keep glancing around as if looking for someone more important to keep company with.

"You will hear much good of this gentleman," Beata said, a touch of melancholy in her voice. "And all of it is quite true. You will also hear gossip about the two of us, for we were, for a considerable time, lovers. But as must all relationships based in passion and regard but absent of love, our liaison was drawing to a close before he went out to India. Indeed, I believe he may have chosen that way to put an end to it before there could be regrets. There are none, I assure you. Indeed, with no brothers or close male relations in the line of inheritance, it is past time he took a wife and set about producing sons."

Oh, dear.

Mira was scrambling for an excuse to take her leave when the blond gentleman bowed to the ladies he'd been speaking with and started toward the fountain. To where she stood like a sacrificial lamb, because there was no question in her mind about Beata's intentions.

"Quid times?" her father used to ask her. Still asked her, from time to time. *What do you fear?* Some days, she had to confess, nearly everything. Of late, Michael Keynes, for reasons she dared not explore. And now this splendid man drawing close to her, his gaze on his former lover as it should be, his attention—she knew it, she *knew* it—on her.

"Caro mio," said Beata when he arrived. "You have kept us all waiting. Now the audience requires a gesture, so I shall lean forward and permit you to kiss my cheek."

Mira saw amusement and resignation in his jade-green eyes as he obliged. From a distance he had been striking, but close up, he was—she had to admit it—breathtaking. The music played on, people continued dancing and talking and strolling around the ballroom, but all gazes were focused on the little scene taking place inches from where she waited to play her own unscripted part.

None of this matters, she reminded herself. *Not this man, nor anything else that stands in the way of what I have to do.* She felt ice closing in around her. Welcomed it. By the time he turned to her, she could face him without the slightest dismay.

"Derek," said Beata, deliberately caressing his Christian name, "I wish to present to you Miss Miranda Holcombe."

It sounded as if Beata were serving her up on a silver platter. Mira produced an impersonal smile.

"Mira, this is Derek Leighton, Lord Varden, known as the Ar—"

"As Varden," he interrupted smoothly. "You must pardon Signora Neri. She enjoys embarrassing me, and I don't mind it, but you needn't be made to guess how you ought to respond. I shall change the subject by complimenting you on your costume."

"It suits her, does it not?" Beata said, staking her claim to the providing of it. "She is, of course, a Vestal Vir—"

"The Oracle of Delphi," Mira said quickly.

"Oh, excellent," said Varden, smiling. "And have you a prophesy for me, Lady Oracle?"

"Certainly not. To learn your fate you must come as a pilgrim to the temple, bearing an offering."

"I will gladly do so, when you tell me what form my offering should take. But for now, may I request the honor of a dance?"

"Yes, yes, do run along," said Beata, satisfaction in her voice.

Varden offered his arm, his left arm, and Mira could think of no excuse to shy away from him. "I appreciate the rescue," she said as he led her from the dais, "but I'm afraid I do not dance."

"Or will not?" he asked with a smile.

"To be precise, I cannot. This is my first venture into Society, and I lack the accomplishments of a proper young lady."

"Do pardon me, Miss Holcombe. I seem to have left my manners in India. I have three sisters, and I am used to teasing them. They pay me no mind, of course."

Sisters ought to have reassured her, but she had seen the look in his eyes. It was not the look a man would give to a sister. Nor, she realized, was it the hungry gaze burning in Michael Keynes's eyes. And truly, she must stop wringing herself dry with fear of every man who paid her a little attention. When she failed to respond, they would soon enough move on to a more receptive female. It seemed unfair, though, that Lord Varden should be escorting the likes of her through crowded parlors and salons while women who longed to be in her place enviously watched them pass by.

"I don't at all object to being teased," she said when they were in a place quiet enough for her voice to be heard. "My father teases me all the time. But he does it in Latin."

"I am silenced, then. Well, unless you are amused by fragments of Caesar's Gallic Wars and a legal tenet or two, which is all I remember from my long-ago classes. Shall we leave these overheated rooms, Miss Holcombe, and stroll in a quieter section of the villa? Beata is especially proud of her Limonaia."

Not there! Michael Keynes had nearly kissed her there. But she couldn't very well say that, so she permitted him to make the turn into a passageway lined with French windows. Beyond, in the Maze Courtyard, colored lanterns swayed in the cold air. She was mentally riffling through excuses to leave him when they made another turn, this one into a dim passage, where a familiar vibration tingled at her ears.

Dear God.

"We should go back," she said urgently.

But it was too late. A little way down, a dark shadow detached itself from the wall and advanced toward them.

Chapter 15

Lord Varden let go of Mira's arm and moved in front of her. A protective gesture, she thought with annoyance, typical of his class and entirely unnecessary. By nature and intent, she was far more deadly than he. But good intentions must be indulged, so she took a position beside him, poised to spring between the men if they came to blows.

It seemed inevitable that they would. The air crackled with their hostility. She held her arms in the position she had practiced, the one that would put her dagger swiftly into her hand.

They were standing in a dim space between wall sconces where the light created silhouettes and painted edges. Of Michael Keynes she could see only the outline of his body, a bronze glow on his jaw and cheekbones, and those preternatural, wolfish eyes. And then his even white teeth, when he flashed a wolfish smile. He was pure animal tonight, confronting the model of a civilized man.

"Well?" he said. "Shall I expect a constable at my door? Shackles on my wrists? A noose around my neck?"

"Most likely, and in that order. But this is neither

the time nor place to air our differences. There is a lady present."

Keynes acknowledged her with a nod. "Miss Holcombe and I are acquainted. She already knows me for a rotter. But you will do well, madam, to take yourself off. The wild creatures are in the woods tonight."

"I'm fine where I am," she said. "You mustn't fight."

"We won't. We already tried that, to no effect. I am here, believe it or not, armed only with sweet reason."

"And your knives."

A moment later, she could not have said how, a knife appeared in each of his large, ungloved hands. He flipped them so that he was holding the blades and held them out for her to take. "You never fail to disarm me, Miss Holcombe."

After a hesitation she took the sleek handles, felt the warmth of his body on them. Wished it were Beast Keynes standing there, weaponless, at her mercy. She took a step back, the knives held at her sides, and waited for the men to get on with it.

"What is it you want?" Varden said, impatience rough in his usually gentle voice.

"To know your intentions. What charges will be brought against me, and when?"

"How can I say? I have only just made my preliminary report to the Consortium. Or should I assume you eavesdropped on our meeting?"

"I considered it. Figured it would be less trouble to ask you directly."

"But why do you require to ask? You know what you did."

Keynes laughed. "And that's the point, isn't it? *I* know, while *you* keep stumbling around nosing for evidence and not recognizing a bloody thing you find."

Mira saw Varden go stiff, as if a blow had struck

home. "Do you deny that your mercenaries preyed on English commerce?"

"Certainly. At least, I deny the euphemism. English commerce and the business endeavors of the East India Consortium are not necessarily equivalent. We attacked only Consortium riverboats, most particularly the ones owned by my brother, and liberated the cargo. To be more exact, we destroyed it."

"And stole the boats."

"Well, yes. But my men required to be paid, so I had to steal something I was willing to sell. And unlike you, I decline to smuggle opium into China in exchange for tea. The Chinese are as entitled to their laws as we are to ours, and the opium trade is illegal there. Nonetheless, your Consortium exploits those who produce opium in India by paying a fraction of its market value, and then you bribe officials in China to let it across their borders."

"England requires tea," said Varden, a trifle uncertainly. "And the Chinese government will accept only silver bullion in payment. We cannot funnel all our hard currency into the Orient, so we must seek other means to develop trade. Would you bankrupt your own country?"

"Given the alternative—enslaving the people of a distant country to opium—I'd drink something other than tea. But you had no idea—did you?—what the Consortium was up to. And you're too damned self-righteous to admit you got yourself tangled in a nest of vipers."

"Mind your language," Varden shot back. "You forget we are in company."

The transparent eyes turned to Mira. "Have I shocked you, Miss Holcombe? I apologize. But be warned. *Graviora manent.*"

It's about to get worse.

He was reminding her, in a way only she would

recognize, that what she saw of him at any time was not all there was to see. He conversed, sometimes, with her father in Latin, but she never liked to think of him as educated. It contradicted all the wildness in him.

He seemed to be her opposite, the dark twin of her soul, his rough exterior concealing a spirit unlike the one he showed to the world. He was a trickster, like she had become, except in reverse. His darkness shielded what she expected was a great light, while her angelic appearance hid the malevolence of a killer.

All of this she understood in a flash of insight that she would deny if she found herself thinking of him again. She must not engage with this man. With either of these men.

They were speaking again. She forced herself to pay attention.

". . . slander some of the finest gentlemen in the country," Varden said.

"Some of the greediest, at any rate. They keep themselves ignorant, deliberately so, while their investments pay off beyond reasonable expectation It's no surprise they dispatched you, the most ignorant of them all, to investigate why the windfall profits were drying up. You would—and did—presume the innocence of your confederates and the guilt of anyone who opposed you. But this debate grows tedious, and you should be dancing with your lady. What charges, and when?"

"Are you in so great a hurry to come to trial? I should think you would be arranging to leave the country."

"But I just got here. Why does everyone keep advising me to take a runner?" He gave a grim chuckle. "I'll tell you what I told my brother—I'll go when I've finished what I came here to do. In the meantime, Archangel, think on this. You have fallen in with bad company. Cut loose while you can, or they will drag you down more surely than a lead weight hung around your neck."

And then he was gone, his long stride taking him along the passageway and to a turn that carried him from her sight. She realized that her hands were fisted around the silver handles of his knives.

"Well," said Varden with a wry smile, "I expect that demolishes any chance I had of making a good impression on you."

"Not at all," she said, her thoughts on the man who had just left. "But I think it would be difficult now to continue our stroll. Perhaps some later time."

"Tomorrow afternoon?" His eagerness exasperated her. "A drive in Hyde Park?"

"It sounds lovely, but my father's physician is coming up from Tunbridge Wells to examine him. I can make no other plans for the day."

"The next afternoon, then, at two o'clock?" By silent agreement, they had begun to walk back in the direction of the salons. "It will be a treat for me, after six months on ship, to enjoy a London park and the company of an English lady. But you look wary, Miss Holcombe. I promise, we shall simply share a pleasant drive in my curricle and the most trivial of conversations."

"Very well, sir. I shall look forward to it." Lies, she had noticed, no longer felt rough in her throat. "Might I ask one question? Was the Duke of Tallant present at your meeting?"

"No. I understand he is not in London. Are you acquainted with him?"

"I just wondered if Mr. Keynes was likely to encounter his brother this evening." Another lie, smooth as cream. Only her disappointment was jagged, but she didn't think it showed. "Lord Varden, you must excuse me now. I can scarcely return to the party carrying these knives."

Not waiting for a reply, she slipped into the court-yard and wound through the maze to a door at the opposite end. From there she made her way through a deserted wing of the villa and out into the cold night. The sky was never clear in London. She looked up at a fuzzy half-moon and stars blurred with the haze of smoke from thousands of coal fires. The damp winter grass brushed against her sandaled feet.

It was only a short distance to her cottage, and well before she let herself through the door, the air had begun to hum.

Michael Keynes. She had rather expected him.

He was not waiting inside the cottage, although it wouldn't have surprised her to find him there. She paused, tuning to his location, no longer questioning how it happened she could track him with a fair degree of accuracy. She sometimes wondered about the range of her perception, about how close he had to be before she could detect him. But it didn't matter. So far as she could tell, the power—if such it was—had little discernible value. She merely became aware of his presence before she saw him.

This time, he'd approached the cottage from the back and was drawing near the window of her bed-chamber. She hurried into the room and was raising the window when he arrived.

The look of astonishment on his face delighted her. With a degree of pleasure she carefully aligned his knives, handles pointed in his direction, on the windowsill. "You needn't have come for these," she said. "I would have sent them back with Mr. Singh."

"They are not why I am here."

Despite the cold, he had stripped down to shirt-sleeves and waistcoat. Heat pulsed from him . . . or perhaps she was the one overheated. He had that effect on her, had done so from the first. She noticed what she had failed to mark before, that when he was close to her, the vibration that she'd felt beforehand vanished, as if it had done its job and was no longer necessary.

"Why, then?" she said. "Or am I supposed to guess?"

"Varden was right. I should not have interrupted you. Insulted him in your presence. I came to apologize."

"Have you apologized to *him?*"

"When hell freezes over."

There wasn't enough light to read his expression or his eyes. It seemed important to her, what he was thinking, although it ought not to be. "Your offense, if there was one, has nothing to do with me. Do you wish to come inside?"

The heat radiating from him increased, as if she'd said something provocative. "I'd better not. Let me say this quickly, while I still have hold of a rare decent impulse. What I said about Varden was true, and I don't mean to take it back. So long as he continues to trust the wrong people, he'll continue to get into trouble. Maybe he'll come to his senses, although I'm not counting on it. The point is, he made a bad mistake and has already paid a heavy price for it. You mustn't judge him by that one incident."

"How could I? I haven't the slightest idea what occurred."

"I'm saying this wrong." He raked his fingers through his overlong hair. "When Varden came after me in India, neither of us had hold of what we were dealing with. We met only once, under unfortunate circumstances. I thought he intended . . . Dammit. There's no explaining what happened that night. You've seen his hand. That's how it ended. I was responsible."

"But you didn't begin it." Why was she sure of that?

"That would depend on where it began. I'm not here to make excuses for myself. For whatever I do, I accept the consequences and don't question the fairness of them. Varden, I have learned since returning to England, is not . . . well, not what I had assumed him to be. He is, in fact, precisely the sort of man you ought to be keeping company with. If he sheds his unsavory associates, he might almost be good enough for you."

She was astounded. And a little hurt. "You came here to give him a *recommendation?*"

"Put that way, it sounds absurd. I thought I might have ruined something for you, that's all. I wanted to put it right again."

"There is nothing between us. Nothing whatever. We'd only just met, were taking a stroll to escape the crowds and the attention."

He leaned forward, his hands planted on the sill, and the light from the front room caught his eyes. "Do you imagine," he said intently, "that I do not recognize when another man desires a woman? I expected him to hate me for what I did to his hand, but that was a poor second to why he really wanted to kill me in that passageway. It was because I belittled him in your presence, because he thought you might reject him on account of what I said."

"I make my own judgments, sir."

"Yes. I should have realized that before coming here and making an ass of myself. I was thinking no more clearly than Varden."

"And I was simply another thing to fight about."

He appeared to consider that for a time. "You might have been. Another woman would have been. But this was different."

"I cannot see how. It is common, I believe, among many species of animals, for males to fight mindlessly for the right to mate with a female who happens to be within reach. There is nothing personal about it. Any female will do."

"Perhaps you are correct, Miss Holcombe, although I have never before had the slightest inclination to do battle for a bedmate. This much is true. If fighting Varden were all it required to possess you, I would slice him up and feed him to the pigs.''

She looked into his fevered eyes and knew he meant every word of what he said. He gazed back at her, stripped of deception, the passion in him leashed by sheer will.

And then, as if he had never been there, he was gone.

Of a sudden she felt the icy air streaming into the room. Outside, where he had stood hot as a brazier, there was only cold and emptiness.

This cannot be, she told herself. She seemed always to be telling herself to dismiss him from her thoughts. He was a distraction, a temporary obstacle. A temptation.

She had not a moment to spare for temptation. Soon Hari Singh would bring her father, and she would feed him, and lie to him about her evening, and settle him to sleep. Tomorrow was for her father as well, and for Mr. Callendar, and for what she expected to be devastating news. No sleep for her, although her bones were melting. She had to prepare herself. Make plans.

But she lingered at the window, shivering. The winter night called to her, and the fearful thing that was about to happen. If only she knew what it was, and what she was supposed to do. What was the use of prowling the back alleyway, walking the pavement of Berkeley Square as if she had a reason to be there at strange hours of the night, or skulking in the park, hoping to spy an unmistakable silhouette at a window? More than a dozen times she had answered the call, gone to the square, and found nothing.

No knocker on the door meant the duke wasn't there. But if he didn't want company, he might leave off the knocker, and for her to see him enter or leave the house would be most unlikely. Except that she was drawn there, and knew she was meant to be there.

Or fancied it. She thought, sometimes, that she was clinging to reason with her fingernails.

Chapter 16

If not for the heavy weight of what she had learned the day before, and all that it implied, Mira might have enjoyed her drive with Lord Varden. The brisk air refreshed her, and the change of scenery, and the sunshine. Her father had selected the ensemble for her very first outing with a gentleman, a soft wool dress of bishop's blue that matched the cloak Lady Jessica had given her, and her frivolous bonnet had drawn a smile and a compliment from the earl.

From the moment he arrived at the cottage, she understood he had set himself to put her at ease. He spent several minutes with her father, keeping his conversation light and impersonal. He'd a lovely, bemused sense of humor that very much appealed to her, especially when he described how it had been to grow up the lone male and youngest resident in a household of females that included two grandmothers, his formidable mother, three sisters, and assorted aunts.

There were few riders and carriages in Hyde Park, but everyone they passed appeared to be acquainted with Lord Varden. To her relief, he politely acknowledged them while ignoring their attempts to wave him over for conversation. Instead, he treated her to a bit of gossip about each one, always fascinating but in no way malicious. A kind man, Lord Varden, not to mention intelligent, amusing, and remarkably picturesque.

She wondered if he pursued her, for unmistakably he was pursuing her, because she presented a challenge to him. As he steered the curricle out of the park and into the late-afternoon London traffic, she began to prepare herself for the awkward moments to come. Already the light was fading, and it would be nearly dark by the time they returned to Palazzo Neri. Then, she supposed, he would ask her for another engagement, and she would decline. Those would be almost the only words she spoke to him all afternoon.

Sure enough, when they turned onto Paradise Row, he slowed the horses to a walk. "I have very much enjoyed our drive, Miss Holcombe. Will you think me too bold if I ask you to dine with me this evening? Well, not with me alone. My eldest sister is getting ready to fire off her twin daughters, which involves a campaign only a little less complex than the invasion of a small country, so they have come to London for a bit of reconnaissance. We would all be pleased to have your company."

She was surprised by a longing to escape, if only for a few hours, her obligations and the tightening bands of dread. To listen to young girls chatter about their first London Season—

But she could not. "You are most kind, sir," she said, finding a smile for him. "I am required to be home tonight with my father."

Color rose on his face. "Now you will be quite sure I am too bold, and if I have offended you, I apologize. But while you were donning your cloak and bonnet, I asked Mr. Holcombe's permission to escort you to dinner."

"Which he gleefully granted, I am sure. And did you then ask Mr. Singh to watch out for him until my late return?"

"Ah. I *have* offended you. It all transpired in just

that way, but I confess to taking encouragement from your father's enthusiasm."

"To speak frankly, sir, he is in a great hurry to marry me off. Any gentleman who chances by is apt to be caught up in the whirlpool, and if he passes my father's critical inspection, there is no help for him. But the consequences are no more than a little awkwardness, such as we are experiencing now. I am not at all offended, Lord Varden. In other circumstances, I expect I should be flattered."

"That sounds ominously like a dismissal." He hesitated. "Might I inquire if another man has captured your interest?"

A dark, saturnine face at her window. Long fingers scraping through black hair as he studied the chessboard. *No!* She wrenched her attention to the man seated beside her, searching for words to give him a fair answer, if not a truthful one. "My father is extremely ill," she said eventually. "There are many things I must attend to. I cannot be distracted."

"But you could allow me to help you."

"Yes. Perhaps there will be such an occasion. I shall think on it. For now, though, I must ask you to leave me on the path I have taken."

He nodded, smiling with gentle regret, too much the gentleman to press his suit. "As you wish, Miss Holcombe. But I refuse to withdraw my friendship, which you may call upon at any time, for any reason. Now here we are, too soon back at the Palazzo."

He was about to pass the reins to a footman when she put a hand on his forearm. "Sir, you must not leave your horses to stand. The servant will help me alight, and you can be on your way."

His arm tensed. She had insulted him, she knew, but a growing sense of foreboding had taken possession of her. She was in the wrong place. She had to—

"Ma'am?" The young footman was holding out his hand.

Once on the pavement, she turned back to Lord Varden, who doffed his hat and gave her a kind smile. "Don't forget, Miss Holcombe, a friend may be called upon at any time. Please give my regards to your father."

She smiled back, but her thoughts had flown to the hackney coach coming up the street behind him. There could be no harm. It was early yet, barely four o'clock, and thanks to Lord Varden, her father wasn't expecting her. Mr. Singh would see to his needs.

And she had to go. Compared to this summons, the others had been merely rehearsals. It was *now* she must be there.

At her gesture, the coach pulled over and the helpful footman lowered the stairs. She gave the flamboyantly red-bearded driver her direction and looked after Lord Varden, whose curricle was still visible at the end of the street. Then she was inside, the door closed behind her, and on her way to Berkeley Square.

What she was to do there, she could not imagine. She had scarcely been able to string two thoughts together since yesterday afternoon, when Mr. Callendar had examined her father. Afterward he spoke to her in private, giving her the news she'd half expected. Although her father's spirits remained high and his mind lively, the decline of his health had begun to accelerate. By the doctor's estimate, he would not survive beyond a few months.

So soon. She knew he was having difficulty drawing breath, and she had already seen the awareness in his eyes. The effort he always made to disguise it from her.

If only she could take him to Seacrest, let him spend his last days tasting the salt air, looking out over the water, sleeping at night in the home where he had spent nearly all the sixty-five years of his life.

But Seacrest had been closed down, and besides, neither of them would be safe there. Nor anywhere, she supposed, remembering the linen closet and the duke, blood dripping from his murderous hand.

When I return, the vise will close.

For so long she had been driven by one compulsion—kill him before he could do more harm to anyone. It was her last thought at night, her first when she awoke. She had sworn to do it. Resigned herself to the consequences, the worst of them being her father's suffering when she was taken away to prison and trial. She would spare him that if she could. He had so little time now. Perhaps she would be permitted to spend it with him in peace.

Last night, after the doctor had left, she'd resolved that she would not seek out the duke, as she had intended, nor make an opportunity to slay him. Not until her father was gone. She had only to decide if it was better to remain at the Palazzo or find a place to hide, somewhere that would not endanger anyone else. That ruled out Mr. Callendar's hospital in Tunbridge Wells, despite his plea that she bring her father there for his last weeks. And the pair of them were too conspicuous to be concealed, like the Duchess of Tallant, in the Rookeries.

Finally, as the sky began to lighten, she had come to a reluctant decision. She would ask Michael Keynes for help. He was to play chess with her father after lunch, and she had spent the rest of the morning rehearsing her speech and scraping up the courage to deliver it. But it was Hari Singh who came, with news that Mr. Keynes had business to attend to. She had been too proud to ask when he would return, and he'd not done so before Lord Varden arrived to take her driving.

Now here she was in a hackney, answering a mysterious call to a place she had been summoned before, only to have nothing happen. Those times, though, she'd been dressed in her widow's weeds and it was late at night, with no one there to pay her any mind.

In her blue cloak and fashionable bonnet, walking alone, she was sure to draw notice.

So be it. She didn't mean to stay long, and when the coach pulled up at the end of Berkeley Street, she asked the driver to wait while she delivered a message to a friend. Then she set out briskly, aiming herself for the far end of the square. Not far ahead, to her right and behind a low wrought-iron fence, stood Tallant House.

The square was dark, save for the streetlamps and the light streaming from windows. In the center, a vine-covered fence encircled an oblong park studded with trees, most of them bare of leaves, some hedges and bushes, the remains of flower displays, and a few benches. She had spent the better part of one evening seated on one of those benches, directly across from Tallant House but concealed by the shrubbery, wondering how to get herself into the house unseen. Later she had walked around the back, examined the high wall that enclosed the garden, and decided she could not scale it while wearing a dress.

So much time spent plotting and planning, to the point she had begun to doubt she would ever bring herself to actually *do* something. Even the notion of waiting until after her father's death had filled her with an unwelcome sense of relief, as if she'd been handed the perfect excuse to postpone a difficult task.

Really, she had to stop thinking herself silly. Debating herself into knots. A scholar's daughter made a damnably ineffective avenger.

She kept her head bowed and her cloak drawn tight around her as she proceeded along the pavement. A few vehicles and horses came into the square, and several pedestrians jostled past her in their hurry to get home. Only when she drew even with Tallant House did she lift her head, turning her gaze to the door. A pair of lanterns hung to the right and left of it, illuminating the elaborate brass knocker. The duke was in residence.

Heart galloping in her chest, she lowered her head again and continued quickly on, making a left turn at the corner and coming around the other side of the park.

He was there. She had her knife.

But in residence did not mean he was, at the moment, in the house. And he knew she carried a knife. Even if she knocked on his door and was admitted to his presence, direct confrontation could not possibly succeed. The first thing he'd do was take away her weapon. Add it to his collection of her weapons.

But if she was not here to kill him, why had she been summoned?

She turned, pretending confusion, pretending to be looking for a particular house at the narrow end of Berkeley Square. And saw, at the other end, someone climbing into the carriage that was supposed to be waiting for her. Saw the carriage come up as far as Bruton Street and turn, leaving her stranded. It seemed to her an omen, an injunction to remain where she was.

Omens. Forebodings. Portents. She'd never been the least bit fanciful before these past few weeks. Not once had a premonition warned her of trouble in advance. There had been no change in the atmosphere, no hum that wasn't a sound, when certain persons came into her vicinity. As for being summoned to a place again and again for no apparent reason, the experience was entirely new to her.

What was she to make of it all? And where was the gift of prescience when she had truly needed it? Why hadn't she received a warning before the greatest disaster of her life sprang upon her? Of a sudden odd things were occurring, and she'd no idea what they meant or what to do about them.

Or perhaps they were only the product of an over-strained mind and exhausted body. She hadn't been at her best for so long that she'd almost forgotten what it was like. She used to be clever and resourceful, even a little bit brave.

For example, across the street, just where the fence curved around the park, was a spot where no light reached. She could likely remain there for a time without it being too obvious she was scrutinizing Tallant House. Most of the traffic that entered the square did as the hackney had done and left it at Bruton Street. Most of the pedestrians as well, she had noticed. It must be a shortcut to somewhere else.

Only one carriage went by as she hovered in the shadows, intently watching the door, waiting for it to open, cursing herself for being so foolish. And then, to her astonishment, the door did open, and a small figure flitted out, bounded down the stairs, fumbled for a moment with the gate before it opened, and sped across the street. It turned in Mira's direction, paused after a few steps, and in a blink, vanished.

From her earlier ventures to Berkeley Square, Mira knew there were two gates opening to the fenced park—one just where the cloaked person had entered and another directly across from it. Mira hurried around the opposite corner from where she had been, expecting to see the figure emerging or already running down the street. But save for a plump man walking in the other direction and a woman holding a child's hand coming toward her, she saw no one. Whoever had come out of Tallant House in such a hurry was still inside the park.

Mira went quickly back to where she'd been. That side of the square was deserted. Nobody had emerged from Tallant House in pursuit. Deciding to approach from the other side, careful not to draw attention to herself, she walked to the gate, gingerly raised the latch, and quietly entered.

Almost no light made its way inside the tall ivy-coated fence. The lone pathway, which reached from gate to gate, was graveled, so she moved onto the grass and poised there, scarcely breathing as she listened for a telltale sound. It came sooner than she'd expected, from a dark place to her left. Squinting, she made out the trunk of a large tree and the clumps of several evergreen shrubs.

She had trained herself to move silently. Lifting her cloak so that the hem would not brush against the brittle grass, she picked her way in the direction of what sounded like a spent animal panting for air. As she came nearer, she detected a dark shape huddled against the base of the tree. And beneath the panting, like an undertone, a low, despairing whimper.

Halting a short distance away, she waited for some reaction to her presence. There was none. But she already knew, or thought she did, whom she had found. "Lady Corinna?" she said.

A gasp. The figure uncurled, scuttled a little way, sank to the ground again.

"Don't be afraid," Mira said, holding very still. "I'm a friend of your mother. She asked me to help her find you. I promise you are safe with me."

No response.

Mira, prepared to give chase if the girl bolted, moved slowly forward. The ambient light of stars and distant lamps revealed a slim body curled on its side, knees drawn up, arms wrapped around them. This close, Mira could smell the odor of sweat and clothing too long worn. And there was another scent, coppery and sweet. Blood.

Oh dear God. Mira knelt beside the girl and sat back on her heels. "Are you hurt, Lady Corinna?"

After a beat, a faint "No."

"Are you able to walk, then?"

"To where?"

Good question. Mira thought rapidly. If she recalled

correctly, Sothingdon House was nearby. And closer still, the house where David Fairfax rented the upper two stories. She had been there once and thought she could remember which house it was.

"A friend lives not far from here. We'll try there first, and if he is not at home, I've another friend a little distance away." Mira unhooked the clasps at her throat. "You are exceedingly cold, Lady Corinna. I believe you should wear my cloak. Will you give me your pelisse in exchange?"

"It's . . . dirty."

"I don't mind. If someone comes looking for you, they'll not be watching for a blue cloak and bonnet. And when people observe me, they see only my hair. Let me undo the buttons. We should hurry, I think."

When the pelisse had been removed, Lady Corinna tottered to her feet and allowed Mira to fasten the cloak. "Do you always speak so quietly?" she asked as Mira was securing the bonnet.

"I'm afraid so. But it makes me a useful conspirator, don't you think?" Mira picked up the pelisse. It would not fit her, she could tell, so she swung it over her shoulders and felt something heavy strike her on the hip. "We have only a short distance to walk. When possible, we should avoid passing directly beneath the streetlamps."

Turning a little sideways, Mira slipped her hand into the pocket and felt the cold metal and distinctive shape of a small pistol. "Take my arm, if you wish. And although we needn't say anything, we should now and again pretend to be conversing. Are you ready to set out?"

The girl visibly straightened her shoulders. "I'll do well enough. But why can't we go to my mother? Where is she?"

"In London, but rather far from here." They began walking toward the gate. "We arranged for her to stay in a place where she would not be discovered. There was concern that she might be in danger."

"I expect she was. From my father."

"Yes. But she is safe, I promise you."

Pausing, Lady Corinna looked up at Mira. The lights from across the street illuminated her eyes. Keynes eyes, colorless and transparent, like pools of deep water. "I know," she said without expression. "He's dead."

Chapter 17

"Say nothing more." Mira drew a steadying breath. The Duke of Tallant dead, and this child had killed him. "Let us go quickly."

David Fairfax's residence on Mount Street was closer than she had expected, but even the short walk left Lady Corinna clinging for support to her arm as they waited for someone to answer their knock. After a considerable time, just before she had resigned herself to continuing on to Sothingdon House, the door cracked open and a face with a blindingly white chin appeared.

"Mira?" The door swung wide. "What's wrong?"

It was David, wearing his small clothes, a towel slung over his shoulders and soap lather on his face. Catching sight of Lady Corinna, he flushed to the roots of his hair. "Oh, my. I beg your pardon. Please come in."

He led them upstairs and fled into his bedchamber, leaving Mira to settle Lady Corinna on a chair near the fire. When the cloak and bonnet had been removed, she saw in full light the girl's torn, blood-stained dress and her hair, black like her father's and unevenly cropped, probably by her own hand. Her

face was thin and sharp angled, mottled with scratches
and bruises. She looked as if she'd not slept or eaten
properly for a considerable time.

"Are you injured, Lady Corinna?"

"No. Do not, please, address me as Lady Corinna.
At school I was Cory. I wish to be Cory." Her voice
faded at the end, and she appeared to close up around
herself, like a sea anemone.

David returned then, wearing a dressing gown, the
lather scrubbed from his chin. When he opened his
mouth to speak, Mira put a finger to her lips, drew
him into the next room—the music room—and closed
the door.

"I'll tell you everything later," she said, "when I
have questioned her. She requires something bland
to eat—gruel or plain biscuits or soft bread—and a
hot bath."

"There's a bath on the way. I ordered it earlier, for
myself. That's Corinna, right?"

"Yes. She says her father is dead. But let us first
care for her, and then we'll figure out what to do next.
She needs something to wear and a place to sleep."

He had caught her urgency. "I'll order the bath to
be set up in the spare bedchamber at the top of the
stairs, and a fire built, and I'll bring linens and a robe.
Food as well. But by all that's holy, how did you
find her?"

"*Later*, David. Oh, and send a message to Helena
Pryce. We shall require her help."

The servants arrived shortly after with a hip bath
and kettles of steaming water, and when they were
gone, Mira led Cory upstairs. She appeared listless and
withdrawn, as if she had come to the end of her resources. After fumbling with the ties on her gown, she
dropped her hands and permitted Mira to disrobe her,
disclosing more bruises and scrapes on her pale skin.
At the last, Mira loosed the waist ribbon of her knee-

length linen drawers, which slid down her narrow hips and no farther. The fabric had become caught on something attached to the outside of her left thigh.

Puzzled, Mira tugged the drawers loose and saw bands of torn material wrapped around the blade of a knife, and then around her thigh to hold it in place. She swallowed a gasp. The hilt, silver inlaid with onyx, was like one she had seen before, in the large hand of Michael Keynes as he carved on a piece of wood.

Mira unwrapped the knife, set it on a table, and helped Cory into the bath.

Half an hour later, bundled in one of David's dressing gowns, Cory sat by the fire drying her hair while Mira gathered paper, a pencil, and her wits. A cup of chocolate and some plain biscuits had put a little color on Cory's cheeks, and like Mira, she seemed to be preparing herself for an ordeal.

For that's what it would be, Mira was sure. She drew up a chair near to the small sofa where Cory was sitting with her legs curled under her, her eyes shadowed with dark thoughts. "You are very tired," Mira said carefully. "We needn't talk of everything now, only what is necessary. Perhaps it will go more easily if I ask questions."

"As you wish," Cory said. "I've nothing to hide. Not any longer."

Mira had already decided to begin slowly, leading her step-by-step to the killing. "Your mother has explained that you left her in Scotland, and I have seen the message you wrote. You needn't tell me of the journey. When did you come to Tallant House?"

"What day is this?"

"Tuesday evening."

"Then, Saturday. At first I watched the house to see who came in and out, and at what time. Saturday night I scaled the back wall and hid in a small shed used by the gardener. Sunday, when most of the servants left for church or to visit their families, I looked for a way to get inside. The doors and French windows on the ground floor were locked, so I climbed a tree that stands between two balconies and tried the windows there. One was unlatched. It opened to a room with the furniture in Holland covers, and that room connected on both sides to other unused rooms. I had plenty of hiding places."

"And you've been there all this time?"

"Waiting for my father to return. I'd thought he would be there when I arrived, but only a few servants were in residence. They rarely came upstairs. Father used to . . . to bring me to London during school holidays, so I know where the servants' doors and stairs are. There is piped water to the dressing rooms, but I was afraid to go looking for food in the pantry or the kitchen. At night, I'd climb down the tree to the kitchen garden and dig for carrots and turnips. The climbing is how I got most of my scratches."

Admiration held Mira speechless for a moment. This intrepid girl had come alone all the way from Scotland, found a place to lie in wait, stalked her father with knife and gun. A Keynes hunter, like her father and his brother. Like Mira herself, except that Corinna Keynes had been more relentless and far more brave. "You meant to kill him?" she asked at length, amazed at how normal the question sounded to her ears. "With the pistol?"

"I'm an excellent shot," Cory said. "I've been practicing for years."

Her cool demeanor cast its own chill across the room. Mira went to the dwindling fire and fed it with a log. "When did the duke return?"

"Late this morning." Cory gave a short laugh. "It seems a year ago. I don't think the servants expected him. It was chaotic at first, him shouting and them running about trying to please him. Well, most times were like that, I suppose, with my father. I was concealed under a draped sofa in the chamber next to his, waiting for him to be left alone in there. Then I planned to use the servants' door to enter his room and put a bullet in his head.

"It appeared, though, that he meant to go out. He was berating his valet and seemed concerned about his appearance, and I began to worry that I'd not have a chance at him alone. Then he was brought a message, I think. I cannot be sure. Something happened, and he said he was going to his study and wished not to be disturbed under any circumstances."

"And you went after him?"

"Not for a considerable time. As I said, the servants were swarming like bees, so I could not use their stairs or the main passageways. There is a private staircase leading from the duke's bedchamber to his study that I could take, except I couldn't get to it because his valet stayed and stayed and stayed. Finally a servant summoned him to dinner, and I was able to go through the bedchamber to the secret door."

Mira wondered briefly how the girl had come to know of a hidden passage between two rooms used almost exclusively by the duke. But Cory was leaning forward, absorbed by her memories.

"I took care to move silently," she said. "The pistol was in my hand. It is pitch dark on the staircase and in the narrow corridor that leads to the study. I could hear my heart pumping and the sound of my footsteps, though I was treading softly. Then I saw the barest slice of light, where the door did not quite meet the floor, so I went ahead on tiptoe and pressed my ear against the door. There wasn't the least bit of noise from the other side.

"Despair seized me. What if he had gone out after all? My every thought was on killing him, on how to do it, on getting it done quickly. If you are wondering, I assure you I had no moral compunctions, nor any concern about what would become of me afterward.

He required to be dead, and I had come to see that he was."

Mira had not been wondering. She felt precisely the same as Cory had felt, except that Cory had not hesitated, Hamlet-like—*Mira-like*—to take decisive action.

"Then I worried that he'd locked the door from the other side. There's a concealed mechanism to do so, just as there is a lever inside the corridor that raises the latch. But it was no good drooping about or fidgeting. I pressed the metal rod, the door came loose, and I pushed it a little open. That put me just to the left of the desk, where I'd rather expected to find him. I had positioned myself to aim and fire before he noticed anything amiss. But the chair was empty and tilted against the wall, as if someone had lurched from it and knocked it halfway over."

Mira found herself dreading what was to come. "Cory, it's important now that you describe everything you observed, no matter how insignificant it may seem. Later, the details will not be so clear in your mind."

"I expect I shall try to forget them. But you shall hear all of it. I pushed open the door and came inside, pistol raised, looking around for him. It's a fairly large room, rather long and narrow, mostly lined with bookshelves and cabinets. I smelled a sour odor and saw that something had been spilled on the desk. Then I saw a wineglass on the carpet."

"Broken?"

"No. The carpet is thick. There were dark red stains near where the glass lay."

"Was there a bottle or a decanter?"

"Not on the desk. Perhaps elsewhere. I didn't notice." Cory frowned. "There was practically nothing on the desk, now that I think on it. Pens, an ink bottle—it was open—a blotter. But no paper, no sealing wax. In any case, I came around the corner of the desk, and then I saw . . ." She took a deep breath. "I saw him, but just as I did, my foot caught on something—a box—and I tripped. I tried to catch myself, but I toppled forward, nearly onto him. I fell on hands and knees, and dropped the gun, and got his . . . his blood on me."

His blood on the pelisse, Mira realized. Some of it now on her own dress, and on her hands before she had washed them. After a moment, she returned to her chair. "Do you wish to stop for a time?"

"There's no need." Cory stared into the fire. "He was lying head and shoulders on the hearth. There was blood on the corner of the mantelpiece and on the flagstones. His hair was matted with blood. And his eyes were open. I hadn't expected that. He was on his back, and I landed just short of falling atop him." She shuddered. "It's all I saw, his face, and his eyes staring up at the ceiling. And I thought, 'What if he's alive?' So I found the gun, and stood, and pointed it at him. Then I saw the knife. Here." She put a hand to her chest. "Someone had stabbed him with a knife."

Surely she did not draw the blade from his chest! Mira glanced over at the table where she'd placed the pistol and the knife Cory had been carrying. "You took it?"

Cory gave her a startled look. "Not the one in his heart. I took the one in the curtain."

"I beg your pardon?"

"When first I came into the house through the unlatched window, I had to push the curtain aside. The hem was weighted, like most curtain hems, but this one made a *clunk* when it hit the wall. So I examined it and discovered the knife. The killing knife was different. More slender. I could see only the hilt, of course. It was ebony, set with a single jewel. A ruby."

From "slender," Mira had expected the rest. Her own knife, the one Tallant had taken from her. Ironic, *unbearable,* that her blade had killed him, but not her hand. With all her being, she wished that it were otherwise.

A blessing, though, that Cory was free of the crime. But not of the punishment, if anyone had seen her. She couldn't account for why she'd been hiding in the house when the murder occurred, nor prove that she had been elsewhere.

Never mind. Never mind. All that was for later. Mira rose again and went to a side table, where she half filled a glass with brandy. "What did you do next?"

"I fled. I'm not sure why. I'd no idea where I was going, and I didn't mind if I was caught. Indeed, I opened the door and went into the passageway and ran to the entrance hall without ever looking to see if anyone was there. No one stopped me, at any rate. And you know where I ran to, because you found me there." Cory looked over at her, eyes filled with puzzlement. "How did you come to be in the park? Were you watching the house, searching for me?"

I was summoned. But Mira could scarcely tell her so, not until she understood it herself. Probably not ever. Leaving the brandy, she took up a pencil, paper, and a book. "Before we leave your father's study forever, I would like you to sketch for me what you saw, and how things were positioned, and describe for me anything else in the room that you recall."

She spoke firmly, worried that Cory would object, or question her, and God knew she could not explain why she required the information. But with a little shrug, the girl accepted the book handed her, set a piece of paper atop it, and began to draw.

After a few moments, Mira sat beside her on the sofa, watching the figures take shape. The door, the desk, the wineglass on the floor. Just around the corner of the desk, the box Cory had tripped over. "What was that made of?" she asked as Cory sketched in the last few lines.

"Metal. It was on its side, most of it under the desk, and open. My foot went into the corner that was sticking out. He had boxes like it at Longview as well, and the locks require two keys. This one was empty."

Cory drew the fireplace and marked how the duke's body was placed. She marked the blood as well, and the position of the knife. "I forgot this," she said, pointing to the area of his throat. "His neckcloth and collar were twisted, as if he'd been trying to loose them."

There were a few other details as well—what he was wearing, a narrow rope of blood from the corner of his mouth to his chin, the tinderbox fallen to the hearth.

"That's all I remember," she said, handing Mira the paper. "Will you give this to the authorities?"

"No." Mira folded the paper, slipped it into her pocket, and went to fetch the brandy. "They must never know you were in the house." She paused, saw that her hands were shaking, feared her next question. Perhaps she ought to trust her instincts and spare Cory the ordeal. But for Cory to contain her secrets inside her would be immeasurably worse. Of that, Mira had no doubt whatever. Look what keeping her own secrets had cost.

Pulse hammering, she went back to the sofa and placed a glass on the table beside Cory. "Drink this, if you wish," she said. "It will help you sleep. But first, I hope you will tell me why it was you set out to kill your father."

There. She'd said it. And Cory did not seem the least surprised. More like resigned, as if she'd charged through the worst already, leaving only the cleaning up of the devastation in her wake. Even so, it was a long time before she spoke.

"If I tell you, how many others must know?"

"That is for you to say. I'll not betray anything you have told me tonight, unless I must do so in order to

protect you. But I believe that if you confide in me
now, you will find it easier to confide in someone else
when the time comes that you wish to. It is the first
step, I have learned, that seems impossible to take.
After that, the journey . . . Well, I cannot be sure. I
never got past the beginning."

A sad smile curved Cory's lips. "The ending is not
so wonderful, either. But you have been kind, and if
you wish to know, I shall tell you." She took a sip of
brandy. "Ever since I can remember, I have wished
him dead. Did you know that people called him the
Beast? It was true. He was a monster. He beat the
servants and struck my mother if she displeased him,
or just because he was out of temper. Mostly he ignored me and my sister, Catherine, who is three years
younger than I, and Mother tried to keep us out of
his way. But when I was twelve, he . . . he—"

Mira held still, scarcely breathing. *I did this to you.*

"He said he had a birthday present for me, and
took me to his bedchamber, and it hurt so much I
could not even cry. It made him angry that I bled, but
he said in future I would not. And he said if I told
anyone, or even if someone found out without me
telling, he would rid himself of us, all of us, and get
himself a new family. I thought that meant he would
send us away, which I wanted more than anything.
But then he laughed, and told me how he'd make it
appear an accident, and that no one would even miss
us. For Mother's sake and Catherine's, I must always
do as he wished and try hard to please him. He said
he would teach me all the things that pleased him.
And from that time on, except when I was away at
school, I did whatever he told me."

Save for the first words—"when I was twelve"—she
had spoken calmly, as if describing a commonplace
event. But . . . *twelve.* How had she endured it?

"It is strange," Cory said reflectively, "that when
there is no other choice, one can become accustomed

to nearly anything. I did try once to starve myself,
thinking that if I made myself ill or ugly, he wouldn't
want me. But I only succeeded in terrifying Mother,
who took me to the seashore until I was well again. I
was happy there. Every day I thought of walking into
the sea, but it would have meant missing the next day,
and the next. And if I could not die when living was
unbearable, how could I give up my life in the very
moments I was tasting happiness?"

Another sip of brandy. "But I have not answered
your question. In the past year, my father paid me
little attention. I was growing too old, I think. And a
few weeks ago, he told Mother that she and I were
to open the house in Scotland and remain there,
which I rejoiced at . . . until he said that he was
bringing Catherine home from school. I knew then
that he meant to do to her what he'd done to me.
So you see, I had to kill him. It was the only way to
protect her."

Cory bowed her head, done with her story, come
to the end of a long nightmare. "What happens
now?" she asked in a dull voice. "Might I sleep a
little first?"

"Of course. I shall help you settle in bed, and then
David Fairfax and I shall decide how best to proceed.
Your mother must be told you are safe, and then I
expect we shall spirit you both out of London for a
short time. No one must know either of you was here
when the duke was murdered."

"You should take my mother away," Cory said.
"And above all things, I want her and Catherine to
keep clear of me. It's possible I was seen, and there
are servants at Longview who know what my father
and I did together. Perhaps in London as well. Suspicion is certain to fall on me. I left some of my belongings in the shed, and when the house is searched, it
will be clear someone was hiding there. Really, things

will go better for everyone if I simply take myself to the authorities."

Mira felt her throat constrict. "But you did nothing wrong. And if you bring attention to yourself, they might draw the wrong conclusions and fail to seek the real killer."

Cory looked up, her eyes bleak with resignation. "Yes. That's precisely what I want. For all my determination, I might have failed. Probably I *would* have failed, and what he'd have done to me would be infinitely worse than anything I am facing now. But my friend, because the person who got to him before me is my greatest friend in the world, spared us all. Now Cathcrine will be safe, and my mother can be at peace. If I confess, and all is done swiftly, it will be over. And I will have saved my friend."

Horrified, Mira shook her head. "You cannot mean to take responsibility for your father's death. Think how your mother and sister would feel. And it would not be so easy as you imagine. You would have to perjure yourself—"

"Good God, what matters a lie to someone who set out to kill her own father? As for the rest, there will be a little sadness, I know, and scandal as well. But at the end of the day, my family will be better off without me."

After a moment she began to tremble, and wrapped her arms around herself. "Don't prevent me, I beg you. Let me do what I must. I am *nothing*. There can be no life for me now, no purpose. I am ruined, and empty, and immeasurably afraid. I wish only to disappear and be forgotten. I wish not to *feel* anything, ever again."

And then the tears began to wash down her face, and she was shaking as if she'd fly apart. Mira rushed to her side and gathered the despairing girl into her arms. She was keening for a childhood ripped from her, for all the years of brutality and shame that she ought not to take upon herself. But she did. Mira knew it, and understood, and as she held the sobbing Corinna, she came to an irrevocable decision.

Some time later, when the shivering began to abate and the weeping quieted, Mira heard, as if from somewhere far away, a gentle melody being played on the harpsichord. It sounded to her like birdsong, and the sea rustling over pebbles and shells, and rain on flower petals.

Cory lifted her head, turned watery eyes to Mira's face. "Do you hear music?"

"That is Mr. Fairfax, and he is playing your grandmother's harpsichord. She gave it to your Uncle Michael, and before he went out to India, he gave it to David."

"I never met him. My uncle. He left before I was born."

"He has returned to England, and it was to him your mother came after you ran away. He has been looking for you."

"Will he take care of my mother and Catherine, do you think?"

"I'm sure of it. And he'll care for you as well." Mira brushed Cory's shaggy hair from her face. "You mustn't let him intimidate you, though. He can be a bit gruff, and I'm afraid he looks rather like your father. It's best to be prepared for that. The resemblance quite startled me when first we met."

"I don't want to meet him. I told you what I want to do."

"Cory, in this you cannot have your way. Your father was an evil man who did terrible things, but he has no power over you now." Mira handed her the brandy glass. "You have been, for so long, incalculably brave. This is no time to give up. When you wake tomorrow, you shall begin your new life. At first it will be difficult, but not so bad as you fear, and you have family and friends to support you."

"Will you be there?"

I did this to you. "My father is very ill," she said carefully, "and I must care for him. Mr. Fairfax and Miss Helena Pryce will see you reunited with your mother and provide you a story to tell if you are questioned. You may trust them. Mr. Fairfax has been my friend since I was a child, and Miss Pryce is something of a marvel. I think the two of you will rub along famously. Do precisely as they tell you, Cory, and all will be well."

Cory, looking doubtful, finished her brandy and set the glass aside. "When we arrived, Mr. Fairfax called you Mira, but you haven't told me who you are. Is that another secret?"

"Dear me, no. I ought to have introduced myself." Mira went to the bed and began turning down the covers. "I am Miranda Holcombe, but my friends call me Mira. I hope you will."

"Holcombe?" Cory appeared beside her. "A family by that name lives close by to Longview. Or used to. I never met any of them, and I think they've all gone now."

"Yes. My father and I are the only ones left, and we departed several years ago."

A silence. "Did you know my father, then?"

"I knew of him, of course. I had a cousin who knew him well, but he died in India." She slipped the dressing gown off Cory's narrow shoulders. Underneath was one of David's nightshirts, the sleeves rolled up and the hem dragging on the carpet. "In you go."

When Cory was under the covers, looking small and, for the first time, frightened, Mira sat beside her and took her hand. "Lady Corinna, there is something of great importance I must say to you. From this time on, you must tell no one what you have told me to-

night. Not the authorities if you are questioned, not
your mother, not even Mr. Fairfax or Miss Pryce. No
matter what occurs, no matter how greatly you feel
compelled to tell the truth, you will withhold it. More-
over, you will persuade those who badger you for information that you have none to give. You are clever,
and you will find a way to satisfy them while revealing
nothing. Do you understand?"

"Yes. All except the reason why you ask this of me."

"And that, for now, is *my* secret. Will you give your
word of honor to do as I have asked? It means that
no matter what occurs, no matter how difficult it is or
how wrong it seems, you must keep your promise."

"What if I don't promise? What happens then?"

Obstinate, incisive, extraordinary. So much like her
uncle. "I don't know," Mira said honestly. "But consider what you set out to do in order to protect your
sister. By assuming guilt for a murder you did not
commit, you will lay on her a great burden of responsibility for the consequences. Were you not willing to
kill for her? You are now willing to die for her. I am
asking you to *live* for her, Cory, and to give a promise
it will take great courage to keep."

"Well, if you put it that way." Squeezing Mira's
hand, she flashed a brandy-driven smile. "Word of a
Keynes. No, that has never been worth a cup of dirt.
My word, Mira Holcombe, and I shall keep it."

Mira sat with her a few minutes longer, until certain
the girl was asleep. Then she extinguished all but one
lamp and hurried downstairs to speak with David.

It was another difficult, prevaricating conversation,
but at the end, she was fairly certain he believed what
she wished him to. And because David sometimes got
confused when he was nervous, she wrote out preliminary instructions for Miss Pryce. From here on out,
all would be in their hands.

"You're *sure* Lady Corinna didn't kill him?" David
inquired—again—as he escorted her to the street.

"Absolutely sure. Her long journey and the shock of stumbling upon her father's body has disordered her mind, which accounts for her confusion. There is no doubt that she is entirely innocent. Also fragile, so I count on you to stand as her protector."

At David's gesture a hackney pulled over. "I shall," he said, handing her into the carriage. "But who, Mira, is to protect *you*?"

Chapter 18

With her course firmly laid out, Mira required no protector. But she did require help, and while it mortified her to hold out her begging bowl to virtual strangers, pride was the least of what she meant to surrender now. So after a few hours of restless sleep, she rose before first light to pen letters to Mr. Callendar, Helena Pryce, Michael Keynes, and Lady Jessica Duran.

Next, she packed up her father's clothing and those things he would consider essential, hoping that someone—perhaps Beata—would be kind enough to ship the rest to Mr. Callendar in Tunbridge Wells. She packed her own belongings as well, those that would fit in two portmanteaus, moving silently so as not to wake her father in the next room.

All the while, she plotted her story and mapped out what bits of it she would tell straightaway, and which details she would withhold. The longer she kept the authorities preoccupied with her, the better.

And amid her plotting—*My fault. My fault.* It was a constant refrain. She had always known she'd done wrong. What she had failed to imagine were the consequences, the destruction and pain wrought by her cowardice. By her failures.

At eight o'clock the breakfast tray arrived. Following her usual routine, she fed her father, gave him a sponge bath, and dressed him, talking all the while about her drive with Lord Varden and the people she had met in Hyde Park. It felt to her a century had passed since then. She fended off his interest in the dinner she had supposedly shared with Varden, and was greatly relieved when Hari Singh came by earlier than expected.

On her return last night, he had agreed to take Mr. Holcombe up to the villa for the day, while she attended to a matter of business. She'd failed to mention that she wouldn't be returning. But Helena Pryce would come by sometime later, to assume responsibility for her father and see him transported to Tunbridge Wells.

All was in place, as best she could manage it. She asked Mr. Singh to put her letters with the outgoing post, although she'd held back the one for Mr. Keynes. It would be left where Mr. Singh could not fail to notice it when he returned.

She longed to embrace her father, dared not risk it, and settled for a smile, and a wave as he was wheeled from the cottage. Then she finished packing his things and placed his luggage next to hers. Nothing more to do, no excuse to put it off any longer. She donned her cloak and was tying the ribbons of her black bonnet when someone knocked loudly at the door.

Bother!

A large man with pouchy eyes and a crooked nose filled the doorway, looking unhappy to see her. "Miss Miranda Holcombe?"

"Yes."

"Your presence is required by the chief magistrate," he said stiffly, "concerning the matter of the death of His Grace the Duke of Tallant by foul and criminal means."

She nearly laughed. "That is . . . convenient. Might I fetch my reticule before we leave?"

"Aye, but I must be coming with you."

The reticule lay on a nearby table, so they were soon on their way across the lawn in the direction of the river, and from there the long way around to Paradise Row. He was sparing her the embarrassment of encountering someone at the Palazzo, she understood, grateful for the kindness. And then she saw a sleek curricle, a familiar pair of white horses, and the handsome, solemn man striding forward to greet her.

"Miss Holcombe, please know that I deeply regret this misunderstanding and am certain it will be cleared up after a few words with the magistrate. He granted me leave to escort you, on the condition we do not speak about the . . . the—"

"Murder? This gentleman has already explained why I am in custody, Lord Varden. You needn't come along. I am quite prepared to follow the usual procedure, whatever that might be."

"It is too late for that, I'm afraid. The patrolman has only his horse, and there is no hackney in sight. Besides, my presence is required there as well."

She would rather have done this alone. She was accustomed to being alone. Save for her father, of course, and she must not think of him now. His last few months of life were to be made unhappy—there was no other way—in exchange for a girl's frail hope of healing and a new life.

With little choice, she let Varden hand her into the curricle and endured the drive to Bow Street, which he was considerate enough to let pass in silence. She used the time to shape new layers of ice over the core of ice at her heart.

When they arrived, the earl offered his hand to help her alight. Cold as winter, she accepted it. "You will be questioned by Sir Richard Burnie," he said, as if the name tasted sour on his tongue. "He is ambitious, autocratic, and reputed to be vindictive if he thinks he's been made to look a fool. But in this matter, he is sure to tread carefully. One misstep could throw him out of an office he achieved only a short time ago, and if ever there was a case apt to seize the public's attention, this is it. Under such scrutiny, he will be both fair and relentless."

And she would be lying and delaying, which was certain to displease Sir Richard.

Well, too bad for him. "Thank you," she said as Varden led her through the tangle of rooms and passageways to the door of the chief magistrate's office.

Small eyed and pudgy faced, Sir Richard regarded her the way he might a bug pinned to a blotter. "Sit there," he said with a faint Scottish burr, pointing her to a straight-backed chair across from him. "You may remain, Lord Varden, on condition you speak only if addressed. As for you, Miss Holcombe, let us come directly to the point. You will account for your activities between four of the afternoon yesterday until the present time."

"I recall nothing of importance," she said.

"Speak up. The clerk cannot hear you."

At his gesture, she looked to her right and saw a young man seated at a small writing table, his pen poised to record the proceedings. "I can speak no louder than I am doing now," she said. "Perhaps he should move closer."

Another gesture from Sir Richard, and the clerk began to relocate his implements and the writing table itself. During the interval, she took note of several items arrayed on the desk in front of her—a folded cloth, a sheet of paper covered with writing, an open metal box.

Sir Richard, clearly a man of little patience, was running out of his small supply. "Since your recall is poor, allow me to refresh your memory. Shortly before four o'clock, having been left off at Number Five, Paradise Row, otherwise known as Palazzo Neri, by the Earl of Varden, you entered a hackney coach and instructed the driver to conduct you to Berkeley Square. For that information we have the testimony of Lord Varden, who saw you enter the hackney, and who was able to provide a description of the driver."

He pushed the sheet of paper closer to her. "This is the recorded testimony of John Crabb, also called Big Red because of his distinctive appearance, and signed by him this morning. According to his account, you asked him to wait, but after doing so for a considerable time, he accepted another fare and departed."

Considerable time was a blatant lie, but she could deny none of the rest. "I did go to Berkeley Square," she said.

"And what did you do there?"

"I have nothing more to say."

"Are you aware that the Duke of Tallant resides in Berkeley Square, and that he was murdered yesterday afternoon?"

"The officer who took me into custody made reference to the murder."

"Did you enter the duke's residence?"

"I have nothing more to say."

The magistrate's face reddened. "By God, young woman, you will answer my questions. Failure to do so is an admission of guilt."

"I am unacquainted with the law, sir. But I don't believe I have admitted anything other than riding in a hackney to Berkeley Square."

Sir Richard glanced behind her, to where the earl was standing, and when he spoke again, his tone was milder. "Since being roused from my bed with news that servants had discovered His Grace's murdered body, I have undertaken a swift and thorough investigation. Although it is still in the preliminary stages, a number of individuals have already given testimony. Everything I have learned thus far points to your involvement. This is your opportunity, Miss Holcombe, to spare yourself a great deal of trouble. Can you provide witnesses that you were elsewhere at the time of the killing?"

"What time was that, sir?"

He ground his teeth. "The coroner has not yet completed his examination. But as we already know your whereabouts from two o'clock, when Lord Varden took you driving, until approximately four-thirty, when you arrived in Berkeley Square, why do you not begin there and tell us where you went and with whom you spent time?"

This was going well, she thought. Things were playing out just as she had hoped they would. He was convinced of her guilt, but now understood that he would be forced to prove it, step-by-step. "I have nothing more to say," she repeated, looking him directly in the eyes.

"Not from lack of knowing anything," he fired back. Taking hold of the folded cloth, which appeared to be a napkin, he unwrapped the object within it and held up a dagger, its ebony hilt embellished with a single ruby. "Do you recognize this?"

"It is a knife."

"*Your* knife. We have testimony that you attacked His Grace with this very knife not long ago."

Stunned, she took care to maintain her composure. How could anyone have known what happened in the linen closet? She'd no intention of denying the knife was hers, although she had meant to postpone the admission until a search of her possessions revealed three daggers exactly like it, except for the gemstones—one emerald, one sapphire, and one diamond. The matched set, sent from India by her cousin Robert, had been contained in an enameled gold case, but she'd given that to Helena Pryce to sell for her. Dear heavens, she was tired. Her mind had begun to wander, thinking of her knives. For the first time in more than a year, she had left off the sheath in her glove and the one usually bound to her thigh. She'd assumed the police would search her, but so far, it hadn't occurred to anyone that she might be carrying a weapon. The very same people who reckoned her a murderess—

She became aware of Lord Varden's voice, and his hand resting protectively on her shoulder. ". . . badger the young woman," he was saying. "I must protest, Sir Richard. The tale of Miss Holcombe slashing the duke's hand with a knife is no more than hearsay."

Oh, don't start defending me now. She hadn't wanted to admit so much so soon, but Lord Varden was trying to divert suspicion from her, which was the last thing she wished. "But it is quite true," she said. "The duke accosted me, I drew out the knife to protect myself if he persisted, and he wrenched it from my grasp. In the process, his hand was slightly cut."

"He returned the knife to you?"

I ought to have admitted nothing. "He kept it, sir."

"And I suppose you have not seen it since then, until today."

"If you say so."

"No, no. What do *you* say, Miss Holcombe? Did you drive this blade into the Duke of Tallant's heart?"

"I have nothing more to tell you, Sir Richard."

Lurching to his feet, the magistrate looked about to launch into a tirade when something caused him to snap his mouth shut and storm from the room. The door slammed shut, and she glanced around to see that Lord Varden was gone as well. Beside her, the clerk, his face the color of a ripe red apple, was scribbling furiously.

Although she hadn't dared to eat a bite of breakfast, she feared she was going to be sick. She glanced down at her hands, still folded calmly on her lap, and wondered how it was that separate parts of her were having such different reactions to all of this. Over the years she had achieved a degree of self-control that disturbed her father and kept others at a distance, but

she had never altogether mastered her feelings. They
kept breaking out, in one fashion or another, like prisoners refusing to stay where she'd caged them.

At some other time, with only herself to bear witness, she would open the gates and let them all run
riot. She ought to experience, in every way, the consequences of what she had done and left undone. How
could there be forgiveness without suffering? To deny
herself the pain, the terror, and the loneliness she deserved would be yet another act of cowardice, like the
one for which she was condemned.

She must pay for her sin. Not the murder, although
for that she was surely guilty by intention, if not by
fact. It was an older sin for which she was to be punished, a sin that had cast a long shadow over her life
and, she should have realized, over the lives of others
as well. Their suffering multiplied her guilt a
thousandfold.

Yes, she was deathly afraid of what was to come,
but she also welcomed it. At last, there would be
atonement. Absolution. Perhaps, at the end, peace
of heart.

Sir Richard returned, accompanied by a stern-faced
Lord Varden and the officer who had taken her into
custody. "Well, well, Miss Holcombe. It appears you
have a champion. While it is my own inclination to
send you directly to Newgate, where the conditions
have a way of inducing cooperation, Lord Varden has
persuaded me to allow you a respite here, where you
may contemplate the advantages of speaking the truth.
Meantime, I am sending to have your residence
searched for evidence."

"Will your father be there?" said the earl gently.
"Shall I bring him to my home until this matter is
resolved?"

His kindness, she feared, would undo her. "Thank
you," she replied in a cool voice, "but I have arranged
for him to be put in the care of his physician."

Sir Richard scowled. "Because you were expecting to be arrested, Miss Holcombe?"

"Because he is dying, sir."

Color flagged his plump cheeks. "That is regrettable. But I must say, you have picked a pretty time to commit murder, young woman. Well, you will have several hours to think on what you have done. Go along with the officer."

In silence, her escort led her up a flight of stairs and locked her in a small, damp room with a square wooden table, two armless chairs, and an adjoining privy room. A barred window looked out to a brick wall.

The room was cold. She paced for a time, to warm herself and ease the tension in her limbs, pleased that more hours were to pass with attention focused on herself. More hours for Cory and her mother to escape London, for Helena to arrange her father's journey to Tunbridge Wells, for Lord Varden to become reconciled to her guilt.

After a while, bundled in her cloak, she sat on a chair and sent her thoughts into the empty place where she had spent so many days and nights, a place of no thinking, no sensation, a landscape in which she had nothing to do but endure.

The door swung open, hitting the wall with a thud.

Mira, startled from the half-conscious state in which she had passed the time—she'd no idea how much time—looked up to see the chief magistrate glowering at her.

"You are free to go," he said as if dredging the words from the bottom of a mine. "Lord Varden will convey you home. I won't pretend I'm glad of it. To the contrary, I am not at all satisfied with your failure to account for your whereabouts last night. But under the circumstances, Miss Holcombe, I have no choice but to release you."

Her heart gave a lurch. "M-might I ask what circumstances you speak of?"

"Why, the murderer has confessed."

Oh, Cory, Cory. Could you not keep your promise?
"I see."

"Walked into the police court on Great Marlborough Street two hours ago." He sounded disgruntled. Robbed of a successful investigation with himself at the helm. "Word just now came to me, not five minutes ahead of the broadsheets. The news is already out, by God, and the rabble are clamoring for a public hanging."

"Oh, you mustn't." She bit her lip. "That would be . . . horrible."

"I've no doubt he would agree. Better the ax than—"

He? She drew a relieved breath. *Not Cory, then.*

Sir Richard was still speaking. ". . . put him safe in the Tower for the time being. It will be a speedy procceding, I expect, what with the confession. No point dragging things out to please the scandalmongers."

"Who is it, sir, that killed the duke?"

"What? Didn't I say? Him that's the new duke, but he won't be that for long. Michael Keynes it was, killed his own brother."

Chapter 19

"I wish to see him," Mira told Lord Varden shortly after he had threaded his curricle through the crowd surrounding Number Four, Bow Street, where they'd come for a glimpse of the duke who had killed a duke.

On every street corner, boys hawked broadsheets and hastily printed newspapers emblazoned with garish headlines. CAIN AND ABEL IN LONDON! DUKE OF TALLANT SLAIN WITH DAGGER! LAST TALLANT DUKE CONFESSES MURDER!

"It isn't possible for you to see him," said Varden. "Nor would it be wise. Sir Richard remains suspicious of you, and the surprising confession delivered to his subordinate has frustrated his ambition to use this case to his advantage. Now he chafes to uncover something overlooked by everyone else. If he can find a way to implicate you, Miss Holcombe, he will leap on it."

She quite agreed with his assessment of the situation, except that to her, it was irrelevant. "Nonetheless, I must speak with Mr. Keynes. Can you arrange it?"

"I *will* not. How could I agree to help you do yourself harm?"

"You mean well, I know. But I do not wish to be protected. Nor am I in league with Mr. Keynes, who

will not be pleased to see me appear. Even so, if Sir
Richard is correct that he will be quickly brought to
execution, I cannot let pass my last chance to recover
the property stolen from my family by his brother."

Lord Varden whistled softly. "I was unaware you
had such a quarrel with Tallant. It is as well you keep
that information private, Miss Holcombe. Sir Richard
will seize upon it as a motive for conspiring to kill the
duke, if not carrying out the crime yourself."

"Let him think what he will. My father has only a
short time to live, and his greatest wish is to spend
his last days at Seacrest. That is our home in Kent."

It seemed to her a sacrilege, using this particular
excuse to secure the earl's assistance.

But she was resolved to see Michael Keynes, even
if it meant scaling the Tower walls and searching every
dungeon and cell until she found him.

"I am sorry for it," Lord Varden said. "But you
have no hope whatever of recovering your home. A
murderer forfeits his personal property, which includes
any land that is not entailed. Even if Keynes wished
to oblige you, he could not sign over the property."

"But that's the point, don't you see? The Duke of
Tallant held vouchers for gaming debts owed him by
my cousin, who went out to India and disappeared.
So Tallant laid claim to my father's land, as well as
the nearby estate he'd inherited from his brother.
More than that, he pillaged the houses for anything
of value and prevented us from setting foot in our
home. But his claim is not valid, and no court has yet
made a ruling. If Michael Keynes withdraws the claim
on our land and acknowledges my father as the right-
ful owner, it will be ours again."

"And you believe he will grant you this favor?"

"Why should he not? He has been kind to my father. Played chess with him, read to him. I'm sure he
will agree, if only I can speak with him. And it must
be right away, before he is condemned. After that, it

will take years for the courts to separate our claim from his forfeited property." By his time, she barely knew what she was talking about. She only hoped the earl sensed her urgency and could overcome his own dislike for Michael Keynes long enough to arrange access to him.

Grim faced, Lord Varden said nothing until making the turn onto Paradise Row. "Very well, Miss Holcombe. But as you are not related to Keynes, and because of the public clamor surrounding this case, permission must be secured from the chief magistrate." A sigh, quickly suppressed. "I shall leave you off at the Palazzo, return to Bow Street for a grant of entry, and pick you up again as soon as may be. Then we shall go together to the Tower."

That won't do at all. "I mean to beg of him a favor, sir, and at a time when he can care nothing for my concerns. If I arrive in your company, he is certain to refuse me. Indeed, he must not learn that you have assisted me in any way."

"But no gentleman would permit you to confront him alone, Miss Holcombe. In addition to his other crimes, which I am continuing to investigate, he is a self-confessed killer."

"And a prisoner under guard. I wish to go to him alone and speak with him alone."

They had come to the entrance of Palazzo Neri, where the earl reined in his horses and turned to her with worried eyes.

She pressed her advantage. "Once, not so long ago and on this very spot, you gave me reason to believe you would stand my friend. You said I could call upon you for help at any time. I am doing so now. I ask only for an appointment with Mr. Keynes, and I would be glad of written authorization to present when I arrive at the Tower. Will you help me, Lord Varden, as you promised?"

He exhaled slowly. "You leave me, in honor, no

other choice. Wait in your cottage for now. When I
have spoken with Sir Richard, I'll dispatch a servant
with his reply."

Gratitude burned in her throat, but she dared not
express it. Even after all that had occurred, the longing in his eyes reached out to enfold her. "Here is a
footman to help me from the curricle," she said
briskly. "I shall await your messenger."

His jaw tightened, as if receiving a blow. But when
she looked back at him from the pavement, he gave
her a reassuring smile.

Such a good, good man. And yet, if all could be
different, if she were capable of falling in love, she
would not have chosen him.

It was drawing near three o'clock when a young
man wearing the green-and-gold livery of Varden arrived at Mira's door. He brought with him the letter
of authorization she had requested, a parcel, and a
note from the earl explaining that the items taken during the search of her cottage were being returned, save
for the gown she had worn to Berkeley Square. It was
stained with what appeared to be blood, and for the
time being, the magistrate had decided to keep it.

"Lord Varden instructed me to secure for you a
hackney," said the young man. "It is waiting at the
entrance to the Palazzo."

"Thank you. I shall make ready to depart." Taking
the parcel with her, she opened it on reaching her
bedchamber. Why the officials had taken its contents
in the first place she could not imagine. Well, except
for the dagger, but only one of the three that had been
in the cottage was there. Her sheaths were missing as
well, and the large knife she was nearly sure belonged
to Michael Keynes. That, of course, had been packed
in her luggage, which was also missing.

She assumed that while she was at Bow Street, Helena Pryce, or someone sent by her, had come to col-

lect Edgar Holcombe. By mistake, her own luggage
must have been gathered up along with his. She was
going to be short of clothing, not that she expected to
require very much of it.

After donning her cloak and bonnet, she selected
two books from her own small collection, added the
compact chess set her father used when they were
traveling, and accompanied Lord Varden's servant to
the coach.

It was a long distance from Chelsea to the Tower.
She'd thought to spend the time preparing herself, but
it was no use rehearsing an encounter with Michael
Keynes. He would strike past her makeshift defenses
in a heartbeat. So she looked out the carriage window,
watching people going about their everyday lives,
shopping and doing business and heading home to
their families. How she envied them. This seemed to
her another world entirely, one she passed through
without ever touching anyone or anything that dwelt
there.

By the time the White Tower, tinged with the gold
of the late-afternoon sun, came into view, her nerves
were all on edge. They always were, at the prospect
of seeing him. Just ahead was the stone bridge across
the moat that surrounded the Tower, and a line of
men in blue-and-red uniforms holding back the surg-
ing crowd.

She alighted and strode directly to the bridge as if
she'd every right to cross it. A guard quickly moved
forward to prevent her, but when she showed him her
document, he escorted her to the Middle Tower gate
and handed her over to an amiable, bearded warder
who examined the items she was carrying.

"I'd have been required to search your person as
well," he told her as they proceeded through one gate
after another, "save that His Grace is here of his own
accord. A man what turns himself in and confesses
ain't likely to escape, is my theory. Not that he could

take himself free of the Tower, mind you. Newgate, well, there's a prison like a Swiss cheese, criminals slipping out like mice through the holes. But a man what comes here, stays here, until he's pardoned or executed. This one will be executed, mark my words. I hope it's here, but they'll likely send him to Newgate for a hanging, where more people can watch. Got a great fondness for executions, have the people of London."

She did not wish to think of that. She thought instead of the menagerie somewhere within the Tower, and how she had intended to bring her father to see the lions and tigers and leopards and bears.

"Here we be," said the warder, his gold-laced scarlet coat and skirts flapping as he guided her across a courtyard to a Tudor-framed building. "The Lieutenant's Lodgings," he said, "where Anne Boleyn was kept before they lopped off her head. There's a room next the Council Chamber where His Grace be stored for now."

She wasn't sure what she'd expected. A dungeon, perhaps, or a grim cell with a tiny slit of a window and moss growing on the walls. Not this refined edifice, more suited to a wealthy resident than an imprisoned murderer.

Who was also a duke, she had to keep reminding herself. It was difficult to imagine.   •

And even more difficult a short time later, when the warder unlocked a door and stepped aside to let her enter. "Your Grace," he announced, "it's Miss Holcombe come to call."

The humming in her head that had intensified while they were walking up the two flights of stairs arrowed her attention to the table and chair at the center of the room. Then, as always when she came face-to-face with him, it disappeared.

He was gazing up at her, the first expression of surprise quickly transformed to a sardonic smile. He looked as she had often seen him, tousled hair, stubbled chin, shirtsleeves rolled halfway up his arms.

"Well, well," he said, propping his elbows on the table and templing his hands. "Entertainment. I hope you've come with brandy, but gin will do. I'm in no case to be particular."

A fleeting instinct to curtsy passed swiftly by. "Thank you for receiving me," she said, setting the books and boxed chess set on a nearby chair. "I did bring entertainment, but not the sort you'd rather have. I should have remembered that you prefer above all things to be drunk."

"Not above *all* things." The oil lamp on the table cast wavery shadows over his face. "But I don't expect you are here to indulge my fantasies. Why *are* you here, Miss Holcombe?"

"To ask you that very question, sir. I am informed you have confessed to killing your brother, and I know very well you have done no such thing."

One black brow went up. "But of course I did. Why, it says so right here in these newsrags. Have a look." He sifted his fingers through the papers spread across the table, drew one of them out. " 'Brother Slayer!' Or this—'A Knife Through the Heart!' Chock full of gruesome details. It seems I carved my initials in his forehead, although I don't remember doing that. Was I crazed with bloodlust, do you suppose?"

What she did with cool indifference, he did with sarcasm. Different tactics, but the goals were the same—avoid questions, hold others at a distance, and if necessary, drive them away. "They are taking their cue from you," she said. "What possible reason could you have for doing this?"

"My brother and I didn't get along. Are you going to continue standing there glowering at me, or would you care to be seated?"

"Thank you, no." She had an unnatural impulse to start throwing things at him. Perhaps a chess set would knock some sense into his head. But she did approach the table, curious to see what information he was gleaning from the newspapers. "I was referring to why you confessed to the murder."

"Boredom. And they'd have got me sooner or later. I've been heard to threaten the duke, I've a long history of making trouble for him, and I stand to inherit his title and fortune. I'm the logical suspect. Can you blame me for declining to be chased down like a hare? Where's the dignity in that?"

"Where's the dignity in lying while the real murderer goes free?"

"We appear to be speaking at cross purposes, Miss Holcombe." He jabbed a finger at his chest. "Killer. Guilty. Execution to follow."

"You would not have killed him," she said, "with my knife."

His lashes flickered. "Is that what it was? I grabbed what was handy from his desk. Thought it was a letter opener."

"Can you describe it?"

"Sleek. Black hilt. Red stone. Sharp blade. Slid right in. Is this a private inquisition, or should I be telling all this to the magistrate?"

She picked up a handful of papers and carried them to a stand of candles across the room. Three of the broadsheets described her knife, and two of them quoted servants who claimed to have seen it in the duke's chest. He was piecing together the details of his story from what he read. But most was pure speculation and, as he'd admitted, lurid theatrics. Forced to pick and choose from what was being reported, he was bound to go wrong some of the time. Then again, he had not expected his confession to be challenged.

"Why," she said, "would you go unarmed to your brother's house if you intended to kill him?"

"I didn't think he'd be there." Rising, he laced his fingers together and stretched his arms over his head.

"It's after dark, Miss Holcombe. You should go home now."

"If you didn't expect him, why were you there?"

"I was counting the silverware." He chuckled. "By God, I think you may be as stubborn as I am. It happened I was in the neighborhood yesterday afternoon, got to wondering if our duckling had dropped by Tallant House, and decided to have a look." He regarded her speculatively. "You haven't found her, I don't suppose?"

"Lady Corinna? No. And apparently she wasn't where you were searching, either. Did you simply knock on the front door and ask to be admitted?"

"That didn't occur to me. I went over the back wall, up a tree, across to a balcony, and through a window."

Her breath caught. Had he been there after all? Got in the house the same way Cory had done? It explained, or perhaps it did, his knife in the curtain hem. But the timing was all wrong. Or Cory had lied, or he was lying. *She* certainly was. At this point, it seemed likely that all three of them were lying.

She aligned the papers she was still holding and returned them to the table. Michael Keynes had gone to the window and was standing with his hands clasped behind his back, gazing outside.

"Are you satisfied?" he said after a time. "I assure you, the officials will be. And the good citizens of London are already queuing up for the execution. Why have you such difficulty accepting that I killed him? I have killed a great many men, and not a one of them so deserved to die as my brother. Let it be, Miss Holcombe. In all of this, what I cannot bear is to see you distressed."

"What you see in me is *anger*, sir," she told him, wishing—as she so often did—that she were able to produce a forceful noise. Her mind shouted, but her voice whispered. It was no wonder he refused to take her seriously. "You cannot have put the knife in him.

I know that because I was the one who stabbed him, with my own dagger, and watched him die at my feet."

He spun around. "The hell you did."

"You think me incapable of murder?"

"I'd put nothing past you. Nothing but the strength to physically overmaster a brute like Jermyn Keynes."

"Which is why I relied on misdirection and stealth. You may as well withdraw your false claim to guilt now, for when you are questioned, you'll not be able to describe the scene of the killing with any degree of accuracy. And because I can do so, down to the smallest detail, it is my story that will be believed. My confession that will be accepted."

"Stalemate," he said softly.

"Oh, no, Your Grace. It's checkmate."

"We'll see." As he moved forward, the light caught his eyes, those strange Keynes eyes that never failed to send a shiver along her spine. "Consider your father."

"I always have. But you must have seen that his illness grows worse." She folded her hands, which had begun to tremble. "I would have stayed peacefully with him until the end, save that Tallant threatened us both with worse, far worse, than what we face now. Sometimes we have only bad choices. And I would rather be hung at Newgate, and have my father watch it, than endure what the Beast would have done to us."

"Understood. But neither fate confronts you now."

"I have my hands on the rope," she said. "I will put it around my neck. And you will assume your position as Duke of Tallant and head of your family, for that is your duty."

He looked startled, as if the notion had never occurred to him.

"Consider this. You've a niece still missing, another all alone, and a sister-in-law who will be left without a home or funds to care for her children. You can't imagine your brother provided for them. If you are condemned for this crime, they will be left with nothing."

That, more than anything she had said, appeared to affect him. But only for a moment.

Shrugging, he crossed to where she stood, compelling her to hold her ground with all her will as he loomed over her, dark and wild and resolute. "You need not have been frightened by my brother's threats. I said I would protect you. Did you not believe me?"

She looked up and up, feeling smaller than she was, the ground beneath her unsteady as her heartbeat. "I know only how to rely upon myself."

"We have that in common. And we are both wrong, I think, to refuse help when we need it. But being wrong has not stopped you, and in this circumstance, it certainly won't stop me."

"*I* will stop you. It is your family that requires your protection, sir. I am nothing to you, and can never be."

A storm raged in his eyes. She started to turn away, but his hands, large and bare, clamped on her shoulders. She froze. Gazed up at him openmouthed.

He let her go. Took a step back, hands open-palmed and lifted in a gesture of apology.

She took a ragged breath, and another. "I thank you for your kindness to my father," she said when she could speak in a level voice. "If you wish to do something for me, then try to make what is to come easier for him. For now, the chief magistrate is already half persuaded of my guilt, and I am on my way to provide him the evidence to convict me."

"Don't do this."

"You cannot prevent me. Good-bye, Your Grace."

She was at the door when he spoke again, softly. "Thank you for the books."

She oughtn't to have done it, but she turned, just

for a moment, and looked at him one last time. At his eyes, that spoke of all the things she could never have.

It was only when she'd closed the door behind her that she realized he had been smiling.

Nightfall and a cold drizzle had dispatched the curious and bloodthirsty citizens home to their suppers, leaving the area outside the Tower walls nearly deserted. The warder walked with Mira across the stone bridge, still chattering about infamous prisoners and their dire fates while she looked around for a hackney.

There was only one vehicle on the street, with two men huddled under broad-brimmed hats and caped coats on the driver's bench. They straightened when the warder waved his arm, and brought the carriage forward, and one of them jumped down to open the door. "Number Four, Bow Street," she told him.

After thanking the warder, she entered the coach, which was far nicer than any hackney she'd been in before, and settled back on the soft leather squabs. These would be her last few minutes of freedom. At least she would spend them in comfort, she was thinking when the door on the opposite side opened and a large figure filled the space.

"I beg your pardon," said Hari Singh, taking his seat just as the coach pulled away. "I did not mean to startle you."

And then he did so again, reaching past her to pull down the window shade. He closed the one on his side as well, while she stared at him in confusion. Light from the lantern overhead fell over his white turban, bearded chin, and cheeks the color of plums. His eyes were apologetic and sad.

"How did you know I was at the Tower?" she demanded, profoundly suspicious.

"Michael asked me to collect you. He feared you intended to do something . . . inadvisable."

How had Michael Keynes known of her plans? Or

that she would come to him in the Tower? "You are not taking me to Bow Street, then?"

"Nor to the Palazzo. We shall be traveling for perhaps two hours. I cannot disclose our destination."

"You are *abducting* me?"

His face grew impossibly redder. "Conducting you, rather, to a place of safety. Your possessions—those you had packed—are there now, as is Mr. Holcombe."

She shook with fury. All the while she had been in that prison with Michael Keynes, defying him, informing him of her intentions, assuring him he'd no choice but to accept her decision, he had known she would fail. Had already *arranged* for her to fail. No wonder he had been smiling when she left him.

Mr. Singh regarded her with evident concern. "Michael said you would not take easily to this change of plans. I regret being the cause of your distress, but where we are going, my friends will make you comfortable and welcome."

"For how long? Until they hang him? Are you instructed to release me when he is dead?"

"Not in those words. But should it come to that, yes."

"Then disobey him! He is your friend. I am nothing, except that I can save him. You must let me go free to do it."

"I cannot." Gentle, but final.

"Because you believe he really did murder the duke?" she asked after a time.

"He has not said so. But for as long as I have known him, he has dedicated himself to the destruction of his brother. When he returned to England, it was with the purpose of killing him."

"But don't you understand? He may be executed for a crime he did not commit."

"It is possible. But I have no power to prevent him, Miss Holcombe. Michael will not be led, nor will he be guided. He can only be accompanied."

Chapter 20

In the Tower, the long gray morning wore on. After a sleepless night, most of it spent pacing the room or running in place, Michael left his breakfast untouched and lounged on a comfortable chair by the fireplace, brooding. A book, facedown, lay across his lap with his hands resting on the leather binding. He wasn't in the mood to read, had not even looked at the title. But it was a book she had brought to him, and he wanted to be touching it.

She was safe now. A coded message from Hari confirmed that she had been intercepted and taken to a place where she would not be found and from which she could not escape. She'd probably try, though.

His greatest regret was that he would never see her again.

He had no other immediate regrets, none to speak of, except his failure to consider what was to become of Norah and her daughters. They had not once entered his thoughts until Miranda put them there, and now they joined the other dark spirits that haunted his nightmares.

There had been time, if he'd thought to use it. Instead of galloping directly to Great Marlborough Street to turn himself over to the authorities, he could have delayed long enough to settle his brother's financial affairs and make sure the family was provided for. But it hadn't occurred to him to do so.

Hell, it hadn't even crossed his mind he'd become the ninth Duke of Tallant until some oily official at the police court began Your Gracing him. The first time it happened, he had looked around to see who had come into the room behind him. He wasn't sure he'd ever get used to it. Conveniently, he wouldn't have to.

The news that Miranda Holcombe had been taken off to Bow Street Court had knocked every coherent thought from his brain. From that point on, his only aim had been to get her out of there.

A good thing he had been having her watched. After Beata told him Miranda had drawn a knife on his brother, he'd put one of Hari's Punjabi friends to guard her, certain that Jermyn would seek retribution. Lakhbir could not always follow where she went, but he had been concealed near the cottage when a court officer arrived to collect her. And he told Hari, who told Michael on his return to the Palazzo late that morning.

Yesterday morning. It seemed months ago. But then, he had never dealt well with being closed in. The sooner this was over with, the better.

There was a knock—everyone was amazingly polite to a titled murderer—and he glanced over to see the door swing open. He swore aloud.

Varden. Looking sleek and perfectly groomed as a show horse, wearing an expression that said he'd just placed last in a field of hacks.

Ominous, that. He ought to be looking pleased. He ought to be gloating.

"Your Grace." Varden bowed.

Worse and worse. Michael sensed bad news on the way.

"I have just handed over to the Yeoman Warder the order sent by the chief magistrate. You are free to go."

What the devil? Michael's fingertips curled over the book on his lap, but he otherwise held still. Put a mildly interested expression on his face while swallowing a blast of oaths in Hindi, Punjabi, and Arabic. Damned if he'd give Varden the satisfaction of his confusion. "Murder is no longer a crime in England?" he inquired when he could speak.

"It is. But we only punish the guilty. There are penalties for making a false confession, of course, but the magistrate seems disinclined to pursue charges."

Michael would have preferred to remain as he was, insolently stretched out on a chair with his stockinged feet propped on an ottoman, but a storm was gathering inside him. He closed Miranda's book, set it reverently on the side table, and lowered his feet to the carpet. "Should I have made myself more clear? Is there something about 'I killed my brother' that he failed to understand?"

"The part that tells him you could not have been there at the time. You have doubtless enjoyed making fools of the authorities, not to mention the newspapers and the citizens of London who accepted your claim of guilt. But it is a reckless game you have played with us, because it has hindered the investigation and perhaps allowed the true killer to escape."

"*Tsk tsk.* I would be ashamed of myself, really I would, if I knew what in *hell* you are talking about. Since I drove a knife in Jermyn's chest, how can I not have been there when he died?"

"Because you were seen in a tavern outside the village of Elmstead on the afternoon he was killed. You could not have got back to London and Berkeley Square in time to have done it."

"You are mistaken." Michael rose, stretched, and slouched over to the window. It was a gray, miserable day. "Who claims to have seen me?"

"The men I hired to follow you. I have not abandoned the investigation I began in India. You were an outlaw there, and I'd no doubt you would take up some unlawful venture here."

When the implication of that pronouncement had sunk in, Michael broke out in laughter. In his dogged effort to prove Michael Keynes guilty of something—*anything*—Varden had stumbled into proving him innocent of a capital crime.

"Will you deny you were in the south of Kent, Your Grace? You need not bother. The man you met in the tavern was known to one of my . . . my—"

"*Spies?* Good God, you needn't be ashamed. Over the years I have employed spies, beggars, thugs, whores, and even children to do my dirty work. When the cause is sufficiently compelling, most men would do the same. But what makes you think I failed to return to London in time to do the killing? Your spies weren't tracking me at that point."

A slight flush stained Varden's smooth complexion. "You knew you were being followed?"

"Of course." He just hadn't guessed who had sent them. "For the most part they were of no great concern, your pair of sleuths. When they became a nuisance, I shook them off."

"After meeting with the Runner. Will you tell me the reason?"

"Giving myself an alibi?" Michael wondered if the Runner had been interrogated. "I wish I'd thought of that. But your timing is all wrong. I was in London, in Berkeley Square, and in my brother's study, face-to-face with him when he died."

"That is not possible."

"I have a fast horse. I don't always take the roads. And you can't have measured either the route or the time it would require to cover it."

"In fact, Your Grace, you've no idea what information I possess. You can only accept that I, and the magistrate, have determined that it exonerates you."

"Then why in hell would I put my neck on the block? Does your *information* explain that?"

"I am entirely ready to believe you did it for your own amusement," Varden said evenly. "But Sir Richard believes you are conspiring with the true killer, whom he thinks to be Miss Miranda Holcombe."

"Good God. I can think of any number of things I'd like to do with the delectable Miss Holcombe, but conspiring is not among them. What gives you the idea she is entangled with me?"

"Excepting the Sikh, she has been your only visitor."

"What of it? She sure as hell didn't come here for a celebration. As a matter of fact, I could never quite make out what she wanted. In the company of Miss Holcombe, my thoughts invariably turn to coarser matters."

Varden gave him a look of contempt. "She wishes you to withdraw your brother's claim to her family home."

"Ah. She did keep nattering on about debts and property, so I figured Jermyn owed her money. But Miss Holcombe is indebted to me? Very nice. Very nice, indeed. You seem to know all about this, Archangel. What will she offer me, do you think, in exchange for her home?"

"You are despicable."

"Undeniably. But we have digressed from the reason you are here. What cause has the magistrate to suspect Miss Holcombe of murder most foul? She hardly seems the sort to attack a man twice her size and strength, and she could not bring him down with a puny little dagger."

"She had a quarrel with him—"

"About the property. So you say. But killing him would not put it in her hands. And my brother had a great many enemies. If motive to eliminate him is all it requires, the queue of suspects will stretch from Berkeley Square to Brighton."

"There is, as well, suspicious behavior. Miss Holcombe went to Berkeley Square late in the afternoon, about the time we think Tallant was killed."

"What time would that be?"

"If you had killed him, you would know."

Michael gave himself a mental kick. "I do, which is my point. She had not come to the house when I left it, and by then, he was dead. Did anyone see her when she arrived?"

"Not . . . precisely. A woman was seen departing through the main door, but only from the back, and the servant admitted he was some distance down the passageway. We can secure no firm identification, nor can he recall the precise time."

Thank God for that. Michael realized he was standing by the fireplace with no idea how he'd got all the way across the room, while Varden, in better control of himself, stood where he had originally planted his well-shod feet. "In short, you have no evidence she was ever there."

"Her knife. The testimony of the hackney driver. She does not deny going to Berkeley Square, but she refuses to disclose her reason, or why she failed to return home until many hours later."

Michael laughed, in part from relief. "Can you not imagine why a young woman would steal out of an evening and decline to explain where she's been? Or with *whom* she has been? It was clearly an assignation, and not, alas, with either of us. Our hopes are dashed, Archangel. The delightful Miss Holcombe prefers another fellow."

"You insult her, Your Grace."

"And accusing her of murder is *not* an insult? Better a killer than a whore?" Michael reined in his stampeding temper. "I'd take her if she were both, and gladly. But she won't have me, nor, I expect, you, so we may as well leave her in peace."

Varden finally moved, to the table where the latest broadsheets were spread out, and sorted through them with his one useful hand. Lacking information to feast on, the newspapers had resorted to invention, including one story that involved, mysteriously, a chambermaid, a missing necklace, and a pair of ferrets. News of the duke's release from the Tower was going to send them into a frenzy of speculation.

He wanted a head start, before the news hit the streets. And to rid himself of the Archangel, who roused all his most violent instincts. But Varden was not so easily intimidated. Most men would have taken their leave before now.

Time to ratchet up the provocation a few notches. "Was there anything else? If you're too miserly to buy your own, you may take those papers with you."

Varden glanced over at him, his demeanor perfectly contained. "One more thing, Your Grace. Miss Holcombe and her father have vanished. Do you have any idea where they might be?"

"None whatever. So, how do I go about making you vanish?"

"For your convenience," Varden said as if Michael had not spoken, "and because a crowd is assembled at the entrance, you will be escorted to the watergate and transported by a riverboat to Palazzo Neri."

"Will I indeed?" Michael advanced on him, hands fisted, not terribly surprised when Varden held his ground. In one of the future lifetimes Hari believed in, the two of them might be friends. But in this one, no question, they were implacable enemies. "I will decide where I go, you pompous fool, and how I get there. It's long past time you stopped poking your aristocratic nose in my affairs. You ought to have learned your lesson in Calcutta. Hell, you carry the evidence of it at the end of your right arm. Yet here you are again, flailing about in waters far above your head."

"Also seeing to your release," Varden pointed out.

"And how that must gall you." Michael was face on with him now. "First you stumble onto proof of my innocence, or so you imagine, and then your precise conscience won't let you keep quiet about it."

"I do my duty," Varden said with maddening calm.

"You like to think so. Me, I do whatever I like. Now pay attention, Archangel, to your last warning. You may walk out of here and turn the key behind you. I give you leave to try me, convict me, and lop off my head. But if you choose to do none of those things, then let me be. I'll tolerate no more of your infernal *meddling*."

Jade-green eyes flashed with anger, but there was no other perceptible response from the earl.

Michael found himself envying his self-control. Varden had not been born with a volatile temper, or a roiling anger in his belly, or a longing so deep it would one day rend him to pieces. He didn't know how lucky he was, sailing through life on untroubled seas. Or nearly so, until the debacle in India, but that was less than a year ago. He'd enjoyed a damnably smooth ride until then.

Not so for the Devil's son, who had been fighting a war with himself for as long as he could remember. He'd trained his body to do his bidding, but he had little control of his passions. Always, he burned and burned and burned. Perhaps that was why he was drawn to Miranda Holcombe's icy composure, and why he wanted to shatter it and light a fire inside her to match his own.

Perhaps he hated Varden because he wanted to be like him.

And when had he become so bloody self-absorbed?

Disgusted, he took himself back to the window and clamped his hands around the bars.

"Nevertheless," said the golden earl in a plummy tone that grated on Michael's nerves, "the boat will be waiting for you. Direct the oarsmen wherever you choose."

"You'd better have paid them, then. All my blunt has gone to bribing the warders."

"I'll see to it." Varden went to the door, paused as if he'd something to add, and appeared to change his mind. On his way out, he left the door conspicuously open.

The reprieve would be useful, Michael was thinking while he gathered up Miranda's books, the chess set, and the few things Hari had brought him. He stowed them in the small portmanteau, put on his boots, greatcoat, and hat, and took a last look around the room. He would soon be back.

A warder escorted him to the traitor's bridge and the skiff manned by two oarsmen who were eyeing him with undisguised curiosity. Not many self-confessed murderers exited the Tower in this fashion, he supposed.

Drizzle, thick and gray, made the air nearly as wet as the Thames. They'd gone only a short distance when he had the watermen put him off at All Hallows Lane and set out on foot for the bank.

Although it was barely past eight o'clock when he arrived, the reliable Charles Whitehead was already at work in his office. And from the look on his face when Michael was ushered in, he'd read the most scurrilous of the broadsheets.

"Sit down, man," said Michael, pulling off his hat and giving it a good shake. "I only slaughter my relations. And anyway, the magistrate wouldn't give me back my knife."

"Mist . . . er, Your Grace, how may I be of service?" A thin film of sweat coated the banker's upper lip.

Michael dropped onto a chair. "I want control of my late, unlamented brother's records, finances, property . . . everything he owned, managed, and controlled, above the table or beneath it. I want all of that in the hands of a reliable, honest, tenacious firm of solicitors by noon today."

"But that's—"

"Impossible. I know and you know. But don't tell them. They'll get hold of what they can and advise me how we get hold of the rest. Now this is the important part. By late today, I want to have made provisions for the widow and her two daughters. Lavish provisions, secured against any possible challenge from, let us say, the Crown. Everything else can wait, but the solicitors don't need to know that."

"Did you have a firm in mind, Your Grace?"

"The one you recommend."

"Hmm." Mr. Whitehead pulled off his spectacles and began to polish the lenses with a handkerchief. "The chaps who drew up your will and the trusts were adequate for the needs of a wealthy man, but not for a duke. No, no, not for a duke. And I shouldn't trust the fellows the former duke employed, either. No, not them."

"Agreed. Do you happen to know who they are?"

"Oh, yes. Yes. It's a small world, finance and banking and the legal community. I have a firm in mind for you. Strictly honest, aggressive, skillful. Choosy about their clients, though. They represent, oh, the Duke of Devonshire, the Marquess of Blythe, Lord Philpot, Lord Varden. Hmm. I'm not sure they'll have a Tallant, though. Oh, dear."

Fussy little man. Good at his job, though, and for all his dithering, he had a needle-sharp mind.

"Well, talk them into it, " Michael said. "Tell them I want hard work for a short time and will pay extravagantly for it. And that I won't expect them to retain me as a client overlong. Just find someone to handle this. What is required to arrange the handover of my brother's records and assets?"

"I shall have papers drawn up that will authorize

your solicitors to act in certain matters on your behalf. We can fill in their names when we know them. I'll send a messenger to the firm I have in mind. Their offices are nearby. Yes. And arrange for the papers. Yes. Can I provide refreshments, Your Grace, while you wait?"

"Paper, pen, ink, and the use of a writing table," Michael said. "And I require a messenger to deliver my letter straightaway."

"Make yourself free of my desk, Your Grace. I'll see to the rest."

It was two hours before matters were well enough along that Michael could leave for a time. The letter to Miss Pryce had long since been dispatched, the persnickety firm of solicitors had been persuaded to accept him, and after a few abortive fumbles, he'd got used to signing "Tallant" to a slew of documents.

He sucked in deep breaths of cold wet air. It was a relief to be striding through the soggy streets of London again, his pockets plump with cash, a wide umbrella borrowed from Whitehead in his hand.

For his sins, he was required to return later in the day for yet more paper signing and ducal folderol. A good thing he wouldn't have to be a duke for long, because he'd be a damnably bad one. Business bored him. He wanted it taken care of without him. And most of it *would* be, he was learning, because apparently dukes didn't have to lift a finger if they didn't wish to.

Chapter 21

"Can it be?" In a swish of taffeta, Beata Neri swept up to where Michael, with no choice, waited for her greeting. Pausing a little distance away, she first surveyed him head to toe and rolled her eyes in mock despair. Then, with the grace of a courtesan, she sank into a profound curtsy. "Your Grace. How is it you are here, and not in the Tower? I had thought you killed your brother."

"I thought so, too. But I am informed that I did not, on account of being elsewhere at the time."

She frowned. "You did not confess, then?"

"I expect I did, on the principle that I'm usually guilty. After the second bottle, I'm capable of just about anything. Well, except remembering later what I did earlier."

"You play games with me, my wolf. And now I expect you will be leaving my *villeta* for the great house in Berkeley Square."

"Not until they've scraped the bits and pieces of my predecessor from the flagstones. For now, being of a sudden wealthy, titled, and rid of a troublesome relative, I'm going out to celebrate."

"Excellent." Her eyes gleamed. "Celebrate *here*, where you will not be mobbed by the rabble."

"But I *am* the rabble, signora. Permit me a few nights of debauchery among my own kind. Then I shall return and let you teach me how to behave."

"Mah! I wish you here tonight, as my trophy. But promise you will make it up to me, and I shall send to you a bath."

He left her with a grin instead of a promise, but she sent the bath anyway, and an hour later he was in her stable, hiring one of her small carriages for the day. It had begun to rain again, one of those slow, relentless rains that would last for hours and provide him a little concealment. It would also make for the men following him an uncomfortable day, which gave him a degree of malicious pleasure. Had they been enemies, he'd have found a way to render some of them incapable of keeping up with him. But they were decent men hired to do a job, so it was going to require ingenuity and effort to elude them.

First, though, he'd bore them silly.

Beata, who liked to see everything, had protruding mirrors on her coach panels to accord passengers a view to the front and rear. He put them to good use, and by the time he entered his bank for the second time that morning, he had marked the two chaps assigned to stick close to him and the skinny fellow who followed at a greater distance. There were others on his trail, he was certain, but they would reveal themselves soon enough.

For now, he made life easy for them. Already conspicuous in a black multicaped greatcoat and a wide-brimmed beaver hat, he carried a silver-handled sword cane and wore, for effect, a crimson wool scarf around his neck. News had not been slow to leak out. On every street corner, urchins hawked broadsheets telling of his startling release from the Tower, his false confession, and the mysterious woman in widow's weeds who had visited him and remained the entire night. He only wished that last bit were true.

He proceeded across the entrance hall, aware of heads swiveling in his direction, and caught sight of a straight-backed female wearing smoked glasses and carrying a leather case. She marched past him as if he weren't there.

In his banker's office, he read the message Miss Pryce had left for him and burned it in the fireplace. What she had planned would require hours for her to arrange, but as it happened, he needed every one of those hours. There was another message, informing him that while his brother's solicitors had granted access to the Tallant records, they refused to give over the records themselves without instructions, in person, from the new duke.

So it was off to Lincoln's Inn for an unpleasant confrontation with several lawyers who almost certainly had a lot to hide, and then to Doctors Commons and the nearby street where his own solicitors kept their offices.

Under the circumstances, he doubted his brother's affairs would ever be entirely sorted out. And with his life measured in days, he must concentrate on arranging for the welfare of his sister-in-law and her daughters. Miranda had been right. The records disclosed that little provision had been made for them, save for the bare minimum required by law.

He gave instructions for everything unentailed to be secured for them in ways least subject to challenge after his conviction for the murder. Then, with several hours to pass while the assets were inventoried and papers drawn up, he took a meal at a crowded tavern, dropped by a jewelers, poked around a bookshop, and with his arms full of parcels, wandered aimlessly, or so he hoped it appeared, through the various offices and courts that made up Doctors Commons. All along, his goal was the office kept by the Archbishop of Canterbury, where he quickly purchased what he had come for and moved on.

By late afternoon, when the papers had been read

and signed, his carriage entered the part of the city
known as the Rookeries, wound its way to a street in
Seven Dials, and pulled up in front of a tall building.
Behind its staid exterior, Madame de Beauvoir, formerly known as Molly Buttons, presided over London's most notorious brothel.

He was in a hurry now. Within a few minutes, bare
chested and with a drink in his hand, he showed himself briefly at a third-story window. A thoroughly bare
female wrapped an arm around his waist and used her
other hand to draw the curtains. Then she sat him
down and applied a droopy brown mustache beneath
his nose, a wart to his chin, a wig to his head, and a
kiss to his mouth. All in all, he decided while pulling
on tattered wool trousers and a shirt reeking of garlic
and beer, this had been the best part of his day.

Soon he was curled up in a cart under a pile of
dirty sheets and being wheeled along a dark alleyway.
Inside a laundry room, someone added a filthy coat
and hat to his costume and sent him through a series
of cellars connected by secret doors. When he
emerged from the last building into the street, he bore
a pole over his shoulders with a bucket attached at
either end. A beer wagon drawn by a sullen horse was
waiting for him, and he drove it to the stable marked
on a map someone had slipped to him.

By this time, he had shaken all his pursuers. When
he rode out of the stable on a horse far better than
its looks suggested, no one he passed gave him a second glance. And later that evening, a man of his
height and wearing his expensive clothes would
emerge from the brothel and return in Beata's carriage to the Palazzo, where he would pass the night
in Michael's Casina.

Even so, Michael spent another hour laying false
trails before heading north to a place called Finchley
Common where Hari Singh's friends and distant relations from the Punjab had formed a small community.

And where a caged tigress waited to spring on him the moment he appeared.

It required two hours' hard riding to get there, not counting the stop at a tavern to stock up on the brandy that the master of the house, for all his hospitality, would not provide. The bottles were stashed in his saddlebags when Michael approached his destination.

A light streaming from a window guided him to a gatehouse set in the high wall surrounding the property. Anticipation, scratching under his skin for most of the day, sent a new rush of energy through him. Until Varden brought news of his release, he'd not thought to ever see her again. But she was there, just beyond the wall.

His prisoner.

His *furious* prisoner. He couldn't help smiling. There would be no warm welcome from Miranda Holcombe, no gratitude for his efforts on her behalf. And he'd have felt the same, had anyone done to him what he'd done to her.

But she was safe, and he would keep her safe, and for a brief time, he would be in her company. He asked little more of life than that.

A gangly young man ran out to open the gate. They'd got word of his release, Rasbir told him as they walked together to the stable, but were not sure he would come to them. The young lady and her father were well. Syr-Sahib looked different than he had done at the wedding.

Michael—Syr-Sahib—remembered how Rasbir had followed him around that night, tongue wagging the entire time. Retrieving the saddlebags and their cargo, he left the horse to the boy's care and set out for the house. Plain, square, and two stories high, its pale stone walls were set with small mullioned windows. As immigrants who are unwelcome in their new country sometimes do, the Punjabis had built for themselves a protected enclave. All the beauty of the home was inside.

The boy who admitted him, bouncing with excitement, led him to a large room laid out with Kashmiri carpets and low divans piled high with cushions. "It's Syr! It's Syr!" cried the boy from the doorway. A score of astonished faced turned to look.

Michael paused at the entrance, whisked off his hat and wig, and bowed respectfully to his hosts. "My apologies for this crude disguise. I would make a proper greeting, but I'm fit only for a barn. Can someone find me a basin of water and a change of clothes?"

Birindar, the middle-aged patriarch of the extended family, rose and crossed to him, smiling. "*Sat sri akal,*" he said. Welcome. "Your freedom brings us joy. Now tell me everything you require, and it will be provided."

Hari joined them, a question in his brown eyes.

Michael shrugged. "They've decided I didn't do it. How is Miss Holcombe? Fulminating?"

"I do not know that word," said Hari. "She is sitting with Mr. Holcombe until he falls asleep."

"Well, when she's free, I want to speak privately with her. See to it, will you? And it might be better if she comes unarmed."

Chapter 22

An hour later, when Michael was well into his second glass of brandy, Nageena Kaur brought saucers of olives, chupatti, dal paste, and dried apricots into the room where he was to contend with Miss Holcombe. "The young woman will be here soon," she said, placing the dishes on a sideboard. "Is there more I can do for you?"

"See to it we are not disturbed, if you will. No matter what you hear." He smiled at Birindar's wife, who was practically vibrating with curiosity. "I will not dishonor her. You know that. But I'll probably make her angry."

"She is angry now, Syr. But she has not shown it to the family, and she has been kind to the children. We are pleased to have her in our home."

It was Miranda Holcombe who needed kindness, he was thinking as Nageena Kaur left the room. But she wouldn't be getting any from him. His intentions were precisely the opposite, and telling himself he would be cauterizing a wound made it no easier. Hell, he wasn't at all sure what to do, except that the other possibilities seemed even worse than the course he had chosen.

First he meant to rouse her temper, the one she pretended not to have, and prod her into a fight. He was rather looking forward to that. Then, with her too angry at him to notice, he would draw in the net, a little at a time, until she was irrevocably trapped.

He took his bottle and glass to a low cushioned bench, where he settled himself cross-legged with the fire at his back. The loose muslin trousers Birindar had provided were too short for his legs, the tunic fit snug across his shoulders, and his feet were bare, but the wine-colored banyon embroidered with gold thread made him look marginally civilized . . . so long as you ignored a day's growth of beard. He hadn't thought his hand steady enough to shave.

Holding out his glass, he watched the brandy undulate. Focused his mind. Willed himself to grow calm.

After a while, the surface of the liquid became smooth and still, like a mountain lake. The lake at Naini Tal, at the end of the tiger's path, where the goddess had come to live.

He reached to the deepest part of him, to where things he must not reveal huddled in silence, and drew them out. One by one he consigned them to the lake, giving each what time it needed to sink into the black water, for some flaws were more difficult than others to release. Small rituals. Preparations for battle. Hari had taught him how to let go of all but his purpose, to count neither the cost nor the punishment, to be at peace with what he must do.

Empty at last of what he feared and what would make him weak, he raised the glass and tipped the brandy down his throat. Drowning the monsters, he'd used to call it, until he acknowledged the monsters that could never be extinguished. After that, he gave up the name, but could never hit upon a good reason to give up the drinking.

Miranda would disapprove, he supposed. Was there anything about him that she *would* approve? And why ask, when he bloody well knew the answer?

She arrived just as he was refilling his glass, entering

so silently that he, who had been watching for her with every nerve end on edge, missed the opening and closing of the door. When he glanced up, expecting to see nothing, there she was. The goddess of the lake.

In an instant, he drank in the whole of her. Gloved hands held motionless at her sides, she stood demure as a nun in her unadorned sage-green gown. Demure except for that wanton tumble of silver-gilt hair over her shoulders, and the fierce passion held barely in check, and the blue eyes fixed on him like a pair of bayonets. If a glacier could go on fire, it would look exactly as she looked at this moment.

His hands started shaking again.

"You summoned me, Your Grace?"

It always amazed him how much expression she could put into that whispery voice. With no perceptible increase in sound, she could shout at you, or rebuke you, or curl your toes with her sarcasm. He'd once confronted, alone and unarmed, a band of Thugees with less trepidation than he felt at this moment.

"You'd have come after me anyway," he said. "Drink?"

"I expect you'll drink enough for the both of us. You recanted your confession, I gather."

"It stands, except I have to refine it a little, to account for my absence from London at the time of the murder. A simple matter, and I'll get around to it shortly. In the meantime, there's *your* confession to deal with."

"But you've done that already, by preventing me from delivering it. For the time being. You can't hold me here indefinitely."

"Why not?" He rested his hands on his knees, trying to look relaxed and in control of the situation. "Besides, it won't be all that long. Once the murderer is executed, no one will care what you have to say. The authorities sure as hell won't admit they hanged the wrong culprit, and they won't rush out and hang you as well, just because you insist on it. They'll rule you mad, Miss Holcombe, and put you away where madwomen are put."

She paled. "The truth should be told, sir."

"Maybe. But it won't come from either of us, will it? The only question is, which lie will win the day? And since I've answered that by having you brought here, what have we left to talk about?"

"Nothing whatever." She came a little forward, the fingers curled against her skirts betraying more than she realized. "If you won't listen to reason."

"I'm all ears, Miranda. Have at me." The use of her first name was deliberate, and the flash in her eyes told him she recognized the opening move of an aggressive campaign.

"I mean to," she said with undisguised scorn. "By what authority do you interfere with where I go or what I do? You have no right, *none*, to meddle in my affairs."

"I don't deny it." How could he? That very morning, he'd said much the same to a meddling Archangel. "But what is that to the point? I've done what was necessary, and I'll get away with it because you cannot prevent me."

The next he knew, a missile was sailing in the direction of his head. He jerked aside just in time. The object whizzed past his ear, shattering against the fireplace. Shortly after, he heard a sizzling noise and smelled burning olives.

Miranda, eyes round as the saucer she'd thrown at him, looked shocked.

He clicked his tongue. "Is that the best you can do?"

"Is it your habit to ride roughshod over helpless females? Abduct them. *Imprison* them?" She had clasped her hands behind her back, as if to keep them from misbehaving.

He wanted her to misbehave, to do worse than that.

The habit of discipline was too strong in her. "Helpless? I very much doubt it. And you are the one resolved to dive into a prison cell. I merely changed the venue from Newgate to this house. Resign yourself, Miss Holcombe. From here on out, you will do as I say."

This time he was ready. He saw her quiver, as if she'd break apart and fly off in all directions. And then she directed her fury to a single action. In a flash, another saucer was skimming toward his head.

It struck his cheekbone hard, ricocheted off, and bounced across the carpet. Its contents, a stack of flat chupatti bread, landed on his lap.

The blow hurt, undeniably, and must have cut open his cheek. He felt a warm trickle of blood making its way down his face.

Miranda, another saucer in her hand, gazed at him with astonishment. "You didn't duck," she said. It was an accusation.

He shrugged. "Nothing you can say or do will stop me, but you have every right to be angry. Go ahead. Throw all of them. I promise to hold still."

"That . . . rather removes the incentive." She looked down at the saucer she was holding. After a moment, she laid it gently on the side table and picked up a napkin. "Your face is bleeding, sir. Shall I tend to it?"

The prospect of being so close to her, of being touched by her . . . But it was an indulgence he couldn't afford. They had too far to go on this journey, and for much of the way, she must continue to despise him. "That's not necessary," he said. "But I'll take the napkin."

Flushing slightly, she brought it over to him and then backed away, but not so far as she had been standing before.

Progress of a sort, he supposed, pouring a little brandy over the napkin before pressing it to his cheekbone. The cut burned like the devil. Reckoning that it would please her, he produced an exaggerated wince.

"Explain to me," she said, "because truly, I do not understand. Why will you not permit me to make my own decisions? What is it to you if I accept responsibility for my crime? I am perfectly willing to do so. And why do you refuse to accept that I killed the duke?"

"In order, then," he said amiably. "You are making bad decisions, and I suspect you rarely do. I've made it my business to obstruct your plans because mine are better. And as for you killing—"

"Don't tell me it's because *you* did it." The anger was back in her eyes. "I know how you look at me, how everyone has always looked at me. You see a . . . a plaster statue in a church. A fresco on a convent wall. A soft-voiced, light-haired female with deformed hands and an otherworldly father to care for. And because I appear gentle and virtuous, you think me incapable of hatred. Of devious schemes and murderous intentions. Of vengeance."

He regarded her for a time, considering. "As a matter of fact, I think you more than capable of plotting a murder and carrying it out. But not, my dear, for the sake of stolen property."

"A stolen home. A stolen *life*. No, many stolen lives. My cousin, entrapped and exploited by the Beast. My uncle, robbed of the money to pursue his dream. My father, so desperate he—" Her hands twisted together. "The strain was too great for him to bear."

"I know all that." He braced himself. "I've made enquiries about your family. Cousin Robert was betting on long shots before he was out of short pants, and if Jermyn hadn't done it, someone else would have plucked his feathers. Your uncle was an eccentric with a score of failed enterprises behind him before he elected to restore a fallen-down castle without the time, funds, or expertise to manage it. And your father is a remarkable gentleman whose ill health we all deplore, but do you imagine he would approve of what you are doing? Does he even know what that is?"

She flinched. "I wrote him a letter."

"I know. I read it, and the one you sent to his physician, and all the others as well. Hari had the presence of mind not to put them in the post."

"It seems," she murmured, "that I have been betrayed by everyone."

"Thwarted, more like. Hari wouldn't betray a housefly. Lay all on the blame on me, Miss Holcombe. He followed my instructions, and I want to point out that he never feels obliged to do so unless he sees good reason. I put him to keep an eye on you, and because he could not always be in attendance, I employed other watchdogs as well. Not enough of them, I regret to say, because you trotted off to Berkeley Square unobserved, perhaps more than once. I underestimated you."

"Everyone does. Shall I assume you were informed I'd been taken off to Bow Street? Was that the reason you turned yourself in and confessed?"

"It was the reason I did so at that particular time. Otherwise, I'd likely have enjoyed a run-through of the seven deadly sins beforehand. But there could be no delay, because once you were in custody, even if it later proved to be a mistake, your reputation would be destroyed."

She looked, for the first time, amused. "Your Grace, I *have* no reputation. I am of modest birth to a family spared absolute obscurity because of my eccentric uncle, God rest him. What money and property we had has been squandered or stolen. For the time being, I enjoy a degree of privilege as one of Beata Neri's rescued strays, and all her friends are polite to me. But very soon I won't be able to afford a cottage at the Palazzo, and when my father is gone, I shall be quite alone."

Another woman might be appealing for sympathy. This one spoke dispassionately of what she perceived to be true. "No one knows who I am," she continued in a level tone, "and no one cares. There is no reputation at stake here, I assure you, save your own."

He found an unbloodied segment of the napkin, dipped it in brandy, and pressed it to his cheek. "No Keynes male has a reputation," he said, "without the word 'demonic' attached to it. And you are forgetting the Archangel, who is eager to wrap his wings around you."

"A temporary infatuation," she said, dismissing it with a wave of her hand. "I am accustomed to them. They never last. I never want them to."

That did surprise him. Varden, it had seemed to him, was probably the stuff of every young woman's dreams—handsome, wealthy, titled, intelligent, and apt to remain faithful to his wife and devoted to his family. Miranda Holcombe could have all that. He'd seen the desire, and the longing, in Varden's eyes.

Hell, he'd seen the same in his own eyes, just from thinking about her. Which was why he took care not to look closely into the mirror when he shaved.

"Are we done quarreling about which of us killed my brother?" he said. "It's old ground, most of it covered in the Tower. And it strikes me you are asking all the questions."

"We can take turns," she conceded with a bland expression he knew better than to trust. "I'll go first. Where were you, that the authorities say you could not have made it back to London in time to do the murder?"

Like a dog with a bone, she was. But this was his chance to turn the subject. "You were not the only one I set watchers on, Miss Holcombe. I hired a Runner to lurk in the neighborhood of Longview on the chance Corinna turned up there. Or Jermyn, for that matter. Yesterday . . . no—" He rubbed the bridge of his nose. "It was two days ago. A message came from the Runner, who'd sniffed out some local gossip and required to speak with me directly. He also wanted to remain close enough to watch over the younger daughter still in residence there, and for that reason asked me to meet him at a nearby inn. I rode south, heard what he had to say, gave instructions, and rode back."

"If you were near Longview, then you were, indeed, several hours from London, with few decent roads in between." She gave him a calculating look. "What did he disclose to you?"

"What happened to taking turns? Tell you what, kitten. Come sit over here, beside me or on the fur rug, and we'll have this out."

"Meaning you'll tell me the truth? All of it?"

He had to think about that. "I'll try," he said eventually, expecting the displeasure on her face. "Best I can do. I don't know where this is going to lead, and it might take us to a truth I'm not prepared to give you."

"Which is, no doubt, the truth I most need to hear. Very well, sir. We are agreed. I shall lie to you if I think it necessary, and you will do the same. Which fairly leaves us where we started, does it not?"

"I said I'd try." He pointed to the rug. "Please."

"I'll not sit at your feet," she said, drawing up a ladder-back chair instead and placing it at an angle to his left. "What did the Runner tell you?"

The chair, standing higher than his Moorish bench, put her at eye level with him, a place he was glad to have her. If he got lucky, those glorious eyes would at long last give something away. "If I answer that," he said, "I'll have to lie. It was mostly local gossip, always unreliable, and a family matter."

The next-to-the-last word had burned on his tongue. And Miranda's gaze had dropped to her hands, which were pressed tightly together. She had guessed what it was, then. He was on the right track.

"My turn for a question," he said before she could recover her balance. "Who are you protecting?"

"What?" She glanced up, startled as she was meant to be, and quickly shifted her gaze to a point somewhere beyond his shoulder. "I don't know what you mean."

"Of course you do. But if it will make this easier for you, I'll begin with a little guesswork. Corinna has been found, I expect by you, perhaps at Berkeley Square on the night of the murder. I haven't figured how you knew she was there. Or maybe you showed up to kill Jermyn and wound up jostling for the privilege with his daughter."

"She di—" Mira shook her head. "Why do you think this?"

"That counts as a question," he advised her. "I had a note from Miss Pryce concerning another matter, and she made a passing reference to the safe departure of my sister-in-law. Norah would be going nowhere unless Corinna had been found, and Miss Pryce seemed to think I knew all about their plans. That leaves you and David to tell me of them, and David has gone missing. He's with the ladies, yes? And you have masterminded all of this."

Miranda had regained her composure. It was the goddess of cold lakes and empty skies sitting across from him now, her eyes the color of blue glacier ice. "Should any of that be true," she said, "you could not have been the killer."

"Are you sure? When you and Corinna arrived, Jermyn was already toes up on the hearth." He grinned. "Or, neither of you ever went into the house, and I came along later and did the deed. For every objection, I'll find an answer. I won't turn her in, Miss Holcombe. Really I won't. If she put the knife in him, she has my congratulations and all my support."

"I thought you were convinced I'd done it."

"And I thought I was convinced *I'd* done it. So round and round we go. Did Corinna kill him?"

She took a deep breath. He watched her release it, sensed the debate raging in her excellent mind, knew when she'd come to a decision. He released the breath he'd taken with her and held longer still as he waited for her to surrender.

"Cory says that she did not. I believe her."

"You *almost* believe her. Or you suspect there is evidence against her. Were she free and clear, you'd not think it necessary to provide her a shield."

Another long breath. Then, "She was in the house for a considerable time, more than two days and nights. With the duke gone, there were few servants in residence, and she knew places to conceal herself. But she might have been seen, or left something behind that—"

"That what?"

"I just remembered. She told me of a bundle she'd stashed in a work shed at the end of the garden. I wonder if it's been found."

"I haven't heard so. Varden mentioned that a female was seen departing the house through the front door."

"It was Cory. She ran into the park. From there I took her to David's rooms, and Miss Pryce saw to the rest."

"And why were *you* there?"

She made an impatient gesture. "Does it signify? You should have someone look into the work shed and remove the bundle if it is still there."

"I'll see to it. Meantime, Corinna is unlikely to come under suspicion, to say nothing of the impeccable alibi I expect Miss Pryce has arranged for her. Have you further reason for concern?"

"I don't know. She did intend to kill him. And I . . . I fear she may try to take the crime upon herself."

"Splendid." He mauled his hair with stiff fingers. "Just what we need. Another humbug confession. Why the devil is *she* jumping into this stew?"

"I cannot break her confidence, sir. But to a degree, I understand why she feels as she does. We both set out to commit a murder, and it doesn't greatly matter whether or not we succeeded. We are guilty in our hearts and must accept responsibility for our intentions."

"Fine. Have it out with the deity when you meet him. Meanwhile, has it occurred to you that while the three of us twist and turn in this *danse macabre* with the authorities, the killer scampers off scot-free?"

She gave a faint smile. "Do you know, I don't care if he is ever found. Or she. Whoever killed the Duke of Tallant did a service to everyone who ever came in his reach or who might have done so in the future. The law would not touch him because he was too wealthy and powerful. No one could deter him. No one even dared to try, except the one who plunged the knife into his heart. And because I should have been that one, I am more than willing to take his place on the gallows."

"I expect better reasoning from you, Miss Holcombe." He leaned forward, elbows propped on his knees, and rested his chin on his folded hands. "I am aware, from Hari and from my own observation, that your father has only a short time to live. It was my impression that you are fond of him. So why are you hell-bent to abandon him when he most needs you?"

Her head jerked back as if he'd slapped her. "How can you say that? Of course I don't want to leave him. I want above all things to be with him."

"Except . . . ?" He raised a brow.

"Dear God but you are brutal. Why say this now, when you've made it impossible for me to make any choices at all?" Her eyes looked fevered. "You don't understand. I owe a debt. People have been hurt because I was a coward. Because I said nothing when I should have, did nothing when I might have prevented . . . oh, all that happened afterward. I should pay for what I failed to do."

What had been difficult for him was near to impossible now. It felt as if knives were twisting in his gut, and he nearly backed away because she was hurting so greatly that he could not bear to make it worse. But he had to go on, because at this time, he was thinking more clearly and seeing farther ahead than she.

"You are free to do so, then." He kept his gaze fixed on hers, forcing her to engage him, forbidding her to look away. "Yes, I mean it. You can go. I'll have Hari take you back to Bow Street so you can hand yourself over to the magistrate. He'll be glad to see you again. He alone continued to suspect you after receiving a confession from someone else, and his ambition will be served by the public spectacle of your execution. Which means, my dear Miss Holcombe, that only Sir Richard Burnie profits from your self-immolation."

"Don't." She looked brittle, like glass about to shatter. "Don't do this."

"What? Am I not giving you what you want? But of course, I am only guessing what that is. I had figured—how to put it?—absolution by martyrdom. Which is, of course, an entirely selfish way to evade responsibility."

"Selfish? How can it be? I am *accepting* responsibility."

"If you think so, you are deluding yourself. I know more of failure and guilt than you can begin to imagine. And I know, to my regret, that there is no absolution to be found in willful suicide. Were there the slightest possibility that death would free me from my demons, I'd not be here, now, tormenting you."

"Was not your confession willful suicide?"

"Folly of a quite different sort, I'm afraid. Take it from me, Miss Holcombe. There is no peace in oblivion. No salvation in escape. There is only duty, and honor, and endurance. If you have debts to pay, then pay them to your father."

Silence for a time, save for the crackle of the fire and the blood rushing through his veins. In the overheated air, he felt as if he were drowning. He should have been appointed to kill his brother, or wrestle bears, or pound his head against a rock. To do anything but what he was doing now.

"I see the difficulty," she said. "I have drawn attention to myself, and if found, I shall be taken into custody. You wish me to stay here, with my father, until the end."

"In fact, no. Your disappearance appears to confirm your guilt, and it's no help that I vanished soon after. Burnie will assume we conspired to kill my brother and have been playing games to confuse the authorities. Which means Varden will soon be on my trail, and he has the resources to discover I've spent time with the Punjabi community in London. A short shot from there to this branch of Birindar's family, and he's on you. Even if I returned to London, they'd not stop tracking you. And you're devilish hard to hide, what with your appearance and a paralyzed father. Nor do you wish to move him more often than you must."

"What, then?" Distress contended with impatience on her face. "Since I cannot hide, what must I do?"

"If you desire freedom, Miss Holcombe, you must surrender it. I can keep you safe for a considerable time, certainly long enough to care for your father. But only if you put yourself entirely under my protection."

"You mean you will help me if I become your *mistress*?"

She looked so horrified at the prospect that he nearly gave up then and there. But the calm of the lake was again strong in him, the battle focus absolute, and no other purpose had ever driven him so hard. "Much as the idea appeals to me," he said, "that wouldn't help. What you require is immunity from prosecution. I can provide it by convincing the law of my own guilt, and if that is what you choose, I will gladly do it."

"Wait! How did your death sentence become *my* choice to make?"

"All the choices are yours, except the one to die. That is the one thing I will not grant you. If you wish to go on the run, with or without your father, I'll arrange it. That would be your second choice."

"No. I won't leave him. And as you say, he ought not to travel now. What else?"

"The third choice, and the last." He rose, removed a folded sheet of paper from his sash, and held it out.

After a moment's hesitation, she took it.

He watched the play of expressions on her face as she opened the document, began to read it, realized what it was.

She looked up at him, her mouth a little open. "You cannot mean this."

"I'm quite sure that I do."

Rising in agitation, the paper clasped between her thumb and forefinger, she looked around the large room as if an answer would start writing itself on the walls. "No," she said. "It is impossible. Unthinkable."

The paper slipped, unnoticed, from her hand as she struck out for the door. There she paused, hand on the latch, and looked back at him. "I'm sorry," she said. "I cannot do this. I cannot."

She left then, in a rush that stirred her green skirts and her bright cloud of hair.

"I know," he murmured, watching her go. "I didn't expect that you could."

Chapter 23

Ever since her idyllic childhood crashed to an end in a muddy ditch, Mira had become accustomed to trouble and adept at coping with it. She even took a queer sort of pride in her unwished-for talent, and in her ability to remain composed and detached in all circumstances.

Until now. Until this night, when the Devil's son had looked into her soul and offered her three choices, all of them insupportable. And forced her to acknowledge that the choice she had made only yesterday, the one he'd deprived her of, was even worse than the alternatives he'd provided.

How could she have thought to do it? At the time, it had seemed so right. So inevitable. She'd been given a chance to make amends, and perhaps to help one of those who had suffered because of her. She would die, Cory would go free. . . . How could this be wrong?

But he had seen, with those too-familiar eyes, past her self-justification, even beyond her very real guilt and her yearning for absolution. He had seen the despair in her.

For that, she resented him beyond measure. And was grateful to him, for he had prevented her from doing the unthinkable. Absorbed in her misery, she

had condemned her father, helpless and beloved, to
the anguish of mourning his child even as he confronted his own lingering death.

The irony of her situation was bitter in her mouth.
Caring for her father and killing the duke had been
all she permitted herself to want from life. But willy-
nilly, one goal had been achieved without her, and
the other would be taken from her hands within a
few months.

What was she to do? She had made herself a suspect
and encouraged the authorities to believe her guilty.
Now her only escape was to accept one of the choices
Michael Keynes had ticked off like a shopping list.

She could condemn a man who might or might not
be guilty—she still wasn't sure—to execution for a
murder she had wanted to commit.

Or she could flee with a dying father from bolt-hole
to bolt-hole, the authorities hard on her heels.

Which left marriage to a man she feared.

Three options that gave her no choice at all. Whatever Michael Keynes had said, it was not given her to
ordain his death, nor could she subject her father to
hardship because she feared to suffer herself. Like Sis-
yphus, she could only go to the boulder and put her
awful hands on it and with all the will she possessed,
begin pushing it once again up a steep and futile
mountain.

How very theatrical, a mocking voice said from the
small corner of herself not given over to self-pity. *If
you feel badly about your fate, consider the unfortunate
man who will be saddled with you. It might be kinder
to send him to his death.*

She became aware of her arms wrapped around her
waist, of the red-gold light cast by an oil lamp and a
pair of braziers, of a moist fragrance in the air. Without realizing it, she had come into her father's room.

She moved quietly to where he slept, half sitting
against a bank of pillow on a narrow bed, and lowered

herself to a chair beside him. To help clear his congested lungs, a healer among the Punjabi women had mixed oils and spices in copper bowls and placed them on the braziers. The room smelled of mint and lemon, cloves and half-a-dozen elusive scents. It smelled of the oils and spices used to anoint the dead. She glanced up and saw her father looking back at her, a question in his pale blue eyes.

"Oh, Papa," she said, wanting to ask him what to do and reluctant to lay her burdens on him. He liked it when she stroked his head, and for several minutes, she simply sat with him and let him feel her touch. But as the time passed, she sensed in him a growing agitation, as if he required more from her.

He always knew when she ached inside. She wished he did not, so that he could be spared her problems. But perhaps she cheated him by withholding them. In his place, she would demand to know everything. To share everything. What if he wanted that as well?

He hadn't used to. After her mother's death, he dove like a fishing bird into the past, into the history of ancient civilizations and troubles too long ago and far away to touch him. He still did that, she knew. What else was there for him now?

Except her. He cared about her, and what he thought his illness had cost her, and what would become of her when he was gone.

If ever she was to open her heart to him, the little of it there was, she must find the courage to do it soon. "Papa," she began, with a smile so that he would not fear bad news, "Michael Keynes has asked me to marry him. I scarcely know what to think of it. Now that he's a duke, he should be looking higher for a wife, and more to the point, I have never wished to be a wife. But he cares nothing for that, and he is in a great hurry besides. Ought I to wed him, do you think?"

Instead of the enthusiastic "Yes" she had expected,

he used his finger to ask for the alphabet card. With a degree of reluctance, she brought it to him, added pillows at his back to raise him up, and positioned his hand. "No fr me," he picked out.

Not for me. The shorthand they had developed spared his strength. "Of course not, although he is fond of you, I'm sure. All is in disarray after his brother's death, and people expect he will carry on where the former duke left off. I think he wants a wife to lend him respectability, and I am conveniently to hand. It would be purely a marriage of convenience."

"Lov?"

"No love at all, but how could there be? We hardly know each other. I thought you would be pleased, Papa. You have wanted me to find a husband this age."

"Gd man."

"Well, yes, I would prefer a good man, but—"

The finger moved again. "He gd."

"Oh. I misunderstood you. In many ways, I expect he is good. Vastly difficult, though, and autocratic. And as you know, I am used to making my own decisions."

"Stbrn."

"Which of us do you mean?" She was relieved to see the gleam of humor in his eyes. "Papa, I may decide to accept him. Not for your sake, and not for love, and not for any reason I can put my finger on, except that I can see no great harm in it. First, though, I must discover if we can come to terms on a number of things. If the negotiation goes well, then perhaps—and only perhaps—I shall consent to become a duchess."

A long pause. Then he wrote, "B wis."

She wasn't sure if he meant she ought to marry the duke, or if he was urging her to think carefully before doing so. "Be wise," he had said. Too late. She had made so many bad decisions that no matter which direction she turned now, a trap waited to close on her.

"I'd better go speak with him before he goes to b— before it's too late." The image of Michael Keynes in bed had sent heat roaring to her face and neck. Moving from her father's line of vision, she removed a few pillows, helped settle him down, and slipped the card off his lap. "This may take a long time, and probably nothing will be settled tonight. I shall come first thing tomorrow and tell you all that occurred. Sleep well, Papa."

Still unable to face him, she went to the door and paused there, careful to remain in the shadows. "Because you are my father," she said, finding it extraordinarily difficult to speak of her feelings, "I have always been loved. And although I have been neglectful in telling you so, I love you as well, Papa. I very much love you."

He could not respond, of course. She waited a few moments longer, as if listening to him speak without words, as she knew he was doing. Then, with a respectful curtsy, she withdrew.

Her bedchamber lay directly across the corridor. She went there first, to splash cold water on her face, pass a brush through her hair, and rummage through her half-unpacked luggage for combs to hold it back from her face. She found something else as well, something she thought had been taken from her at the cottage. Wearing fresh gloves and not as apprehensive as she probably ought to be, she set out for the room at the opposite corner of the house.

It was well after midnight. He might be gone by now. She wasn't sure whether or not she wanted him to be there, but she knew that if this failed to be settled straightaway, she would lose her courage altogether. And then she'd end up doing whatever he wished, because the fight in her had already begun to seep away.

When she opened the door, near darkness met her eyes. Only two colsa lamps still burned on the pier tables, making small islands of golden light on either side of her. The fire had dwindled to coals. A chill was on the room.

The bench where he had sat was empty, the brandy bottle on the table beside it nearly so, but the familiar vibration assured her of his presence. And then she found him, a tall figure slouched against the wall in the far corner, a glass dangling from his fingers. He'd removed the embroidered robe and loosened the drawstring ties on his tunic, exposing his neck and a vee of muscled chest. Clearly he had not been expecting her to return, nor had he noticed that she had done so. She was so often in and out of her sleeping father's room that she had learned to move silently as a wraith.

Already the door was closed behind her. To get his attention, she deliberately raised the latch and dropped it again.

He looked up.

From clear across the large room, she felt him the way she might if he were hovering directly over her. Hands clasped at her back, she leaned against the door for support and chose an opening move he would not be expecting. "Why do they call you Shear?"

A hesitation. He must be surprised she was there at all. "When I first went to the Punjab," he said as if he found the subject tedious, "I attached myself to a troop of Ranjit Singh's cavalry. Sikh men all have the same surname, you'll have observed, but not because they are of the same family. The guru who established their faith had no use for caste, so the men all got rid of the surnames that marked the caste they'd been born into and took instead the name 'Singh.' It means 'lion.' "

His voice was a little slurred. "The women all have a middle name, 'Kaur,' which means 'princess.' You should ask them to explain their beliefs to you. Theirs is an egalitarian society, far more so than our own, with virtually no distinction between men and women in rights and privileges. You would like that, I expect."

He'd neatly turned the subject, no more willing to answer a personal question than she ever was. So she asked it again. "Why Shear? What does it mean?"

A sound that might have been a laugh. "I was new and green, had done something spectacularly stupid in an effort to prove myself, and when it worked out well, the others welcomed me into the troop with a Punjabi name. But I couldn't be a lion, not in a regiment of Singhs, so they dubbed me Syr."

"Which means—?"

A long pause. "Tiger."

Why had he been so loath to reveal it? She'd begun to expect something quite different. "Jackal," perhaps. Or "rat."

He emerged from the dark corner, but only to take up the bottle and pour the last of the brandy into his glass.

"You drink too much," she said.

"I know." He lifted the glass in a toast. "But it's never enough."

It must have been defiance, she was thinking when he swallowed every last bit of the brandy in a single draught. Well, she oughtn't have criticized him. Not when she had set out to win concessions from him. Although . . . he might be drunk enough to grant them, and too drunk to remember in the morning what he'd promised the night before.

"I fail to understand," she said, "why you have proposed that we marry. If the authorities decide to prosecute me, how will my being married to you stop them? What is there in our marriage to protect either of us?"

"I am always protected, Miss Holcombe, if I choose to fight the charges. Rank, they say, has privileges, and one of mine is to be tried by my peers in the Lords. That right devolves as well upon my wife."

"But you, or I, can be as easily condemned there as in a common court."

"Not easily, I assure you. The lords are notably reluctant to sit in judgment of one of their own. The precedent makes them vulnerable, especially those with dirty hands, and their best safety lies in protecting one another. To be sure, Jermyn was unpopular and a severe embarrassment. Under ordinary circumstances, they would be delighted to see the last Tallant duke strung up and the title gone into abeyance. But these are not ordinary circumstances, and the last Tallant duke happens to be me."

"You are not unpopular and an embarrassment?"

"I expect I will be, soon enough. What I am *now* is a threat. A good many of my potential judges are heavily invested in the India country trade, particularly the opium-for-tea smuggling that so enriched my brother. In that, of course, they are scarcely unique. But even those not directly involved turn a blind eye to the fraud, evasion of taxes, exploitation, bribery, extortion, and far greater crimes perpetrated by hirelings so that they and their fellows can reap a grand harvest."

"Are you saying you have evidence against them? And that you would use it to prevent being tried for your brother's murder?"

"Yes to both, assuming—as I said before—that I choose to fight the charge. In this one way, Jermyn has proved useful to me. For the last dozen years I have been tracing his private activities and those of the shells he used as covers, including the East India Consortium. In general, I cared nothing for anyone else's crimes, but when Varden targeted me for investigation, I cast a wider net. Some little of what I hauled in, I carried here with me, and my associates were delegated to pursue the inquiries after my departure. They have already sent plenty of damning information, which is now in the safekeeping of my banker. Long before I can be brought to trial, Miss Holcombe, I'll have incontrovertible evidence against a score of my putative judges. They will not, I assure you, allow that evidence to be brought to light."

She was afraid to ask. "And Varden himself?"

"So far as I know, innocent as a gamboling lamb. He might *ought* to have known what the Consortium was up to, but practically speaking, the information was not accessible to him. Nor to most of the investors, I expect, although Jermyn cannot have orchestrated all their activities on his own. If I elect to, I can probably ferret out the principals. But this is nothing to the point. Have I answered your question?"

She'd all but forgot what it was. Every time she spoke with this man, she discovered unexpected qualities, good and bad, in him. Tonight she had learned that to get what he wanted, he would ruthlessly manipulate the courts and the law, blackmail his peers, and if it suited him, protect a murderer. She was rather more impressed than appalled.

"Fairly well," she rallied herself to say. "But what if I was brought to trial and took advantage of the opportunity to confess?"

He chuckled, no humor in the sound of it. "Do you imagine, my dear, that you would be permitted to speak for yourself in an English court? Your legal identity is absorbed into that of your husband. And were you to blurt out a troublesome admission, I should be forced to acknowledge that my brother's persecution and your father's illness had unsettled your fragile female mind. In their kindness, the lords would undoubtedly permit me to confine my demented duchess where she could do no one, not even herself, any harm."

"I think you would really say that," she said with a degree of furious awe.

"Let us agree, then, that you will not put me to it."

One by one, he closed off every means of escape . . . not that she had anywhere left to go. Swallowing her indignation, she turned her mind to practical considerations. "What happens after my father is . . . no longer a factor? Or if someone else is convicted of the murder? I presume we could then secure an annulment of the marriage?"

"I'm afraid not." He went to the hearth, selected a log, and placed it across the firedogs. "The magistrate already thinks we conspired to commit the murder and protect each other from the consequences. Our marriage will be regarded with suspicion, and all the legalities checked down to the last jot and tittle. There are surprisingly few causes that can trigger an annulment. We'd not get away with faking any one of them."

"We wouldn't need to." A cold knot of pain tightened in her stomach. "Many years ago, I was badly injured in a riding accident. Later, I overheard the doctor say it was unlikely I'd be able to bear children. So you see, I could confess that I had deceived you before the wedding. No one would expect you to remain married to a woman unable to give you an heir."

He had hunkered down and was placing tinder on the coals to get the fire restarted. "Are you certain of this, Miss Holcombe? If you make such a claim, you will be subjected to an unpleasant examination, and only a severe deformity would stand as evidence of infertility."

She wondered what a severe deformity would consist of, and how it could be detected. But she could hardly ask him straight out. "I see. Or rather, I don't quite see. You appear to know a great deal about these matters."

"Only because I have just spent the better part of the day with my solicitors. I took the opportunity to ask them every pertinent question I could think of, along with those I anticipated receiving from you."

"But are you not concerned about my deformities, detectable or otherwise? You have a responsibility to your name and family, sir. You are expected to continue the line."

"I am? By whom? Although I am unacquainted with Norah's daughters, I'd guess they are decent chits who keep themselves out of trouble. Well, if you except Corinna's attempt to kill her father. But there hasn't been a shred of decency in any Keynes male for the last several generations. I have no wish to reproduce myself, Miss Holcombe. The sooner this line dies out, the better."

"Then you should not object to helping me annul our marriage. In the spirit of cooperation, sir, I will go first. But if the physical examination discloses nothing of use, then we'll just have to resort to you. I mean, you could . . . that is, what would it cost you to swear that you are . . . um, incapable of—"

"No."

She lifted her chin, undaunted. "I quite see how you would find such an admission difficult to make. But it's not as if the information would become public. And later, with me gone and unfindable, you could have a miraculous restoration of your powers."

"And you, Miss Holcombe, have a somewhat limited comprehension of male reproductive functions and the law. Even were I willing to swear myself impotent, the word of a Keynes already suspected of duplicity would scarcely hold up in the ecclesiastical court. Any examiner worth his credentials would put you in a room with me and instruct you to remove your clothing. In a remarkably short time, I assure you, all doubts about my capacity to perform would be extinguished."

Having nursed her father over a period of years,

she was not unfamiliar with male reproductive organs. Nor, having observed horses and other farm animals in rampant display, was she unacquainted with the transformation wrought by instinct and, she assumed, passion. She quite understood, generally speaking, what this formidable male had just described to her. She altogether grasped the reality of it and the pain that it would cause in her, and her own terror of the whole . . . procedure.

And yet, with this man, with *him*—

She reeled in her wits and baited another hook. "Very well. I accept the unlikelihood of an annulment. So how about a divorce?"

His laugh this time was genuine. "What other woman, I wonder, would ask that question before consenting to be wed?" The fire caught then, licking over the log, crackling as it consumed the dry bark. He rose and turned to look at her. "You may have a divorce upon request, Miss Holcombe. But only when I am persuaded you can never be indicted for the murder."

"Oh." She found it unaccountably insulting, how little he minded being quit of her. "A divorce would be a terrible scandal, you know."

"We Keyneses thrive on scandal. But if I am to file for dissolution of the marriage, you will first require to be convicted of adultery. That means proof that will stand up in court, so when you are ready to stray, my dear, remember to arrange for witnesses."

"You are surely jesting."

"No, indeed. I'm not certain if the spectators must observe you in *flagrante delicto,* or if seeing you arrive and depart will suffice, but you can consult a solicitor about all the messy details. Just don't count on me to play any part in your scheming. Should I catch you with a lover, in or out of *delicto*, I'd put a knife in his back."

He was mocking her now. Raking up her anger, just

as he'd raked up the coals of the dying fire in the hearth. It was almost as if, in the process of tightening his grip on her, he was at the same time making himself so intolerable that she'd cut free and run.

Was that really what he wanted?

Was that what *she* wanted?

She'd no idea what she was to him, or what—if anything—she wanted to be. She knew only that it was her turn now, and that she had some conditions of her own to put on the table.

"Are you willing to settle for a marriage in name only?" she said. "And do I need to explain what I mean by that?"

"I'm not sure." He had taken up a poker and was half turned back to the fire when she spoke. He paused, not looking at her. "I assume you mean I am not to touch you. That there will be no consummation of the marriage. Is that right?"

"Yes. Exactly that."

After a moment, he completed the motion he'd begun and started punching at the fire. "Your demand is not unexpected. Nor can I blame you for it."

Her breath caught. *Nor can I blame you.* What did he mean by that? Could he possibly—?

"I accept your terms unconditionally, Miss Holcombe. Add to them at will."

And how was it, she wondered, amazed, that in the very act of surrendering, he seized control of her yet again?

"I do not understand you!" She found herself in the middle of the room, her hands still fixed behind her back, her fingers tightly wrapped around the hilt of his knife. "You are throwing away your every chance of a true wife, of children, of building a future for your family. Don't you realize this? Don't you *care?*"

"About those things, not at all. I have never considered the future, Miss Holcombe. Only the task immediately to hand." He turned to face her, his legs slightly apart, his silhouette limned by the fire. "At one time, I sought funds to complete my studies. Then funds for passage to India, and to develop the skills I was going to require. Then the funds to buy for myself a mercenary force. Next, one after the other, I dealt with each mission as it arose. I planned and prepared the raid or the robbery or the ambush. I executed it. And if I survived, which as you see, I invariably did, I devised another scheme and began again. Reachable targets. Short-term goals."

He balanced the poker on the palms of his hand like a votive offering. "Only one long-term purpose absorbed me, had done since I was a child, and that was the destruction and death of my brother. To my chagrin, it was achieved without me. And now I have no purpose, my dear, except to keep you from going to the gibbet. You may be sure I will achieve it."

She had, by this time, no doubt of his determination or his abilities. But why her? Why would he trouble himself with *her?* "It is not in the nature of human beings," she said, "to act without at least a degree of self-interest. And since I bid fair to bring you nothing but trouble for your efforts on my behalf, I cannot help but be suspicious of your motives and your intentions. Once I am legally in your power, I cannot prevent you from doing as you like with me."

"More or less true," he conceded. "I could exile you to a remote and unpleasant place. Beat you if I'd a mind to. Spend your money, if you had any. Take you to my bed. Take you anywhere I wished, for that matter, and in any fashion, as often as it pleased me. Do you think I will do any of these things?"

She could only gaze at him, stunned to silence.

He let go one end of the poker. It struck the flagstone hearth with a sharp sound.

She jumped. Recovered quickly, but not soon enough.

He gave a harsh laugh. "You are quite right to fear

me, Miss Holcombe. You would be a fool to trust me. A greater fool still to marry me and put yourself in my hands."

"You were close to having me there," she said. "Why of a sudden try to frighten me away?"

"*Try?* You've been frightened from the first moment you saw me. Frightened of what I want, and let us both be perfectly clear about what that is. I want you naked and under me and open to me." His expression hardened. "Don't be shocked. Every man who sees you wants the same thing. Even your Archangel, although he'd tell you so in euphemisms while neatly folding his silk underdrawers."

With all her strength, she held her ground. "You haven't answered my question."

He was leaning his weight on the poker as if it were a walking stick. "You already know the answer. You know what could happen, what I could do to you. What I want, profoundly want, to do *with* you. You fear me. But you are still here. Why is that, do you suppose?"

"Because you have given me no choice." A stream of cold sweat streaked down her back. "Because for my father's sake, I must stay alive to care for him. And I can do that only by marrying you."

"Oh, no. You won't slip away from your responsibility by putting it all on me. I admit to deceiving you, but only a little. Your choices are not so dark as they first appeared. Say, for instance, you tell me to go to the devil. To turn myself in and put my head on the block. What I didn't explain is how nicely everyone will profit from my not-unwilling demise. I've made generous provisions, thanks to your counsel, for Norah and her brats. And the provisions I've made for you are nearly as bountiful, although I'm not quite so independently wealthy as Jermyn was."

"You have willed your own money to *me?*"

"I had to do something with it. Even with the funds put aside for Hari and David, you'll have a consider-

able fortune to go along with the property that right-
fully belongs to your family. Independence can be
yours. A chaste bed as well, until some lucky man
lures you into his. I cannot provide health to your
father, but all else I have to give is yours on a say-so."

His smile sent a chill through her. "Isn't that good
news? You needn't marry me after all, Miss Holcombe. You are not called to be a martyr."

And there it was. All she had to do in exchange for
what he'd offered her was . . . send him to his death.
And he didn't mind dying. She accepted his word on
that, because she had shared his readiness to do the
same. But at the time, she'd had very little reason
to live.

Did he feel the same, this powerful, beautiful, tormented man? She couldn't bear to think of it.

What had been, before this moment, impossible
choices, now seemed to her irresistible temptations.
Fear and longing tumbled inside her. She could not
have everything. But he had offered her more than
she had dared to hope for, and she need only select
what she most deeply desired.

Not without risk, though. Not without paying a terrible price.

Apples in Paradise. Serpents twisting around her
ankles, slithering around her thighs. *I want you under
me, open to me.*

His death, in exchange for her freedom. Or his life,
in exchange for her surrender.

She looked up at him, seeking an answer in his
haunted eyes.

Chapter 24

She had a knife.

Not one of her sleek daggers, Michael could tell in spite of the poor light. He'd caught the flash of the blade when her hands, tucked behind her back for all this time, finally dropped to her sides. Now the knife was half concealed by her skirts, but he'd no doubt that in an instant, she could drive it at a target—some portion of his anatomy—with supreme accuracy. She would have trained herself to use her weapons, as he had done.

He wondered, not for the first time, if she really had killed his brother.

Her eyes, fixed on his, were cold, merciless as a feral cat's. God but she fascinated him.

More than that. Enthralled him.

Would probably be the death of him.

She would be worth it, though. She was worth the voyage to England, in spite of his failure to kill Jermyn. Worth all he'd done to earn the money he would provide her. In his better moods, there was nothing he would not do for her, and that included keeping his hands off her.

But his better moods were infrequent, and his noble impulses rarely lasted longer than the time it took them to flash through his imagination. He was a Keynes. In him, the dark blood ran true.

He could protect her from every enemy but himself. When he reverted to the savage he was, Miranda Holcombe would be entirely on her own.

The delay, as they studied each other and considered their next moves, had restored her confidence. Like a character from a Greek tragedy, she stood proud and defiant, the knife of an avenger in her hand.

He directed the tip of his poker toward it. "Do you intend using that on me?"

"I'd planned on returning it to you," she said.

That got his attention. "One of mine, then?"

"It appears to be. I took it from the hem of a curtain in your brother's house."

Bloody damn hell. She *had* been there. And that meant—

For some reason, he'd kept assuming she hadn't done it. He'd thought she was protecting Corinna. "If you had a decent weapon, why use that absurd dagger on him?"

"Because this is difficult to conceal." She raised the knife and sighted a throw. "Not a saucer this time, Your Grace. Will you duck?"

"Send it at me and find out."

After a moment, she gave a throaty laugh and lowered the knife. "There's no use me assuming a posture, is there? You've too much practice. Men are trained to it from birth."

"And women to compliance, but you don't appear to have taken the lesson." If not for the stakes, which escalated with every thrust and parry, he might have enjoyed himself. "Does Varden think you are guilty?"

The change of subject sent her off balance, but not for long. "I don't know. What does it matter what he thinks?"

"He was the one took you off to Bow Street. I'm trying to figure how he fits into all of this."

A feminine shrug. "Since I was preparing to go there anyway, I suppose he fits in by saving me the price of a hackney. And lurking about during the interrogation. And arranging for my visit to the Tower."

"Rather like a jumped-up servant." Michael heard the rasp of jealousy in his voice. He needed to come to the point before he lost the will to do it. "There is another option for you, Miss Holcombe. One we have not discussed, because it is not in my power to give it you. But I think it may be possible to arrange, and if I can do so without letting you slip the net, I will try."

She appeared less eager to hear it than he had expected. But she said nothing, so he marched ahead, barefoot on hot coals. "Varden would marry you, I think, even if persuaded of your guilt. And as his wife, you would have the same protection I am able to offer you."

"Not counting extortion and intimidation of the judges."

"Not counting that," he agreed with a reluctant smile. "What I accomplish by threat and deceit, he achieves with an impeccable reputation and a blinding patina of virtue. Archangels don't marry murderesses, everyone will assume. If he vouches for your innocence, he will be believed."

"But what if he was not sure of my innocence? Would he lie on my behalf?"

"For the privilege of lying on your body, most men would sell out their honor and a good deal more besides. But we'll only know if you put him to the test. I advise you to do it. You'll not find in England a more suitable suitor, and he'll treat you far better than I ever would. Varden will defer to your will, grant all of your wishes, nurture you like a rare orchid. You will never have cause to fear him. So what do you say? Shall I propose to him that he propose to you?"

Head tilted, she regarded him suspiciously "If you wish me to accept Varden, then why dance me through the alternatives? Especially the horrible ones, like hauling my poor father from place to place, one step ahead of the authorities?"

"Because it would occur to you. Because all the choices I presented would occur to you."

"Sending you to the gallows in my place would not. Marrying you would not! Nor would marrying Lord Varden, for that matter."

"They would have done, when it was too late. At the time we began this dance, you were blind to anything but absolution and self-destruction. You required options. A puzzle to solve. Temptations. A glimmer, perhaps, of hope. I wish I could give you more than that. Varden is your best chance, and you should take it."

There. He'd done what he hadn't thought he could do. Varden was always her first choice, and he'd withheld it until the last possible moment because he knew she'd leap for it, and he didn't want her to. He wanted her to choose *him*, which no sane female would do if Varden were on offer. And now he was, and Michael Idiot Keynes had put him there. Because that was Miranda's nearest chance for a happy life, which was the only thing he valued more than the chance to spend a little of his own benighted life in her company.

Well, so much for that. One of these days, perhaps in the next century, he'd be proud of himself for handing her over to a decent man.

"Before I scurry off to Lord Varden," she said, "will you explain one thing to me? When first you suggested a marriage of convenience, you promised I could set the conditions. I thought, briefly, we had come to terms. Then you . . . you turned on me, and led me to believe I could not trust you to keep your promises."

"That's right."

"*What* is right?" Her eyes blazed with indignation. "Which is it? Can I trust you, or can I not?"

"I mean everything I say to you, Miss Holcombe . . . unless I am lying. Or unless a minute or two has passed, at which time I may not mean it any longer." He set the poker gently on the low table in front of him and stood bare-handed before her, bare-handed and very still. "If Hari were here, he'd tell you a peaceable Buddha story that sounded meaningful until you tried to figure it out. My stories, what few I know, are straightforward, and I'll tell you one that answers your question . . . to the degree there is an answer."

"We've had enough quibbling, don't you think? The story, please. The straightforward one."

"Very well. It is a fable, really, and begins with a fire that drove a camel and a serpent to the bank of a wide river. 'Carry me across,' begged the serpent, 'for if you do not, I will surely die.'

"The camel shook his head. 'Every creature that has let you come near was made sorry for it. How can I know you will not slay me as you have done all the others?'

"The fire was so close that it singed the camel's coat and the serpent's scales. 'Do me this service,' said the serpent, 'and I swear I will not harm you.' So the camel, being of a generous and trusting nature, took the serpent on his back and plunged into the river.

"When they were at its deepest point, where the current was so fierce that only the strongest of camels could forge its way through, the serpent coiled around the camel and sank its fangs into his neck.

" 'But why?' gasped the camel as the venom surged through his veins and weakened him so that he could not swim. 'Now I will die, but so will you. Why did you do this?'

" 'Because it is my nature, foolish camel. Did you not understand that I am a snake?' "

Silence. *Snake snake snake* echoed in his ears. Her lucent gaze held him transfixed. The India sun burned into him, the dust of Sher Ka Danda scratched at his eyes. The scent of tigress roused his manhood.

"I take your meaning," she finally said, moving to the low table and placing his knife beside the poker. Then, after a hesitation and a deep breath, she slowly peeled the gloves from her hands, one by one. They were laid on the table as well, and she stepped closer to him, closer still, and lifted her arms. Her hands, inches from him and at the level of his chest, were smooth and white as milk.

"You should have changed your story," she said, "and made the camel a duck with feet webbed like my hands are webbed. The deformity runs in the Holcombe family. All the fingers of my cousin's hands were joined together. He once had a surgeon separate two of them, but the wounds became inflamed and were long in closing. I have not been brave enough to try it for myself."

From the nature of her three-fingered gloves with the large middle sheath, he already knew what to expect. The third and fourth fingers were perfectly shaped, as was every portion of each small hand, except they were fixed together as if by glue. "Is there pain or discomfort?"

A little frown. "No."

He kept his gaze on her hands. "Will you turn them over?"

She did, exposing her palms.

"Do you find it troublesome to use them? Are you required to make a great many adjustments?"

"I—no. They've always been like this, so I grew up using them as they are. Most things are simple enough. I couldn't play the harp, I suppose, or the piano. But I used to play the lute, and . . . No. They give me little trouble."

He held out his own hands, large, dark, monstrous

hands with long fingers and a sword-wielder's knuckles. And scars. A great many scars. "As you see, I'll win no prizes for elegance with these. But they do the job they're intended for, and yours do the same. So why are we having this demonstration?"

She withdrew her hands, color flagging her pale cheeks. "I thought you should know. The condition is inherited."

"Which will not, as I understand things, affect me in the slightest." Tension was making him more abrupt than usual, and his usual was bad enough. "What else, Miss Holcombe?"

She braced herself, the way a soldier does before advancing into enemy fire. For the barest moment, her small white teeth bit at her lower lip before disappearing again.

He held his breath. What would it be? "Go to hell"? "I need more time to consider"? Worst of all, "Varden"?

And then she drew closer still, her face a mask of concentration, her gaze focused on his left shoulder and arm as if she'd never seen anything like them before.

He knew better than to move. That was about all he did know. Small bare fingers moved to his arm where the too-small *kurta* fitted around his bicep. Her fingertips touched the hard surface, skated down it, then up to his shoulder. She explored the shape of him, the swell of muscle, the taut sinews. The muslin shirt felt like armor between his flesh and hers. There was pressure as she stroked him, but the intimacy of skin to skin was denied him, and just as well. He could not have borne it—

She was there. The tip of one finger crossing to his bare chest, tickling at the wiry hair before sliding up to his throat, and then the whole of her hand against the side of his neck. He held perfectly still, as he would have done for the stroke of the headsman's ax.

She held still as well, for what seemed an endless time. She must feel his pulse beating in his veins, the air searing his throat when he drew it in as if through a reed, him underwater, hiding from an enemy.

His eyes had closed sometime along the way. He sensed nothing but what he felt where her hand touched him. The universe gathered there, starlight and moonlight and spinning planets. His head was spinning.

The hand left him. Then came the feather brush of her fingers over the stubble on his chin. He nearly broke. Nearly pushed her away before he lost all control and wrapped his arms around her and carried her to the floor.

He felt nothing. Heard the faint sound of her slippers on the carpet, sensed cool air where she had been. He opened his eyes.

She'd not gone far. Only a short way, just beyond arm's reach, where she was standing quietly, looking at him from intent blue eyes.

"I will cross the river with you," she said.

Expecting something altogether different, he didn't at first take her meaning. And then he understood, and his heart lurched, and the ground opened under him. Or his feet left it, he could not be sure. He'd slipped his anchor, that was certain. And she . . . ah, she had blessedly lost all her caution and good sense.

"Very well," he said, commendably restrained, as if she'd consented to no more than a stroll in the garden. "I'll see to the arrangements. We should act quickly"—*before she can change her mind*—"and have the wedding here"—*because he did not trust what she'd say or do beyond this prison.* "Is that agreeable?"

" 'Twere well it were done quickly," she quoted with a humorless smile. "Have you instructions for me?"

Jagged teeth and claws now, to hold him at bay.

Not *all* her good sense had gone missing. "A request, rather. Hospitality is embedded in the bones of Punjabis, and they will find, even in a marriage of convenience like ours, an excuse for a celebration. If you can bear to do so, I hope you will allow them the pleasure of it. But if you prefer, I will ask them to let this arrangement pass without notice."

"I've no objection," she said after an interval, "so long as we needn't pretend to some sort of romantical feelings for each other."

"Of course not. They would catch us out immediately. Have you any requests for yourself? Questions?"

"What should I call you? Tallant? Your Grace? What do you prefer?"

"It doesn't matter." Using his Christian name, he supposed, would imply more familiarity than she was ready to accept. "But I'm not accustomed to either of those, so don't be surprised if I fail to respond."

"You should call me Miranda," she said, "or Mira. And while we are here, at least when we are in company, I'll use the name your Punjabi friends use. How is it spelled?"

"S-Y-R."

"I would not have guessed that. Well, if there is nothing more, Your Grace, I shall bid you good night." Her curtsy sparkled with frost.

He understood that she was reclaiming what territory she could, setting boundaries, advising him that acceptance did not mean surrender. And he knew that what he had intended to tell her, the words of reassurance he'd meant to give her, would be unwelcome now. The last decision belonged to her, and the last word as well.

He bowed, saying nothing, and watched her move with feminine grace to the door. Then she was gone, taking with her all his strength. Sinking cross-legged onto the white fur rug, he buried his face between trembling hands.

Chapter 25

Mira awoke, glanced over at the clock on the mantel-piece, and sat bolt upright in bed. Past noon! She could not remember when she had slept so late. For a dozen years, her nights had been restless, wretched, plagued by nightmares. She invariably woke before dawn, exhausted and with a heavy sense of dread at what the day would bring. But not today.

Today she had nothing to do but what others wanted her to do. She cast around for some resentment at that and, to her surprise, found none. But after the life-altering decision to cross the river with His Grace the Serpent of Tallant, she'd probably exhausted her capacity for making hard choices.

For now. He would not always have his way, nor would she always be so compliant.

Her wedding day. How had it come to this? And his friends, who were going to make a great fuss of it, must be wondering if she ever intended to come out of her room. She leaped from bed, dressed quickly in the dress she'd worn the previous night, and went in search of her father.

He was sitting in a square of sunshine by a window that looked out on the courtyard, one of his favorite spots because the children often played there. A young boy, perched on a chair beside him, was taking his turn reading aloud, as all the boys had been instructed to do on the excuse that they needed to practice their English. But it was done as a kindness to her father, she knew. All the people in this household had been extraordinarily kind, and today she would have a chance to repay them in small measure by playing the part of a not-unwilling bride.

When she came into the room, the boy closed the book, jumped to his feet, and gave a shy bow.

"Where is the duke?" she asked, horrified to hear the question come out of her mouth. She had resolved while brushing her teeth to pretend no interest in his whereabouts.

"Gone, *memsahib,* before sunrise. To find a . . . a guru, I think."

Someone to marry them. Every time she thought about binding herself to Michael Keynes, the air around her grew thin.

"Thank you, Balvan." His grin confirmed she'd got his name right. "Will you tell Nageena Kaur that when I have spent a little time with my father, I shall be glad to help make ready for the wedding?"

"I think it is they who will make you ready, *memsahib.* That is how it was for my sister, who was a bride only a short time ago. But perhaps it is different for English ladies. I will take your message, though."

He put the book aside, respectfully, and then scampered off. In the silence that followed, she became aware of female voices, like the chatter of birds, rising from every part of the house. Some of the women were preparing a feast, she could tell from the odors wafting into the room—cinnamon and ginger, cardamom and cloves, roasted meats and oils and the clarified butter they called ghee.

There was music too, of a sort. Instruments being tuned. Flutes and bells. Somewhere, a drum thumping. A group of children practicing a song.

Oh, dear. She turned to her father, who was regarding her with concerned eyes. *Curtain up,* she thought. *Act One of* The Wedding Farce. With a smile that probably didn't fool him in the slightest, she put the alphabet card on his lap and set about to convince him that she was content to wed Michael Keynes and was certain that in time, she would come to love her husband.

Which was about as likely as her becoming prime minister.

Three hours later, Mira had been bathed, scrubbed with rough sponges, scoured with hard-bristled brushes, and manicured. An elderly woman called Yaya brushed her hair so hard she was surprised any of it remained attached to her scalp. Kohl was applied to her lashes, and then, to her profound dismay, rouge to her nipples. Even worse, the ladies anointed her with delicate perfumes in places where she didn't like to admit she *had* places.

All of this, she understood, in preparation for her wedding night. All for the pleasure of her husband.

And that caused her to imagine him stroking her soft, clean hair. Uncovering her body to reveal her well-buffed skin and the pinker-than-usual tips of her breasts. Bringing his face close enough to detect subtle fragrances in out-of-the-way crevices and folds.

He had warned her that the time might come when he could not resist taking what he had every legal right to take. And these treasonous women were doing everything they could to make her irresistible.

By midafternoon she was standing on a knee-high wooden stool, surrounded by the seamstresses who had spent much of the day assembling her *salwar-kameez.* The embroidered trousers and loose calf-length tunic were scarlet—an auspicious color—and topped with a mantle that she was supposed to drape over her head during the ceremony. Perched on an adjacent stool, one of the women was arranging an ornament in her hair so that a jeweled pendant hung over her forehead.

Chafing to escape all this kindhearted pampering, Mira welcomed the vibration that told her rescue was at hand. Not long after, her bridegroom was standing in the doorway, regarding her with candid appreciation.

"I am *not*," she informed him, "wearing a nose ring."

"I am sorry to hear it," he said, grinning. "I had intended to lead you around by the chain."

Nageena Kaur approached him then, and they spoke together quietly while the last of the pins were set in the hem of Mira's *kameez*. A disappointed expression on her face, Nageena left the room.

Curious, Mira watched the unkempt duke come over to her and extend his hand.

"I ran into some difficulties," he said, leading her into the passageway. "At the first two parishes, the cleric took one look at the name on the Special License and refused to perform the ceremony. They'd got word of my incarceration in the Tower, it seems, but not of my release, and figured I was on the run."

"We are not to be married, then?"

"Don't look so pleased. The third parish was the charm, and if Reverend Filbert doesn't change his mind in the interim, he'll be here after choir practice. I'm estimating eleven o'clock. He didn't much care that I might be a murderer, but he declined to conduct a wedding in a pagan household until I agreed to repair the church roof, supply the rectory with new curtains and carpets, and endow the steeple with a brass tenor bell."

"He strikes a hard bargain. What will he think to see me in this costume?"

"He won't. I just explained to Nageena Kaur that the ceremony must be private—you, me, your father,

and Hari—and that we'll be wearing proper British
attire. That's the other reason I was gone so long. I
had to find a tailor, who is stitching something together for me. Hari will bring it back, along with a
carriage and a driver. Immediately after the wedding,
we'll set out for London."

"I see. Do you ever intend to consult me, Your
Grace, about where I am to be taken, or when?"

He cast her a puzzled look. "I'm consulting you
right now. I made the arrangements because they had
to be made, but you are free to object, or to propose
an alternate plan."

"To which you will pay absolutely no attention."

"You'll have my full attention, Miranda. You always do. Nonetheless, we have to be in London tomorrow. I've directed announcements to the
newspapers, but the chief magistrate will demand to
see the marriage lines before calling off his hounds.
And I have a lot to do there. Jermyn requires to be
buried. Norah's younger girl, Catherine, is at Longview, alone except for a few servants and the Runner
I hired to watch out for her. I want to bring her to
stay with us until her mother and sister arrive, which
could be at any time. And—"

"Very well, sir. I accept London. But must we reside
at Berkeley Square?"

"The Palazzo, I think. You'll need to stay with me,
to keep up appearances, so Hari will relocate to your
cottage. Until we're settled, your father will remain
here. We don't want to move him more often than is
necessary, which is why we're not marrying in the
church. Is there anything I have failed to cover?"

She repressed a snarl. "There is only one thing
worse than you arbitrarily making all the decisions,
and that is me not finding any reason to quarrel with
you about them. It's maddening."

"I know. Hari used to do the same to me, except
his rulings came attached to a sermon."

They were nearly at the quarter of the house where she and her father had their rooms. "There is one ritual," he said, "that usually takes place among the women the night before the wedding. I have asked Nageena Kaur to give it over to me. Will you come, in an hour's time, to the room where we spoke last night?"

A female ritual, and this primal specimen of masculinity wished to take it on himself? Just when she imagined she'd deciphered his character, Michael Keynes did something altogether unexpected. "Of course," she said, deplorably curious. "Shall I change first into . . . into *Christian* clothing?"

He laughed. "The Reverend Filbert would be pleased to hear that. But no. We'll honor our hosts by wearing traditional clothing until time for the ceremony. Agreed?"

"A turban for you, then?"

"I am not of the blood or of the faith," he said, dismissing her with a gesture. "But they'll deck me out in garish colors, and put a knife in my sash and a sword in my hand. If you laugh at me, I'll have you fitted with that nose ring."

When Mira set off an hour later for her rendezvous, all the silks and ornaments had been put aside. For this appointment, she had chosen a spinsterish dove-gray dress and matching gloves, and taken the precaution of scraping her treacherous hair into a tight knot at the back of her head.

There was nothing seductive about her now. Nothing to draw the heated look he'd cast on her when she stood before him in crimson silk and filigree silver. She'd made sure of it in front of her mirror. The only visible remnant of her adorning, the kohl on her lashes, gave her the appearance of a startled doe, but otherwise, she looked exactly like what she was—a tense, angry, fearful woman.

In the large parlor where she had sealed her fate last night, Michael Keynes waited for her, looking ominously relaxed and confident. He was sitting back on his heels, the plush white fur rug beneath him, his hands loose on his knees. All the light in the room was there—a score of short, fat candles scattered across the large table, a pair of tall candle holders at each corner, burning logs in the hearth behind him. At her entrance he rose in a fluid motion, templed his hands beneath his chin, and bowed.

The women must have been sewing for him as well. The loose trousers and straight-cut tunic were silky, lamb-white, and fit his lean, muscled body exactly. For color, a wide, sleeveless, hip-length waistcoat, scarlet to match her *salwar-kameez*, was embroidered with silver thread and trimmed with sequins. He looked exotic. Alien. Magnificent.

Also like a Keynes—strong-willed and savage.

She approached him with all the confidence she did not feel. Within a few hours, she would be his wife. In his power. And the worst of it was, she was growing used to the idea.

Avoiding his potent gaze, she looked down at the large table. Square and little more than a foot high, it was laid out with basins and a water pitcher, towels and napkins, metal devices and glass bowls, and small ceramic dishes containing . . . well, she'd no idea what, except for the lemon.

His knife was there as well, the one she'd returned to him, and a block of wood. He'd been whittling, but had produced only a number of wands no larger than stickpins except for one end, which was wider and flatter than the other.

"This is the Mehndi ki Raat," he said. "The Night of Mehndi, in which the women gather to sing traditional songs, adorn the hands of the bride, and enlighten her about the mysteries of the wedding night and how to please her bridegroom. I thought, given

our circumstances, that you might wish to be spared
the lesson, not to mention the teasing that goes along
with it."

"Yes. But why do any of this? For Nageena Kaur?"

"The feasting and music and dancing are for the
family. But this, Miranda, is to honor you." His voice
carried a note she had not heard in it before, a reso-
nance of uncertainty. "Will you permit me to perform
the service?"

"I suppose so." She sounded prickly. Felt brittle
and resistant, as she always did when she'd no idea
what to expect. Darkness licked at the edges of the
private world he had created here, a world encompassed by fire, made lavish with fur rugs and tasseled
cushions, mysterious with strange potions and ancient
rituals. She feared it, longed for it. "What am I to
do?"

"Sit here."

She lowered herself onto a satin cushion and curled
her legs to one side. "Adorn the hands with what?"

"A dye," he said, moving the tall candleholders and
oil lamps until she was embraced by their light. "It's
made from a shrub that grows in desert climates. The
leaves are dried, powdered, and mixed with oils,
cloves, and coffee or tea into a paste that is applied
to the hands and sometimes to the feet."

"My heavens. Is it . . . permanent?"

"Don't worry." He settled cross-legged directly in
front of her, so close that even in the midst of candles
and lamps, she felt only the heat that radiated from
him. "At most, the dye lasts a few weeks, and not so
long unless the paste is blended a day or two beforehand and left to dry on the skin for many hours. We
haven't the time for that, nor, I expect, would you
wish it. May I remove your gloves?"

Teeth clenched, she raised her arms and held her
breath while he peeled the glove slowly from her right
hand and then from her left. They dangled there for

a moment, her hands, as if wondering what to do with themselves, until she let them drop onto her lap. Her horrible hands that had made her schoolfellows laugh and the farm children skulk away when she approached, because they believed she had been cursed. But she had been a self-assured child and hadn't minded their foolishness, had not begun to care until much later. How odd she should now remember the sideways glances and the whispers behind her back.

He had poured water into a basin and added a few drops of perfumed oil. At his nod, she dipped her hands into the water. It was warm and smelled of roses. A little steam wafted from the basin, hovered between them, vanished on a puff of air as he leaned forward to pick up a towel. He held it out, and as if they had done this at some other time and place, she knew to place one hand onto it, let him fold the soft fabric around her fingers and palm and wrist, gently pressing it before releasing her.

There was a fresh towel for her other hand, but this time, he kept hold of her wrist when he was done. Lifting it atop two brown fingers placed where her pulse beat madly, he suspended her hand in the air.

"Relax," he said. "Allow your hand to drift as it will. See there? A bird. A flower. A feather borne on a breeze. For many years I lived with a nautch dancer who told stories with her body, but most especially with her hands. Each position, each motion, expressed more than I ever understood, although her gestures conveyed to her countrymen legends that were centuries old. When first I saw your hands, they reminded me of *her* hands and the way she held them. Except that she trained herself for years and practiced daily, while for you it is natural. Your hands were created to be birds and flowers, and to dance."

Stunned, she could only gaze wide-eyed at him as he let go her hand. It fluttered to her lap like a leaf falling from a tree. *Who are you?* She longed to ask him, didn't dare to, didn't know how. Mercenary. Duke. Scholar. Serpent. Tiger. Poet. All of those things, all of them dangerous. All of them seductive.

He had already turned away from her, his attention directed to the table. "Nageena Kaur mixed the paste early this morning," he said, taking up his knife and slicing the lemon neatly in half. "Lemon juice and a little sugar will improve the color and help it to set."

"You seem to know a great deal about this," she said, watching him squeeze half a lemon over a bowl containing a thick, dark paste.

He sprinkled sugar over it and stirred the lot with a spoon. "I've seen it done a few hundred times," he said. "When Priya was to dance, she generally painted her hands and feet. I never paid any mind to the process, though."

"She was your mistress?" Mira loathed the woman for no accountable reason. "You must be sorry to have left her."

"She left me," he said. "And who could blame her? But she has no place here, Miranda. I only thought of her because of the henna. That's what it's called in English, the paste, and this morning, Nageena Kaur gave me a lesson in how to finish blending it and how to apply it. She also sketched patterns for me to follow. You should be warned that I have no skill at this sort of thing, as anyone who has seen my efforts to carve wood will testify."

Again, that slender current of uncertainty beneath the usual confidence in his voice. She wasn't even sure it was there, or if she was interpreting it correctly. But she felt somehow that she was learning to tune herself to him, the way, long ago, she had tuned the strings of her lute to one another. "It will be . . . fine." *Half-wit!* But what else could she say?

"Probably not. The dye will soon fade, though, and in the interim, no one will see the damage. Shall we start with your right hand? It will help a great deal,

Miranda, if you hold perfectly still." He draped a towel over his lap. "Place the hand here, on my knee."

Each time he touched her, and each time she found the courage to touch him, she was sure she could not bear it. Her throat tightened, her pulse raced, her mind went blank with terror. And then, nothing intolerable happened.

Something much worse than intolerable happened.

She wanted to touch him, or be touched by him, again.

Except that she couldn't possibly want any such thing.

He spread a sheet of paper inscribed with drawings beside him on the table, dipped one of the wooden wands into the paste, and bent his head over her hand. A swatch of black hair, thick and shiny, fell across his forehead.

With a tentative stroke, he swabbed a line of paste on the back of her hand. Dipped, painted, dipped, painted. She couldn't see the paper well enough to make out what he was copying, and from the streaks on her hand, it could have been anything from an escutcheon to a plate of mackerel.

She watched him instead. The chiseled lines of his face. The bronzed skin. The nose that must have once been broken. The long dark lashes, longer and darker than her own kohl-blackened lashes. The beat of a pulse on his jaw. The strong neck. The ferocity of his concentration.

The air was heavy with fragrances—lemon and smoke, cloves and coffee, soap and roses and melting wax. She closed her eyes, letting the sensations wash over her. Heat emanating from candle flames. Hard male bone and muscle where her palm rested. The light scratch of wood on her hand, the sound of his breathing, the beat of her aching heart.

He'd moved to her fingers now, narrow curving lines from the feel of them, and small images set along them like jewels on a bracelet. She understood, for the first time in her life, how a man's touch on one innocent part of her body could echo on her throat, at the tips of her breasts, on her thighs. And between them.

No!

Her eyes flew open. She looked down at his hand. It was so dark, so large and rough, with a hint of black hair where his white sleeve met his wrist. And it wasn't touching her at all. Only the wand met her skin, creating another tiny leaf on the vine that snaked down her forefinger.

She released her drawn-in breath. It was lovely, what he had done. Delicate as tracery in a stained-glass window. Vines trailed down all her fingers, and at the back of her hand, a starburst of a flower.

"That's it, then," he said, setting the wand on a saucer. "Are you out of patience, or shall I do your other hand?"

Pride demanded she thank him politely and take her leave, but she could not have moved if elephants were charging in her direction. "It's beautiful. What is the flower?"

"A lotus. The Buddha sits on a lotus, which is a symbol of enlightenment. Hari would approve." A hesitation. "Do you wish to continue?"

In response, she removed her painted hand from his knee and replaced it with her other hand. He shifted his position then, putting him nearly side by side with her, and this time he began with her fingers. More vines, she thought at first, but these bloomed with small flowers.

"Look away," he said when he got to the plane of her hand. "The centerpiece is a surprise."

She closed her eyes instead, drifting again into the world of pure sensation, except this time his shoulder was touching her shoulder and the scent of him was strong in her nostrils. No enlightenment for her, she thought. No abandonment of earthly pains and desires. She was only just beginning to understand the nature of desire. And as it coiled around her and tightened its grip, she knew there would never be, for her, an end to pain

But for now she drifted like a feather on the wind or a bird riding a current of air, more contented than she could remember being in a long, long while.

At some time, when she had lost herself in a fantasy that she would never admit to herself she had enjoyed, his voice called her back to where he really was, seated beside her. Not where he had been just seconds earlier, in her volcanic imagination. She'd no idea, until it manifested itself, that she even had the capacity to imagine such a scene.

He must have noticed the change in her. The fluttering pulse, the flaming cheeks, the moisture on her forehead. Michael Keynes missed nothing, damn him. He seemed to be waiting for her to come to herself again.

Her palm was still resting on his. She looked down, saw the picture he'd dyed on the back of her hand, and after a gasp, broke into laughter.

Three wavy lines for the river. And coiled on top, with a smug look on its pointy face, an impertinent snake.

"But where's the camel?" she asked when she could speak.

"Here, and there, and everywhere. You are the camel. You are the hand under the water, under the land, supporting all that lives on the earth."

"How very lyrical of you." She wanted to laugh and weep, all at the same time, which must be why she continued to fight him.

"Or I couldn't draw a camel. You can scrub it all away, Miranda. Nearly all, because a little of the stain will remain for a few days. Alternately, you can let it dry for an hour or two before the wedding supper and be decorated for a longer time. Do as you like. And because of your gloves, I won't know what you decided, nor would I care in either case."

But . . . she wanted him to notice and care. Except . . . she didn't. She was losing herself, the core of herself, in his kindness, and she resented him for it.

Except . . . she didn't.

She resented herself for needing his comfort and yielding to the cloak of safety he wrapped around her. She had stayed strong for such a long time that strength had become all she was. He made her feel weak. Or perhaps she *was* weak, and he had done no more than make her realize it.

She rose, and put her hands together beneath her chin, and bowed. "Thank you," she said, meeting his upturned gaze. "Whatever becomes of us in the future, Syr, I shall never forget this night."

Chapter 26

The summons came with bells and cymbals and laughter. A tidal wave of women and children swept Mira up, bore her into the courtyard, and dropped her off just outside the open gate. Arcing on either side of her like wings, they left her to wait, in a circle marked out with salt, for the coming of her bridegroom.

The night sky, clear and cold, blazed with stars and a crescent moon. Orion ruled the heavens, Orion the Hunter, putting her in mind of what the Beast had said of his brother. "Michael is a hunter as well."

And so he was. A good one, too. By his arrangement, the prey of the evening was standing right here at the gate, staked like a chained goat for him to pounce on.

I want you under me, open to me. Why could she not put those words, that image, from her mind?

In the distance, light bloomed on the hillside. Moments later, it illuminated horses and riders and the men running alongside, bearing torches. Boys leaping and dancing like fauns. She heard drums and flutes. Male voices raised in rough-sounding songs punctuated with laughter.

As the procession drew closer, the riders peeled

neatly off, adding their half-circle to the one formed by the women. And into the center, prancing like a show horse, came a splendid white steed caparisoned in red and silver with bells on its halter. The rider, a masterful black-haired man, sat at ease in the high-pommeled saddle.

She could not have moved if her life depended on it, which it probably did. A duke's prize, less reluctant than she ought to be, she stood alone before the man who had laid before her a frightful dilemma.

He would take her in marriage, or he would die for her.

What impoverished, despoiled scholar's daughter had ever before been offered such a choice? And she had nothing to offer him in return. *Nothing*. Not even herself, because she had been taken from herself a long time ago. No man could want what was left of her—a husk of ice and at its core, a bitter heart.

But he, unaccountably, did want her. Had gone to impossible lengths to acquire her. She might at least fashion for him a smile.

She did, and got in return a smile that curled the toes in her embroidered felt slippers. Then he was off the horse in a liquid motion and crossing to her with arms extended. What he said, not in English, must have been part of the ritual. There was an answer from the crowd, another pronouncement—firm and possessive—from him, and a shout of joy in return.

"You have come to claim me, I gather," she said, not expecting him to hear her in the clamor. But his eyes flashed with amusement at her remark, and in spite of the continuing noise, it suddenly seemed to her they were alone together.

"The Punjabis make much ado about arrivals and departures," he said. "Our send-off will be nearly as riotous, if only because most of them will be drunk." His eyes softened. "Is this a great ordeal for you?"

She felt foolish then, and mean-spirited. "No. It's quite wonderful, actually, although it should be happening for someone else."

"But it's for us," he said, offering her his arm. "And they do love a party. Let's repay them by enjoying it."

When she slid her arm around his, he glanced down at the hand resting on his forearm. Went still. She put her other hand on his wrist so he could see the whole of her offering to him. On her cold white hands, the henna vines and flowers he'd painted, the lotus and the river and the snake, shone rust colored in the torchlight.

He looked over at her. Their gazes locked. She experienced a communion with him at that moment beyond any she'd ever experienced, even with her father, who communicated to her mostly with his eyes.

This was different. Physical. A look that became a touch that became an act of—

She didn't know what. Not love. Not honesty. A gift from her to him, perhaps, and his acceptance of it, but more than that. He understood, as no one else could understand, what it had cost her to expose her webbed fingers to so many people.

Birindar Singh and his wife came forward then, their arms full of hothouse flowers—orange and red and white—that had been strung into garlands. Birindar draped one around her neck, and Nageena did the same for Syr. Then the celebration moved inside to the largest room in the house, rectangular in shape and lined with long, low tables. There were cushions for the guests to sit on, but otherwise the polished wooden floor was bare. Birindar led the wedding party—bride and groom, Hari Singh and Mira's father, Nageena Kaur and her newly wed daughter and son-in-law—to a table elevated on a platform.

She was to be on exhibit, Mira understood, glad of the salwar trousers when she settled on the plump cushion and arranged her legs. Laughter and chatter filled the room as the others arrived and took their places. The children, all but the very youngest, had a noisy table of their own, and a pair of well-behaved dogs began to prowl the room, alert for a handout.

The feast arrived in waves, platters appearing and vanishing as if by magic, but nothing was offered directly to her. Syr accepted a little of everything until his plate was piled high with exotic, colorful, mostly unidentifiable foods. "I am to serve you," he said. "With my fingers."

She became glad of the bowl filled with rosewater by his plate. "Is that necessary?"

"It symbolizes my servitude to you, which comes to a resounding halt after the marriage. From then on, you are expected to provide food for me, not necessarily by your own hand."

"Just as well, then. You'd starve." She accepted an olive and chewed it thoughtfully. "I thought men and women were equal here."

"In many ways, yes, because they are of the Sikh faith and tradition. But the men and women have different tasks and responsibilities. Also, some customs are passed down through families, and this ceremonial feeding is one of them. Hari spent an hour lecturing me on proper deportment so that I wouldn't embarrass him. He hasn't said so, but I think he means to join Birindar's clan by way of the doe-eyed beauty sitting at two o'clock."

She looked in that direction and saw a girl with her gaze fixed about where Hari was seated. Love was in the air, it seemed . . . except for the air surrounding the bride and groom.

Syr went on feeding her, selecting morsels, telling her what the dish was called and what it contained, giving her small bites and not many of them. His words sounded like music—*mah ki dal, sarson ka saag, roghan josh, makhee ki roti*. She was too apprehensive to enjoy them, and he seemed more interested in his brandy glass, kept filled by one of the men, than the supper.

"Am I supposed to do anything for you?" she asked at one point.

"Not now." He waggled his brows. "You are supposed to be saving your strength for the wedding night."

Flushing hotly, she turned her attention to another platform where musicians were beginning to take their places and tune their instruments. She saw drums and flutes, instruments with one string and instruments with many strings, earthenware vessels, wooden clappers with bells on them, and lots of happy faces.

Platters and dishes began to disappear, to be replaced with saucers of nuts and candied fruits and honeyed cakes. Syr's brandy remained, of course, and from the corners of her eyes she watched his large hand on the glass, remembering the Mehndi painting, imagining his hands elsewhere on her body. Knowing that if he tried to put them there, she would draw out her dagger—now sheathed at her waist—and use it.

She wanted, and she could not accept. That's how it was for her, how it always would be.

To her left, Birindar stood and raised his hands. Immediately all voices stilled. He spoke a few words of welcome in his own language, repeated them in English for her sake, and asked Hari Singh to lead the company in a toast to the bride and groom.

"Here it comes," muttered Syr, reaching for his glass. "Another bloody Buddha sermon."

And it was, but she found it beautiful as Hari, in his deep, resonant voice, recounted the tale of a wedding to which the Lord Buddha was invited. As the guest of honor, he asked the family to go into the streets and welcome anyone who wished to join the celebration. There wasn't food and drink enough for all who came, yet everyone ate and drank to the full, and always there was more.

Hari had moved to the center of the room and stood facing her and the man beside her, who had put down his glass to listen respectfully. "And to the bride and the groom," Hari said, "the Lord Buddha gave his blessing and these words:

" 'A mortal man can imagine no greater happiness than the bond of marriage that ties together two loving hearts. Be you married unto the truth.

" 'For the husband who loves his wife and desires an everlasting union must be faithful to her, and be to her like truth itself, so that she may rely on him and revere him and minister to him.

" 'And the wife who loves her husband and desires a union that shall be everlasting must be faithful to him so as to be like truth itself, so that he may place his trust in her, and for all his life, he will provide for her.'

"So said the Lord Buddha." Putting his hands together beneath his bearded chin, Hari bowed, and the other men stood and bowed as well. The silence that followed, though brief, carried prayers and blessings.

Then Birindar called on Syr, who uncoiled himself, offered a hand to raise up his bride, and spoke a few sentences in what she presumed to be Punjabi. Laughter followed. He spoke again, and the room rang with laughter and cheering.

"What did you say to them?" she demanded as he helped her resettle on the cushions.

"That your beauty was matched only by your obstinacy, and your intelligence far outmatched by your reluctance to obey me. But that you would be tamed, in the way a man tames his woman in the bedchamber, and that I expected you to become before very long a humble and dutiful wife."

"Rubbish!" She gave a short laugh, stopped, and looked over at him. "You didn't *really* say that. Did you?"

He grinned. "Pay attention now. The children are about to sing."

And they were, a chorus of about fifteen boys and

girls, with the younger ones tending to totter off in the direction of whatever got their attention. A little boy broke loose to chase after one of the dogs, and another stood crying for no perceptible reason. But they sang so beautifully that Mira wanted to cry as well, even though she'd no idea what their songs meant. When they finished, to loud applause and little parcels of sweets tied up with ribbons, the smallest of them were led off by their mothers.

Next the women danced, elegant and fierce as they moved to the beat of a drum, and the rhythm of their sandals on the bare floor, and the clapping of their hands.

"The *gidda*," Syr told her. It was easy to think of him as the Tiger tonight. Impossible to think of him as anything else. "When the women dance, they tell a story in pantomime. This one is about a put-upon wife who teaches her loutish husband how to behave."

Then came a dance between two men carrying staves, which they tapped together in what looked like a ritual joust. "The *dankara*," he said, "always part of a wedding celebration. I've never been sure why. Are you enjoying yourself?"

She was. The excitement carried her back to a time when she had been fearless and exuberant, when new experiences made every day an adventure. It was the life she had wanted to lead, filled with challenges and discoveries and passion. But she'd been diverted, and after that, her adventures were confined to the practical. Her body existed to work. She lived only in her mind, and in the echo of her dreams.

Until this man, and this night. Nothing awful could happen while she sat quietly and pretended to be a part of this. No one would know how much it meant to her, or detect the moment when she sealed it away in the corner of herself where she kept her few happy memories. She would revisit this night many, many times in the years ahead.

The men were on their feet now, and the energy

mounted with every beat of the dhol drum. The other musicians played from their platform, but the drummer with his two sticks and the dhol suspended over his shoulders with a leather harness had moved to the center of the floor. The men, about twenty of them, young and old, danced in a circle around him.

"Bhangra." Syr was smiling, vibrating with the drum. "It's going to get wild now."

At first, it didn't seem so. The tempo was slow, the men graceful and precise, beating the rhythm with their feet. But almost imperceptibly, the tempo began to gather speed. Their arms went up, bent at the elbows, and their hands were lifted, fingers splayed. Always the circle moved, but now the men began revolving individually, and jumping, and landing in the position of a man on horseback.

Tongs and flutes and hands beating on earthenware pots. Women clapping, their bangles clicking and jingling. *"Haripa!"* the men shouted. *"Balle! Balle!"*

"What does that mean?" she asked, not expecting to be heard.

He turned immediately to her. "Something like 'hurrah.' Or did you mean the *bhangra?* It used to be a harvest dance. Now it's—uh, oh."

She looked up to see what had caught his attention. Four men had broken from the circle and, calling to him in Punjabi, appeared to be summoning him to the dance.

"I'm expected to show off for you," he said, removing his garland as he rose and dropping it onto her lap. "Try not to laugh."

He sprang over the table, landing in front of the men, and they led him into the circle. All the men were displaying for their ladies, bending and straightening, hopping on one leg as they whirled, sometimes dropping into a crouch and extending one leg after the other so that it seemed to her no part of their bodies touched the ground.

She was breathing heavily, her blood pounding with the dhol, its rhythm a frenzy now. Men were leaping onto other men's shoulders, keeping a precarious balance as the fellows beneath them jumped and revolved and pretended to try and dislodge their burdens.

But she could scarcely pay them any mind, her gaze fixed on the man whose body flowed with athletic control through the exuberant dance. A stallion among stallions, virile and confident, he was laughing as the circle whirled with him and around him like a galaxy of stars.

"Balle, Syr!" they called. *"Balle, Syr!"*

Everyone was standing now. She was standing too, and clapping her hands, and hadn't even known it. She could feel the climax approaching, the great shout of the drum and the clamor of the instruments rushing to their jubilant peak.

The circle broke at one side. Two men, crouching, joined hands as if to vault someone onto a horse. Then Syr came at them in a run, one foot finding its target, and the men threw him into the air. He spun, two backward flips that had to be impossible, and landed the other side of the room. His knees bent to take the jolt. His arms went up in good-humored triumph.

The women made a high-pitched noise in the backs of their throats. The men, sweating and panting, clustered around him, pumping his hand. He said something that made them all laugh. They followed him as he moved from table to table, greeting the ladies, pausing to speak to each one. Bidding them farewell, she knew. It was nearly time for the wedding.

Mira, dazed, went to her father's side. His eyes smiled at her. "It was wonderful, wasn't it?" she said. His finger made a "yes."

Shortly after, Hari came up to her. She realized he had not been in the dance, or even in the room since she could remember. Nageena Kaur was gone as well.

"The reverend's vehicle is approaching, *memsahib*. Will you come to change clothing now?"

"Of course." She found Syr, his back to her as he hunkered down in a ring of children, and understood that she would not see him again until they stood together and made their vows.

And then he took a small girl up into his arms, and Mira's eyes burned with sadness for him.

No children for you, Michael Keynes. Not if you marry me.

Mira, wearing a dark blue woolen dress, gloves, and her half boots for traveling, arrived with her father at the parlor door just as her bridegroom was coming down the passageway from the opposite direction. He'd changed into the garments made for him that day by a local tailor, black and simply cut and not a very good fit. He had washed his hair, which lay sleek and glossy on his head, the drying ends beginning to fluff out at his collar. She thought it rather endearing, almost boyish, until he came close enough for her to see his eyes.

Nothing boyish there, nothing endearing. She saw only determination, and possessiveness, and a touch of triumph. Or perhaps she only fancied seeing them, because there was never anything to be read in the eyes of a Keynes, not for certain.

To her surprise, he went immediately to the foot of her father's chair and dropped onto one knee, putting the two men at eye level. "Sir, I owe you an apology. In a short time I shall wed your daughter, and I have never thought to ask your permission to do so. Nothing will change, I'm afraid, if you deny it. But I should like to know if you can accept this arrangement, and me as your son-in-law."

Mira already knew the answer. Her father was over the moon at seeing her married at all, and he'd become fond—*fond!*—of this predatory male. "He's not losing a daughter," she said. "He's gaining a chess opponent. Shall we get on with it, Your Grace?"

"Is she always like this?" he asked her father.

The finger waved a treasonous "yes."

So they went into the parlor, which was the same one where she'd negotiated this marriage of *his* convenience less than twenty-four hours earlier. It was ablaze with light from what must have been hundreds of candles, and perfumed with vases overflowing with flowers. The hothouse must be empty of blossoms now.

Clumped around a table in front of the fireplace were four men and two women, all with glasses of wine in their hands and nervous expressions on their faces.

Michael Keynes, direct as always, went up to them and addressed a pigeon-shaped man with a neck that overflowed his starched collar like a pink ruff. "Thank you," he said, the tone of a duke like steel beneath his words, "for coming out on this cold night so that my bride's father could witness her marriage. Mr. Holcombe, may I present the Reverend Filbert? I shall leave it to him to introduce his companions."

The vicar had brought along his rail-thin wife, the parish clerk, the church organist, and two members of the choir, all of them warily eying Hari Singh, who had just entered the room and taken a position by the door. *Heathen,* their expressions said. *Extremely large heathen.*

"William," said the wife. "You have something to say to the duke."

"Er, yes. That is, Your Grace, my Marigold has brought to my attention the impropriety . . . That is, I ought not to have implied—not that I *meant* it, you understand—that an offering to the church would be appropriate due to the, er, unusual circumstances of this marriage. Of me conducting it, that is."

"What he means," put in Marigold Filbert, "is that extortion is not the province of a man of God. He will be pleased to marry you and your lady, and there's an end to it."

"But I've no objection, madam, to our agreement."

"You are missing the point," Mira said. "There is no *prior* agreement."

"Ah. But afterward, he might do me the honor of accepting a tenor bell for the steeple, repairs to the roof, and new carpets for the rectory. Do I have it right?"

"And curtains," Mira said.

"I forgot the curtains. Perhaps, Reverend Filbert, we should rely on the ladies to work this out between them. In the meantime, shall we proceed with the marriage?"

They moved to a stand of floor candelabra and took their places in front of the vicar, whose hands trembled as he opened his prayer book. Then, her bridegroom tall and solemn to her right and her father's chair drawn up to her left, she prepared herself to give her life away.

She had heard the words before, when neighbors were married in the little church near her home. They were beautiful words, most of them, and until now, they had never caused her pain.

But when the reverend began to enumerate the purposes for which God had ordained marriage, she was overwhelmed with guilt. How could she be standing here, prepared to take vows she did not mean to keep?

"First, it was ordained for the procreation of children, to be brought up in the fear and nurture of the Lord, and to the praise of his holy name."

Must she try, then? Whatever the cost, despite their agreement, was she obligated by divine ordinance to accept her husband's seed? Michael Keynes had permitted her to set boundaries, although he'd warned her he would likely try to cross them. But there was no negotiating with God, not when taking a solemn vow.

"It was ordained for a remedy against sin, and to avoid fornication; that such persons as have not the gift of continency might marry, and keep themselves undefiled members of Christ's body."

She strongly suspected that Michael Keynes lacked the gift of continency. To an extreme. And if she did not accept him into her body, he would go elsewhere and . . . and *fornicate*. Just thinking of it set her neck and her cheeks on fire.

She had not, until this moment, realized how much of the marriage ceremony was devoted to carnal matters.

There were more words from the vicar, which she scarcely heeded until he seemed to be looking directly into her deceitful eyes.

"I require and charge you both, as ye will answer at the dreadful day of judgment when the secrets of all hearts shall be disclosed, that if either of you know any impediment, why ye may not be lawfully joined together in matrimony, ye do now confess it. For be ye well assured, that so many as are coupled together otherwise than God's word doth allow are not joined together by God; neither is their matrimony lawful."

She ought to speak. She knew of impediments. She *was* an impediment. This marriage was not according to God's word, which meant it could not be lawful. She stared back at the vicar, ice clogging her throat, and said nothing.

More words floated past her on a cloud of guilt and shame.

Then the vicar's gaze shifted to the groom, and she drew her first breath in a considerable time.

She heard a firm "I will" from the duke, and wondered what he had just promised. Her knees shook.

She felt light-headed and wished he had not let go of her arm.

". . . to live together after God's ordinance in the holy estate of matrimony? Wilt thou obey him, and serve him, love, honor, and keep him in sickness and in health; and, forsaking all others, keep thee only unto him, so long as ye both shall live?" He was looking at her again, a little impatiently.

"I w-will," she murmured.

More words, the vicar's and her bridegroom's and her own. "Better or worse." "To love and to cherish." "To obey." "And thereto I plight thee my troth." She stumbled along as best she could, expecting lightning to strike her down for the hypocrisy of it all.

Michael Keynes was holding her hand. She hadn't even noticed when he took it, her right hand into his. Not until he let it go and placed something on the closed prayer book. Her eyes were swimming with tears of remorse. Against the black leather, a glimmer of gold.

Dear God, a ring. And she without a ring finger to put it on.

Then her left hand was lifted, and she gazed up helplessly into his transparent eyes.

"I wasn't sure which you'd prefer," he said quietly, "so I brought two. They'll not fit well over your gloves, but take them now and decide later. Perhaps you'll want them both."

And as he spoke, echoing the vicar's words with one correction, he slipped bands of gold over her little finger and over her forefinger. "With these rings I thee wed, with my body I thee worship, and with all my worldly goods I thee endow."

After that, she felt as if someone else inhabited her flesh. Another person wandered through the last part of the ceremony, made polite remarks to the guests who paid her compliments and conveyed their good wishes. She tasted wine. Her husband—her *husband!*—was a granite pillar at her side. She clung to him without touching him, requiring his support and feeling it like invisible girders holding her erect. Keeping her moving where she was supposed to move.

At some point, she promised Marigold Filbert a stained-glass window for the church. She spoke to her father, and kissed his cheek, and bade him farewell. There was a cloak around her shoulders, a fur-lined hood over her head. She was outside, surrounded by people, and saying her thanks to Birindar Singh and Nageena Kaur. A carriage had pulled into the courtyard. Music. Drums. Singing. Someone held out a bowl. A voice spoke into her ear.

"Take rice in both hands," her husband said, "and toss it over your shoulders. It is meant to bring prosperity to those you are leaving behind, and to the new family you will create."

She did, and looked back through a sheen of tears at her father's glowing face. His happiness gave her the strength to enter the carriage and not to flinch when the tiger she had wed climbed up and settled beside her.

"Don't worry," he said as the coach began to move. "I didn't mean any of those vows either."

But she looked down at the two rings on her left hand and knew he *had* meant them. And nothing in her life, not even the worst thing that had ever happened to her, frightened her more than what this man offered to her now.

Chapter 27

Word got around fast, Michael was thinking as he skimmed the message just delivered to him by one of Beata's servants. While not quite a summons, the letter requesting the Duke of Tallant's presence at Number Four, Bow Street, referred to "matters of extreme urgency."

Barely eight in the morning, only a few hours after their arrival at Palazzo Neri, and already the chief magistrate knew they were there. Well, knew *he* was there. Sir Richard had not mentioned Her Grace, the Duchess of Tallant.

Since he'd meant to call at Bow Street anyway, he sent the servant off with a note advising Sir Richard to make himself available at ten o'clock, rapped on the door to awaken his bride, who had spent a chaste night in what used to be his bed, and went back to Hari's room to finish shaving.

The bride emerged an hour later, austere in a high-necked black dress. "We are officially in mourning for your brother," she said when he raised a brow.

"Speak for yourself, Duchess. Breakfast is on its way, and the carriage will be here in half an hour. We have an appointment with your old friend the magistrate."

He left then, to confer with Hari and, briefly, with the manager of Beata's stable, returning in time to escort a wintry Miranda to the carriage.

"It's as well you have become a duke," she said. "You aren't used to answering to anyone, are you?"

"Not for the last decade or so. When you're running a band of mercenaries, most of them outlaws, command must be absolute. I gave the orders, they obeyed them. And while they wouldn't admit it, they preferred it that way."

"I'm sure."

She had withdrawn again, which did not greatly surprise him. From the moment they'd arrived in London, he had sensed her fear of what lay ahead of them. And for Miranda, fear translated into antagonism. "I'll come about," he said, trying not to sound overly patronizing. "Give me a little time."

"Humph."

Which took care of the conversation until they reached Bow Street, leaving him free to make even more plans she wasn't going to like. And to mentally list the things he did intend to discuss with her, because they concerned the females he'd inherited from his brother. Norah, Corinna, and Catherine. He didn't know how to deal with any one of them, let alone all three. And when they got together with his wife and ganged up on him, as they were bound to do, he wouldn't have a snowflake's chance in hell.

They arrived at Bow Street, the wall still up between them. His duchess, who had permitted him to take her arm, was impressively disdainful when they were ushered into the office of the chief magistrate. The last time she'd been here, he remembered, she was just shy of being a prisoner and not at all certain she would ever walk free again.

Sir Richard, florid faced and pompous, rose when they entered, as did the gentleman who had been seated to one side of the massive oak desk. Varden.

They both bowed while Michael gritted his teeth and Miranda edged the slightest bit closer to him, as if closing ranks.

He would have liked to keep her there, but he'd cobbled together enough manners to guide her to a chair and help her settle on it. When a clerk sprang from his writing table to pull over another chair, Michael waved him off. For this encounter with two men who'd as soon see him at the end of a rope, he meant to take control of the room from the start.

"Well?" he said, roaming to a small window and planting himself in front of it, looking out. "You sent the invitation. Why am I here?"

Someone cleared his throat.

"It concerns the murder of your brother, of course," said the magistrate, his voice bristling with frustration. "The details are not fit for a young lady to hear."

"You mean *this* young lady?" Michael turned and gestured to Miranda. "The same one you interrogated—no, *bullied*—only a few days ago? I expect she can stand up to whatever you have to tell me now." His gaze flicked over to Varden, who stood stone-faced a little behind the magistrate's chair. "But before we get started, gentlemen, I expect I should inform you that Miranda Holcombe has done me the honor of becoming my wife."

Varden's stony expression never altered, but his eyes blazed with a mix of fury and sorrow that might have roused Michael's sympathy if he hadn't hated the man. At the same time, he understood how Varden must feel to have lost Miranda, and worse, to have lost her to his greatest enemy.

Michael had felt much the same when he offered to arrange her marriage to Varden, certain she would prefer the Archangel to the Devil's whelp. In agony he had waited for her inevitable rejection. But she hadn't rejected him, at least for the purposes of a celibate marriage of convenience, and he still could not take it in. She had made the wrong choice. She was smarter than that. She ought to have known better.

"Have you all lost your wits and your tongues?" said the Duchess of Tallant, breaking into the silence like an ice pick. "What have you to tell us about my brother-in-law's murder?"

"Ah, yes." Sir Richard flipped open a leather-backed folder. "We have received the examiner's report. It appears the late duke did not, in fact, succumb to a blade through his heart. There *was* one, of course, but the stabbing occurred at some time after his death. No blood came out of him from that wound, you see, although to be sure there was blood smeared over his coat and shirt. Blood was found on his chest as well. A clever ruse, but our examiner is that much more clever. He determined that the blood was applied later, since none of it was found where it most ought to be, on the minute portion of the blade that failed to penetrate the duke's chest."

Michael started fitting together the pieces of the puzzle. "What killed him, then?"

"Poison." This from Varden, who had apparently grown tired of playing wall ornament. "A wineglass was found beside his desk. It was probably half full when it landed, given the stains on the carpet. From what we can tell, he lurched to his feet, toppling the glass in the process, and came around the desk, aiming himself for the door. Near the corner of the desk he tripped and stumbled in the direction of the fireplace. His head struck the corner of the mantelpiece as he fell onto the hearth. Facedown, because his nose was broken and there were marks on his chin and fore-head. Later, he was turned onto his back and the knife inserted into his heart."

"What kind of poison?"

A pause. "We're not sure. The decanter was only half full, and the duke smelled heavily of wine, although none had been spilled on him. He must have drunk rather a lot before succumbing. We assume, therefore, a diluted solution in the wine or a slow-acting poison, but we have not determined its nature or source. The wine was tested by . . . by the usual method—" Varden glanced over at Miranda. "The results indicated a length of time until a toxic accumulation in the system, then a sudden and deadly consequence."

Michael had begun to pace the room. "But why stage a fake murder scene by stabbing him? To fuddle up the time of death and establish an alibi?"

"I'm more inclined to think he was concealing the motive. If we had put down the killing to a vengeful female with cause to despise Tallant—begging your pardon, Your Grace, but we nearly did so—then we might not inquire too deeply into other possible reasons for the crime."

"If that theory is correct, the murderer had to know the dagger belonged to my wife."

Varden's gaze went to Miranda. "You told us that the weapon in question was taken from you by the duke, and several others of similar design were found when we searched your cottage. Is it widely known you possessed them?"

"I shouldn't think so."

"Beata knew," Michael said. "About the one my brother snatched, at any rate. It's likely that he boasted of it, or made a jest, but I'll ask the signora how she came by the story. I also want a copy of the examiner's report."

Varden and Sir Richard exchanged glances. "That can be arranged," Sir Richard said distastefully. "But you cannot expect to be made privy to details of our investigation, given that you have impeded our inquiries by falsely confessing to the murder. I should like to hear the reason for your inexplicable behavior, Your Grace."

Michael advanced on the desk, pleased to see the magistrate begin to shrink back. "*Inexplicably,* then, it's simple enough. Your errand boys"—a meaningful glance at Varden—"had dragged my betrothed before you to answer for the crime. What else is a gallant swain to do but fling himself between his fair maiden and the reckless arm of the law?"

"We would have arrived at the truth. As you see, we have done so. There was no need for you to interfere with justice."

"What *justice* would that be? You smoked out very little of the truth, from all I can tell. Does Her Grace remain a suspect?"

"It has been ascertained," said Varden as if pronouncing sentence, "that neither of you can have been at Tallant House when the wine was poisoned. Not long after the duke's return, a servant procured a bottle of wine from the cellar, removed the cork, and filled a clean decanter, which he then placed in the study. The duke went there an hour later, about one o'clock. You were well on your way to Kent hours earlier, and the duchess's movements on the day in question have been accounted for. Perhaps she arrived in time to put the knife in him, but she could not have poisoned the wine."

"I might have arranged to have it done," Michael pointed out.

"That possibility remains open, and I would not be displeased to have it proven. But I think it unlikely. You are, by nature, a man who acts directly."

"If it suits me." Michael's attention was diverted by his bride, who had gone stiff. Or perhaps he only sensed her disquiet, because she had not moved, looked no different. She was overset, though, or—more than likely—furious. He was fairly sure he knew why. "Am I free, then, to remove my brother's remains for burial?"

"I have prepared authorization," Sir Richard said. "The papers you requested will be delivered to you when they have been transcribed. There is one more matter to discuss, however. I gather you have not yet called at Tallant House?"

"No. Is there a problem?"

"Yesterday morning, a foreign young man delivered a letter, purportedly from you, instructing the servants to close down the house and enjoy a paid holiday until further notice." He pulled a wrinkled sheet of paper from the folder and held it out.

"I needn't look at it. That's my letter, and those were my instructions."

Sir Richard frowned. "We'd thought it a ruse. Last night, with only a maid and a footman still in residence, two men broke in and ransacked the house."

"Was anyone hurt?" Miranda asked immediately.

"The footman, I'm afraid," said Varden. "He was knocked unconscious, but has recovered and is at home with his family. The maid found a hiding place and remained there until the intruders were gone, at which time she ran outside and located a member of the Watch."

"It might have been a robbery," Sir Richard said, "but I expect otherwise. Although valuables were taken, the men appeared to concentrate on places where papers and records would be stored. They found a wall safe behind a picture frame and blew it open with some sort of explosive. More to the point, when the duke's study was examined after the murder, virtually no papers or ledgers were found in his desk or on the shelves, and an empty lockbox lay open on the floor. I believe the murder and the robbery are connected."

The man wasn't entirely a fool, then. "So do I," Michael said. "I want, now, the direction of the footman and the maid. By nine of the morning tomorrow,

I want every other piece of information you have, including whatever you learned from searching the house."

"We intend to pursue the investigation," Varden said.

"Meaning I should keep my nose out of it? Don't count on that. I intend to protect my wife from your inept inquisitions, and to reward whoever did me the kindness of killing my brother." Michael held out a hand. "Your Grace?"

Miranda put her hand on his, rose gracefully, and smiled at the chief magistrate. "You were doing your duty, I know, to interrogate me. And you, Lord Varden, have been of service to us all. Thank you."

The tug on his hand told Michael she was ready to go, and he let himself be taken outside to where the carriage pulled up only moments after they appeared. He was beginning to appreciate the convenience of his elevated position. The young clerk arrived as he was handing Miranda into the coach. He took the folder the clerk had brought him, extracted the papers with the information he wanted, gave the rest to his wife, and closed the paneled door.

Miranda's face immediately appeared at the window. "Where are you going?" she demanded, blazing with all the anger she had been concealing for the past half hour.

From the safety of the pavement, he grinned at her. "Duchess, I'd take you with me, but I have a lot to do in a short time and will move faster on my own. I'll tell you all about it later, just before you tear into me."

Chapter 28

The tearing into began shortly after Michael's return to the Palazzo.

Informed by a footman that Her Grace could be found in the Sala Fiorentina, he'd crept the opposite direction and taken refuge in the library, meaning to evaluate what he had learned that afternoon and come to several decisions he'd been postponing. But with the uncanny way she had of locating him, she arrived moments after he did and towed him around lines of bookcases and screens to a narrow room he'd never seen before. Outside a large window, trees cast their long shadows over the winter grass. Purple clouds scudded across the darkening sky.

"One day!" She backed him to a picture-strewn wall and pinned him there with her blue-eyed fury. "A few measly hours! If you hadn't rushed the marriage, if we had waited just a little longer, we would not be . . . be—"

"Stuck with each other?"

Her scowl told him what she thought of his attempt to lighten the situation. "Precisely that. Did you know about the poison? That we were certain to be exonerated?"

"No on both counts. But I don't blame you for being suspicious."

"I should think not. And now that our sole reason for being *stuck* has vaporized, how do we extricate ourselves? It's been only sixteen hours. Would Reverend Filbert and the witnesses agree to forget the wedding ever happened? Perhaps in exchange for . . . Oh, I don't know. New pews?"

"Not likely. They brought the parish register, remember? Our marriage has been duly recorded and we have inscribed our signatures. Considering it's a felony to tamper with the Register of a License of Marriage, and that the punishment is death, I don't expect new pews would turn the trick. Not to mention that Hari and your father wouldn't lie under any circumstance."

"An annulment, then?"

"We've been through all this. There are no grounds."

She whirled, paced for a few moments, and turned back on him. "In that case, Your Precipitate Grace, I want a divorce!"

"Very well."

"You said that you would giv . . . *what*?" She looked as if she'd just run into a wall. "What did you say?"

"If you wish a divorce, I will cooperate. We mustn't appear to be in accord about it, collusion being an impediment, but I expect we can devise a credible scheme. Except for the adultery portion of the entertainment, which you must, I'm afraid, arrange entirely on your own. Try Varden. Since he'll find himself bedding a virgin, *mirabile dictu,* he might even consider making you Lady Archangel. Well, once the scandal has died down, but you won't be wanting to rush into another marriage. Look where the first rush got you."

"*Rush* and *push* are two quite different things. I was pushed. By you."

"Dragged, pushed, coerced. To protect you, there was nothing I would not have done. But your life is no longer in danger, Miranda, and I would not override your wishes for any lesser reason."

"Rubbish. You override them all the time."

"To be perfectly accurate, I ignore them. I am not used to considering what someone else wants, nor have I generally cared. You'd not have put up with that for very long, I am sure, and rightly so. But my behavior is no longer your concern."

"No." Teeth appeared, nibbled at her lower lip, and vanished again. "Not when the marriage is severed. That will take some time, I imagine."

"Oh, yes. But I'll not require you to keep up pretenses in the meantime. In fact, we should separate as soon as possible, to demonstrate that the marriage is insupportable to us both."

She put her hand on the back of a chair. "As you say. Pardon me if I appear to be quarreling with you. I'd not . . . not expected you to be so eager to be rid of me."

"My eagerness is to please you. Only that. My own wishes are irrelevant here."

"That's not fair. Of course they are relevant. If given your choice, what is it you would want?"

"That's easy enough. Easy to answer, at any rate. I'd want to be married to you for all of my life."

"Oh." She flushed. Looked down at her wriggling hands, clasped together but about to fly apart. "I had no idea. Before the wedding, you agreed to a divorce. You just agreed again."

"Because you asked it of me."

"Then . . . well, what if I decide it should not happen right away? That we should wait until the scandal of the murder has died down. Perhaps after your sister-in-law has been settled, and Corinna has found a place for herself, and Catherine as well." Her gaze slid up again, meeting his. "Or must we separate immediately?"

"Not my call, Duchess. This is your game. You set the starting time, and the finish."

"So that if I go wrong, it's all my fault." She resumed her pacing. "I'll think it over. A rash decision got me into this, but from what you have told me, only careful planning will get me out of it. *Us* out of it. Better not to rush into another hasty decision."

"If you say so."

"I don't mean to inconvenience you," she said so earnestly that it tugged at his heart. "You mustn't order your life according to my uncertainties. I understand that gentlemen are . . . that is, they have . . . *needs*. And given the terms we have agreed on for our own mutual . . . lack of . . . Well, naturally, I would expect you to take a mistress."

"Thank you."

She shot him a glare. "Are you being sarcastic?"

"Grateful. Infidelity can be expensive, or so I'm told by straying husbands. Jewelry, carriages, expensive trinkets, and that's just to pacify their wives."

"As if I'd settle for any such thing." She stalked the short distance to the window. "Why will you never deal with me on level ground? You knew from the start that I was spoiling for a row, didn't you? And you have been humoring me all along, haven't you?"

"You don't expect me to answer that, do you?"

She whirled around. "Don't make fun of me. I'm serious about the divorce."

He knew it. The knife twisting in his chest told him so. "I find it hard to come to terms with, that is all. But the divorce will be yours, if I have the power to deliver it, whenever you choose."

"Settled for now, then." She sounded confused. Unhappy. "Tell me what you learned today."

The knife settled in, not moving, not until she resolved to twist it again. He could live with it there, so long as he was permitted to live with her. But he was tired. Had been sleepless or nearly so for days and

nights on end. There was a wingback chair with a
footstool by the window, where the last traces of light
were pale echoes in the sky outside. He went to the
chair and slumped on it, putting his feet up, trying to
order his thoughts.

"What did I learn?" he said. "Not enough. I went
first to see the footman who was attacked at Tallant
House. He has a headache and a lump from the blow,
but he didn't see who struck it. Someone large, he
thinks. When he heard a noise from behind him and
started to turn, he got the impression of a tall figure.
The maid did better. I called on her next, at her sister's home. Perhaps I'd better tell you that after the
other servants departed, she and the footman had remained to enjoy a little privacy. He'd gone downstairs
to fetch something to eat and was accosted on the
way. The girl heard heavy footsteps, knew they
couldn't belong to her barefooted lover, and had the
presence of mind to dive into an armoire. Through
the keyhole she saw two men, but only from midchest
down. Large, the both of them, and one had a slight
limp."

"Not enough information to be useful, then," said
Miranda.

"That depends. She thought their voices sounded
familiar, and one of them had an accent that might
have been Scots or Irish. They didn't speak like gentlemen, was all she could say, and she was fairly sure
she'd heard them speak before."

"A Welsh accent, perhaps?"

He looked up at Miranda, who had seated herself
on the window bench. "Clever girl. The same thugs
Norah described, the ones she and Corinna managed
to elude. It's a good possibility. Jermyn would have
turned them off, or worse, for letting the prisoners
escape. They might have decided to take him down in
return, or they might have found employment with
one of his adversaries."

"If they were looking for something specific," she said, "and if they didn't find it, would they try next at Longview?"

He had already come to these conclusions, but still it felt as if he were trailing several steps behind her. "Perhaps. I wouldn't be too concerned, except that Catherine is there and I don't know how reliable the servants are. Not very, I suspect. There's a Runner in place nearby, and I hired two more this afternoon. They'll be there tonight."

"You should have sent Hari as well."

"Except that he's arranging transportation for Jermyn's body, and a place to store it until I figure out where to dig the hole. And I'm thinking of sending him north to intercept David and the women, except I don't know where they are. Or where I want them to go. Nowhere our large friends can get at them, that's certain. I meant to tell you that the bundle Corinna left in the gardener's shed has been retrieved. Some of Birindar's kinsmen have begun a thorough cleaning of Tallant House, and any trace of her stay will soon be eradicated."

He leaned back his head and let his eyes close. "I'm not sure how to proceed from here," he said after a time. "There are too many things to do all at once. Too many things, I'm afraid, that I haven't taken into account."

"Well, you can't do anything more at the moment," she said in a brisk sort of whisper that made him want to smile, if he could have summoned the energy. And if she would not have taken it as smug and patronizing.

She continued to speak long after he'd lost sense of her words. He heard only the sound of wind over water, of gentle rain on grass, of a bird taking flight.

And then, though he could not be sure of it through the veil of sleep muting his senses, the soft sounds of her departure.

*   *   *

Three hours later, when Mira returned to the library cubbyhole, her husband was exactly where she'd left him and in nearly the same position, except that his eyes were open. So much for her attempt to sneak up on a man who had spent much of his life, Hari once told her, with a price on his head.

He still looked tired, too tired to stir without an immediate threat to confront, his hands limp on the armrests and strands of black hair drifting over his forehead. Black stubble on his chin. Blackness everywhere in the room, save for the one lamp she'd left to burn on the mantelpiece.

The room had gone cold, but she was afire with energy and accomplishment. "I have a plan," she said. "Plans, rather. Do you feel up to discussing them?"

No perceptible reaction.

Finally, "About the divorce?"

"Were you not listening before? I'm speaking of the matters we need to deal with immediately." She lofted the sheaf of papers she was carrying, the ones with all her notes and lists. "For example, I know where you should dig the hole."

His eyes widened. "What is the hour? And where have you been?"

"It's a little after seven," she said, using a tinder stick to light candles and lamps. "I sent a messenger to Helena Pryce, who came here straightaway. There's much to tell you, but we're pressed for time, so I shall summarize the information of most immediate importance."

When there was sufficient light to read by, she sat on a chair across from him. "Your father, purportedly a suicide, could not be buried in hallowed ground, but the rector of a small church not far from Longview fenced a plot outside the cemetery wall and put him there. It's large enough to accommodate your brother as well. I have the direction.

"Next. I wished to send Hari to find the duchess's party and escort them south, but that proves to be unnecessary. Miss Pryce arranged for several body-guards to accompany them from the start—the driver, an armed guard on the coach, and four outriders. The men aren't 'gentry trained,' she told me, but they'll not allow their charges to come to harm."

"A terrifyingly efficient young woman, Miss Pryce. Does she happen to know where they are at the moment?"

"I'm afraid not. It had to seem they were in Scot-land, or perhaps starting on their way back to London, when they got news of the duke's murder. They went north in an unmarked coach and are returning in a fancy one, but it will be a few more days before they can reappear without raising suspicion. Miss Pryce will dispatch messages to the last two posthouses where they are to stay, instructing them to proceed directly to Longview."

At that, he sat up.

"Because we shall be there," she said. "Catherine will have heard of her father's death, and she must be confused and frightened. I think we should leave for your estate first thing in the morning, taking your brother with us for burial. The others can join us there."

"You've decided this, have you?"

"Miss Pryce is arranging for the ducal carriage to pick us up, because we must begin to conduct our-selves according to our rank, and for a cart and driver to transport the coffin. We didn't know precisely where Mr. Singh is to be found, but if you are able to get word to him, perhaps he will oversee that part of the business."

She'd been rushing through this, giving him no time to object or interfere. In fact, most of what she had concluded would be parceled out later, in slow install-ments. As Miss Pryce had advised, "Gentlemen require careful handling. After a limited number of decisions taken without them, they feel compelled to assert their supremacy. Allow them the opportunity to do so in matters of insignificance, and reserve all your patience and tolerance for those things you wish to control."

Having spent most of her life acting hostess for her father and a horde of male guests and hangers-on, Mira already knew how to get men to do as she wished. But Michael Keynes was like no other man she had ever encountered, and while she was plotting how to manipulate him, he generally went ahead and made all the decisions for the both of them.

This time she was turning the tables, using his own tactics against him, and she had no idea how he was going to react. So far he had been mostly speechless, but that was, she suspected, when he was most dangerous.

She risked the first direct look at him since he'd sat up in his chair and appeared to be paying attention. His eyes were bright, his lips moving in an odd way. She thought . . . but no. He could not be trying to contain a laugh.

"Shall I go on?" she said, suddenly unsure of herself.

"By all means."

His voice had been a trifle unsteady. She was reading too much into that. She never knew what to think of him, or what he was thinking. For that matter, in his company she rarely knew what *she* was thinking.

"I have told Beata," she said, "that we shall make our only public appearance in London at her rout this evening, after which we shall withdraw to the country for the duration of the mourning period for your brother. It was not a capricious decision. Our last impression must be favorable, to counter the reputation you have inherited and the one we both gave ourselves in the last few days. Primarily, though, we must build a foundation for the duchess and her daughters, who will one day enter the society your brother withheld from them."

"My best chance of making a favorable appearance," he said, "is not to appear at all."

"But you will, and you'll be properly dressed, and you'll not intimidate people or make sarcastic remarks."

"Very well. And I'll send a message to Hari. What else?"

"You don't mean to object?" She had prepared herself for everything but this . . . this astonishing *capitulation*. "Not even to negotiate?"

"I will if you like. Let me see. One hour playing duke at Beata's party. No longer."

"Three hours."

"Two." He rose, stretched, and grinned at her.

"Is this a trick? You are going to let me direct what we do and when we do it?"

"I'm concerned with results, not with how they are achieved. If a mongoose popped up from the bushes with an answer to a problem, I'd take its advice. So why not yours?"

"A m-mongoose! Of all the . . . Oh." Her cheeks went hot. "You are teasing me."

"A little retribution, on account of you dragging me to Beata's exhibition." He offered his arm. "Come along, Duchess. There's a lot of work to be done if I'm to be made presentable."

Chapter 29

As the crested carriage wound its way into Kent, Mira reflected on what Helena Pryce had said to her the previous afternoon.

"You must decide if there is one thing you want more than all other things, and if it is worth the price you must pay to have it. You must accept that even if you pay that price, you may not get what you wanted. You must risk everything you have, and everything you are, to achieve your goal. If you have considered all this and elect to proceed, you must lay plans, prepare yourself in every way, and take the journey step-by-step."

"Have you done this?" Mira asked.

"Several times." Miss Pryce gave one of her near smiles. "I have achieved all the goals that were achievable, and each, in its way, has prepared me for the last great gamble. As to that, I have not decided whether I shall take it. Do not underestimate the difficulty, Your Grace. To risk everything for what you may never attain should not be lightly undertaken."

"What if you attain it, and you have not chosen wisely?"

"Ah, yes. The greatest reversal of all, to pursue an improvident course because you have been self-deceived. I believe the secret, if there is one, is to ensure that your goal includes the happiness of someone else. Then your own disappointment may be another's fulfillment."

Self-deceived. That word had struck a chord deep inside Mira, beyond the shield of ice she kept between her mind and her feelings. Always, she had assumed she knew herself very well indeed, while everyone else mistook who and what she was. Now she had begun to question all her assumptions. She had lost trust in herself.

Improbably, the disconnection had freed her. Well, to a degree. She was ready to imagine changing, but into what? When her mother died, she had become the image of her mother, managing the household, playing hostess for her father. When he fell ill, she became, in a way, his mother as well. Now, practically overnight, she had become a wife of convenience and a duchess. But who did she *want* to be?

And then she thought of Michael Keynes in the Tower, a man she scarcely knew, taking her place there. She thought of him at Birindar's house, offering marriage to protect her, accepting her terms and her unsatisfactory self, asking nothing in return.

It's not who I am, or what I want to be. It is what I can give that matters. I shall be what I do.

That was what she had concluded at the end of a sleepless night, and she didn't much care if it was the right conclusion. It would at least get her started, and perhaps a more profound truth would disclose itself along the way.

Now, with the better part of a day to spend alone in the carriage, she was examining her bright new goal from every perspective, testing it against her own powers to achieve it.

The prospect was bleak. Thinking about the goal only discouraged her. So she narrowed her vision to what Miss Pryce had recommended—the laying of plans, the preparations, the first steps. With a traveler's writing desk on her lap and a sheet of blank paper waiting for the first note, she took up her pen and wrote *Horse*.

Since her fifteenth birthday, she had not ridden. What had happened to her was not Caliban's fault, of course. She still wondered, on occasion, if he'd found a home, been treated well, gave a whinney for the girl who rode him once and never saw him again. To ride again would be a first step, no great thing except it frightened her. But if she could not overcome this small fear, the later, harder steps would be altogether beyond her reach.

Tallant—she had decided to call him that to help him get used to it—came alongside just then and looked at her through the glass window. She returned a smile and a wave, and watched him canter ahead, the capes on his coat fluttering, the wind sifting through his hair.

Dance, she wrote. Last night at Beata's rout, he had astounded her, and probably himself, by conducting himself with surpassing . . . *dukeness.* She wasn't exactly sure what that was, not having moved in aristocratic circles, but she knew it when she saw it. Last night she'd seen it in him, although even when impeccably groomed, he put one in mind of a jungle cat loosed in a drawing room.

But he had manners when he chose to use them, and she was probably the only one who saw the effort it required to contain his impatience with fools and toadies. When he caught her eye with an I'm-on-my-best-behavior-for-you expression, it felt almost like a caress.

Dance was meant literally, since she didn't know how and neither did he. Persuading him to accept lessons from a dance master was going to be . . . challenging.

But *Dance* stood as well for all she had to learn

about being a duchess, meaning everything there was. She decided on a full page for *Dance*, with room for plenty of subheadings. Perhaps two or three pages.

The Family, she wrote. Her father, of course. She wanted to bring him to Seacrest, and the house must be made ready. She accepted the decline of his health and what lay ahead, but she had not prepared herself to face it.

Norah Keynes and Catherine. Little she could do on their account except discover their wishes and see them carried out. The duke would begrudge them nothing, she was sure.

Corinna. As always when she thought of Cory, guilt wrapped around her throat like fingers, squeezing until she could not breathe.

She leaned her head against the plush leather squabs. So much to learn. So much to do. She felt entirely inadequate. And she hadn't even got to the impossible duties, the ones she dared not put into words, let alone inscribe on paper.

After a time, she rallied her spirits and got back to work, and when she'd run out of paper, she decided that the duke would require several wives to accomplish all the tasks she'd outlined for herself. Just about then, the coach slowed and he drew even with the window. She lowered the pane.

"The driver tells me the road for St. Swithin's is directly ahead. I've no idea how long this will take, but I'm hoping to get it over with tonight. Don't be concerned if we are delayed."

They had agreed his brother's coffin should not be taken to Longview, and last night, he had dispatched a messenger to the rector with his request for immediate interment. That meant she would be required to make her first appearance at the estate alone, but she knew how anxious he was to get the burial done with. "Take care," she said, smiling.

The shadow of apprehension in his eyes vanished.

"You as well, Duchess. See that my instructions have been followed, will you?"

All rooms that bore the stamp—or the stench—of his brother were to be closed off. "I'm sure they have. The staff will wish to make a good impression, and so do I. We shall dust and polish and make ready for the Master of the House."

"Duchesses don't dust," he said, laughing as she had meant him to do. "I'll be there soon, and we can muddle along together."

For Mira, the first hours at Longview passed in a blur. Primarily she was astounded at the size of the estate—the Beast had bought up nearly all the land for miles around, excepting Seacrest—and the sullen resentment of the servants, who proved that some people, even when miserable, dislike change. They were certainly unimpressed by her, for which she could not blame them, but most of their rancor was earmarked for the new duke. Clearly they expected one much like his predecessor, or worse.

Her own preoccupation was with Catherine, a coltish fourteen-year-old with the hair and eyes of a Keynes, and the temperament as well. She wished to be called Cat, demanded to know the whereabouts of her mother and sister, had no interest whatever in her murdered father. She was very like her uncle, Mira decided, especially when she relaxed enough to chatter about her obsession with horses.

She liked archery as well, and was showing Mira the bow she'd carved and primed for herself when the butler, unhappy to be at work after midnight, announced that His Grace had arrived. Catherine went stiff then, and gathered up her bow and arrows and skittered off to a corner.

Mira had sensed his approach for several minutes and looked up as he came into the room, flinging off his hat, greatcoat, and gloves and letting them drop to the floor. She could tell immediately that he'd been drinking.

"Done," he said. "Cost me a new baptismal font and an organ, and I had to help dig the grave myself, but he's planted. Hari said a prayer. I said 'Good riddance.'"

Oh, dear. "We're not alone here," she said before he could go on. "You will wish to make yourself known to your niece."

He swore under his breath, glanced in the direction she had pointed, and gave her a rueful shrug. Then, grim faced, he strode to the far end of the room and halted, hands clasped behind his back. "Lady Catherine. I beg your pardon. This is not how I should have preferred to make your acquaintance."

"I do not expect drawing-room manners," she said, chin lifted. "I have no expectations at all. Well, perhaps one. I have been promised a good riding horse."

He glanced at Mira over his shoulder. "By Her Grace?"

"She described your horse and said you were an excellent judge of quality."

"And by that, you extrapolate that I should select a mount for you? Or am I meant to redeem the poor impression I have made? You should know from the first, young woman, that extortion is wasted on me."

"That's too bad." She flashed a self-mocking grin so very like Michael's grins that Mira nearly laughed. "It was worth a try. But while I have your attention," she added a shade less confidently, "I would very much like to return to school."

"Indeed? Then discuss it with your mother when she arrives. Did you bring that here to shoot me with?"

She lifted the bow and arrows. "I made these myself and brought them to show Aunt Mira . . . Her Grace. In this house, it has always been a good idea to carry a weapon."

"I can quite imagine." He took the bow and ran his fingers over it. "Nice work. I've wanted to carve a bow for myself and haven't come around to it. Perhaps you can help me get started." He handed it back. "As for a horse, you'll need to show me what you can handle. If you rise early enough, I'll introduce you to Loki."

Her eyes shone. "I always rise early, to make up for going to bed late. Good night, Your Grace. And call me Cat, please." She curtsied, after a fashion, and sped from the room.

"There are four other Catherines in her class at St. Bridget's," Mira explained. "She's very like you, don't you think?"

"She's a clever, greedy, impertinent chit." He dropped onto a chair. "I've been at the gatehouse taking a few wee drams with Hamman MacFife, who has been keeping her in his sights. She's more than once led him a chase."

That explained why she had sensed her husband nearby for an hour before he came into the house. "Will you retain him here to watch her?"

"Yes, and to watch out for our elusive friends. Mac-Fife says there's been no sign of two large men, one with a limp, in the area. The Runners I hired yesterday—was it only yesterday?—will start interviewing the locals tomorrow."

"You still think they will come here?"

"I don't know that I ever thought so. But I'll take the necessary precautions, and that includes you and Cat securing an escort before you leave the property. No more excursions like the one that took you alone to Berkeley Square." His gaze fixed on her. "Which, by the way, you have never explained to my satisfaction."

She'd been hoping he'd forget all about it. "I doubt that I can," she said carefully. "I felt . . . summoned there, as if I was supposed to do something, or be

witness to something. The sensation was overwhelm-
ing, and I did not consider resisting it. I thought, to
be honest, that it meant I would encounter the duke
and have an opportunity to kill him. That was my
greatest wish, had been for many years, so perhaps I
was summoning myself." She gave a little laugh. "Do
you believe in mysterious occurrences beyond our own
power to create or understand, but intended to guide
us in some way?"

The immediate "no" she'd expected did not arrive.
He seemed to be looking past her now, his thoughts
elsewhere. "One cannot live in India for any length
of time," he said slowly, "without wondering how it
is so many people credit signs and portents, spiritual
upwellings and otherwordly contacts. If it can be con-
ceived of, someone or other is certain to believe it is
true. But you should have this conversation with Hari.
He is a warrior saint in the true Sikh tradition, although his beliefs encompass all benevolent philoso-
phies. He claims to have prescient visions. On the
other hand, he never understands them until they have
come to pass, which makes them pretty much useless."

"Perhaps one day I'll speak with him," she said,
rising. "It's very late. You wished to keep clear of
your brother's rooms, so we'll be staying in the old
wing of the house. The servants opened it up and
cleaned the suite of rooms that belonged, I think, to
your grandfather. In the next few days, we'll make
them more habitable, but they'll do for now. Shall I
show you the way?"

"I remember it," he said. "I'd as soon sit here by
the fire for a time. You go on ahead."

And she understood, from that simple remark, that
in the future he intended to keep his distance from
her. Even the slight intimacy of going in company to
their separate bedchambers seemed beyond him, or
perhaps he wished to spare her the awkward moment
of an impersonal "good night." In fact, she had been

dreading that very thing, with the stab of guilt she felt for denying him what he had every right to expect from her.

Step-by-step, she reminded herself. Perhaps she would arrive where he wished her to be, and perhaps she would never make it so far. But she meant to try. Tomorrow, when Cat helped her climb aboard a horse for the first time in a dozen years, she would put herself to the first test.

Under an azure-and-apricot sky, Mira set out for the stables just in time to see her husband vault into the saddle, reach down for Cat, take her aboard in front of him, and set off in an explosion of speed. Heart in her throat, she watched Loki soar over a fence, land without breaking stride, and streak across the stubbled field before disappearing through a screen of bare-branched trees.

She went back to the house for a solitary breakfast.

An hour later, the small mare she meant to ride saddled and ready, she saw Loki and his passengers returning from the opposite direction. The duke paused long enough for Cat to slip to the ground, waved at Mira, and rode off again for what she knew would be a day-filling round of visits to tenant cottages.

Bright eyed and grinning, Cat came to her on unsteady legs. "I have learned a great lesson today," she said, with the frankness Mira had come to expect from every Keynes, male or female. "Loki is a splendid horse, and I wish above all things to have one just like him for myself. But I have much to learn first. I am not yet ready. And my pride can barely stand to admit it."

"I know precisely how you feel," Mira said, watching the Duke of Tallant vanish over the horizon. *I want him just for myself, and I am not yet ready.*

But after a good deal of quivering hesitation, Mira

clambered aboard the oldest, laziest nag in Kent and steered it around the fenced paddock for all of seven minutes. After lunch, fortified by sardonic encouragement from Cat Keynes, she navigated the paddock for eleven minutes. And then she selected a slightly livelier mare for her outing the following morning, which she took with Cat riding alongside of her.

Slow steps, taken one at a time. She no longer feared to ride, wondered why she had ever feared it. Riding wasn't to blame for what had befallen her. It was what had happened after she'd fallen.

On the third night, she and Cat joined forces to convince the duke they required the purchase, or at least the hire, of more spirited riding horses for themselves. By the afternoon of the next day, he had provided them.

Mira also got in a lot of practice at the archery butts. At first she used one of Cat's older bows, but Hari Singh brought her a yew bow more up to her size and experience. The sense of accomplishment and physical exercise went a long way to improve her confidence, which she required in order to herd the recalcitrant servants into line. When she found the courage to send off several troublemakers, including the butler, morale greatly improved.

Each day, the duke rode out early and came home late. She thought—no, she was sure of it—that he was deliberately exhausting himself with work. What leisure time he took for himself, the hour after a solitary meal taken in his study, he spent with Cat. He'd decided that while she was out of school, she should read history under his supervision, and fairly soon, Mira found herself jealous of the lonely young girl who had begun to thrive under the critical attention of her uncle.

Mira was lonely, too, although her days were crowded. She missed her father, missed her husband's focused regard, wondered when she had become so selfish. She had so much more now than she had ever had, and still she burned for what, God help her, she had rejected.

Her remarkable husband. When he was in the house, she sensed his every movement. When he left, she felt him go, and when he returned, she knew without seeing him that he was on his way. But by her choice, because she could make no other choice, they lived together as virtual strangers. And she profoundly feared she was going to lose him before she had gathered the strength to do what she must to keep him.

Five days after they arrived at Longview, everything changed again. The carriage arrived shortly before sundown, flanked by an odd assortment of armed men who were taken to the kitchen for supper while the widowed Duchess of Tallant, her daughter Lady Corinna, and the Honorable David Fairfax, were made welcome by the new Duchess of Tallant.

The duke was gone, as usual.

Mira had misgivings about acting as hostess to Norah, as she insisted on being called, in what used to be her home, but the widow quickly put her at ease.

"I am very tired," she said as they settled together over a pot of tea, "but the adventure was a rare change from my incarceration here. I even enjoyed my stay in the Rookeries, although I was terribly worried about Cory at the time. She looks well, don't you think?"

It had been hard to tell. Bundled under a hooded cloak, Cory had gone directly from the carriage to find her sister, and neither of them had been seen after that. "Quite well," Mira said. "Travel appears to agree with her."

Norah stirred sugar into her tea. "I believe so. At times, I feel I hardly know her. She would tell me nothing of where she went or what she did after running off, except to say I needn't worry about her. But I do, of course. Ought I to press her for the truth?"

Mira had tried to prepare herself for this sort of question, without success. "At her age," she said tentatively, "I expect she is disinclined to answer questions or take advice. There is no hurry, I think, to make decisions now. She will reveal what she wishes, when she wishes."

"But not to me. I have not earned or deserved her trust. Still, we must look to the future. For the longest time, all decisions were made for us by the duke. Perhaps that has not changed. We have nothing of our own, do we? No home, no money, and a reputation that will close every door to us."

There was no self-pity in her tone. Only a practical evaluation of her circumstances, viewed from the perspective of the Beast's wife. Mira took a lesson from that. Compared to this woman's suffering, and Cory's, her own troubles were insignificant.

"We must all deal with the family reputation," Mira said. "It will take time, but I expect we shall eventually be accepted in most drawing rooms. As for homes, you are always welcome at Longview and Tallant House. If you wish a residence of your own, that can be arranged as well, and there will be provision made for your needs. His Grace will agree, I am sure. We can do without many things, Norah, but not without our family."

Norah's eyes glistened with unshed tears. "I have always been a proud woman, despite my circumstances. I cannot go to the duke with begging bowl in hand, nor do I wish you to do so on my behalf. But I shall go on my knees before him, if I must, for the means to create a decent life for my daughters."

"You will need to do no such thing."

"In the spring, Mr. Fairfax will travel with the Duke of Devonshire to Italy, and he has suggested that we accompany him and remain there until the autumn. Do you suppose that would be possible?"

"It sounds ideal," Mira said with enthusiasm. "Much more exciting than waiting out the year of mourning in the country. And educational as well. By the time you return, the scandal of the duke's murder will be all but forgotten. I think, though, that Cat wishes to return to school."

"Oh, yes. I meant only Cory and me." The prospect had put color on Norah's cheeks, softening her face, making her look almost lovely. "And . . . I don't know if I dare say this, but I suspect that Mr. Fairfax has fixed his interest on her. It's early yet, too early to know if it will come to anything, and I doubt she has even noticed. Still, he's a lovely young man. So considerate, and of a good family."

To cover her astonishment, Mira picked up a scone and begin to spread jam on it. *Too soon. She will require time to heal, if that is even possible.* But she could say nothing of that to Cory's mother, so she returned the subject to their proposed trip, and where they might stay, and whether Devonshire would agree to take them along.

That evening after supper, while David played for them on the pianoforte, Mira watched Cory select a chair apart from everyone else, and saw how she pretended to be working on a piece of embroidery while listening attentively to the music.

Mira had been observing David as well, and how he behaved when in company with Cory. He was kind, of course, but that was his way with everyone. He never singled her out, but he noticed when she required something at the table and quietly directed a servant to supply it. And when Cory's attention was diverted, he looked at her with a gentle hunger in his eyes that Mira recognized. It was the way her father had looked at her mother, his beloved wife.

She decided to encourage the trip to Italy. Cory

must not seclude herself like damaged goods, the way she had done.

The next day, when Norah and Cory had provided descriptions of the men who had accompanied them to Scotland, two of the Runners set out for London to organize a wider search.

Hari, who had been gone for several days on the duke's business, returned with news of her father. His breathing had noticeably improved, he was eating better and putting on weight, and except for missing his daughter, he was in excellent spirits. He'd even dictated a letter to her, filled with stories about the family who had made him welcome while she and her husband enjoyed the first few weeks of their marriage.

In fact, she had seen a good deal more of her husband *before* they were wed. But over the next several days, she crossed item after item from her detailed list, and saw that Corinna and Norah and Cat were drawing closer to one another, and knew that the time for her next great trial had arrived.

Chapter 30

The only thing Mira planned was what she'd wear, and that was simple enough. She'd precisely one non-flannel nightdress, the cream-colored silk night rail and dressing gown provided her by Lady Jessica, un-adorned and modest so long as she stood perfectly still. But when she moved, and she could scarcely avoid doing so, it had a lamentable way of clinging to parts of her anatomy she'd rather not call attention to.

Her hair would provide a distraction. After her bath, she'd washed it and brushed it out by the fire until it shone. No perfume, though, and no rouge where the ladies of Birindar's household had applied it nearly three weeks ago, in preparation for her wedding night. Even the henna dye on her hands had faded, save for the barest outline of the coiled snake.

She could not seduce him, never gave thought to trying. This would be a negotiation, like the one that preceded the marriage, except that on this occasion, only she had anything to lose.

No. She had *everything* to lose. Even so, she re-hearsed none of what she would say, nor did she dare to imagine what would follow. If she kept thinking about it, she would almost certainly fail.

Firelight gleamed off the gold bands on her forefin-

ger and her little finger—twin promises she'd yet to
keep—and she thought of how he had looked at her
when he placed them there. For his sake, whatever
the cost, she must do this.

The short walk through the sitting room that lay
between their bedchambers felt like a hundred miles.
Her palms and forehead were damp, her knees shook,
her mouth was dry as ashes. He had returned late, she
knew, gone directly to his rooms, and ordered a supper tray. That was two hours ago. Perhaps he was
asleep. Probably he was drunk.

The door loomed before her like the portal to the
underworld. Now her heart was jumping in her chest
like a March hare. She reached for the brass knob,
wondered for the first time if the door was locked,
decided she ought to be polite and knock.

No response.

Then she wondered if he might have a woman in
there with him. One of the maids, perhaps. She'd
seen how some of them looked at him. Or the mistress she'd told him he should acquire. She hadn't
thought he might bring his mistress to the house, but
it was, after all, *his* house. She knocked again, a trifle
louder, her courage sifting away with appalling
speed.

Before it entirely disappeared, she grasped the knob
and turned it. The door swung open.

Beyond it, she could see almost nothing. Her gaze
went to the orange-red coals in the fireplace to her
right. She moved inside. Shivered. It was like stepping
into an icehouse.

She blinked as her eyes adjusted to the darkness.
The outlines of furniture took shape before her. Atop
a three-staged platform in the center of the room rose
an enormous canopied bed. Along the wall to her left
she saw tall armoires, what looked to be stands of
drawers, and side tables. Heavy oak and mahogany

furniture from a bygone era, if it was anything like the furnishings in her own bedchamber.

What was missing, in this room where she'd never been, was her husband.

She sensed him, though, and followed the vibration deeper inside, directly to the bed. It was empty. So she went around it, and saw at the far end of the long, long room, a shaft of light pouring in through a pair of open French windows. On either side, curtains billowed in the midnight breeze.

She felt like an iceberg sailing across the great North Sea. But she had come this far, and her goal, her last and enduring goal, waited for her on a small balcony, facing into the night, head lifted to the sky. The full moon lit his bare, scarred back and wide shoulders. Loose white muslin trousers, tied with a drawstring, hung low on his narrow hips. On the marble railing, a glass of brandy glowed like an amber coal.

At the sound of her slippers brushing over the carpet he stiffened, the muscles in his back bunching like fists. He didn't look around.

She moved to him, took her place beside him. His chest and arms, sprinkled with curling black hair, were silvered bronze. His breath fluttered like gauze in the winter air.

"I love the moon," he said quietly, as if they'd been standing together for a long time. "It's so alone, hanging there between the earth and the stars, wondering which direction to go. Some nights it comes to earth, round and full, and I want jump on it and ride it back to the stars."

His deep voice, achingly gentle, pulled at her until she surged like the moon-snared tide. In that one turbulent moment, drawn to his shining, tempting sky, she almost broke free to go with him. But another night, moonless and cold, was less gentle than his soft voice, its terrors more real than his call to star flight.

She was rooted in the frozen ground, in her guilt, in the duty she owed to a future she had not expected to have. "I've been thinking," she said.

"I'm afraid to ask." A touch of self-mocking humor in his voice. "What will it cost me?"

Straight to the point, as always. Well, she was a Keynes now, at least by name. She threw him back a Keynes answer. "The rest of your life."

"You've got greedy, Duchess. And you must be cold. Come inside and I'll build up the fire."

She looked up at the moon, at the star-spun sky, and thought it might be easier here, where the cold of her skin matched her cold heart. "I'm well enough," she said. "And it's too beautiful a night to walk away from."

"Then wait a moment."

He was gone only a short time and returned wearing a black silk banyon loosely belted at the waist. He'd brought a velvet dressing gown, also black, and helped her slip her arms into the sleeves. The heavy fabric enveloped her, the sleeves dangling well beyond her hands, the folds of velvet pooling around her feet. He was smiling a little as he wrapped the woven tie twice around her waist and secured it in front with a little bow.

"If you stand on the hem," he said, "your feet will keep warm."

She did so, and then it felt as if he entirely enveloped her, as if his body and not his robe were wrapped around her. He adjusted the collar, rolling it to protect her neck from the cold, and stepped away. "Now then. What's this about?"

She should have rehearsed. It was all so clear in her mind, but she could not think how to begin. "The f-future," she began. "With what we need to do."

Silence. He picked up his glass, examined its contents. "Are we back to the divorce?"

"No. Well, not yet. It isn't what I want."

His gaze flicked over to her. "What, then?"

"I want us to build something, to create something good and productive and enduring. You must admit, sir, that we have, the both of us, spent the better part of our lives seeking destruction. We were avengers, and no matter how right it was that Beast Keynes be prevented from doing more harm, we have let him rule us."

"Not precisely rule, but yes, I was committed to bringing him down. It was necessary. My real crime was not killing him years earlier."

"That's as may be. I feel much the same. But we must contrive to escape the hold he has on us, and the prison, if you will, of what occurred in the past. It has had me in its grip for nearly half my life, and when I was not plotting a fanciful revenge, I was hiding myself behind my father. I would still be hiding, had you not compelled me to marry you. But everything has changed now, and I must change with it."

"Into what, Duchess?"

"Into precisely that. A duchess. The murder, the marriage, all happened so quickly I never truly considered what I had landed into. Then, at Beata's party, when Lord Gretton asked when you would make your first speech in the Lords, and what subject you would address, I thought I'd choke. You are to be part of the government!"

"Not if I can help it. And if I make a speech, my first and last, I can say only that it will be short. You are taking this all too seriously. The government wants no part of me, I assure you."

"We can discuss that later." She had let herself wander afield, trying to impress him with how impressive he was and could be. "I have been useless and a coward. You have been neither, but you are the last male—Helena Pryce told me this—of your family, and because your four predecessors squandered all that the earlier generations had built, it now falls to you to restore the Keynes legacy. It is no small thing to be a duke, sir. There are responsibilities, to the land and to its residents. To the country itself."

"Do you think I have not considered that? What else have I been doing these last weeks?"

"What you always do. Setting short-term goals and achieving them. But what happens when the land is profitable and the servants and tenants are thriving? What will you do with yourself then?"

He sliced her an unamused grin. "I've a feeling you are about to tell me."

"That's what I've been trying to do. Except it has sounded like a lecture, when I know very well that you will see your duty and fulfill it." Her hands were tightly clenched. "The question is, am I able to fulfill mine? I don't know the answer. In small ways, I have been testing myself, and sometimes I have succeeded. I believe I can learn to manage your household, here and in London. You have made me unafraid to exhibit myself in society. I am not confounded by our notoriety, or my insignificant birth, or my voice, or my hands."

"You shouldn't be. But you look as if you're about to shoot off sparks like a fireworks display. What *does* confound you?"

Here it was, then. No more distractions and evasions. She took a deep breath of frosty air. "I do not know," she said, "if I can be a true wife to you."

"We've covered this ground. You said it was likely you could not bear a child, and I told you I care nothing about producing an heir."

"You should. You *must*. I—"

He gripped her shoulders, not ungently, and looked steadily into her eyes. "Get this straight. I understand about your . . . accident, and that you may have been damaged. But many perfectly healthy men and women fail to have children. Nor are there any guarantees about providing an heir to the title. My brother sired only females. It's a gamble, Duchess, for every man and wife, a gamble I'm more than willing to take with you."

"But—"

The fingers tightened. "If you're about to insist I replace you if you fail to breed, don't. We are not livestock. On those grounds, I will not give you a divorce."

"Very well. It would be an offense, I suppose, to second-guess the Creator. But that's not the same as my fears getting in the way of tossing the coin at all."

His hands slid from her shoulders, fell to his sides. "I'm sorry. I ought not have touched you."

"Of course you ought. I made with you a devil's bargain, one I had no right to demand. And I wish to rescind it, except that I'm not at all sure I can. We may never have a child, Your Grace, but the reason cannot be my unwillingness to come to your bed. I am here, now, to tell you that I wish to try, and that I may fail unpleasantly, and that if I do, I am willing to keep trying until I am sure that . . . that it is . . . hopeless."

Her voice had all but vanished at the last words. She felt soul-naked before him, offering herself like some sort of unwilling sacrificial lamb with sharp teeth and fast legs.

And he was no help. His jaw tight, he stared at her from those wolfish eyes, tormented and repelled. It was no good. She should have known his pride would not allow him to bed her on such conditions as these. She had offered herself as a martyr, to establish a dynasty he did not want.

Why had she thought this a good idea? That her goal encompassed his happiness, when clearly it only brought him to anger and pain? Taking hold of the long dressing gown, she disentangled her feet and fled.

Michael, frozen in place, felt the emptiness where

she had been. It seemed a long time before he could bring himself to move, but when he went into his bed-chamber, she had only just reached the far end of the room. Along the way she had discarded his dressing gown, and now she glowed like a specter, her white gown edged with orange light from the dying fire as she swept toward the door that would take her away from him.

Perhaps forever.

She had offered herself. And he had nearly refused, because what she offered him was not what he wanted. As if it mattered what he received from her.

For those few moments, he'd forgot there was nothing he would not give her.

"Mira." He started after her. "Don't go."

Her hand, reaching for the doorknob, lowered to her side, She stood for a time, head bowed, and finally turned to face him. He was only a few feet from her by then, unsure if he ought to draw closer, no idea in his head what he should do next.

"I've disappointed you," she said. "Or angered you. I didn't mean to."

"You took me by surprise, is all. I didn't handle it well."

"I was surprised, too. I had been given to believe that males always wanted—" She made a helpless gesture. "You know what I mean. You told me yourself that if we were enclosed in a room together, and if I removed my clothing, that you would—" Another gesture. "So you see, I thought you would be pleased."

A hundred ways to twist the knife, and she was mistress of them all. "Of course," he said, finding a smile for her. "But not if it means hurting you."

"Oh, I don't mind." Her eyes, earnest and pleading, turned the blade yet again. "Pain is no great thing. And you probably won't. After the . . . my accident, I am not, in the traditional sense, precisely a virgin."

"But you fear what is to occur. You fear *me*. It is too soon. Perhaps after more time has passed, it will not be so difficult for you."

"Time will only make it worse. Truly. Since deciding I must bring myself to do this, every minute has stretched to an hour, every hour to a week. This morning I finally resolved to approach you, and it has been the longest day in history. Longer than the day in which God created all the animals."

More and more encouraging. He began to think he would not leave this room with a shred of male pride.

And because he was weak and selfish, he stole for himself one moment, made one small gesture of his love for her. Raising his right hand to her cheek, he stroked it gently, with lingering fingertips. "As you wish, Duchess. All will be as you wish."

The relief in her eyes, although it did not banish the fear, heartened him. "I wish it to be swift," she said in a breathless rush of her own. "And because I do not know how I shall deal with it, or how I might react, I should prefer not to be concerned for you as well."

"You needn't be."

"What I *mean*," she said, her face red as strawberries, "is that this should be as impersonal an event as possible. Nothing . . . intimate. Nothing fancy. Nothing *extra*."

"I take your point," he said finally, through a screen of pain that all but blinded him. "But unless your body is prepared to accept mine, you will be hurt. And I cannot do that. You must let me guide you, to a degree, in how we proceed."

"Yes. Well, I suppose you are the expert. What must I do first, then? Shall I remove my dressing gown? My night rail?"

Clearly the thought of doing so horrified her. "That depends. What are you wearing underneath them?"

"N-nothing."

"Then leave them on, at least the night thing, if you prefer. And let us spend a little time together, without touching, until you feel more at ease."

"In bed?" Her lower lip trembled.

"Or on it. You go make yourself comfortable there. I'm going to pour myself a drink."

He was on his way to reclaim his glass from the balcony when she caught up with him. "I'd like one as well, if you please. Perhaps it will help."

She left him off at the bed, and when he'd got his glass and started for the sideboard, he paused to watch her climb the three steps up to the platform like a maiden on her way to the guillotine. Dear God, how was he to manage this? He understood, too well, that for her this was a sexual gauntlet she must run again and again until she'd proven to herself she could endure his touch, his body inside her body.

What if she could not?

He lifted the decanter, spilled brandy on the carpet, managed to fill the glass. Took his time, to let her settle, and when her back was to him, untied the drawstring and slipped out of his muslin trousers. He was already barefoot, and the banyon covered what she most feared.

What if *he* could not?

Given that he'd desired her from the moment he first saw her, it seemed impossible that he would be unable to claim what had consumed his imagination for so long. But . . . not to stroke her. Tantalize her. Rouse her desire. Not to kiss her. Simply to enter her and leave her as quickly as he could. A man expiring of thirst in a desert, with only the mirage of a fountain to save him.

"It is the way of nature," Hari had told him. "The tigress calls when it is time, and her mate responds because he must."

He swallowed half the brandy and topped off the glass again before slogging toward the bed. Even from a distance he could see that she had nested there, stacking pillows against the headboard for him, co-cooning herself in a cave of sheets and blankets. She was sitting upright, cross-legged, her white face peering out from the veil of covers draped over her head like the embroidered mantle she'd worn the night of their marriage. She looked small and frightened and heartbreakingly brave.

"It turns out I have three decanters, but only one glass," he said, slipping his hairy legs between the sheets at a distance from her and resting his back against the pillows. "We'll have to share."

She took the glass from his hand, sniffed at it, wrinkled her nose, and like a child taking medicine, managed a quick swallow. Her eyes widened. Her lips pursed. "Oh, my. That's *awful.*"

"You wouldn't say that if you knew what it cost. Prime cognac, Duchess. I admit, it's an acquired taste."

"But why would anyone wish to acquire a taste for something that tastes bad, when there are so many things that taste wonderful right from the start? Lemonade. Champagne. Especially champagne." She gave him back the glass. "What an odd sensation, though. As if it got heated up on the way to my stomach."

"One of its better effects." He could think of nothing to say to her. He didn't know where to look. Not at her, a shadowy figure in her hideaway save for the wisps of hair and the wide eyes illuminated by the distant moon. It hurt too much to look at her. Perhaps she had the right idea. Perhaps he should lay her down under him and get it over with. He took another drink, felt the glass being lifted from his hand. Heard a little choking sound.

"I don't like the taste," she said after a moment. "But I rather like the feeling. Hot, and then numb. If I drink a good deal more, will I become numb all over?"

"That's the general idea. But it affects people in different ways."

"What do you like about it, then? You drink more than anyone I've ever known."

She had made herself so vulnerable to him that he felt obliged to be a little honest in return. But only a little. "I always think it will help," he said. "It never does."

"You must be taking lessons in obscurity from Mr. Singh." Another swallow of cognac. "Perhaps it would taste better if I'd eaten something. I could not, all day, except the bit of toast at breakfast."

"In that case," he said, reclaiming the glass, "you need to go easy."

"If you say so. But I remember one of the historians who stayed with us for a summer got foxed one morning, and he was not a gentleman who often tippled. He said he wished to dull his sensations because he was on his way to have a tooth drawn."

The lady knew how to put him in his place, Michael thought, distantly aware that she'd snatched back the glass. "I told you it never works," he said.

"But it might put me to sleep. And then you could do it, and I wouldn't mind, and it would be done with."

"No." With effort, he kept his voice level. "Even if you prefer it that way, I draw the line at bedding an unconscious female."

"I suppose you are right," she said with patent regret. "If I didn't remember, I might feel compelled to do it all again. For the first time, I mean. Not for the only time. This won't be a token gesture, you understand. No matter what, I mean to soldier on."

She was taking him near the end of his endurance. The moon, conspiring with her on its skyward course, had sent its light all the way to the bed. Heated by the cognac, she'd let the covers fall from her head and shoulders. Her hair, her glorious hair, begged his fingers to slip through it, to draw her face to him for a kiss. But kisses were forbidden. And passion. Pleasure. Every expression of love and trust and true union. All was forbidden him except the penetration of her unwilling body.

"I wish you had known my father before his illness," she said, dashing cold water on his painful fantasy. "Our home was always filled with his protégés, the new untried ones and those who had fulfilled the promise he saw in them. He had the gift of making everyone feel important, even when they were perfectly silly, like Lord Galworth, who wrote poetry about pigs. His family raised them, and had got rich on them, so he thought they ought to be celebrated. 'No pig so fine as a Hampshire swine.' Really!"

The last of the cognac went down her throat. She coughed, gave him the glass, and smiled. Within half an hour, he judged with an expert eye, she would be cheerfully senseless. Ought he to take action? But she was already babbling again—

". . . interested in too many things to make a reputation for himself, but in his way, my father was a great scholar. Of course, he could never remember where he left anything. One evening he came downstairs to dinner in full dress, except for his pantaloons. He even had his shoes on. All the guests were standing in the foyer when he made his grand entrance. I thought Mother would choke.

"The prime minister was there, and it was his first visit so everyone was out to impress him. Father gave one of his better bows, but his bony knees stuck out and his white legs positively shone against the black marble staircase. I'll never forget that sight as long as I live.

"His bow took him over far enough to see what everyone else was gaping at, and he stared at his bare legs as if he didn't know what they were doing there. His mind always was miles ahead of his body.

" 'Dear me, I seem to have forgot my trousers,' he said. 'I'll be back directly.' And up he went, cool as lemonade, to finish dressing. He really thought nothing about it, and by the time he returned, no one else did either."

"Is there supposed to be a lesson in this for me?" Michael said. "A 'Buddha Holcombe' story?"

She gave the question some thought. "Not when I started. But I may have stumbled across a truth of sorts. Or not. Everything feels strange now, and all my ideas have fuzzy edges. I was thinking that when I was growing up, I adored my father and wanted someday to marry a man just like him. But here I am, married to you."

"And I am nothing at all like your father."

"I was thinking that as well, and then I realized that in rather a lot of ways, you have the qualities in him I most admire."

It seemed the wrong time to correct her. To do anything but proceed before she became insensible. But that she believed him to be a finer man than he was touched him deeply. It was the one moment of this night he would not try to forget. He reached over to set the glass beside the bed, and when he sat back up, she had drawn closer, her gaze riveted to a spot below his neck.

He glanced down. The motion had pulled the banyon apart, baring an expanse of chest. She was regarding it with a look of befuddled curiosity.

"Such an odd place for hair to grow," she said. "May I touch it?"

"You may always do so." He felt a little breathless at the prospect. Altogether breathless when her pale hand crossed the gulf between then and gingerly stroked the sprinkle of hair, and the flesh beneath.

"You're very hard," she said.

Indeed he was. A good thing the folded bedcovers

concealed the evidence, which would frighten her to see.

She had turned her attention to his arm, pushing the wide silk sleeve up to his shoulder and examining his biceps with flattering amazement. Then she shrugged out of her robe and raised her pale, sleeveless arm next to his, measuring them side by side. "Just look at that. We might be two entirely different species. Mine is a . . . a noodle, and yours is a mahogany *log*."

She didn't know the half of it. How to deal with this? Unless he moved quickly now, it would all be over . . . without her. What had it been? Eight months? Ten? Too long for a man of his sort, and the last weeks of it wrung out with desire for this remarkable woman.

He slipped his arm around her waist, put his other hand on her shoulder, and drew her to him. He felt her trying not to resist him, trying to cooperate even though she was taut as a gazelle scenting danger.

Her arm was bent up between them, her hand on his chest as if she'd push him away. And yet, she lowered her head to his shoulder. Her breath was warm against his neck. "Is it time?" she said.

"Yes. It has to be. Unless you wish to call this off."

"Oh, no. I've got this far. But I do not know how I shall react from here on out. You must finish. No matter what I say or do, sir, you *must* finish."

"I understand that you may be resistant, physically, and not mean it. But if you tell me 'no,' if you tell me to stop, I will. You must be complicit. I won't take the choice from your hands."

She looked up at him, her eyes full of sadness. "Might I at least put a handkerchief in my mouth? I do want this. I *will* it. But my body may have other ideas. And that includes what I say."

He thought, then, that he could seduce her, and

considered it as she relaxed slightly in his arms. But that wasn't what she'd asked of him, and they had conducted too many negotiations already. This time, never mind she was wrong, he would do precisely what she thought she wanted.

He slid down the bank of pillows, taking her with him, until they lay together side by side, her head resting on his outflung arm. "I desire you," he said quietly. "Will you let me lead your body to accept mine?"

He felt her nod against his arm, decided she had sealed her lips to prevent an inadvertent protest. He brought his hand to her slim waist, rubbed her back until the tightness left it, and then found the swell of her breast. Only the side of it, swathed with silk, until he was sure she would accept a more intimate touch. A light touch, not at all threatening. With his fingers he shaped the soft, feminine mound, letting his thumb brush over the nipple once, and again, and again. It tightened in response. Her head inclined closer to his, a secretive female demand for a kiss she would not permit him.

She had been, yes, very wrong. Her mind had decided to have him. Her body, she must be realizing, wanted him. But the great barrier, unspoken between them, could only be overcome when she trusted him with the truth. Perhaps not even then. He'd built walls around himself as well.

When her leg moved against his, he recognized the unconscious signal, her invitation to the place he most wanted to be. He was ready, too ready, had been for too long.

He sent his hand along her flank, around to the irresistible curves of her buttocks, down to where the silk left off and silky leg began. He glided upward, hand under the nightgown, up the dip behind her knee and the back of the thigh until he reached the place where her legs joined and where his fingers could enter between them.

They did, and she went stiff. Squeezed her thighs together. He paused, felt the act of will by which she pulled herself past resistance and gradually moved her legs a little apart.

"Like this," he whispered, lifting her knee, bending it, and bringing it to rest over his side. Better this way, he had decided early on. Better that he not climb on top of her, large and dark and powerful, while she was so afraid.

Now she was open to him, the scent of cognac and female desire hovering in the air around them. From behind her, he let one finger begin a gentle exploration of the soft folds and dark mysteries at the center of her, a little moist already with instinctive welcome.

She moved restlessly against him. He would have to hurry now. But she wasn't quite ready. Not for his size, not for the depth in her he would reach if he could not help himself. His fingertip moved back and forth lightly near her opening, coaxing the filmy moisture to flow in her. He came to the little valley, and to the slope that led upward to her hooded nib, swollen just enough to tell him what he needed to know. He pressed, rubbed, remembered she would resent taking pleasure after all her certainty that she could do no more than endure.

He drew his finger back to her damp core, welling with female recognition of what belonged there. What he was about to put there. He brought his hips forward, placing a wide-spread hand on her buttock to hold her in place. She gave a little moan of dread.

His cock slid between her thighs, engorged with his passion for her, found her opening and homed in on it, pushed inside.

Immediately she froze. Her hand, that had somehow got inside his banyon to rest against the scars on his back, seized up. Her nails dug into his skin.

He went still, waiting for her to speak, to say "No!"
To cast him away.

Instead, she gave a little sigh. Loosened her death
grip on his back. Tightened her knee on his waist to
keep him inside her. He went deeper, and deeper still.
He heard his own breathing, like that of a panting
animal. She enclosed him. Gripped him inside her, the
pleasure now so intense he nearly broke with it.

Mira. He might have said her name. Beyond control, he felt his whole self rush to his loins, to the
heated, throbbing staff moving inside her, and too
soon, the pulsations began, one after the other. Mindless as he climaxed, he held her close and poured himself into her.

After a time, she stirred restlessly against him. He
realized he was still clasping her against him, that he
was still inside her. Carefully he slid away, put some
distance between them, and propped himself up on
his elbow.

She was looking at him, wide-eyed. "Is that all,
then? Are you finished?"

"I'm afraid so."

"Oh." Relief bloomed on her face. "Well. That
wasn't so bad."

"I'm glad you think so."

"If only you knew what I'd been imagining! I was
sure it would take a great deal longer."

"It . . . sometimes does." He didn't know whether
to laugh or beat his head against a heavy piece of
furniture. "That's not altogether a bad thing."

"If you say so," she said doubtfully. "But it's better
to proceed slowly, I believe, as I did when I began to
ride the horse. This was something like it, really, like
riding around the paddock . . . a bit unnerving at first,
but after a time, of very little consequence at all. In
fact, I believe that in the future, and without requiring
brandy to lend me courage, I shall be able to ride
around the paddock again."

"You'll let me know when I'm to saddle up."

"Yes. Well, not . . . Oh." An entirely uncharacteristic giggle. "You're making fun of me. But I don't mind. I'm feeling quite full of my success, actually."

Full of brandy, Duchess, and full of my seed. But he knew better than to say it. "Teasing a little, perhaps."

"I deserve it." A frown knitted her brow. "Why is it my tongue has grown so large? And my head is packed with feathers. I'd better get on with this while I still feel brave and self-satisfied. Might I request another favor?"

"Of course."

"I should like you to come with me to Seacrest. Papa will wish to stay there, and the house is in poor repair. I must make it ready for him."

He winced. "I've been meaning to tell you, but it kept slipping my mind. The men in Birindar's family, most of them, are builders. Under Hari's supervision, they have already completed the major repairs . . . roof, pipes, that sort of thing. Local laborers will be hired to finish the work. We can go see what progress has been made, if you like. And you'll want to decide about paint and furnishings. My brother left very little intact, although the books were still there, crated up. I expect he meant to cart them to London for auction."

Her eyes lit up. "I never dreamed Papa would see his library again. It's something for us both to look forward to." Then, as if it had never been there, the light in her eyes was gone. "There is another place I want to take you first. It's a little out of the way. I've been there only once before, but I think I can find it. Will you accompany me? Tomorrow?"

"You're apt to have a headache tomorrow, Duchess. And a few other symptoms of overindulgence."

"You would know," she said. "But if we don't do this straightaway, I'll probably change my mind. Decide to put it off. And once I do that, I'll just keep putting it off. It's better that I commit to a firm plan

and a deadline, Your Grace. Please. Give me tomorrow."

He recognized another act of courage, another
gauntlet she must run. "As you wish. I'll need to make
an early call, to cancel other arrangements I've made,
but then we can be on our way."

"Thank you." She sat up and begun rummaging
through the twisted covers. "Where is that dressing
gown?"

"Must you go?"

She glanced up in surprise. "Aren't I supposed to?"

He wasn't used to asking anything for himself. He
felt a little sick doing it, dizzy because he wanted it
so much. "I'd rather you stayed." He sounded curt,
as if snapping an order to one of his mercenaries.

"Oh. I hadn't thought—" She regarded him warily.
"You won't . . . *do* anything?"

"I will never *do* anything, until you ask it of me."
He laid himself down, his head on the pillow, still
a distance from her. "Will you stay? Will you give
me tonight?"

Without seeming to move, she drew closer and laid
her head on his outstretched arm. Her hand went to
his chest in a familiar gesture . . . an intimate touch
that at the same time held him away. She didn't seem
to mind, though, when his other arm wrapped around
her. "It seems only fair," she whispered sleepily.

He didn't think he could sleep at all. He didn't want
to miss out on a moment of this night, the night she
trusted him with her body, the night she admitted,
without knowing he understood what she was doing,
that she now felt safe enough with him to reveal her
deepest secrets.

But those hardships were for tomorrow. For tonight,
there was only Mira in his arms, and the stirring of
what must be happiness in his heart.

Chapter 31

Mira watched Cory's arrow fall short and wide of its target, joining half a dozen arrows scattered around the archery butt.

"I have no talent for this," Cory said with characteristic Keynes impatience, striding forward to reclaim the fallen arrows.

Mira went to retrieve her own arrows from the target. "You're not as bad with a bow and arrow as I am with a pistol," she said. They had decided to instruct each other, usually during the first hour after dawn while the duke was out riding with Cat.

She had awakened that morning alone in her husband's bed, just as sunlight began to steal through the windows. He'd drawn open all the curtains, built up the fire, and left a lit candle on a table to mark his scrawled note—*Back at nine o'clock. The rest of the day is yours.*

Porridge for breakfast had helped dispatch her headache, but no amount of tea quenched her raging thirst or moistened her parched mouth for longer than a few minutes. New item for her list—no more overindulgence in spirits.

As for the other sensations, the oddly pleasant ache between her legs and the echo of his hard body against hers, well, she didn't mind them. Rather the contrary, she had to admit, plucking the last arrow from the bull's-eye.

"My father didn't touch Cat," said Cory from just behind her. "I've meant to tell you, but kept waiting until there could be no doubt."

Arrested, Mira turned. "Did you ask her, then?"

"I didn't need to. Do you think I could not tell, looking into her eyes? But I thought she might suspect how he'd dealt with me, and if she did, I would be forced to speak of it with her. Otherwise, it would lie between us always, and I do need her friendship, annoying as she is. But she doesn't know, and if my mother does, she will never acknowledge it, even to herself. So now, we proceed from here."

"Thank you for telling me," Mira said. "I have . . . wondered. And worried."

They shot another round, and this time, two of Cory's arrows stuck the outer ring of the target. A little at a time, Mira thought, pleased to hear her laugh with delight at her accomplishment. One step after another.

Half an hour later, when Cat and the duke thundered into the stable yard, Mira was waiting with her mare, a large picnic hamper affixed behind the saddle. Lacking a riding habit, she wore a brown wool dress, a darker brown redingote, a small fur-lined hat, and leather half boots. She thought she looked fairly presentable, in spite of reddened eyes and the hot flush on her cheeks. Just seeing him caused her to remember what they had done together—well, what *he* had done while she waited for herself to go into a panic— and how foolish and silly he must think her to be.

For other reasons now, the fear was back, its talons sunk into her as deeply as ever before, the last great obstacle looming only an hour or so away. Forcing her hands to unclench, she watched him swing lithely from the saddle and stride in her direction, a look of concern on his face. A glimmer of something else in his eyes, she saw as he came up to her. Uncertainty? Shyness?

But he was a Keynes, and as always, he came directly to the point. "How are you? How do you feel?"

"Very well indeed," she said truthfully . . . so far as it went. He was referring to last night, and lingering consequences, but there were none. If she passed the last great test, she might even want another night just like it. Or one in which the main event lasted longer, as he'd told her it sometimes did.

The lines of tension at the corners of his mouth relaxed. "I'm glad to hear it. And I see you are ready to go. Cat thinks it will snow later today. Would you rather wait until the weather is more dependable?"

The air was crisp, she supposed, although the exertion at the archery butts and her apprehension had caused her not to feel the cold. But the pale winter sky was clear, and besides, she could not postpone this for even one more day. "We won't be traveling far," she said. "Perhaps I should fetch my cloak."

"I'll get it for you. Bear with me. I'll be gone for several minutes."

Twenty-three minutes, it turned out, not that she was counting. She used the time to check the map she'd drawn with the help of the stable master, who helped her attach her bow and quiver to the saddle. It was an impulse, taking them along, but once the thought popped into her head, it refused to leave.

Tallant returned wearing a charcoal-colored greatcoat, a wide-brimmed hat, and carrying her blue cloak over his arm. At her request, he bundled it up and tied it to the wicker hamper. Then, raising an eyebrow at the sight of her bow, he tossed her onto the sidesaddle and handed her the reins.

They rose in silence for about half an hour, past fields of newly sewn winter wheat, pastures of sheep and cattle, the occasional cottage. Leaving Tallant land, they turned onto a narrow road that cut through an expanse of woodland. All around were the colors of the season, black and gray, biscuit and brown and fawn, patches of green moss, the red-berried, shiny green leaves of a holly tree, the darker needles of the evergreen yew. Skeletal oaks and birch reached naked branches to the powder-blue sky.

There was space to ride side by side, but barely enough space for a coach and four. She could quite imagine that in a rainstorm at dusk, a driver would fail to see a girl leading a horse along the side of the road. It had been a credible story, and had been believed. But this was never a road she had been on, that she remembered.

They came over the crest of a hill, and at the bottom of a long slope, she saw a single-arched stone bridge. Her hands tightened on the reins. Her skin went clammy. She looked over at Tallant and saw him looking back at her, his expression unreadable.

When they arrived at the bridge, she drew up. The stream, pocked with rounded stones, ran north to south, from her right to her left. It was about ten feet across, swift currented but shallow. From the watermarks on stones and tree trunks lining the bed, she could see that in heavy runoff, the stream would become a torrent. It must have been like that on the stormy night when she was brought here.

Tallant, without being asked, dismounted and helped her down. They walked the horses a little way beyond the bridge, to a spot where the ditch along the left side of the road was not so deep. With care, they picked their way across it and into the woods, tethered the horses, and curved around to join the stream and walk alongside it for about a hundred yards. There it took a turn to the right. Small boulders were strewn along one side of the bend, and just past the curve, the thick, exposed roots of a large tree stretched into the stream. She went still.

All this time, the duke had said not a word. Nor did he now, as she looked at the place where she had been found. It fit the description exactly, even a dozen years later.

A breeze had picked up, stirring the dry grasses and brackens. Water gurgled at her feet. She wrapped her arms around her waist, felt the sheltering presence of her husband at her side, the silence of his attention She sensed that without knowing, he somehow understood.

"On my fifteenth birthday," she said, "my father gave me a horse I had coveted. He forbade me to ride without an escort, as always, but I could not wait. Back then I was willful and spoiled. It had been raining off and on all day, but during a lull, and while the stableman was at his meal in the kitchen, I saddled Caliban and stole away. I didn't mean to be gone for long, but when I took him across a wide field for a gallop, he caught a foreleg in . . . oh, I can't say. A rabbit hole, perhaps. He went down, and me with him. We were neither of us badly hurt, but he'd injured his leg enough to cause a limp. I set out leading him, and then it began to rain, pelting rain, with thunder and lightning. The ground became a quagmire of mud. I kept trying to find a road, and when I did, I had no idea which direction to go. I could scarcely see at all."

It was tempting to stay with the simple part of the story, which had never been a secret. But the rest of it must be told, for the first time, and to this man. "It had gone dark. I had been walking more than an hour when I heard horses coming up behind me, so I moved to the side of the road. A large coach swept by, but a little way past me, it pulled up. A hand came out of the window and beckoned me forward. When I got closer, I saw the crest on the panel. I wanted to run then, because the neighborhood children had been warned to keep clear of the Beast. He was the local bogey man, all the more terrifying because none of us had ever seen him.

"But he was smiling when I got to the window, and spoke kindly to me, and asked where I was supposed to be. When I told him, he said we were much closer to his estate than to Seacrest, and that if I would accept a ride for a little distance, he would send a message to my father where I could be found. A servant took Caliban and tied him to the back of the coach."

She was there again, seeing it, feeling the heavy rain on her body, the mud seeping into her short riding boots, the lure of a dry, well-lit carriage. When the door swung open, she climbed inside. The man . . . the Beast . . . had looked much as her husband looked today, slim and long limbed, a shock of black hair, white teeth, and clear, colorless eyes. She had been embarrassed, streaming water all over the maroon squabs and carpeted floor. Had been about to apologize when the coach set out, picking up speed. Caliban!

"Mira?"

She calmed her breath, which had picked up speed as well. "I beg your pardon," she said, still not looking at him, not daring to look at him. "I'm tangled up in unimportant details. The coach began moving, so swiftly that I protested, and he slapped me. No one had ever struck me before. I was so stunned, I barely reacted when he grabbed me and swung me onto his lap, one leg on either side of him. His hands were so large and strong. I struggled, but he held me with one hand and pushed up my skirts with the other. Did something else. Opened his trousers, I realize now. Put his hand where . . . where—"

She shuddered. It was happening now, as it had happened then. From a distance, she heard her voice, unnaturally calm, relating the tale. "I began to scream, and he hit me again, and put a hand over my mouth. He said that he would do as he wished with me, and that it would hurt, and that he wanted it to hurt. If I pleased him, he would let me go free. But if I did not, he would give me to his servants as well. And if ever I told anyone what had happened, no one would believe me because he was a duke and I was only a foolish girl who had taken a fall and hurt her head. If I told, he would hear of it. Then he'd punish my father, and take everything we had, and put us into dark cellars from which we would never escape. He told me to promise I would never tell, for my father's sake. So I did."

"Mira." Her husband's voice was soft. "You needn't go on."

"I know. But *she* must. She is knotted up inside me, keeping her secrets still. And she was wrong to do what she did, and to never tell of it. Until she speaks, I will always be her and always be wrong. Always be responsible. You needn't hear it. I can tell it to the trees if you'd rather, and to the stones. But I must tell it."

"Then I must hear it."

"Just . . . stay with me a little while longer. Be a stone, and pay no mind to what I say. It helps that you are here."

He said nothing, did not move, and that was what she required of him. Closing her eyes, she dove deep inside herself, to where a young girl had been curled up and weeping for all these years, and gave her a voice.

"I promised to keep silent," she said, "and felt myself lifted up, his hands on my waist, and brought down again. Onto him. I didn't know what had happened. But it hurt so. Oh God, it hurt. And I bit my tongue, because he said I mustn't scream and mustn't mind, but then he . . . he pulled me up again, and down, again and again until I couldn't bear it. And I began to scream and scream and scream.

"His hands went from my waist to my throat. I couldn't breath. Couldn't scream any more, because his thumbs were . . . I don't know. Then he was beating my head against the wood panel, and I heard him shouting, *Bitch. Bitch. Bitch.* And after that, there was nothing."

The blood pounding in her ears like the rush of water at her feet. Like the blood that had flowed between her legs. "I should have told you," she said, "before last night. Before I asked you to . . . to touch me. I thought—" Speech came hard to her now. "If I discovered I could not be a wife to you, then I wouldn't be required to admit the truth. There would have been no reason. I debated for weeks, which to try first. I made the wrong choice, the selfish choice. You didn't know I had been with your brother. What I had become. You had a right to know."

"I did know." Straightforward, without pity, as he always was. "Or rather, I had guessed. Jermyn always preferred young girls. He used to take them, the maids or children of the servants, to the stable. After a time, they would leave the estate, their families with them. There is more, but you needn't hear it. When I sent the Runner to guard Cat, he heard the local rumors about Jermyn's incest with his older daughter and told me of them. Cory had every reason to want him dead. You wanted to kill him as well, and the reason had to be other than the theft of your property. It had to be . . . what it was."

She risked a glance at his face. "You knew? And you didn't mind?"

"In the sense you mean that question, of course not. Except—" He looked off into the distance, frowning. "Except that I would put you in mind of him, and make it all the more difficult for you. It was I who made the selfish choice, by taking you into my bed. Only a woman of your courage could have endured it."

"It isn't like that. Truly. When I look at you, I don't see him. When I am with you, I do not think of him."

"But you did, when first you saw me. You did, when I first touched you. From the beginning, you were careful to stay out of my way."

It seemed years had passed since then. "The resemblance was striking, yes, and for all I knew, you *were* like him. There was no reason to believe otherwise. But your kindness to my father forced me to reconsider. If I avoided you, it was for quite another reason, although at the time, I didn't know what it was. I'm not sure, even now, that I understand why."

"That night, in the Limonaia." His voice held a trace of doubt. "I cannot have mistaken your repugnance."

"It wasn't for you. When you touched me, I—I was in the coach again, with him, and his hands were around my neck. I was *there.* It persuaded me I dare not ever let you touch me again, which is why, later that night, I refused to let you help me through the window. I was afraid, not of you, but of how I would react. Then David fell asleep, and I required your help, and when you touched me, it was nothing."

She looked at him again. "Have I insulted you?"

"I'm getting used to it, Duchess."

But he'd given her an encouraging smile, so she continued. "*Nothing* was not the right word. No moment I have spent with you has been without significance. But you must let me stumble through this by misdirection, sir. I haven't yet got to the difficult part.

"It was there"—she pointed to the nest of entwined roots—"that I was found. I have little recollection of the weeks after that. For much of the time, I remained unconscious. I am told that few believed I would survive. But I did, and when I awoke, I had no memory

of what had befallen me. I could not speak. When he
strangled me, he did damage to my voice. It came
back, after a long time, but only to the degree you
hear."

"I think it lovely," he said.

"Yes. Men do think that. It makes them imagine I
am gentle and docile, when I am nothing of the kind.
But it wasn't only my voice went bad. For nearly a
year I could not read or write properly. Letters got
jumbled around. I would look at a word, like *cat*, and
see *act*. Or *tca*. I could not put words together in
speech, even in a whisper. I thought he had ruined,
not only my body, but my mind."

She looked up. Clouds rode in from the sea on a
freshening wind. There would be snow, as Cat had
predicted. "I remembered, long before I could speak,
what he had done. The images came to me first in
nightmares, so vivid I could feel him. Smell his breath.
Hear my own screams. Then, I could not distinguish
memory from dream. After a time they came together,
until I was sure of each detail until the point I went
unconscious. But I never told anyone. I kept pretending what had once been true, that I could recall
nothing except taking Caliban out, and falling, and
starting to walk him home on a strange road in the
rain."

"It's as well you kept silent," he said. "You could
prove nothing. And my brother would have carried
out his threats."

"He did so anyway, when he got around to it. Had
he not been killed, he would have finished what he
began. My silence bought, for me and my father, a
little time. No more than that. And in the interim,
others suffered because I did not speak. The blood of
every girl he raped is my responsibility."

"You know better than that."

"Knowing has nothing to do with feeling." She was
at a gallop now, the words racing from her tongue

faster than her mind could put them together. "I am not so vain as to think my accusations could have stopped him. But it fell to me to try. The truth was in my hands and I buried it inside me. Worse. I put myself into his hands by going out when I should not have done, and accepting his offer of a ride, and climbing willingly into his coach."

"Once he saw you, he would not have let you go." Impatience in his voice now. "You were not complicit, Mira. Not at fault."

"It doesn't *matter*! I can control only myself, and I did not. I should have spoken, and I did not. Even when it does no good, we must speak out. Tell the truth. Defy evil, and point the finger at it, and if we must, suffer for doing so. Because when we are silent, we make it easy for them, for people like your brother. We say, 'Go ahead. Do what you will, so long as you don't do it to me.' Cory, I am sure, would have been assaulted even if I had spoken out. The others, too. There must have been others. But I am . . . I . . . Oh God. I am guilty. Because I knew. It wouldn't have helped. But I should have *tried*."

Her face was hot. Her cheeks wet. *Wet.* Her eyes felt on fire. She was weeping. Had not wept since . . . she could not remember when. Before she was fifteen. Before she turned to ice.

And there were arms around her, and a warm face against hers, and a heart pounding in rhythm with her heart.

"She was a child," said a voice, soft as her own, at her ear. "You need to forgive her, Mira. As you would forgive Cat, if she'd just told you the story you told me. Forgive her, and set her free."

"*Y-you* don't," she managed to respond after a long time. They were on the ground together, she realized, him sitting cross-legged, she encased in his lap like an egg in a nest. "You haven't forgiven yourself. Guilt is heavy in you as well."

"But I was never young, or innocent, or incapable of killing. Keynes men emerge from the womb with knives in their hands and murder in their eyes. My decisions and failures are not yours, Mira. I think you made all the right choices, and that you are guilty of nothing. But if you feel otherwise, then you must come to terms with your decisions. Hari can advise you."

"Does he advise *you*?"

"Constantly. I never listen. But with you, Duchess, I will strike a bargain. Once you have made peace with yourself, I give you leave to work on me."

A chaffinch swooped by. *Pink*, it called. *Pink*.

She looked up at her husband, at his unsentimental expression, at the steel in his eyes. "What makes you think I shall wait as long as that?"

A smile quirked his mouth. "You needn't. Guilt does not dissolve because we will it to, nor would I hold you hostage to my own regrets. Tell me only that you have confronted the last ordeal, and come through it."

"I don't know. I think I have done. For so long, it has seemed that I was dragging an anchor around with me, but I don't feel it now. Perhaps it's gone. Or perhaps you have taken it from me and onto yourself. You would do that, I believe, if you could."

"Yes." A statement of fact. "Is there more you need to do here?"

She looked around, at the stream that had carried her to shelter, and the roots that had scooped her up and held her safe. "It's astonishing," she said, "that someone managed to find me. I had not realized, until coming here, how unlikely a circumstance that was. Nor been glad of it. They carried me away, but I never left here. Perhaps the anchor kept me tethered to this place for all this time. But today I will leave here forever, with you."

The brush of gloved fingertips against her cheek.

Then he rose in a single motion, carrying her with him, and set her on her feet.

They returned in silence to the horses. He seemed withdrawn, his attention elsewhere, as he unwrapped the reins. She started to speak and he raised a hand to stop her, head lifted as if scenting the air. Then a knife was in his hand. He cut through the twine securing her bow and quiver to the saddle and passed them to her. A pistol as well, taken from his coat pocket.

"Hide yourself. This may be nothing, but don't come out until I return. I'll try not to go far. Use the gun if you need to."

"But I can't shoo—"

"Go!"

She hurried off, glancing once over her shoulder. He was tying a lattice of twigs and shrubbery to the saddle. Over it, he draped her cloak. Then he swung onto Loki, seized the mare's reins, and headed back for the road. Moments later, she heard the beat of hooves as he took the horses to a gallop.

Angling away from the stream, she went up a short rise and concealed herself within a ring of blackthorn and holly bushes. Directly after, hollow thumping sounds as horses—she could not tell how many— passed over the bridge, moving very fast.

Chapter 32

Michael held to the road, which dipped and rose for several miles, letting his pursuers glimpse the two horses and their passengers. He would have to outmaneuver them. The mare was too slow for a getaway, and when he set her loose, there was a risk the men would follow and uncover his deception. Then, with him out of reach, they'd go back after Mira.

He thought there were only two of them, probably the same pair of thugs who had eluded the Runners for several weeks. But why should they come for him? Someone had to be paying them. Maybe the Archangel. He'd hired thugs in Calcutta, brought them to Michael's house, set them on him. It seemed out of character, though. A stupid mistake, not a habit.

It didn't matter. He was getting too far from Mira. Needed to circle around, separate the pursuers, pick them off one by one. But it was open land on both sides now, for about a quarter mile. He kept going. Was lucky to have sensed their coming, he supposed, with the same instinct that had kept him alive for so many years.

When he'd left Mira in the stable yard that morning, he had first dispatched Hari to Seacrest with instructions to make it presentable in a hurry. Then he'd settled on the bed where Mira had lain with him and entered the lake of Naini Tal, preparing himself for the journey she was soon to take him on. The concentration he gathered there had kept him calm when she spoke of the nightmare she'd endured, and the torment of unreasonable guilt, which he understood and lived with every day. The lake held him still when she wept in his arms. And later, it had alerted him to the vibration of the ground as the riders approached, and to the threat in the wind.

Now, all his senses at knife's edge, he saw in the distance a stand of trees, the prelude to another stretch of woodland. The first break was to the left. He passed it by and cut off the road a hundred yards beyond, to the right. Rolling hills ahead, studded with beech and oak. Not much undergrowth, no concealment. Any other time of year, he could have found a way to vanish.

Zigging and zagging like a hare, he used the cover of hillocks to hide his objective. The mare was tiring. He had soon to send her off and hope one of the men went after her while he brought down the other. And found out who had sent them and why, or Mira would never be safe.

Ahead, the woods thickened. He couldn't keep the mare at his side for much longer. They came through a small break, splashed across the same stream that wound its way to Mira's tree, went up a hill. On the other side, denser woodland, thick with undergrowth and shrubs low to the ground. A narrow woodsman's path straight ahead.

He drew out his knife. Let go the mare's reins. Darted the knife bee-sting deep into her hindquarter. *Sorry, girl.* She squealed. Kicked up her back hooves. Plunged ahead, down the path, while he swerved right. Over another hill, and another, looking for his spot.

He saw it on a level stretch of ground between two hills. Nearly impenetrable ground, overgrown with oaks, yews, and spiky holly bushes. Lots of cover.

They'd figure it out, but not before he'd had time to prepare. As Loki approached a tall oak, Michael slipped his feet from the stirrups, crouched on the saddle, stood as they came close to a thick branch, and sprang into the air. Loki continued on, swerved when he got to the screen of shrubs and trees, found space to his right and pounded away. As he had been trained to do.

Michael lifted himself onto the branch and moved in the canopy from tree to tree for about thirty yards before returning to the ground. Nearby, clumps of holly surrounded the base of an oak. He removed his greatcoat, calculated the most probable approach by an enemy, and arranged his coat and hat to make it appear he had concealed himself behind the tree and the bushes. A bit of sleeve, the edge of a hat brim. No more, or it would be clearly a trap.

He backtracked to an old yew, its gnarled bole wide enough to conceal two of him. Dull needles crowded low-hanging twigs, providing more cover. He stilled his breathing. Slipped his knife into his hand. Summoned the goddess of the lake. Waited.

They came a little after he'd expected them, separated where he'd expected them to. One shouted to the other, but they were too far away for him to make out the words. A rough voice, accented.

More waiting. Then the clip-clop of hooves—one horse—ceasing at the top of the hill. He couldn't chance taking a look. It was all by sound now. A dismount. Feet hitting the ground. The crunching of dead leaves as the man moved slowly, cautiously forward. In the right direction, the one that would take him close by the yew tree.

He would be following Loki's tracks, and would see where the horse had veered to the right. He might follow, but Michael had left his own tracks from there to the oak and holly and brushed leaves over the tracks, but not completely, as if he'd been in a rush. He might have been giving his followers too much credit, or perhaps not enough.

What would they do when the other man caught up with the mare, saw the twig-and-cloak ruse? His heart began thumping. He snatched his thoughts from Mira's danger, returned them to the quiet of his purpose.

The man was close now. Michael assumed him to be armed. Heard him stop. Jump to one side. Behind a tree? That would mean he'd spotted the betraying hat and coat sleeve. A rustling sound. He was closer than he had seemed. Almost in reach, just the other side of the yew. Using it to conceal himself, Michael realized with a spike of humor.

"Come out, Y'r Grace. I sees you there!"

Michael readied himself to spring at the next covering sound. It came almost instantly. A gunshot.

Then Michael was on him, one arm across his shoulder and chest, his knife at the man's throat. "Toss the guns." There were two of them, a string of smoke ascending from one muzzle. "Now!"

Both pistols hit the ground about ten feet away. The stench of onions and ale rose from the man's filthy clothes.

For a brief time, Michael considered his choices. In the short run, better to kill this man and go after the other. But he needed information, and as always, balked at a cold-blooded murder. That squeamishness would be the death of him one of these days. Perhaps this day. "Who sent you?"

The man spat. Made a squeaking noise as the knife sliced in, drew blood.

"Make no mistake," Michael said. "I'll kill you if you fail to talk, and talk fast."

"I dunno who it were." The sputtered words tumbled over one another. "He leaves messages and money at a tavern near to the river. We worked mostly for the duke, but a little for t'other man. And after the duke turned us off, we was hired to make it look like we killed him."

"You didn't?"

"Would have done. Hated him. Paid bad, he did, when he paid at all. The message said to go there, and how to get in, and what to do when we got there. He were dead already, just like we was told, and the knife was left on the desk where we could see it. We turned 'im over, put the knife in 'is heart, spread some pig's blood around. We was told to look for papers 'n' bring all we found. Later, we was sent back to get more."

"Someone else poisoned him, then."

"Mebbe. Like I said, he were dead. There's a way into the house, through a bit of wall that opens with a key if you know the right place. Davie has the key. I paid no mind."

"Which tavern? And why come after me?"

"We was supposed to leave the country. Word was that Runners been lookin' for us, so we had to go. The man didn't want no questions asked, paid good to be rid of us. Said if we killed you first, he'd give us more. But it had to be done before Sunday next, when we be takin' ship from Southampton."

The man started to struggle. Kicked out, lost his balance. Shouted an oath as Michael pulled him erect and secured his hold.

Click. Behind him!

Michael whirled, taking his prisoner with him. A blast of sound, a scream. The man sagged in his arms. Michael shoved him out of the way, aimed himself for the discarded pistol, the one that hadn't been fired. A thump as the man hit the ground.

"Hold!"

The gun was beyond his reach. Michael froze in place, half crouching, arms splayed, and turned slowly to face the Welshman.

The new enemy had two guns as well. One had brought down his fellow, and the other was pointed at Michael. The hand was steady, the slanted eyes clear and wary.

"Canny trick with the sticks and the cape," he said. "If the horse hadn't stopped running, I'd be chasing her still. But it weren't of use. We've not been paid to kill the woman. Is he dead?"

"I don't know."

The Welshman's eyes hadn't shifted to glance at his fallen companion. Smart and experienced. In control. Michael figured he had one slim chance to reach the pistol on the ground, but it would only come after he'd been shot. Assuming he could still move, and reach it in time, and fire.

The urgency was not so great now. The Welshman didn't mean to go after Mira. That was all that mattered. "Who sent you?" Michael asked, wanting to know before he died.

"I don't know." A chuckle. "We neither of us know much of anything, do we? Nothing personal, Your Grace, but you're trouble alive and worth a lot of blunt to me dead. That's only if I get away. Somebody passing by might be hearing these shots. Time to pray now."

Michael watched his eyes, all his attention focused there, waiting for the sign to leap. He sensed the finger begin to tighten on the trigger, the clench of muscles, all in the space of a heartbeat—

A whirring noise. *Thwap!*

The gun went off, a bullet sped by his cheek. The Welshman staggered forward.

Michael jumped for the pistol, found it, rolled over, searching for the target.

Whir. *Thwap!* The man jerked upright, eyes wide, mouth open, blood gushing out. He held there a moment, then fell forward. Hit the ground.

From his back pronged two feathered arrows, still quivering with the force of their arrival.

Michael's gaze went to the crest of the hill, to the slim figure poised there, another arrow nocked in her bow, her eyes fixed on the man who lay dead at her hands.

Discipline sent Michael, breathing heavily, first to the man who'd taken a bullet. He felt for a pulse at his wrist and throat, examined the glassy eyes. Dead. There could be no doubt about the fellow Mira had brought down, but he checked anyway.

Finally, letting go the pistol he'd been gripping, he rose and looked directly at Miranda. She had lowered her bow, was standing with her hands at her sides, pale skinned and clearly shaken.

"Diana," he said. "The Huntress."

At his words, color rose in her cheeks. She gazed down at him, directly into his eyes. "We are matched, then. I had hoped we could be."

That meant something to her—he didn't know what—and it seemed to help. He would ask her later, after the shock had worn off. It would be on her soon. He put two fingers to his lips, gave a loud whistle. It startled her. He whistled again.

Loki appeared not long after, while Michael was retrieving his coat—a bullet hole through its sleeve—and his hat. He found a key in the Welshman's pocket and took that as well. Mira had remained where she was, accepting that the men were dead, saying nothing. And he knew better than to speak before she was ready. Even when necessary, killing was never easy. It wasn't supposed to be.

He considered the two horses abandoned by the thugs, the possibility of finding the mare, and decided to take Mira up with him on Loki. He mounted and beckoned to her. She went wordlessly into the circle of his hands, let herself be lifted up, settled across his legs with one arm around his waist and the other clutching her bow.

"I saved you," she murmured, resting her head on his shoulder.

"In every way there is," he said.

Chapter 33

Mira stood at cliff's edge, pearl-gray clouds swirling overhead, the silver ocean below sleek as fur. Fat snowflakes drifted in the air. She breathed deeply, tasting salt in the moist breeze. Soon the pale light would fade, and she would withdraw to the house to wait, as she had already waited the better part of the day, for her husband's return.

She had asked him to bring her here, and not to Longview, although it meant she would be alone. On this day, the day of her rebirth, she wished to be at Seacrest, where she had first been born.

Snowflakes on her cheeks, melting, gliding down like tears. But she felt warmed from within as the silent girl inside her, given a voice at last, began to stretch and move about. Make herself known, springing from the ice like a snowdrop. The promise of new life, a different life.

She wondered if Michael would like the woman reborn in the roots of a tree, in the snap of an arrow from her bow, in the healing embrace of his arms.

She wondered if *she* would like the new Miranda.

He had been reluctant to leave her by herself, but she insisted that Mr. Singh, who had been here when they arrived, accompany him to deal with the after-math of the attack.

She'd used the time to prepare a room for them to stay the night, plundering the attics and walking a mile to the nearest neighbor for the loan of blankets and other necessities. Mrs. Dwindle, whom she had known since childhood, brought her back in a wagon piled with supplies, in case they got snowed in. Mira was hoping they would.

She felt much better now. Earlier, gripped with shivers and nausea, she kept hearing the sound of her arrows, seeing them strike . . . Well, she mustn't think on it now. She'd found mint in the overgrown kitchen garden, brewed it into a tea, and rid herself of the bad taste in her mouth. Later, she'd been able to swallow a few crackers and keep busy enough to distract herself. It wasn't that she regretted what she'd done—how should she?—but she wished never to do violence again. What ghosts must haunt her husband, who had spent most of his life fighting and killing?

Her face under the hood of her borrowed cloak burned with cold. Fire and ice. And now, the anticipation tingling at her awareness. He was on his way. She decided to wait, to greet him here, suspended between earth and water and sky, a place of new beginnings.

A few minutes later, she turned to watch him striding down the long slope of the grassy hill, his greatcoat open and flowing behind him. She held out her hands, and after a look of surprise, he took them. A man unsure of his welcome, she had come to understand. His eyes, the color of the winter sea, regarded her with concern.

"I'm quite well," she said. "Will you tell me what has occurred?"

"We found your mare. I answered the same questions several hundred times, signed papers, and left the rest in the hands of the authorities. In a day or two, I shall be required to go to London. That's about all."

"What of the man responsible? What is to prevent him from hiring someone else to kill you?"

A pause. "He's dead, Mira. There was a message sent me at Longview, and Hamman MacFife had got the word as well, from Bow Street. The investigation is not complete, but it appears the man drank the same poison he used to kill my brother. And he confessed to the murder in a letter apparently written while he waited for the poison to work. It was slow acting, according to the magistrate, and he'd have known that. The handwriting deteriorated as he wrote, the ink is smeared, and the letter is stained with the poisoned wine and his sweat. But it can be deciphered, and it appears credible."

Appears? Mira put that aside for the moment. "Who is he?"

"No one I ever heard of. Mr. Phineas Garvey, shipowner, country trader, charter member of the East India Consortium. He'd lost the better part of his fortune in recent years—I'm to blame for that—and it seems my brother held notes on his property and meant to foreclose. Garvey mentions the notes in his letter, and I'll be required to sift through Jermyn's papers in search of them."

"We can assume Mr. Garvey's hired bullies didn't find them when they searched Tallant House?"

Michael shrugged. "That seems logical. But we needn't make this more complicated than it is. The message I received was from Varden, who knew of Garvey's financial problems and his uncontrollable temper. Varden witnessed an explosion of that temper shortly before setting out for India. Garvey threatened his colleagues, including my brother, and Hugo Duran as well. I see no reason to question what we have learned. Jermyn made a great many enemies, and it was always likely that one of them, pushed beyond reason, would act against him."

"Temper," she said, "does not accord with slow-acting poison. And why would a man bent on suicide hire killers to eliminate *you,* a man he'd never met?"

A harsh laugh. "When you were born female, Duchess, England lost a splendid chief magistrate. The two men who came for me had been hired some weeks ago, on speculation. I presume that when their search of Tallant House failed to turn up the papers Garvey wanted, he reckoned I would at some point come upon them and foreclose on his property, as Jermyn had intended to do. So he put a price on my head. Or perhaps he meant to punish me for my actions against the Consortium in India, which bankrupted him in the first place. Clearly he felt backed into a corner, and with the poison to hand, swallowing it must have seemed an escape from his troubles."

It all sounded logical. There was a suicide, a letter of confession, and plenty of motive for Mr. Garvey to kill the duke. It did not require a great villain to do great harm. Only a man with a grievance, and really, she ought to be honoring the memory of poor Mr. Garvey. He had taken action and eliminated the evil duke while she, obsessed with vengeful plots for a dozen years, had done nothing more than devise imaginary schemes.

And yet . . . "What if he had an ally? Or was being used by someone else? What is to prevent you being a target in the future?"

"I'm used to being a target." A small, heart-stealing smile. "But now I have an incentive to stay out of harm's way. In the event there is more to the story than we presently know, I'll see to it the authorities follow every trail to its end. That's one reason for the London trip, and no, you may not come with me."

Her pulse speeded up. "I'll not be left out of an investigation."

"Yes, you will. As will I. If someone else is involved in Jermyn's death, and we have little reason to believe there is any such fellow, we'll be dealing with a master intriguer who won't be stopped by ordinary means. We first need to make it clear I pose no immediate threat, which ought to hold off another attack and give us time to track him down. But the investigation must be clever, and secret, and conducted by someone else. Someone unexpected."

"You could ask Lord Varden's help. He—"

"No."

"But surely you can't imagine *he* is guilty. And he has all the right connections, while we have none at all."

"Varden is the last man on the planet I will permit to be involved in my affairs. On this, Duchess, there will be no compromise."

"Very well," she said, the lines of weariness around his eyes and mouth telling a story of their own. She had pushed him as far as he would go, for now. At some later time, if the niggling sense he was still in danger persisted, she would wheedle him into a long wedding trip to the Continent. "As you may recall, Your Grace, I played rather a significant part in to-day's adventure. How is it that no one has bothered to interrogate *me*?"

"What for?" His brows went up in mock astonishment. "You are a mere wife. The law directs husbands to speak for their mere wives. Resign yourself to sub-servience, Duchess."

"I never shall, you know. But as it all sounds quite tedious, this legal folderol, you have my leave to do the speaking. I will confine myself to the *rescuing*."

"Ah. I'm never going to hear the end of this, am I?"

His grin sent ripples up and down her back. "Not any time soon. But I will spare you a little, if you will stop protecting me from hard truths. When you leave me to speculate, my imagination conjures every sort of disaster."

"I'll try to do better." He squeezed her hands. "But if you wish honesty from me, you must return the service. You came out of nowhere this morning. How did you travel so far, and so quickly, without your horse? And how the devil did you find me?"

Oh, dear. But she could scarcely demand what she refused to give. "I got there by running. It was only a mile, perhaps two. And I'm afraid I always know where you are, within limits. That was a few hundred yards, until today. I had no difficulty tracking you much farther when it mattered."

His jaw tightened. "*How?*"

"It's impossible to describe the sensation. A vibration, of a kind. A soundless humming. Disturbing at first, but not any longer."

"Not for you. I'm bloody *damn* disturbed. Are you vibrating now?"

"It stops when we're together." His hands were fisted. She'd known he wouldn't be pleased to learn she could pinpoint his location, but he'd insisted on knowing. And it wasn't as if she could help doing it.

"Is it like that *summons* you told me about, the one that sent you to Berkeley Square?"

"A different feeling, but equally strange. Inexplicable. I didn't ask for this, you know, and I cannot simply make it go away. But if you do not wish me to be able to find you, the solution is obvious." Only her new confidence made the next words possible. "Keep me always with you."

His eyes, fixed intently on her, flashed with the humor she loved in him. "You know what will happen if I do?"

"I think I know." She saw the wariness shadowing his gaze, and the longing. "You want me naked, and under you, and open to you."

A muscle twisting at his jaw. A light rising in his eyes. "And what do you want?"

The answer was diamond bright. And with its coming, the last of the ice imprisoning her winter heart melted away, leaving her exposed. She felt a jolt of fear at the promise of a future with happiness in it, and with love. Did she dare believe this could be true? That it could endure? His gaze burned into her.

"Mira?" Softly—"Tell me what you want. Whatever it is, if it is in my power, I will put it in your hands."

And he would. He had proven it again and again. In the heat of his passion, she unfurled like a flower. "Michael," she said, speaking his name for the first time. "I want you naked, my love, and over me, and inside me."

Instantly, strong hands swept her up. Strong arms carried her swiftly to the house, and into the small room she had prepared for them.

Firelight, candlelight, and a bower of blankets and pillows laid out near the hearth. She was on her back then, her skirts up around her waist, his mouth on hers. The kisses deepened, his tongue mating with her tongue in an act of love she had never imagined. Wonderful. Her fingers tangled in his hair.

Mindless with desire, she clung to him as he moved quickly to enter her. Plunged into her with a sigh against her mouth. Raised her knees to his waist and filled her with himself and his need, and then she began to feel a burning urgency where her flesh was joined to his. He drove into her, and she pulled him back and back and back again, wanting more.

Small sounds in her throat. His tongue at her throat, his manhood at her core, his heart pounding against her heart. She knew herself powerful. Confident. Seductive.

The pleasure mounted, like the beat of the dohl drum, like the rhythm of the *bhangra* dance. She strained against him. Something new, his finger on her, just where she needed it. She flamed in his embrace. Felt him explode with her, go still as the waves of pleasure washed over her, and finally turn onto his side, drawing her with him.

Silence then, save for their breathing and the sparking of the fire.

After a time, she dared a question. "Why did you want me, Michael? From the first, I was sure that you did, and that it would pass. Other men have wanted me as well, but with you, it was different. I don't wish for compliments. I have always been more trouble than I was worth, so why was it, when I kept turning you away, that you never gave up?"

His eyes opened, inches from her own. A hand lifted to stroke her hair. "Since you forbid me to tell you that you are lovely, and intelligent, and honorable, and brave, I can tell you only that we have met before. You won't believe me, and I never admitted to believing it either, but it is nonetheless true."

"Met when? Here in Kent, when I was a child?"

"Half a year ago, in India, on the Path of the Tiger. I know, you weren't there. And I've always been a practical man, about as spiritual as a fencepost. But when I saw you, blue-eyed and silver-haired, you held my life between your teeth. And when I saw you again, at the Palazzo with the river at your back, I recognized you immediately."

His hand moved to her face, cupped her chin. "We were brought together, fated to be together. I thought it was for a short time, just long enough to protect you, but it seems I was wrong. Here we are, and perhaps you will be forced to put up with me for a lifetime. Pardon me for hoping so. And that's all I know. I'm not sure what I believe."

She was still on the tiger's path. "You *saw* me? Like a vision of some sort?" She regarded him cautiously. He didn't appear to be teasing her, but—"What was I wearing?"

"Fur." A smile. "You were a tigress then. Hell, you're a tigress now. And a goddess. *Dea certe.*"

Assuredly a goddess. She felt his hand at her back,

undoing the buttons on her dress. "This is all exceedingly odd. I'm not sure I care for it."

"Nor I. Come here. I can't reach where I want to reach."

He rolled onto his back, bringing her with him, stretching her on top of him. Rumpled clothes where there were still clothes, hot flesh where they'd been pulled up, or down, or open. She could tell, from the determination in his eyes, that *naked* was next on his agenda.

"If I can stay out of trouble," he said, "we shall have a great many years to decipher all these puzzles. Or let them remain a mystery, if you prefer. That would be my choice. For now, I still need to prove to you that making love can take longer, much longer, than you have imagined. And that you will enjoy it."

"I already did enjoy it. But first, before you . . . proceed, I have something more to say to you."

"Words, words, words," he said, proceeding. "Have we not said enough, negotiated too much? I will always love you with actions, Duchess. It's the only way I know."

"That's . . . Oh."

He sat her up, pulled her gown over her head, and then her chemise.

"Fine," she said. "Now wait a moment. There are one or two things remaining to be settled."

"You settle them," he said, not waiting. His gaze, and then his hands, went to her bare, fire-lit breasts. "I'll agree to anything."

"No divorce, then. Not ever."

He paused. Looked into her eyes, took a deep breath. "Thank you." Then he returned, with avid concentration, to what he had been doing. This time it was his mouth on her breast.

"And . . . ah. Michael. I am losing myself in you. You must stop for a moment."

"Very well," he murmured, not stopping. "Don't

worry about being lost. So am I. But you will be safe with me, always."

"Yes. What I am trying to tell you is that I know I have much to learn, and I hope you will instruct me, but it may be a while before you find me . . . satisfactory."

"You are eternally splendid. At present, we are waiting on me. It requires a few minutes to . . . to reload the artillery."

She gave an exasperated laugh. "I *mean*, Your Grace, that I am withdrawing my previous offer. In future, I intend to leave you neither the time nor the strength to require the services of a mistress."

He paused then, and placed his hands on her face, and gazed with unmistakable love into her eyes. "Thank you, brave Miranda. Beloved Mira. Duchess. Goddess. Tigress. Wife. You may be sure that I shall exclusively and forever devote myself to the lot of you."

Read on for the final book in
Lynn Kerstan's exciting trilogy.

Coming from Onyx in November 2003

Lord Varden sifted through the thick stack of papers on his desk. Impressive credentials indeed, befitting an earl's private secretary. Too many skills for one person to possess, a dozen recommendations from impeccable sources, and almost nothing in the way of personal information.

Just as well. He had lost his taste for personal relationships of any kind.

A tug on the bell pull brought Quill to the door, his brows waggling with agitation. Staring meaningfully at his employer, the butler jerked his head in the direction of the anteroom as if robbers had invaded it.

"What is it, Quill? Did the last candidate give up and go away?"

Lips clamped together, the butler went on jerking his head. His hands waved X's in front of him, signaling *No*.

"Am I about to be shot? Speak up, man."

"He is trying to warn you," said a clear, crisp voice. "About me."

With a sigh, the butler withdrew to admit a slender, pale-skinned woman wearing a steel gray woolen dress, a matching bonnet, and darkly smoked spectacles.

Varden had seen her before—the spectacles were unmistakable—but he couldn't think where. Rising, his habit in the presence of a female, he watched her stride purposefully to the desk and stand before him, her back straight as a lance.

"You were expecting a man, of course. I apologize for the mild deception, but it couldn't be helped."

"What became of the pugilist fellow I saw waiting in the anteroom?"

"Finn is my driver. I cannot bear to be idle for any length of time, so he held my place while I explored the grounds. Now he is with my carriage, expecting me to arrive there momentarily. I, on the other hand, believe you are fair-minded enough to grant me an interview. We have a bet on it."

He rarely encountered that degree of self-confidence outside the House of Lords. "I fear you are about to lose your wager, Miss Pryce. Or is it Mrs. Pryce?"

"I am unmarried, sir. The 'H' is for Helena."

"Well, it appears you have made the journey to Richmond in vain. For all your considerable experience, I require absolute integrity in the *man* who will become my secretary."

"In a good cause," she said, "I have been known to prevaricate, or dissemble, or tell a downright corker. My references introduce me as H. Pryce to mislead you. I instructed my driver to pretend he had come for the interview, and when the next-to-last candidate emerged, I entered the house and presented myself to your butler. Had you known H. Pryce to be a female, my lord, I should never have been admitted to your study. Will you deny it?"

"Certainly not. But what made you think that bluffing your way into my presence would secure you a hearing?"

"Regard for your character. Confidence in my abilities. The certainty you would find no one better suited for the position." A little curve, the shape of a parenthesis, winked at the corner of her mouth. "You think me vain. Perhaps I am."

They were still standing on opposite sides of his desk, immobile as pillars, and he realized with a shot of astonishment that he was beginning to enjoy himself. It seemed a long time since he had enjoyed himself.

"Very well, Miss Pryce." He gestured to the chair where the other applicants had sat, nervous and inadequate, which this female was decidedly not. "If you insist on prolonging a futile endeavor, please be seated and tell me about yourself."

She lifted her skirts and sat, with graceful precision, on the edge of the chair, folding her hands on her lap. "All you need to know is contained in the papers on your desk. For the last several years, I have been secretary to Lady Jessica Sothingdon, but since her marriage, she has required less of my time. In consequence, I have accepted temporary commissions from several clients, including the Duke of Wellington, Mr. Huskisson, Mr. Canning, Lord Philpot, and the Duke of Devonshire. You have their testimonials."

It occurred to him that he should sit down as well. When he did, he found himself looking directly at the spectacles that entirely obscured her eyes. Crafted to cup her eye sockets, they were hinged at her temples to bend back another inch or so. He found it disorienting, the inability to read her thoughts by looking into her eyes. She might as well have been wearing a mask.

"But you seek a permanent position with me?" he said, because it was his turn to speak. She had the unnerving capacity to let a silence drag on.

"Little in life is permanent," she said. "I wish employment with you for so long as I find the experience rewarding. I should advise you now that my services are prodigiously expensive."

He bit back a laugh. "You continue to deflect my

questions. What is your background? Your education? Your family?"

"I am an orphan, sir, and if I have living relations, they do not know of my existence. I spent my early childhood in London and was sent to be educated at the Linford Sisters' Academy for Young Ladies in Surrey."

"Your age?"

"Eight-and-twenty."

"Where have I seen you before?"

"At Palazzo Neri, most like. I am a friend of Beata Neri's companion, Signora Fannella."

He couldn't have said why he persisted. None of this signified. But she interested him, if only because she posed a challenge he could appreciate without having to deal with it. And because she wouldn't be hurt when he sent her away. Miss Pryce, he suspected, had made herself impervious to insult and rejection. For that, he envied her.

"What is wrong with your eyes?" he asked with uncharacteristic bluntness.

"When it comes to seeing, very little. Nothing that impedes the performance of my duties, unless you require my opinion of a sunset or the quality of a painting. I cannot distinguish colors with perfect accuracy." That beguiling hint of amusement. "Not to be overly dramatic, but the world presents itself to me as through a glass darkly."

It came to him the same way, without the barrier of smoked glass. "Spectacles so encompassing," he said, "are rather out of the ordinary."

"They are designed to protect my eyes. I have a rare and inherited disorder that makes me excruciatingly vulnerable to light. The merest glimmer causes a burning that is all but unendurable. Exposure for any length of time would result in blindness. You will understand, then, why I take care not to remove the spectacles."

"Are they painful to wear?"

The barest pause. "Uncomfortable. But I have grown accustomed to them, as one must when there is no choice."

He glanced down at his leather-gloved hand, lying flat and motionless on his thigh. "Yes."

"In every other way," she said, "I am in excellent health."

Something had troubled him since first she appeared. "You could not have been sent by the agency, Miss Pryce. How did you learn of this position?"

"My predecessor, Mr. Blaine, is soon to be married, and his bride recently inherited a property in Northumberland. On Monday last, he gave you his notice. Presuming you would quickly replace him, I posted my credentials and, as you see, presented myself for an interview."

My predecessor? After hearing that, it took some time for the rest of her speech to register. "Mr. Blaine's marriage and departure is scarcely public information How the dev—how did you *know* all that?"

"I have made a study of you. I am acquainted with your family history, your financial assets, your education and interests, your political activities, and your prospects. After assuring myself it was in your best interest to employ me, I sought an opportunity to bring myself to your notice."

"Well, you have certainly done that."

"I've no doubt you resent my intrusion into your affairs, and I cannot justify what I have done in terms that will satisfy you. On the other hand, I needn't have admitted to investigating you. Be assured, Lord Varden, that your welfare is my sole concern."

"Good God. As if I didn't have a battalion of female relations meddling in my affairs. Was it my mother recruited you, Miss Pryce? The grandmothers? One of the aunts? My pestilential sisters? Or did the lot of them conspire to inflict you on me?"

The trace of a smile at one corner of her mouth, so fleeting he could not be sure he'd seen it.

"I am here because of my conviction that a gentleman raised in a household of women will have learned to respect the intelligence, determination, and capabilities of the female sex."

"And to beware them as well." Helena Pryce had swept in like a force of nature, and he kept wondering what she would do next. As if his life were not already complicated beyond measure. "Whatever your talents, it would be unthinkable for me to employ a female secretary. The scandal—"

"Did not concern my previous employers. The Foreign Secretary and the Dukes of Wellington and Devonshire managed to emerge with their reputations intact." She sat forward on her chair. "You have been treated to the edges of my sharp tongue, sir. You have examined my appearance. It must be obvious that I am not a woman capable of enticing a man. The very notion that the Archangel Earl of Varden would pay me the slightest attention is absurd. No one would credit it."

What was he to say to *that*? Gentlemanly words, reassuring compliments, sprang to his lips and promptly sprang away again. Her diabolical attractions lay beyond the reach of common understanding. Intelligence. Wildness. Leashed energy, pulsing beneath that rigid self-control. She gave no sign of these things, but he felt them. They vibrated in his bones.

They made her dangerous.

With his left hand, he began to fold up the documents and letters of recommendation she had provided. "I am sorry, Miss Pryce, but for all your accomplishments, you do not suit the requirements for this position."

She said nothing. Neither did she look away as he struggled to assemble her papers and slide them into the leather case. From the tilt of her head, she was observing his every move. Analyzing the means by which he adjusted to having only one workable hand.

But she didn't try to help, or take over the job for him, as he might have expected from such a managing female. Instead, she left him to get on about it. And that, more than anything she had said or done, impressed him.

It changed nothing, though. Approving her, feeling unaccountably drawn to her, made her dismissal all the more urgent.

At the end, he was forced to bring up his throbbing right hand to hold open the case while he slipped the papers inside. It required several tries, but at last he was able to rise and hold out the packet.

She rose as well, took it, curtsied. For a moment, just before she turned away, he caught his own reflection in the polished glass of her spectacles. Light hair, troubled eyes, a face that struck him as severe and overbred. He didn't like what he saw.

She moved calmly to the door. Her hand was on the latch. A sense of loss, the certainty he was making a mistake, took hold of him.

"There is one thing," he said, "that you might do for me."

She held still for several heartbeats before turning to face him. "A temporary hire?"

"More of a test. I could hardly refuse to employ a secretary who can do the impossible. I wish to purchase a partly restored castle located in the Mendips, but there is some dispute about the title to the land. In consequence, I am willing to settle for a lease and the right to continue the restoration of the castle until the legalities are worked out, at which point ownership must be signed over to me at an equitable price. Can you accomplish all of that, do you suppose?"

Silence, save for the ticking of the clock. Her full lips tightened as she thought it over. "What if I can?"

"Then you may have the position you came here to secure."

"On my terms?"

"On negotiated terms. You must know I will deal fairly, or you would not be considering my offer."

"Yes. But it is not dealing fairly to assign me all the risk. Even if I fail, Lord Varden, I expect to be paid for my time. The price will be high."

He had a mental image of shoveling gold into a volcano. A vivid image of flames rising up to consume him.

"Very well, Miss Pryce. You want to be my secretary, and I want you to buy me a castle. Let us see if you can work miracles."

About the Author

.

Lynn Kerstan's Regency and historical romance novels have won a score of awards, including the Golden Quill, the Award of Excellence, and the coveted RITA.

A former college teacher, professional bridge player, folksinger, and dedicated traveler, she lives in California, where she plots her stories while walking on the beach or riding the waves on her boogie board.

Visit www.lynnkerstan.com for more about the author, her books, and the times and places in which her stories are set.